HORRIBLE
IMAGININGS

HORRIBLE IMAGININGS

FRITZ LEIBER

OPEN ROAD

INTEGRATED MEDIA

NEW YORK

"Horrible Imaginings" originally appeared in *Death*, 1982 Playboy Publishing

"The Automatic Pistol" originally appeared in *Weird Tales*, May 1940

"Crazy Annaoj" originally appeared in *Galaxy*, February 1968

"The Hound" originally appeared in *Weird Tales*, November 1942

"Alice and the Allergy" originally appeared in *Weird Tales*, September 1946

"Skinny's Wonderful" original to this collection

"Answering Service" originally appeared in *Worlds of If*, December 1967

"Scream Wolf" originally appeared in *Mike Shayne's Mystery Magazine*, February 1961

"Mysterious Doings in the Metropolitan Museum" originally appeared in *Universe 5*, 1974 Random House

"When Brahma Wakes" originally appeared in *Fantastic*, January 1968

"The Glove" originally appeared in *Whispers*, June 1975

"The Girl With Hungry Eyes" originally appeared in *The Girl With Hungry Eyes*, 1949 Avon Books

"While Set Fled" originally appeared in *Amra #15*, 1961

"Diary in the Snow" originally appeared in *Night's Black Agents*, 1947 Arkham House

"The Ghost Light" originally appeared in *The Ghost Light*, 1984 Berkley Books

ISBN 978-1-4976-0808-5

This edition published in 2014 by Open Road Integrated Media, Inc.
345 Hudson Street
New York, NY 10014
www.openroadmedia.com

HORRIBLE
IMAGININGS

Acknowledgments

THE EDITOR WOULD LIKE TO ACKNOWLEDGE THE invaluable assistance of Catherine Brown, Richard Curtis, Stefan Dziemianowicz, Allen Koszowski, Brian Metz of Green Rhino Graphics, Kathy Pelan, & David Read in the preparation of this volume.

CONTENTS

IMAGINE, IF YOU WILL...

OBVIOUSLY, THE AUTHOR OF THESE TALES NEEDS little introduction. Fritz Leiber was a master of imaginative fiction and a profound influence on the genres of horror, science fiction, and heroic fantasy. As comfortable putting his own unique spin on H.P. Lovecraft's as he was creating his own worlds, Leiber's stories display a rare mastery in all the fields he touched.

This collection is another volume of his darker tales, selected from different points in a forty-year career. From his 1940 tale "The Automatic Pistol" to "The Ghost Light" from 1984, this collection presents a retrospective sampling of Leiber's horror fiction. No doubt there are some familiar pieces here; certainly several of these stories have been frequently anthologized and will be familiar to Leiber fans. However, we are pleased to offer up a selection of stories that had vanished into relative obscurity. His short fantasies "When Brahma Wakes" and "When Set Fled" are minor masterpieces of the short-short form. One tale was discovered among the Leiber papers and to my knowledge has never seen prior publication. "Skinny's Wonderful" was found with a note from Leiber's agent implying that he expected a sale to *Esquire* to be forthcoming... To the best of my knowledge, this sale never took place and the story languished in an envelope, unsubmitted elsewhere.

Esquire's loss is our gain; "Skinny's Wonderful" is an excellent Hitchcockian piece that shows Leiber's excellence at the straight psychological suspense tale to great effect. Another rare inclusion is the short and poignant sword and sorcery tale "When Set Fled" from a 1961 issue of the Robert E. Howard journal *Amra*. "Scream

Wolf" is another suspense tale, this time from the often-excellent *Mike Shayne's Mystery Magazine. MSMM* has undeservedly fallen into obscurity under the larger shadow of *Alfred Hitchcock' Mystery Magazine,* but a perusal of 1960s and 1970s issues yields some nice surprises. In any given issue you may find stories by *Weird Tales* alumni such as Robert Bloch, Carl Jacobi, Theodore Sturgeon, and even Robert Barbour Johnson; to say nothing of early appearances by modern masters like Richard Laymon and Gary Brandner.

These are essentially the oddball items in this collection; assuming that you bought the first two Midnight House volumes of Leiber, you're here for the horror... I must apologize and explain the somewhat eclectic nature of this series. When we began, we foolishly assumed that one or two volumes collecting rarer pieces would be adequate and that two volumes each of SF and horror would pretty well cover things. Such has been the popularity of the series that we've decided to forge ahead and collect all of Leiber's non-Gray Mouser tales. There will be one such story published, but it's the early, never-before- published version of "Adept's Gambit", written as a Cthulhu Mythos tale! Sadly, I did not discover until well into the third book that Fritz had assembled a horror collection entitled *Thirteen Dark Dreads.* We will offer this title in 2005, but due to several of the stories appearing elsewhere, the contents will be radically different from what Fritz had envisioned. To that I can only offer up an apology for my eagerness to get *The Black Gondolier* and *Smoke Ghost* into print, and hope that you, the reader find that the dark dreads I've selected meet with your approval.

The other tales from this volume may be familiar to a large extent; "The Automatic Pistol" was so overshadowed by "Smoke Ghost" that many have forgotten what an excellent early story this was. Other inclusions from the *Weird Tales* years are "The Hound" and "Alice and the Allergy". I've tended to leave aside the entire decade of the 1950s in favor of presenting early and still vital work which may be contrasted with three of Leiber's latter-day masterpieces. In the 1970s and 1980s Stuart Schiff's phenomenal little magazine *Whispers* was an infrequently published delight, everything that *Weird Tales* should have been. Artists included the great Lee Brown Coye and Frank Utpatel and authors read like a who's who of the time period. Leiber, King, Campbell, Strieber, Wellman, Aickman, and newer authors like Karl Edward Wagner. David Campton, David Drake, and many others. Leiber's story "The Glove" remains one of the most fondly remembered tales from that great magazine.

Editor Schiff was able to parlay his success from *Whispers* into a series of anthologies, while the *Whispers* series drew mainly from the magazine, his anthology *Death* was a non-themed horror anthology, he rounded up some top-flight authors that he knew could deliver the goods and left them to write whatever pleased them at whatever length. Fritz Leiber responded with the remarkable titular novella of this collection. A story which was also selected as best of the year for 1982 in *The Century's Best Horror*.

There's little I can say about "The Girl with the Hungry Eyes", that hasn't already been remarked on by scores of critics. The quintessential 1950s horror story, it's been reprinted a number of times and is readily available in many anthologies, but I thought it would be a shame to leave it out here.

"Mysterious Doings at the Metropolitan Museum" is more likely to raise a smile than a shiver (at least on initial reading), it's only after the book has been set aside and we start to wonder about the secret nature of things that the chill starts to set in and the horripilations begin.

We end the book with a bit of a contrast, a story from early in Leiber's career that I feel transcends its pulp tropes very effectively and we conclude with his last real masterpiece, "The Ghost Light". "The Ghost Light" is an ambitious work that examines themes and motifs that have been present in Leiber's work for years the dark magic of cities, alcoholism, loss, alienation, and of course our ability (or is it a need?) to create new ghosts for a modern era.

For over forty years no one did a more effective job of showing us our new ghosts than did Fritz Leiber, here are few of them for your enjoyment... Do leave the light on and consider that the gray shape slowly detaching itself from the alley is probably just a shadow. Probably...

John Pelan
Midnight House
Summer Solstice 2004

HORRIBLE IMAGININGS

"Present fears are less than horrible imaginings."
—Macbeth

OLD RAMSEY RYKER ONLY COMMENCED THINKING about going to see (through one-way glass) the young women fingering their genitals *after* he started having the low-ceilinged dreams without light—the muttering dull black nightmares—but *before* he began catching glimpses of the vanishing young-old mystery girl, who wore black that twinkled, lurking in the first-floor ground-level corridors, or disappearing into the elevator, and once or twice slipping along the upstairs halls of the apartment tree (or skeleton) that is, with one exception, the sole scene of the action in this story, which does not venture farther, disturb the privacy of the apartments themselves, or take one step out into the noisy metropolitan street. Here all is hushed.

I mean by the *apartment tree* all the public or at least tenant-shared space within the thirteen-floor building where Ryker lived alone. With a small effort you can visualize that volume of connected space as a rather repetitious tree (color it red or green if it helps, as they do in "You are *here*" diagrammatic maps; I see it as pale gray myself, for that is the color of the wallpaper in the outer halls, pale gray faintly patterned with dingy silver): its roots the basement garage where some tenants with cars rented space along with a few neighborhood shopkeepers and businessmen; its trunk the central elevator shaft with open stairway beside it (the owner of the building had periodic difficulties with the fire inspectors about the latter—they wanted it walled off with heavy self-closing doors at each floor; certainly a building permit would never have been granted today—or in the last three decades, for that matter—for such a lofty structure with an open stairwell); its branches the three halls, two long, one short, radiating out from the shaft-stairwell trunk and identical at each level except for minor features; from the top floor a sort of slanted, final thick branch of stairs led, through a stout door (locked on the outside but open on the inside—another fire regulation), to the roof and the strong, floored weatherproof shed holding the elevator's motor and old-fashioned mechanical relays. But we won't stir through that door either to survey the besmogged but nonetheless impressive cityscape and hunt for the odd star or (rarer still) an interesting window.

At ground level one of the long corridors led to the street door; on the floors above, to the front fire escape. The other long ones led to the alley fire escape. The short hall was blind (the fire inspector would shake his head at that feature too, and frown).

And then of course we should mention, if only for the sake of completists, the apartment tree's micro-world, its tiniest twigs and leaflets, in a sense: all the cracks and crevices (and mouse- and rat-holes, if any) going off into the walls, ceilings, and floors, with perhaps some leading to more spacious though still cramped volumes of space.

But it would be discourteous of us to wander—and so frivolously—through the strange labyrinthine apartment tree with its angular one- and two-bedroom forbidden fruit, when all the time Ramsey Ryker, a lofty, gaunt old man somewhat resembling a neatly dressed scarecrow, is waiting impatiently for us with his equally strange and tortuous problems and concerns. Of these, the black nightmares were the worst by far and also in a way the cause of, or at least the prelude to, all the others.

Actually they were the worst nightmares in a restrained sort of way that Ramsey ever remembered having in the seven decades of his life and the only ones, the only dreams of any sort for that matter, without any visual element at all (hence the "black"), but only sound, touch, intramuscular feelings, and smell. And the black was really inky, midnight, moonless and starless, sooty, utter—all those words. It didn't even have any of those faint churning points of light we see, some of them tinted, when we shut our eyes in absolute darkness and when supposedly we're seeing rods and cones of our retina fire off without any photons of outside light hitting them. No, the only light in his nightmares, if any, was of the phantom sort in which *memories* are painted—a swift, sometimes extensive-seeming flash which starts to fade the instant it appears and never seems to be in the retina at all, something far more ghostly even than the nebular churnings that occur under the eyelids in the inkiest dark.

He'd been having these nightmares every two or three nights, regular almost as clockwork, for at least a month now, so that they were beginning to seriously worry and oppress him. I've said "nightmares" up to now, but really there was only *one,* repeated with just enough changes in its details to convince him that he was experiencing new nightmares rather than just remembering the first. This made them more ominously terrifying; he'd know what was coming—up to a point—and suffer the more because of that.

Each "performance" of his frightening lightless dream, on those nights when his unconscious decided to put on a show, would begin the same way. He would gradually become aware, as though his mind were rising with difficulty from unimaginable depths of sleep, that he was lying stretched out naked on his back with his arms extended neatly down his sides, but that he was *not* in his bed—the surface beneath him was too ridged and hard for that. He was breathing shallowly and with difficulty—or rather he discovered that if he tried to investigate his breathing, speed or slow it, expand his chest more fully, he ran the danger of bringing on a strangling spasm or coughing fit. This prospect frightened him; he tried never to let it happen.

To check on this, explore the space around him, he would next in his dream try to lift up a hand and arm, stretch a leg sideways—and find out that he could *not,* that so far as any gross movement of limbs went he was paralyzed. This naturally would terrify him and push him toward panic. It was all he could do not to strain, thrash (that is, try to), gasp, or cry out.

Then as his panic slowly subsided, as he schooled himself to quietly endure this limitation on his actions, he would discover that his paralysis was not complete, that if he went about it slowly he could move a bit, wag his head about an inch from side to side, writhe a little the superficial muscles and skin under his shoulders and down his back and buttocks and legs, stir his heels and fingertips slightly. It was in this way that he discovered

that the hard surface under him consisted of rough laths set close
together, which were very dusty—no, gritty.

Next in his dream came an awareness of sound. At first it
would seem the normal muttering hum of any big city, but then
he'd begin to distinguish in it a faint rustling and an infinitesimal
rapid clicking that was very much closer and seemed to get nearer
each moment and he'd think of insects and spiders and he'd feel
new terror gusting through him and there'd be another struggle
to stave off hysteria. At this point in his dream he'd usually
think of cockroaches, armies of them, as normal to big cities as
the latter's muttering sounds, and his terror would fade though
his revulsion would mount. Filthy creatures! but who could be
frightened of them? True, his dear wife, now dead five years, had
had a dread of stepping on one in the dark and hearing it crunch.
(That reaction he found rather hard to understand. He was, well,
if not exactly pleasured, then well satisfied to step on cockroaches,
or mash them in the sink.)

His attention would then likely return to the muttering,
growling, faintly buzzing, somehow *nasal* component of the
general sound, and he'd begin to hear voices in it, though he
could seldom identify the words or phrases—it was like the
voices of a crowd coming out of a theater or baseball park or
meeting hall and commenting and arguing droningly and wearily
about what they'd just seen or heard. *Male* voices chiefly, cynical,
sarcastic, deprecating, mean, sleepily savage, and ignorant, very
ignorant, he'd feel sure. And never as loud or big as they ought
to be; there was always a *littleness* about them. (Was his hearing
impaired in his nightmares? Was he dreaming of growing deaf?)
Were they the voices of depraved children? No, they were much
too low—deep throat tones. Once he'd asked himself, "Midgets?"
and had thought, rich in dream wisdom, "A man lying down is
not even as tall as a midget."

After sound, odor would follow, as his senses were assaulted
cumulatively. First dry, stale, long-confined—somehow so
natural seeming he would be unaware of the scents. But then he
would smell smoke and know a special pang of fright—was he
to be burned alive, unable to move? And the fire sirens when the
engines came, tinied by distance and by muffling walls, no larger
than those of toys?

But then he would identify it more precisely as tobacco smoke, the reeking smoke of cigars chiefly. He remembered how his dead wife had hated that, though smoking cigarettes herself.

After that, a whole host of supporting odors: toilet smells and the cheap sharp perfumes used to balance those out, stinking old flesh, the fishy reek of unwashed sex, locker rooms, beer, disinfectants, wine-laden vomit—all fitting very nicely, too, with the ignorant low growling.

After sound and odor, touch, living touch. Behind the lobe of his right ear, in his jaw's recessed angle, where a branch of the carotid pulses close to the surface, there'd come an exploring prod from the tip of something about as big as a baby's thumb, a pencil's eraserhead, snout of a mouse or of a garter snake, an embryo's fist, an unlit cigarette, a suppository, the phallus of a virile mannequin—a probing and a thrusting that did not stop and did not go away.

At that point his dream, if it hadn't already, would turn into full nightmare. He'd try to jerk his head sideways, throw himself over away from it, thrash his arms and legs, yell out unmindful of what it did to his breathing—and find that the paralysis still gripped him, its bonds growing tighter the more he struggled, his vocal cords as numb as if these were his life's last gaspings.

And then—more touches of the same puppet sort: his side, his thigh, between two fingers, up and down his body. The sounds and odors would get darker still as a general suffocating oppression closed in. He'd visualize grotesquely in imagination's light- less lightning flashes, which like those of memory are so utterly different from sight, a crowd of squatty, groping male Lilliputians, a press of dark-jowled, thickset, lowbrowed, unlovely living dolls standing or leaning in locker-room attitudes, each one nursing with one hand beneath his paunch a half-erect prick with a casual lasciviousness and with the other gripping a beer can or cigar or both, while all the while they gargled out unceasingly a thick oozy stream of shitty talk about crime and sports and sex, about power and profit. He envisioned their tiny prick nubs pressing in on him everywhere, as if he were being wrapped tighter and tighter in a rubber blanket that was all miniscule elastic knobs.

At this moment he would make a supreme effort to lift his head, reckless of heart attack, fighting for each fraction of an inch of upward movement, and find himself grinding his forehead and nose into a rough gritty wooden surface that had been there, not three inches above him, all the while, like the lid of a shallow coffin.

Then, and only then, in that moment of intensest horror, he'd wake at last, stretched out tidily in his own bed, gasping just a little, and with a totally unjoyous hard-on that seemed more like the symptom of some mortal disease than any prelude to pleasure.

The reader may at this point object that by entering Ramsey's bedroom we have strayed beyond the apartment-tree limits set for the actions of this story. Not so, for we have been examining only his *memories* of his nightmares, which never have the force of the real thing. In this fashion we peered into his dream, perhaps into his bedroom, but we never turned on the light. The same applies to his thoughts about and reactions to those erections which troubled his nightmare wakings and which seemed to him so much more like tumorous morbid growths—almost, cancers—than any swellings of joy.

Now Ramsey was sufficiently sophisticated to wonder whether his nightmares were an expression, albeit an unusual and most unpleasant one, of a gathering sexual arousal in himself, which his invariable waking hard-ons would seem to indicate, and whether the discharge of that growing sexual pressure would not result in the nightmares ceasing or at least becoming fewer in number and of a lesser intensity. On the one hand, his living alone was very thoroughgoing; he had formed no new intimacies since his wife's death five years earlier and his coincidental retirement and moving here. On the other, he had a deep personal prejudice against masturbation, not on moral or religious grounds, but from the conviction that such acts demanded a living accomplice or companion to make them effectively real, no matter how distant and tenuous the relation between the two parties, an adventuring-out into the real world and some achievement there, however slight.

Undoubtedly there were guilty shadows here—his life went back far enough for him to have absorbed in childhood mistaken notions of the unhealthiness of auto-eroticism that still influenced his feelings if not his intellect. And also something of the work-ethic of Protestantism, whereby everything had its price, had to be worked and sweated and suffered for.

With perhaps—who knows?—a touch of the romantic feeling that sex wasn't worth it without the spice of danger, which also required a venturing out beyond one's private self.

Now on the last occasion—about eight months ago—when Ramsey had noted signs of growing sexual tension in himself (signs far less grotesquely inappropriate, frightening, oppressive, and depressing than his current nightmares—which appeared to end with a strong hint of premature burial), he had set his imagination in a direction leading toward that tension's relief by venturing some four blocks into the outer world (the world beyond the apartment tree's street door) to a small theater called Ultrabooth, where for a modest price (in these inflated times) he could make contact with three living girls (albeit a voiceless one through heavy one-way glass), who would strip and display themselves intimately to him in a way calculated to promote arousal.

(A pause to note we've once more gone outside the apartment tree, but only by way of a remembered venturing—and memory is less real even than dream, as we have seen.)

The reason Ramsey had not at once again had recourse to these young ladies as soon as his nightmares began with their telltale terminal hard-ons, providing evidence of growing sexual pressure even if the peculiar nightmare contents did not, was that he had found their original performance, though sufficient for his purpose as it turned out, rather morally troubling and aesthetically unsatisfying in some respects and giving rise to various sad and wistful reflections in his mind as he repeated their performance in memory.

Ducking through a small, brightly lit marquee into the dim lobby of Ultrabooth, he'd laid a $10 bill on the counter before the bearded young man without looking at him, taken up the $2 returned with the considerate explanation that this was a reduction for senior citizens, and joined the half-dozen or so silent waiting men who mostly edged about restlessly yet slowly, not looking at each other.

After a moderate wait and some small augmentation of their number, there came a stirring from beyond the red velvet ropes as the previous audience was guided out a separate exit door. Ryker gravitated forward with the rest of the new audience. After a two-minute pause, a section of red rope was hooked aside, and they surged gently ahead into a shallow inner foyer from which two narrow dark doorways about fifteen feet apart led onward.

Ryker was the fourth man through the left-hand doorway. He found himself in a dim, curving corridor. On his left, wall. On his right, heavy curtains partly drawn aside from what looked like large closets, each with a gloomy window at the back. He entered the first that was unoccupied (the second), fumbled the curtains shut behind him, and clumsily seated himself facing the window on the cubicle's sole piece of furniture, a rather low barstool.

Actually his booth wasn't crampingly small. Ryker estimated its floor space as at least one half that of the apartment tree's elevator, which had a six-person capacity.

As his eyes became accommodated to the darkness of his booth and the dimness of the sizable room beyond, he saw that the latter was roughly circular and walled by rectangular mirrors, each of which, he realized, must be the window of a booth such as his own—except one window space was just a narrow curtain going to the floor. A wailing bluesy jazz from an unseen speaker gently filled his ears, very muted.

The windows were framed with rows of frosted light bulbs barely turned on—must have them on a rheostat, he thought. The floor was palely and thickly carpeted, and there were a few big pale pillows set about. From the ceiling hung four velvet-covered ropes thinner than those in the lobby. Each ended in a padded leather cuff. He also noted uneasily two velvet-covered paddles, no larger than Ping-Pong ones, lying on one of the big pillows. The dimness made everything seem grimy, as though fine soot were falling continuously from the ceiling like snow.

He sensed a stirring in the other booths, and he saw that a girl had entered the room of mirrors while he'd been intent on the paddles. At first he couldn't tell whether she was naked or not, but then as she slowly walked out, hardly glancing at the mirrors, face straight ahead like a sleepwalker's, the music began to come up and the lights too, brighter and brighter. He saw she was a blonde, age anywhere from nineteen to twenty-nine—how could you know for sure? He hoped nineteen. And she was wearing a net brassiere bordered by what looked like strips of white rabbit's fur. A tiny apron of the same kind of fur hung down over her crotch, attached to some sort of G-string, and she wore short white rabbit's fur boots.

She yawned and stretched, looked around, and then swiftly removed these items of apparel, but instead of letting them fall or laying them down on one of the pillows, she carried them over to the curtained doorway which interrupted the wall of mirrors and handed them through to someone. They were taking no chances on the fur getting dirty—how many performances a day was it the girls gave? He also realized that the right- and left-hand passages to the booths didn't join behind, as he'd imagined at first—there had to be an entry passage for the performer. Good thing he hadn't tried go all the way around and check on all the booths before picking one—and maybe lost his.

The vertical slit in the curtain widened, and the now naked blonde was joined by a naked brunette of the same undetermined youth. They embraced tenderly yet perfunctorily, as if in a dream, swaying with the music's wails, then leaned apart, brushing each other's small breasts, fingers lingering at the erecting nipples, then trailing down to touch each other's clefts. They separated then and began to work their way around the booths, facing each mirror in turn, swaying and writhing, bumping and grinding, arching back, bellying toward. The brunette was across from him, the blonde off to his left and coming closer. His mouth was dry, his breaths came faster. He was getting a hard-on, he told himself, or about to. He was jealous about the time the blonde spent at each other window and yet somehow dreaded her coming.

And then she was writhing in front of him, poker-faced, looking down toward him. Could she see him? Of course not!—he could see the windows across from him, and they just reflected his blank window. But suppose she bent down and pressed her face and flattening nose-tip against the glass, cupping her hands to either side to shut out light? Involuntarily he flinched backward, caught himself and almost as swiftly stretched his face forward to admire her breasts as she preened, trailing her fingers across them. Yes, yes, he thought desperately, dutifully, they were small, firm, not at all pendulous, big nippled with large aureoles, splendid, yes splendid, yes splendid...

And then he was forcing his gaze to follow her hands down her slender waist past her belly button and pale pubic hair and stretch open the lips of her cleft.

It was all so very confusing, those flaps and those ribbons of membrane, of glistening pinkish-red membrane. Really, a man's genitals were much neater, more like a good and clear diagram, a much more sensible layout. And when you were young you were always in too much of a hurry to study the female ones, too damn excited, keyed up, overwhelmed by the importance of keeping a hard-on. That, and the stubborn old feeling that you mustn't look, that was against the rules, this was dirty. With his wife he'd always done it in the dark, or almost. And now when you were old and your eyesight wasn't so good anymore... One

slender finger moved out from the bent stretching ones to point
up, then down, to indicate clitoris and cunt. Whyn't she point out
her urethra too? It was somewhere there, in between. The clitoris
was hard to make out in the midst of all that red squirming...

And then without warning she had spun around, bent over,
and was looking at him from between her spread legs, and her
hand came back around her side to jab a finger twice at the
shadowed sallow pucker of her anus, as if she were saying, "And
here's my asshole, see? My God, how long does it take you dumb
bastards to get things straight?"

Really, it was more like an anatomy lesson taught by a bored,
clown-white cadaver than any sort of spicy erotic cocktail. Where
was the faintest hint of the flirtatious teasing that in old times,
Ryker recalled, gave such performances a point? Why, this girl had
come in almost naked and divested herself of the scant remainder
with all the romance of someone taking out dental plates before
retiring. My God, was that how they got ready for the full act in
private? Where was the slow unbuttoning, the sudden change of
mind and buttoning up again? Where was the enthusiastic self-
peek down her pulled-forward bodice followed by the smile and
knowing wink that said, "Oh, boy, what I got down there! Don't
you wish... ?" Where was the teasing that overreached itself, the
accidental exposure of a goody, pretended embarrassment, and
the overhasty hiding of it, leading to further revelations, as one
who covering her knees bares her rear end? Where the feigned
innocence, prudish or naive? the sense of wicked play, precocious
evil? Above all, where was the illusion that her body's treasures
were just that? her choicest possessions and her chiefest pride,
secret 'tween her and you, hoarded like miser's gold, though
shared out joyously and generously at the end?

The girl, instead of graciously overhearing his racing thoughts
(they must be audible!) and at least attempting to make some
corrections for them in her behavior, last of all seized handholds
at the corners of the window and set the soles of her feet against
the sides and dangled there spread open and bent for a short
while, rocking back and forth, like a poker-faced slender ape,
so he could see it all at once after a fashion: asshole, cunt, and
clitoris—and urethra—wherever that was.

That was the show's highpoint of excitement, or shock at any
rate, for Ryker. Although a third girl appeared and the other
two got her undressed and strung up by the padded straps on

the velvet ropes, and did some things to her with their lips and tongues and the lightly brushing velvet paddles, that was the high point—or whatever.

Afterward he slipped out into the street feeling very conspicuous, but even more relieved. He swore he'd never visit the ignorant place again. But that night he had awakened ejaculating in a wet dream. Afterward he couldn't be quite sure whether his hand mightn't have helped and what sort of dream it had been otherwise, if any—certainly not one of his troll-haunted, buried-alive nightmares.

No, they were gone forever, or at any rate for the next five months.

And then when they did come back, against all his hopes, and when they continued on, and when he found himself balanced between the nightmares and Ultrabooth, and the days seemed dry as dust, there had come the welcome interruption of the Vanishing Lady.

The first time Ryker had seen her, so far as he could recall, they'd been at opposite ends of the long, low entry hall, a good forty feet apart. He had been fumbling for his key outside the street door, which was thick oak framing a large glass panel backed by metal tracery. She'd been standing in profile before the gray elevator door, the small window of which was lit, indicating the cage was at this floor. His gaze approved her instantly (for some men life is an unceasing beauty contest); he liked the way her dark knee-length coat was belted in trimly and the neat look of her head, either dark hair drawn in rather closely or a cloche hat. Automatically he wondered whether she was young and slender or old and skinny.

And then as he continued to look at her, key poised before the lock, she turned her head in his direction and his heart did little fillip and shiver. *She looked at me,* was what he felt, although the corridor was dimly lit and from this far away a face was little more than a pale oval with eye-smudges—and now her hair or hat made it a shadowed oval. It told you no more about her age than her profile had. Just the same, it was now turned toward him.

All this happened quite swiftly.

But then he had to look down at the lock in order to fit his key into it (a fussy business that seemed to take longer with each passing year) and turn it (he sometimes forgot which way) and shove the door open with his other hand, and by that time she'd moved out of sight.

She couldn't have taken the elevator up or down, he told himself as he strode the corridor a little more briskly than was his wont, for the small glass window in its door still shone brightly. She must have just drifted out of sight to the right, where the stairs were and the brass-fronted mailboxes and the window and door to the manager's office and, past those, the long and short back corridors of the ground floor.

But when he reached that foyer, it was empty and the manager's window unoccupied, though not yet dark and shuttered for the night. She must have gone up the stairs or to a back apartment on this floor, though he'd heard no receding footsteps or shutting door confirm that theory.

Just as he opened the elevator door he got the funniest hunch that he'd find her waiting for him there—that she'd entered the cage while he'd been unlocking the front door, but then not pushed a button for a floor. But the cage was as empty as the foyer. So much for hunches! He pushed the 14 button at the top of the narrow brass panel, and by the time he got there, he'd put the incident out of his mind, though a certain wistfulness clung to his general mood.

And he probably would have forgotten it altogether except that late the next afternoon, when he was returning from a rather long walk, the same thing happened to him all over again, the whole incident repeating itself with only rather minor variations. For instance, this time her eyes seen barely to stray in his direction; there wasn't the same sense of a full look. And something flashed faintly at her chest level, as if she were wearing jewelry of some sort, a gemmed pendant—or brooch more likely, since her coat was tightly shut. He was sure it was the same person, and there was the same sense of instant approval or attraction on his part, only stronger this time (which was natural enough, he told himself later). And he went down the hall faster this time and hurried on without pausing to check the stairs and the back corridor, though his chance of hearing footsteps or a closing door was spoiled by the siren of an ambulance rushing by outside. Returning thoughtfully to the foyer, he found the cage gone, but it came down almost immediately, debarking a tenant he recognized—third or fourth floor, he thought—who said rather puzzledly in answer to a question by Ryker that he thought he'd summoned the elevator directly from One and it had been empty when it had reached his floor.

Ryker thanked him and boarded the elevator.

The cage's silvered gray paper and polished fittings made it seem quite modern. Another nice touch was the little window in its door, which matched those in the floor doors when both were shut, so that you got a slow winking glimpse of each floor as you rose past—as Ryker now glimpsed the second floor go down. But actually it was an ancient vehicle smartened up, and so was the system that ran it. You had to hold down a button for an appreciable time to make the cage respond, because it worked by mechanical relays in the elevator room on the roof, not by the instant response to a touch of electronic modern systems. Also, it couldn't remember several instructions and obey them in order as the modern ones could; it obeyed one order only and then waited to be given the next one manually.

Ryker was very conscious of that difference between automatic and manual. For the past five years he had been shifting his own bodily activities from automatic to manual: running (hell, trotting was the most you could call it!—a clumping trot), going down stairs, climbing them, walking outside, even getting dressed and—almost—writing. Used to be he could switch on automatic for those and think about something else. But now he had to do more and more things a step at a time, and watching and thinking about each step too, like a baby learning (only you never did learn; it never got automatic again). And it took a lot more time, everything did. Sometimes you had to stand very still even to think.

Another floor slowly winked by. Ryker caught the number painted on the shaft side of its elevator door just below that door's little window—5. What a slow trip it was!

Ryker did a lot of his real thinking in this elevator part of the apartment tree. It wasn't full of loneliness and ambushing memories the way his apartment was, or crawling with the small dangers and hostilities that occupied most of his mind when he was in the street world outside. It was a world between those, a restful pause between two kinds of oppression, inhabited only by the mostly anonymous people with whom he shared his present half-life, his epilogue life, and quite unlike the realer folk from whom he had been rather purposefully disengaging himself ever since his wife's and his job's deaths.

They were an odd lot, truly, his present fellow-inhabitants of the apartment tree. At least half of them were as old as he, and many of them engaged in the same epilogue living as he was, so far as he could judge. Perhaps a quarter were middle-aged; Ryker liked them least of all—they carried tension with them, things he was trying to forget. While rather fewer than a quarter were young. These always hurried through the apartment tree on full automatic, as if it were a place of no interest whatever, a complete waste of time.

He himself did not find it so, but rather the only place where he could think and observe closely at the same time, a quiet realm of pause. He saw nothing strange in the notion of ghosts (if he'd believed in such) haunting the neighborhood where they'd died— most of them had spent their last few years studying that area in greatest detail, impressing their spirits into its very atoms, while that area steadily grew smaller, as if they were beetles circling a nail to which they were tethered by a thread that slowly wound up, growing shorter and shorter with every circumambulation they made.

Another floor numeral with its little window slid into and out of view—8 only. God, what snaillike, well-frog pace!

The only denizen of the apartment tree with whom Ryker had more than a recognition acquaintance (you could hardly call the one he had with the others nodding, let alone speaking) was Clancy, rough-cut manager-janitor of the building, guardian of the gates of the apartment tree and its historian, a retired fireman who managed to make himself available and helpful without becoming oppressive or officious. Mrs. Clancy was an altogether more respectable and concierge-like character who made Ryker feel uncomfortable. He preferred always to deal with her husband, and over the years a genuine though strictly limited friendship (it never got beyond "Clancy" and "Mr. Ryker") had sprung up between them.

The figure 12 appeared and disappeared in the window. He kept his eyes on the empty rectangle and gave an accustomed chuckle when the next figure was 14, with none intervening. Superstition, how mighty, how undying! (Though somehow the travel between the last two floors, Twelve and Fourteen, always seemed to take longest, by a fraction. There was food for thought there. Did elevators get tired?—perhaps because the air grew more rarified with increased altitude?)

The window above the 14 steadied. There was a clicking; the gray door slid open sideways, he pushed through the outer door, and as he did so, he uttered another chuckle that was both cheerful and sardonic. He'd just realized that after all his journeying in the apartment tree, he'd at last become interested in one of his nameless traveling companions. The elevator-tree world also held the Vanishing Lady.

It was surprising how lighthearted he felt.

As if in rebuke for this and for his springing hopes not clearly defined, he didn't see the Vanishing Lady for the next three days, although he devised one or two errands for himself that would bring him back to the apartment tree at dusk, and when he did spot her again on the fourth day, the circumstances were altered from those of their first two encounters.

Returning from another of his little twilight outings and unlocking the heavy street door, he noted that the hall and distant foyer were a little bit dimmer than usual, as if some small, normal light source were gone, with the effect of a black hole appearing suddenly in the fabric of reality.

As he started forward warily, he discerned the explanation. The doors to the elevator were wide open, but the ceiling light in the cage had been switched (or gone) off, so that where a gray door gleaming by reflection should have been, there was an ominous dark upright rectangle.

And then, as he continued to advance, he saw that the cage wasn't empty. Light angling down into it from the foyer's ceiling fixture revealed the slender figure of the Vanishing Lady leaning with her back against the cage's wall just behind the column of buttons. The light missed her head, but showed the rest of her figure well enough, her dejected posture, her motionless passivity.

As he imperceptibly quickened his stride straight toward her, the slanting light went on, picking up bits of detail here and there in the gloom, almost as if summoning them: the glossy gleam of black oxfords, the muted one of black stockings, and the in-between sheen of her sleek coat. The nearest black-gloved hand appeared to be clutching that together snugly, and from the closure there seemed to come faint diamond glimmers like the faintest ghost of a sparkler shower, so faint he couldn't be sure whether it was really there, or just his own eyes making the churning points of light there are in darkness. The farthest jetty hand held forward a small brass object which he first took for an apartment door key got out well in advance (as some nervous people will) but then saw to be a little too narrow and too long for that.

He was aware of a mounting tension and breathlessness—and sense of strangeness too. And then without warning, just as he was about to enter the cage and simultaneously switch its light on, he heard himself mutter apologetically, "Sorry, I've got to check my mailbox first," and his footsteps veered sharply but smoothly to the right with never a hesitation.

For the next few seconds his mind was so occupied with shock at this sudden rush of timidity, this flinching away from what he'd thought he wanted to do, that he actually had his keys out, was advancing the tiny flat one toward the brass-fronted narrow box he'd checked this noon as always, before he reversed his steps with a small growl of impatience and self-rebuke and hurried back past the manager's shuttered window and around the stairs.

The elevator doors were closed and the small window glowed bright. But just as he snatched at the door to open it, the bright rectangle narrowed from the bottom and winked out, the elevator growled softly as the cage ascended, and the door resisted his yank. Damn! He pressed himself against it, listening intently. Soon—after no more than five or six seconds, he thought—he heard the cage stop and its door *clump* open. Instantly he was thumbing the button. After a bit he heard the door *clump* shut and the growling recommence. Was it growing louder or softer—coming down or going away? Louder! Soon it had arrived, and he was opening the door—rather to the surprise of its emerging occupant, a plump lady in a green coat.

Her eyebrows rose at his questions, rather as had happened on the previous such occasion. She'd been on Three when she'd buzzed for the elevator, she said. No, there'd been no one in it when it arrived, no one had got off, it had been empty. Yes, the light *had* been off in the elevator when it had come up, but she hadn't missed anyone on account of that—and she'd turned it on again. And then she'd just gotten in and come down. Had he been buzzing for it? Well, she'd been pushing the button for One, too. What did it matter?

She made for the street door, glancing back at Ryker dubiously, as if she were thinking that, whatever he was up to, she didn't ever want that excited old man tracking *her* down.

Then for a while Ryker was so busy trying to explain that to himself (Had there been time for her to emerge and shut the doors silently and hurry down the long hall or tiptoe up the stairs before the cage went up to Three? Well, just possibly, but it would have had to be done with almost incredible rapidity. Could he have *imagined* her—projected her onto the gloom inside the cage, so to speak? Or had the lady in green been lying? Were she and the Vanishing Lady confederates? And so on...) that it was some time before he began to try to analyze the reasons for his self-betrayal.

Well, for one thing, he told himself, he'd been so gripped by his desire to see her close up that he'd neglected to ask himself what he'd do once he'd achieved that, how he'd make conversation if they were alone together in the cage—and that these questions popping up in his mind all at once had made him falter. And then there was his lifelong habit, he had to admit, of automatically shrinking from all close contact with women save his mother and wife, especially if the occasion for it came upon him suddenly. Or had he without knowing it become just a little frightened of this mysterious person who had stirred him erotically—the apartment tree was always dimly lit, there'd never been anyone else around when she'd appeared, there'd been something so woeful-melancholy about her attitude (though that was probably part of her attraction), and finally she *had* vanished three times unaccountably—so that it was no wonder he had veered aside from entering the elevator, its very lightlessness suggesting a trap. (And that made him recall another odd point. Not only had the light inside the elevator been switched off but the door, which always automatically swung shut unless someone held it open or set a fairly heavy object, such as a packed suitcase or a laden-large shopping bag, against it, had been standing open. And he couldn't recall having seen any such object or other evidence of propping or wedging. Mysterious. In fact, as mysterious as his suffocation dreams, which at least had lessened in number and intensity since the Vanishing Lady had turned up.)

Well, he told himself with another effort at being philosophical, now that he'd thought all these things through, at least he'd behave more courageously if a similar situation arose another time.

But when the Vanishing Lady next appeared to Ramsey, it was under conditions that did not call for that sort of courage. There were others present.

He'd come in from outside and found the empty cage ready and waiting, but he could hear another party just close enough behind him that he didn't feel justified in taking off without them —though there'd been enough times, God knows, when he'd been left behind under the same circumstances. He dutifully waited, holding the door open. There had been times, too, when this politeness of his had been unavailing—when the people had been bound for a ground-floor apartment, or when it had been a lone woman and she'd found an excuse for not making her journey alone with him.

The party finally came into view—two middle-aged women and a man—and the latter insisted on holding the door himself. Ryker relinquished it without argument and went to the back of the cage, the two women following. But the man didn't come inside; he held the door for yet a third party he'd evidently heard coming behind *them*.

The third party arrived, an elderly couple, but that man insisted on holding the door in his turn for the second man and his own ancient lady. They were six, a full load, Ryker counted. But then, just as the floor door was swinging shut, someone caught it from the outside, and the one who slipped in last was the Vanishing Lady.

Ramsey mightn't have seen her if he hadn't been tall, for the cage was now almost uncomfortably crowded, although none of them were conspicuous heavyweights. He glimpsed a triangle of pale face under dark gleaming eyes, which fixed for an instant on his, and he felt a jolt of excitement, or something. Then she had whipped around and was facing front, like the rest. His heart was thudding and his throat was choked up. He knew the sheen of her black hair and coat, the dull felt of her close-fitting hat, and watched them raptly. He decided from the flash of face that she was young or very smoothly powdered.

The cage stopped at the seventh floor. She darted out without a backward glance and the elderly couple followed her. He wanted to do something but he couldn't think what, and someone pressed another button.

As soon as the cage had resumed its ascent, he realized that he too could have gotten out on Seven and at least seen where she went in, discovered her apartment number. But he hadn't acted quickly enough and some of these people probably knew he lived on Fourteen and would have wondered.

The rest got out on Twelve and so he did the last floor alone—the floor that numerically was two floors, actually only one, yet always seemed to take a bit too long, the elevator growing tired, ha-ha-ha.

Next day he examined the names on the seventh-floor mailboxes, but that wasn't much help. Last names only, with at most an initial or two, was the rule. No indication of sex or marital status. And, as always, fully a third were marked only as OCCUPIED. It was safer that way, he remembered being told (something about anonymous phone calls or confidence games), even if it somehow always looked suspicious, vaguely criminal.

Late the next afternoon, when he was coming in from the street, he saw a man holding the elevator door open for two elderly women to enter. He hurried his stride, but the man didn't look his way before following them.

But just at that moment, the Vanishing Lady darted into view from the foyer, deftly caught the closing door, and with one pale glance over her shoulder at Ryker, let herself in on the heels of the man. Although he was too far away to see her eyes as more than twin gleams, he felt the same transfixing jolt as he had the previous day. His heart beat faster too.

And then as he hurried on, the light in the little window in the gray door winked out as the elevator rose up and away from him. A few seconds later he was standing in front of the electrically locked door with its dark little window and staring ruefully at the button and the tiny circular telltale just above it, which now glowed angry red to indicate the elevator was in use and unresponsive to any summons.

He reproached himself for not having thought to call out, "Please wait for me," but there'd hardly been time to think, besides it would have been such a departure from his normal, habitually silent behavior. Still, another self-defeat, another self-frustration, in his pursuit of the Vanishing Lady! He wished this elevator had, like those in office buildings or hotels, a more extensive telltale beside or over its door that told which floor it was on or passing, so you could trace its course. It would be helpful to know whether it stopped at Seven again this time—it was hard to hear it stop when it got that far away. Of course you could run up the stairs, racing it, if you were young enough and in shape. He'd once observed two young men who were sixth-floor residents do just that, pitting the one's strong legs and two-or-three-steps-

at-a-time against the other's slow elevator—and never learned
who won. For that matter, the young tenants, who were mostly
residents of the lower floors, where the turnover of apartments
was brisker, quite often went charging blithely up the stairs even
when the elevator was waiting and ready, as if to advertise (along
with their youth) their contempt for its tedious *elderly* pace. If *he*
were young again now, he asked himself, would he have raced up
after a vanished girl?

The telltale went black. He jabbed the button, saw it turn red
again as the cage obediently obeyed his summons.

Next afternoon found him staring rather impatiently at the red
telltale on the fourteenth floor, this time while waiting to travel
to the ground floor and so out. And this time it had been red for
quite some while, something that happened not infrequently, since
the cage's slow speed and low capacity made it barely adequate
to service a building of this size. And while it stayed red it was
hard to tell how many trips it was making and how long people
were holding the door at one floor. He'd listened to numerous
speculative conversations about "what the elevator was doing,"
as if it had mind and volition of its own, which one humorist had
indeed suggested. And there were supposed to be certain people
(sometimes named and sometimes not) who did outrageous and
forbidden things, such as jamming the floor door open while they
went back to get things they'd forgotten, or picked up friends on
other floors as they went down (or up), organizing an outing or
party or having secret discussions and arguments before reaching
the less private street. There were even said to be cases of people
"pulling the elevator away" from other people who were their
enemies, just to spite them.

The most colorful theory, perhaps, was that held by two
elderly ladies, both old buffs of elevator travel, whom Ramsey
had happened to overhear on two or three occasions. The
cornerstone of their theory was that all the building's troubles
were caused by its younger tenants and the teenage sons and
daughters of tenants. "Mrs. Clancy told me," one of them had
whispered loudly once, "that they know a way of stopping the
thing between floors so they can smooch together and shoot dope
and do all sorts of other nasty things—even, if you can believe,
go the whole way with each other." Ryker had been amused; it
gave the cage a certain erotic aura.

And every once in a while the elevator did get stuck between floors, sometimes with people in it and sometimes not, especially between the twelfth and fourteenth floors, Clancy had once told him, "like it was trying to stop at the thirteenth!"

But now the elevator's vagaries weren't all that amusing to Ramsey standing alone on the top floor, so after one more session of pettish button-pushing—the telltale had gone briefly black, but evidently someone else had beat him to the punch—he decided to "walk down for exercise," something he'd actually done intentionally upon occasion.

As he descended the apartment tree (he thought of himself as an old squirrel sedately scampering zigzag down the barky outside of the trunk the elevator shaft made), he found himself wondering how the elevator could be so busy when all the corridors were so silent and empty. (But maybe things were happening just before his footstep-heralded arrivals and after his departures—they heard him coming and hid themselves until he was by. Or maybe there was some sort of basement crisis.) The floors were all the same, or almost so: the two long corridors ending in doors of wire-reinforced glass which led to the front and alley fire escapes; these were also lit midway by frosted glass spheres like full moons hanging in space; in either wall beside these handsome globes were set two narrow full-length mirrors in which you could see yourself paced along by two companions.

The apartment tree boasted many mirrors, a luxury note like its silver-arabesqued gray wallpaper. There was a large one opposite each elevator door and there were three in the lobby.

As he ended each flight, Ramsey would look down the long alley corridor, make a U-turn, and walk back to the landing (glancing into the short corridor and the elevator landing, which were lit by a central third moon and one large window), all this while facing the long front corridor, then make another U-turn and start down the next flight.

(He did discover one difference between the floors. He counted steps going down, and while there were nineteen between the fourteenth and the twelfth floors, there were only seventeen between all the other pairs. So the cage had to travel a foot and a bit farther to make that Fourteen-Twelve journey; it didn't just *seem* to take longer, it *did*. So much for tired elevators!)

So it went for nine floors.

But when he made his U-turn onto the third floor he saw that the front corridor's full moon had been extinguished, throwing a gloom on the whole passageway, while silhouetted against the wired glass at the far end was a swayed, slender figure looking very much like that of the Vanishing Lady. He couldn't make out her pale triangle of face or gleaming eyes because there was no front light on her; she was only shaped darkness, yet he was sure it was she.

In walking the length of the landing, however, there was time to think that if he continued on beyond the stairs, it would be an undeniable declaration of his intention to meet her, he'd have to keep going, he had no other excuse; also, there'd be the unpleasant impression of him closing in ominously, relentlessly, on a lone trapped female.

As he advanced she waited at the tunnel's end, silent and unmoving, a shaped darkness.

He made his customary turn, keeping on down the stairs. He felt so wrenched by what was happening that he hardly knew what he was thinking or even feeling, except his heart was thudding and his lungs were gasping as if he'd just, walked ten stories upstairs instead of down.

It wasn't until he had turned into the second floor and seen through the stairwell, cut off by ceiling, the workshoes and twill pants of Clancy, the manager, faced away from him in the lobby, that he got himself in hand. He instantly turned and retraced his steps with frantic haste. He'd flinched away again, just when he'd sworn he wouldn't! Why, there were a dozen questions he could politely ask her to justify his close approach. Could he be of assistance? Was she looking for one of the tenants? some apartment number? Etcetera.

But even as he rehearsed these phrases, he had a sinking feeling of what he was going to find on Three.

He was right. There was no longer a figure among the shadows filling the dark front corridor.

And then, even as he was straining his eyes to make sure, with a flicker and a flash the full moon came on again and shone steadily.

Showing no one at all.

Ramsey didn't look any further but hurried back down the stairs. He wanted to be with people, anyone, just people in the street.

But Mr. Clancy was still in the lobby, communing with himself. Ramsey suddenly felt he simply had to share at least part of the story of the Vanishing Lady with someone.

So he told Clancy about the defective light bulb inside the

front globe on Three, how it had started to act like a globe that's near the end of its lifetime, arcing and going off and on by itself, unreliable. Only then did he, as if idly, an afterthought, mention the woman he'd seen and then got to wondering about and gone back and not seen, adding that he thought he'd also seen her in the lobby once or twice before.

He hadn't anticipated the swift seriousness of the manager's reaction. Ramsey'd hardly more than mentioned the woman when the ex-fireman asked sharply, "Did she look like a bum? I mean, for a woman—"

Ramsey told him that no, she didn't, but he hadn't more than sketched his story when the other said, "Look, Mr. Ryker, I'd like to go up and check this out right away. You said she was all in black, didn't you? Yeah. Well, look, you stay here, would you do that? And just take notice if anybody comes down. I won't be long."

And he got in the elevator, which had been waiting there, and went up. To Four or Five, or maybe Six, Ramsey judged from the cage's noises and the medium-short time the telltale flared before winking out. He imagined that Clancy would leave it there and then hunt down the floors one by one, using the stairs.

Pretty soon Clancy did reappear by way of the stairs, looking thoughtful. "No" he said, "she's not there anymore, at least not in the bottom half of the building—and I don't see her doing a lot of climbing. Maybe she got somebody to take her in, or maybe it *was* just one of the tenants. Or...?" He looked a question at Ramsey, who shook his head and said, "No, nobody came down the stairs or elevator."

The manager nodded and then shook his own head slowly. "I don't know, maybe I'm getting too suspicious," he said. "I don't know how much you've noticed, Mr. Ryker, living way on top, but from time to time this building is troubled by bums—winos and street people from south of here—trying to get inside and shelter here, especially in winter, maybe go to sleep in a corner. Most of them are men, of course, but there's an occasional woman bum." He paused and chuckled reflectively. "Once we had an invasion of women bums, though they weren't that exactly."

Ramsey looked at him expectantly.

Clancy hesitated, glanced at Ramsey, and after another pause said, "That's why we turn the buzzer system off at eleven at night and keep it off until eight in the morning. If we left it on, why, any time in the night a drunken wino would start buzzing apartments until he got one who'd buzz the door open (or he might push a dozen at once, so somebody'd be sure to buzz the door), and once he was inside, he'd hunt himself up an out-of-the-way spot where he could sleep it off and be warm. And if he had cigarettes, he'd start smoking them to put him to sleep, dropping the matches anywhere, but mostly under things. There's where your biggest danger is—fire. Or he'd get an idea and start bothering tenants, ringing theirs bells and knocking on their doors, and then anything could happen. Even with the buzzer system off, some of them get in. They'll stand beside the street door and then follow a couple that's late getting home, or the same with the newsboy delivering the morning paper before it's light. Not following them directly, you see, but using a foot (sometimes a cane or crutch) to block the door just before it locks itself, and then coming in soon as the coast's clear."

Ramsey nodded several times appreciatively, but then pressed the other with "But you were going to tell me something about an invasion of female bums?"

"Oh, that," Clancy said doubtfully. A look at Ramsey seemed to reassure him. "That was before your time—you came here about five years ago, didn't you? Yeah. Well, this happened... let's see... about two years before that. The Mrs. and I generally don't talk about it much to tenants, because it gives... gave the building a bad name. Not really any more now, though. Seven years and all's forgotten, eh?"

He broke off to greet respectfully a couple who passed by on their way upstairs. He turned back to Ramsey. "Well, anyway," he continued more comfortably, "at this time I'm talking about, the Mrs. and I had been here ourselves only a year. Just about long enough to learn the ropes, at least some of them.

"Now there's one thing about a building like this I got to explain," he interjected. "You never, or almost never, get any disappearances—you know, tenants sneaking their things out when they're behind on the rent, or just walking out one day, leaving their things, and never coming back (maybe getting mugged to death, who knows?)—like happens all the time in those fleabag hotels and rooming houses south of us. Why, half of *their* renters are on dope or heavy medication to begin with, and come from prisons or from mental hospitals. Here you get a steadier sort of tenant, or at least the Mrs. and I try to make it be like that.

"Well, back then, just about the steadiest tenant we had, though not the oldest by any means, was a tall, thin, very handsome and distinguished-looking youngish chap, name of Arthur J. Stensor, third floor front. Very polite and soft-spoken, never raised his voice. Dark complected, but with blonde hair which he wore in a natural—not so common then; once I heard him referred to by another tenant as 'that frizzy bleached Negro,' and I thought they were being disrespectful. A sharp dresser but never flashy—he had class. He always wore a hat. Rent paid the first of the month in cash with never a miss. Rent for the garage space too—he kept a black Lincoln Continental in the basement that was always polished like glass; never used the front door much but went and came in that car. And his apartment was furnished to match: oil paintings in gold frames, silver statues, hi-fi, big-screen TV and the stuff to record programs and films off it when that *cost,* all sorts of fancy clocks and vases, silks and velvets, more stuff like that than you'd ever believe.

"And when there was people with him, which wasn't too often, they were as classy as he and his car and his apartment, especially the women—high society and always young. I remember once being in the third-floor hall one night when one of those stunners swept by me and he let her in, and thinking, 'Well, if that filly was a call girl, she sure came from the best stable in town.' Only I remember thinking at the same time that I was being disrespectful, because A. J. Stensor was just a little too respectable for even the classiest call girl. Which was a big joke on me considering what happened next."

"Which was?" Ramsey prompted, after they'd waited for a couple more tenants to go by.

"Well, at first I didn't connect it at all with Stensor," Clancy responded, "though it's true I hadn't happened to see him for the last five or six days, which was sort of unusual, though not all that much so. Well, what happened was this invasion—no, goddammit! this *epidemic*—of good-looking hookers, mostly tall and skinny, or at least skinny, through the lower halls and lobby of this building. Some of them were dressed too respectable for hookers, but most of them wore the street uniform of the day— which was high heels, skintight blue jeans, long lace blouses worn outside the pants, and lots of bangles—and when you saw them talking together palsy-walsy, the respectable-looking and the not, you knew they all had to be."

"How did it first come to you?" Ramsey asked. "Tenants complain?"

"A couple," Clancy admitted. "Those old biddies who'll report a young and good-looking woman on the principle that if she's young and good-looking she can't be up to any good purpose. But the really funny thing was that most of the reports of them came in just by way of gossip—either to me direct, or by way of the Mrs., which is how it usually works—like it was something strange and remarkable—which it was, all right! Questions too, such as what the hell they were all up to, which was a good one to ask, by the way. You see, they weren't any of them *doing* anything to complain of. It was broad day and they certainly weren't trying to pick anyone up, they weren't plying their trade at all, you might say, they weren't even smiling at anybody, especially men. No, they were just walking up and down and talking together, looking critical and angry more than anything, and very serious—like they'd picked our apartment building for a hookers' convention, complete with debates, some sort of feminist or union thing, except they hadn't bothered to inform the management. Oh, when I'd cough and ask a couple of them what they were doing, they'd throw me some excuse without looking at me—that they had a lunch date with a lady here but she didn't seem to be in and they couldn't wait, or that they were shopping for apartments but these weren't suitable—and at the same time they'd start walking toward the street door, or toward the stairs if they were on the third or second floor, still gabbing together in private voices about whatever it was they were debating, and then they'd sweep out, still not noticing me even if I held the door for them.

"And then, you know, in twenty minutes they'd be back inside! or at least I'd spot one of them that was. Some of them *must* have had front door keys, I remember thinking—and as it turned out later, some of them did."

By this time Mr. Clancy had warmed to his story and was giving out little chuckles with every other sentence, and he almost forgot to lower his voice next time a tenant passed.

"There was one man they took notice of. I forgot about that. It could have given me a clue to what was happening, but I didn't get it. We had a tenant then on one of the top floors who was tall and slim and rather good-looking—young-looking too, although he wasn't—and always wore a hat. Well, I was in the lobby and four or five of the hookers had just come in the front door, debating of course, when this guy stepped out of the elevator and they all spotted him and made a rush for him. But when they got about a dozen feet away from him and he took off his hat—maybe to be polite, he looked a little scared, I don't know what he thought— showing this wavy black hair which he kept dyed, the hookers all lost interest in him—as if he'd looked like someone they knew, but closer up turned out not to be (which was the case, though I still didn't catch on then)—and they swept past him and on the stairs as if that was where they'd been rushing in the first place.

"I tell you, that was some weird day. Hookers dressed all ways— classy-respectable, the tight-jeans and lacy-blouse uniform, mini-skirts, one in what looked like a kid's sailor suit cut for a woman, a sad one all in black looking like something special for funerals... you know, maybe to give first aid to a newly bereaved husband or something." He gave Ryker a quick look, continuing, "And although almost all of them were skinny, I recall there was a fat one wearing a mumu and swinging gracefully like a belly dancer.

"The Mrs. was after me to call the police, but our owner sort of discourages that, and I couldn't get him on the phone.

"In the evening the hookers tapered off and I dropped into bed, all worn out from the action, the wife still after me to call the police, but I just conked out cold, and so the only one to see the last of the business was the newsboy when he came to deliver at four-thirty about. Later on he dropped back to see me, couldn't wait to tell me about it.

"Well, he was coming up to the building, it seems, pushing his shopping cart of morning papers, when he sees this crowd of good- looking women (he wasn't wise to the hookers' convention the day before) around the doorway, most of' them young and all of them carrying expensive-looking objects—paintings, vases, silver statues of naked girls, copper kitchenware, gold clocks, that sort of stuff—like they were helping a wealthy friend move. Only there is a jam-up, two or three of them are trying to maneuver an oversize dolly through the door, and on that dolly is the biggest television set the kid ever saw and also the biggest record player.

"A woman at the curb outside, who seems a leader, sort of very cool, is calling directions to them how to move it, close beside her is another woman, like her assistant or gopher maybe. The leader's calling out directions, like I say, in a hushed voice, and the other women are watching, but they're all very quiet, like you'd expect people to be at that hour of the morning, sober people at any rate, not wanting to wake the neighbors.

"Well, the kid's looking all around, every which way, trying ,to take in everything—there was a lot of interesting stuff to see, I gather, and more inside—when the gopher lady comes over and hunkers down beside him—he was a runt, that newsboy was, and ugly too—and wants to buy a morning paper. He hauls it out for her and she gives him a five-dollar bill and tells him to keep the change. He's sort of embarrassed by that and drops his eyes, but she tells him not to mind, he's a handsome boy and a good hardworking one, she wished she had one like him, and he deserves everything he gets, and she puts an arm around him and draws him close and all of a sudden his downcast eyes are looking inside her blouse front and he's getting the most amazing anatomy lesson you could imagine.

"He has some idea that they're getting the dolly clear by now and that the other women are moving, but she's going on whispering in his ear, her breath's like steam, what a good boy he is and how grateful his parents must be, and *his* only worry, she'll hug him so tight he won't be able to look down her blouse.

"After a bit she ends his anatomy lesson with a kiss that almost smothers him and then stands up. The women are all gone and the dolly's vanishing around the next corner. Before she hurries after it, she says, 'So long, kid. You got your bonus. Now deliver your papers.'

"Which, after he got over his daze, is what he did, he said.

"Well, of course, as soon as he mentioned the big television and player, I flashed on what I'd been missing all yesterday, though it was right in front of my eyes if I'd just looked. Why they'd been swarming on Three, why they rushed the guy from Seven and then lost interest in him when he took off his hat and they saw his hair was black dyed (instead of frizzy blonde), and why the hookers' convention wasn't still going on today. All that loot could have only come from one place—Stensor's. In spite of him being so respectable, he'd been running a string of call girls all the time so that when he ran out on them owing them all money (I flashed on that at the same time), they'd collected the best way they knew how.

"I ran to his apartment, and you know the door wasn't even

locked—one of them must have had a key to it too. Of course the place was stripped and of course no sign of Stensor.

"Then I did call the police of course but not until I'd checked the basement. His black Continental was gone, but there was no way of telling for sure whether he'd taken it or the gals had got that too.

"It surprised me how fast the police came and how many of them there were, but it showed they must wearing had an eye on him already, which maybe explained why he left so sudden without taking his things. They asked a lot of questions and came back more than once, were in and out for a few days. I got to know one of the detectives, he lived locally, we had a drink together once or twice, and he told me they were really after Stensor for drug dealing, he was handling cocaine back in those days when it was first getting to be the classy thing, they weren't interested in his call girls except as he might have used them as pushers. They never did turn him up though, far as I know, and there wasn't even a line in the papers about the whole business."

"So that was the end of your one-day hooker invasion?" Ryker commented, chuckling rather dutifully.

"Not quite," Clancy said, and hesitated. Then with a "What-difference-can-it-make?" shrug, he went on, "Well, yes, there was a sort of funny follow-up but it didn't amount to much. You see, the story of Stensor and the hookers eventually got around to most of the tenants in the building, as such things will, though some of them got it garbled, as you can imagine happens, that he was a patron and maybe somehow victim of call girls instead of running them. Well, anyhow, after a bit, we (the Mrs. mostly) began to get these tenant reports of a girl—a young woman—seen waiting outside the door to Stensor's apartment, or wandering around in other parts of the building, but mostly waiting at Stensor's door. And this was after there were other tenants in that apartment. A sad-looking girl."

"Like, out of all those hookers," Ryker said, "she was the only one who really loved him and waited for him. A sort of leftover."

"Yeah, or the only one who hadn't got her split of the loot," Clancy said. "Or maybe he owed her more than the others. I never saw her myself, although I went chasing after her a couple of times when tenants reported her. I wouldn't have taken any stock in her except the descriptions did seem to hang together. A college-type girl, they'd say, and mostly wearing black. And sort of sad. I told the detective I knew, but he didn't seem to make anything out of it. They never did pick up any of the women, he said, far as he knew. Well, that's all there is to the follow-up—like I said, nothing much. And after two or three months tenants stopped seeing her."

He broke off, eyeing Ryker just a little doubtfully.

"But it stuck in your mind," that one observed, "for all these years, so that when I told you about seeing a woman in black near the same door, you rushed off to check up on her, just on the chance? Though you'd never seen her yourself, even once?"

Clancy's expression became a shade unhappy. "Well, no," he admitted, glancing up and down the hall, as though hoping someone would come along and save him from answering. "There was a little more than that," he continued uneasily, "though I wouldn't want anyone making too much of it, or telling the Mrs. I told them.

"But then, Mr. Ryker, you're not the one to be gossipping or getting the wind up, are you?" he continued more easily, giving his tenant a hopeful look.

"No, of course I'm not," Ryker responded, a little more casually than he felt. "What was it?"

"Well, about four years ago we had another disappearance here, a single man living alone and getting on in years but still active. He didn't own any of the furniture, his possessions were few, nothing at all fancy like Stensor's, no friends or relations we knew of, and he came to us from a building that knew no more; in fact we didn't realize he was gone until the time for paying the rent came round. And it wasn't until then that I recalled that the last time or two I spoke to him he'd mentioned something about a woman in an upstairs hall, wondering if she'd found the people or the apartment number she seemed to be looking for. Not making a complaint, you see, just mentioning, just idly wondering, so that it wasn't until he disappeared that I thought of connecting it up with Stensor's girl at all."

"He say if she was young?" Ryker asked.

"He wasn't sure. She was wearing a black outside coat and hat or scarf of something that hid her face, and she made a point of not noticing him when he looked at her and thought of asking if she needed help. He did say she was thin, though, I remember."

Ryker nodded.

Clancy continued, "And then a few years ago there was this

couple on Nine that had a son living with them, a big fat lug who looked older than he was and was always being complained about whether he did anything or not. One of the old ladies in the apartment next to their bathroom used to kick to us about him running water for baths at two or three in the morning. And he had the nerve to complain to us about *them*, claiming they pulled the elevator away from him when he wanted to get it, or made it go in the opposite direction to what he wanted when he was in it. I laughed in his pimply face at that. Not that those two old biddies wouldn't have done it to him if they'd figured a way and they'd got the chance.

"His mother was a sad soul who used to fuss at him and worry about him a lot. She'd bring her troubles to the Mrs. and talk and talk—but I think really she'd have been relieved to have him off her mind.

"His father was a prize crab, an ex-army officer forever registering complaints—he had a little notebook for them. But half the time he was feuding with me and the Mrs., wouldn't give us the time of day—or of course ask it. I know *he'd* have been happy to see his loud-mouthed dumb son drop out of sight.

"Well, one day the kid comes down to me here with a smart-ass grin and says, 'Mr. Clancy, you're the one who's so great, aren't you, on chasing winos and hookers out of here, not letting them freeload in the halls for a minute? Then how come you let—'

" 'Go on,' I tell him, 'what do you know about hookers?'

"But that doesn't faze him, he just goes on (he was copying his father, I think, actually), 'Then how come you let this skinny little hooker in a black fur coat wander around the halls all the time, trying to pick guys up?'

" 'You're making this up,' I tell him flat, 'or you're imagining things, or else one of our lady tenants is going to be awful sore at you if she ever hears you've been calling her a hooker.'

" 'She's nobody from this building,' the kid insists, 'she's got more class. That fur coat cost money. It's hard to check out her face, though, because she never looks at you straight on and she's got this black hat she hides behind. I figure she's an old bag—maybe thirty, even—and wears the hat so you can't see her wrinkles, but that she's got a young bod, young and wiry. I bet she takes karate lessons so she can bust the balls of any guy that gets out of line, or maybe if he just doesn't satisfy her—'

" 'You're pipe-dreaming, kid,' I tell him.

" 'And you know what?' he goes on. 'I bet you she's got nothing on but black stockings and a garter belt under that black fur coat she keeps wrapped so tight around her, so when she's facing a guy she can give him a quick flash of her bod, to lead him on—'

" 'And you got a dirty mind,' I say. 'You're making this up.'

" 'I am not,' he says. 'She was just now up on Ten before I came down and leering at me sideways, giving me the come on.'

" 'What were you doing up on Ten?' I ask him loud.

" 'I always go up a floor before I buzz the elevator,' he answers me quick, 'so's those old dames won't know it's me and buzz it away from me.'

" 'All right, quiet down, kid,' I tell him. 'I'm going up to Ten right now, to check this out, and you're coming with me.'

"So we go on up to Ten and there's nobody there and right away the kid starts yammering, 'I bet you she picked up a trick in this building and they're behind one of these doors screwing, right now. Old Mr. Lucas—'

"I was really going to give him a piece of my mind then, tell him off, but on the way up I'd been remembering that girl of Stensor's who lingered behind, maybe for a long time, if there was anything to what the other guy told me. And somehow it gave me a sort of funny feeling, so all I said was something like 'Look here, kid, maybe you're making this up and maybe not. Either way, I still think you got a dirty mind. But if you did see this hooker and you ever see her again, don't you have anything to do with her—and don't go off with her if she should ask you. You just come straight to me and tell me, and if I'm not here, you find a cop and tell him. Hear me?'

"You know, that sort of shut him up. 'All right, all right!' he said and went off, taking the stairs going down."

"And did *he* disappear?" Ryker asked after a bit. He seemed vaguely to remember the youth in question, a pallid and lumbering lout who tended to brush against people and bump into doorways when he passed them.

"Well, you know, in a way that's a matter for argument," Clancy answered slowly. "It was the last time I saw him—that's a fact. And the Mrs. never saw him again either. But when she asked his mother about *him,* she just said he was off visiting friends for a while, but then a month or so later she admitted to the Mrs. that he *had* gone off without telling them a word—to join a commune, she thought, from some of the things he'd been saying, and that was all right with her, because his father just couldn't get along with him, they had such fights, only she wished he'd have the consideration to send her a card or something."

"And that was the last of it?" Ryker asked.

Clancy nodded slowly, almost absently. "That was damn all of it," he said softly. "About ten months later the parents moved. The kid hadn't turned up. There was nothing more."

"Until now," Ryker said, "when I came to you with my questions about a woman in black—and on Three at that, where this Stensor had lived. It wasn't a fur coat, of course, and I didn't think of her being a hooker—" (Was that true? he wondered) "—and it brought it all back to you, which now included what the young man had told you, and so you checked out the floors and then very kindly told me the whole story so as to give me the same warning you gave him?"

"But you're an altogether different sort of person, Mr. Ryker," Clancy protested. "I'd never think— But yes, allowing for that, that about describes it. You can't be too careful."

"No, you can't. It's a strange business," Ryker commented, shaking his head, and then added, making it sound much more casual, even comical, than he felt it, "You know, if this had happened fifty years ago, we'd be thinking maybe we had a ghost."

Clancy chuckled uneasily and said, "Yeah, I guess that's so."

Ryker said, "But the trouble with that idea would have been that there's nothing in the story about a woman disappearing, but three men—Stensor, and the man who lived alone, and the young man who lived with his parents."

"That's so," Mr. Clancy said.

Ryker stirred himself. "Well, thanks for telling me all about it," he said as they shook hands. "And if I should run into the lady again, I won't take any chances. I'll report it to you, Clancy. But not to the Mrs."

"I know you will, Mr. Ryker," Clancy affirmed.

Ryker himself wasn't nearly so sure of that. But he felt he had to get away to sort out his impressions. The dingy silvery walls were becoming oppressive.

Ryker made his walk a long one, brisk and thoughtful to begin with, dawdling and mind-wandering to finish, so that it was almost sunset by the time he reentered the apartment tree (and our story), but he had his impressions sorted. Clancy had—

possibly—given the Vanishing Lady a history, funny to start with (that "hookers' convention"!) but then by stages silly, sad, sinister. Melancholy, moody, and still mysterious.

The chief retroactive effect of Clancy's story on his memories of his own encounters with the Vanishing Lady had been to intensify their sexual color, give them a sharper, coarser erotic note—an Ultrabooth note, you could say. In particular Ryker was troubled that ever since hearing Clancy narrate the loutish youth's steamy adolescent imagining that his "little hooker" had worn nothing but black stockings and a garter belt under her black fur coat, he was unable to be sure whether he himself had had similar simmering fantasy flashes during his encounters with her.

Could he be guilty, at his age, he asked himself, of such callow and lurid fantasies? The answer to that was, of course, "Of course." And then wasn't the whole romantic business of the Vanishing Lady just a retailoring of Ultrabooth to his own taste, something that made an Ultrabooth girl his alone? Somehow, he hoped not. But had he any real plan for making contact with her if she ever did stop vanishing? His unenterprising behavior when he'd had the chance to get into the elevator with her alone, and later the chance to get off the elevator at the same floor as she, and today the opportunity to meet her face to face on the third floor, indicated clearly that the answer to that question was "No." Which depressed him.

To what extent did Clancy believe in his story and in the reality of the girl who'd reportedly lingered on? He obviously had enjoyed telling it, and likely (from his glibness) had done so more than once, to suitable appreciative listeners. But did he believe she was one continuing real entity, or just a mixture of suggestion, chance, and mistaken resemblances, gossip, and outright lies? He'd never seen her himself—had this made Clancy doubt her reality, or contrariwise given him a stubborn hankering to catch sight of her himself for once at least? On the whole, Ryker thought Clancy was a believer—if only judging by his haste to search for her.

And as for the ghost idea, which you couldn't get around because it fitted her appearing and disappearing behavior so well, no matter how silly and unfashionable such a suggestion might be—Clancy's reaction to that had seemed uneasy, skepticism rather than outright "Nonsense!" rejection.

Which was very much like Ryker's own reaction to it, he realized. He knew there'd been some feelings of fear mixed in with the excitement during all his later encounters with her, before he'd heard Clancy's story. How would he feel now, after hearing it, if he should see her again, he wondered uncomfortably. More fear? Or would he now spot clues to her unreality? Would she begin to melt into mist? Would she look different simply because of what he'd heard about her?

Most likely, reality being the frustrating thing it was, he thought with an unamused inward guffaw, he'd simply never glimpse her again and never know. The stage having been set, all manifestations would cease.

But then, as he let the front door slip from his hand and swing toward its click-solemnized self-locking, he saw the Vanishing Lady forty feet away exactly as he had the first two times, real, no ghostliness anywhere (the name for the material of her coat came to his mind—velour), her shadowed face swung his way, or almost so, and modestly reaverted itself, and she moved out of sight on her black oxfords.

He reached the foyer fast as he could manage, its emptiness neither startling nor relieving him, nor the emptiness of the long back hall. He looked at the Clancys' door and the shuttered office window and shook his head and smiled. (Report this adventure? Whyever?) He started toward the stairs, but shook his head again and smiled more ruefully—he was already breathing very hard. He entered the elevator, and as he firmly pressed the Fourteen button with his thumb and heard the cage respond, he saw the dark gleaming eyes of the Vanishing Lady looking in at him anxiously, imploringly—they were open very wide—through the narrowing small window in the doors.

The next thing he was aware of, the cage was passing Three and he had just croaked out a harsh "Good evening"—the chalky aftertaste of these words was in his throat. The rest of the trip seemed interminable.

When the cage reached Fourteen, his thumb was already pressing the One button—and that trip seemed interminable too.

No sign of anyone anywhere, on One. He looked up the stairs, but he was breathing harder than even before. Finally he got back into the elevator and hovered his thumb over the 14 button. He could touch but not press it down. He brought his face close to the empty little window and waited and waited—and waited.

His thumb did not press down then, but the cage responded. The little window slipped shut. "It's out of my hands," he told himself fatalistically; Tm being pulled somewhere." And from somewhere the thought came to him: What if a person were confined to this apartment tree forever, never leaving it, just going up and down and back and forth, and down and up and forth and back?

The cage didn't stop until Twelve, where the door was opened by a white-haired couple. Responding to their apologies with a reassuring head-shake and a signed "It's all right," Ryker pressed past them and, gasping gently and rapidly, mounted the last flight of stairs very slowly, very slowly. The two extra steps brought on a fit of swirling dizziness, but it passed and he slowly continued on toward his room. He felt frustrated, confused and very tired. He clung to the thoughts that he had reversed the elevator's course as soon as he could, despite his fright, and returned downstairs to hunt for her, and that in his last glimpse of them, her eyes had looked frightened too.

That night he had the muttering black nightmare again, all of it for the first time in weeks, and stronger, he judged afterward, than he'd ever before experienced it. The darkness seemed more impenetrable, solid, an ocean of black concrete congealing about him. The paralysis more complete, black canvas mummy wrappings drawn with numbing tightness, a spiral black cocoon tourniquet- tight. The dry and smoky odors more intense, as though he were baking and strangling in volcanic ash, while the sewer-stenches vied in disgustingness with fruity-flowery, reeks meant to hide them. The sullen ghost-light of his imagination showed the micro-males grosser and more cockroachlike in their hordes. And when finally under the goad of intensest horror he managed to stir himself and strain upward, feeling his heart and veins tearing with the effort, he encountered within a fraction of an inch his tomb's coarsely lined ceiling, which showered gritty ash into his gasping mouth and sightless eyes.

When he finally fought his way awake it was day, but his long sleep had in no way rested him. He felt tired still and good for nothing. Yesterday's story and walk had been too long, he told himself, yesterday's elevator encounter too emotionally exhausting. "Prisoners of the apartment tree," he murmured.

* * *

The Vanishing Lady was in very truth an eternal prisoner of the apartment tree, knowing no other life than there and no sleep anywhere except for lapsings that were as sudden as a drunkard's blackouts into an unconsciousness as black as Ryker's nightmares, but of which she retained no memory whatever save for a general horror and repulsion which colored all her waking thoughts.

She'd come awake walking down a hall, or on the stairs or in the moving elevator, or merely waiting somewhere in the tall and extensive apartment tree, but mostly near its roots and generally alone. Then she'd simply continue whatever she was doing for a while, sensing around her (if the episode lasted long enough, she might begin to wander independently), thinking and feeling and imagining and wondering as she moved or stood, always feeling a horror, until something would happen to swoop her back into black unconsciousness again. The something might be a sudden sound or thought, a fire siren, say, sight of a mirror or another person, encounter with a doorknob, or with the impulse to take off her gloves, the chilling sense that someone had noticed her or was about to notice her, the fear that she might inadvertently walk through a silver-gray, faintly grimy wall, or slowly be absorbed into the carpet, sink through the floor. She couldn't recall those last things ever happening, and yet she dreaded them. Surely she went *somewhere,* she told herself, when she blacked out. She couldn't just collapse down on the floor, else there'd be some clue to that next time she came awake—and she was always on her feet when that happened. Besides, not often, but from time to time, she noticed she was wearing different clothes—*similar* clothes, in fact always black or some very dark shade close to it, but of a definitely different cut or material (leather, for instance, instead of cloth). And she couldn't possibly change her clothes or, worse, have them changed for her, in a semi-public place like the apartment tree—it would be unthinkable, too horribly embarrassing. Or rather—since we all know that the unthinkable and the horribly embarrassing (and the plain horrible too, for that matter) can happen—it would be too *grotesque.*

That was her chief trouble about everything, of course, she knew so little about her situation—in fact, knew so little about herself and the general scheme of things that held sway in this area, period. That she suffered from almost total amnesia, that much was clear to her. Usually she assumed that she lived (alone?) in one of the apartments hanging on the tree, or else was forever visiting someone who did, but then why couldn't she remember the number or somehow get inside that apartment, or come awake inside, or else get out the door into the street if she were headed that way? Why, oh why, couldn't she once ever wake in a hospital bed?—that would be pure heaven! except for the thought of what *kind* of a hospital and what things they had passing as doctors and nurses.

But just as she realized her amnesia, she knew she must have some way of taking care of herself during her unconscious times, or be the beneficiary of another's or others' system of taking care of her, for she somehow got her rest and other necessary physical reliefs, she must somehow get enough food and drink to keep her functioning, for she never felt terribly tired or seriously sick or weak and dizzy—except just before her topplings into unconsciousness, though sometimes those came without any warning at all, as sudden as the strike of pentothal.

She remembered knowing drunks (but not their names—her memory was utterly worthless on names) who lived hours and days of their lives in states of total blackout, safely crossing busy streets, eating meals, even driving cars, without a single blink of remembered awareness, as if they had a guardian angel guiding them, to the point of coming awake in distant cities, not having the ghost of an idea as to how they'd got there. (Well, she could hardly be a drunk; she didn't stagger and there was never a bottle in her purse, the times she came awake clutching a purse.)

But those were all deductions and surmises, unanchored and unlabeled memories that bobbed up in her mind and floated there awhile. What did she really know about herself?

Pitifully little. She didn't know her name or that of any friend or relative. Address and occupation, too, were blanks. Ditto education, race, religion, and marital status. Oh Christ! she didn't even know what city she was in or how *old* she was! and whether she was good-looking, ugly, or merely nondescript. Sometimes one of those last questions would hit her so hard that she would forget and start to look into one of the many mirrors in the apartment tree, or else begin to take off her gloves, so she could check it that way—hey! maybe find a tag with her name on it sewed inside her coat! But any of these actions would, of course, plunge her back into the black unconsciousness from which *this* time there might be no awakening.

And what about the general scheme of things that held sway

in this area? What did she know about that? Precious little, too. There was this world of the apartment tree which she knew very well although she didn't permit herself to look at every part of it equally. Mirrors were taboo, unless you were so placed you couldn't see your own reflection in them; so mostly were people's faces. People meant danger. Don't look at them, they might look at you.

Then there was the outside world, a mysterious and wonderful place, a heaven of delights where there was everything desirable you could think or imagine, where there was freedom and repose. She took this on faith and on the evidence of most of her memories. (Though, sad to say, those memories' bright colors seemed to fade with time. Having lost names, they tended to lose other details, she suspected. Besides, it was hard to keep them vivid and bright when your only conscious life was a series of same- seeming, frantic, frightened little rushes and hidings and waits in the apartment tree, glued together at the ends like stretches of film—and the glue was black.)

But between those two worlds, the outside and the inside, separating them, there was a black layer (who knows how thick?) of unspeakable horrors and infinite terrors. What its outer surface was, facing the outside world, she could only guess, but its inside surface was clearly the walls, ceilings, and floors of the apartment tree. That was why she worried so much that she might become forgetful and step through them without intending to—she didn't know if she were insubstantial enough to do that (though she sometimes felt so), but she *might* be, or become so, and in any case she didn't intend to try! And why she had a dread of cracks and crevices and small holes anywhere and *things which could go through such cracks and holes,* leading logically enough to a fear of rats and mice and cockroaches and water bugs and similar vermin.

Deep down inside herself she felt quite sure, most of the time, that she spent all her unconscious life in the black layer, and that it was her experiences there, or her dreams there, that infected all her times awake with fear. But it didn't do to think of that, it was too terrible, and so she tried to occupy her mind fully with her normal worries and dreads, and with observing permitted things in the apartment tree, and with all sorts of little notions and fantasies.

One of her favorite fantasies, conceived and enjoyed in

patches of clear thinking and feeling in the mostly on-guard, frantic stretches of her ragtag waking life, was that she really lived in a lovely modern hospital, occupied a whole wing of it, in fact, the favorite daughter of a billionaire no doubt, where she was cared for by stunningly handsome, sympathetic doctors and bevies of warm-hearted merry nurses who simply cosseted her to swooning with tender loving care, fed her the most delicious foods and drinks, massaged her endlessly, stole kisses sometimes (it was a rather naughty place), and the only drawback was that she was asleep throughout all these delightful operations.

Ah, but (she fantasized) you could tell just by looking at the girl—her eyes closed, to be sure, but her lips smiling—that somewhere deep within she knew all that was happening, *somewhere she enjoyed*. She was a sly one!

And then, when all the hospital was asleep, she would rise silently from her bed, put on her clothes, and still in a profound sleep sneak out of the hospital without waking a soul, hurry to this place, dive in an instant through the horror layer, and come awake!

But then, unfortunately, because of her amnesia, she would forget the snow white hospital and all her specific night-to-night memories of its delights and her wonderfully clever escapes from it.

But she could daydream of the hospital to her heart's content, almost! That alone was a matchless reward, worth everything, if only you looked at it the right way.

And then after a while, of course, she'd realize it was time to hurry back to the hospital before anyone there woke up and discovered she was gone. So she would, generally without letting on to herself what she was doing, seek or provoke an incident which would hurtle her back into unconsciousness again, transform her into her incredibly clever blacked-out other self who could travel anywhere in the universe unerringly, do almost anything—and with her eyes closed! (It wouldn't' do to let the doctors and nurses ever suspect she'd been out of bed. Despite their inexhaustible loving-kindness they'd be sure to do something about it, maybe even come here and get her, and bar her from the apartment tree forever.)

So even the nicest daydreams had their dark sides.

As for the worst of her daydreams, the nastiest of imaginings, it didn't do to think of them at all—they were pure black-layer, through and through. There was the fantasy of the eraser-worms for instance—squirmy, crawling, sleek, horny-armored things about an inch long and of the thickness and semi-rigidity of a pencil eraser or a black telephone cord; once they were loose they could go anywhere, and there were hordes of them.

She would imagine them... Well, wasn't it better to imagine them outright than to pretend she'd had a dream about them? for that would be admitting that she might have dreamed about them in the black layer, which would mean she might actually have *experienced* them in the black layer, wasn't that so? Well, anyway, she would start by imagining herself in utter darkness. It was strange, wasn't it, how, not often, but sometimes, you couldn't keep yourself from imagining the worst things? For a moment they became irresistible, a sort of nasty reverse delight.

Anyhow, she would imagine she was lying in utter darkness— sometimes she'd close her eyes and cup her hands over them to increase the illusion, and once, alone in the elevator, greatly daring, she had switched off the light—and then she'd feel the first worm touch her toe, then crawl inquisitively, peremptorily between her big toe and the next, as if it owned her. Soon they'd be swarming all over her, investigating every crevice and orifice they reached, finally assaulting her head and face. She'd press her lips tightly together, but then they'd block her nostrils (it took about two of them, thrusting together, to do each of those) and she'd be forced to part her lips to gasp and then they'd writhe inside. She'd squeeze her eyes tight shut, but nevertheless... and she had no way to guard her ears and other entries.

It was only bearable because you knew you were doing it to yourself and could stop any time you wanted. And maybe it was a sort of test to prove that, in a pinch, you *could* stand it—she wasn't sure. And although you told yourself it was nothing but imagination, it did give you ideas about the black layer.

She'd rouse from such a session shaking her head and with a little indrawn shudder, as if to say, "Who would believe the things she's capable of?" and "You're brooding, you're getting into yourself too much, child. Talk to others. Get out yourself!" (And perhaps it was just as well there was seldom opportunity—long enough lulls—to indulge in such experimenting in the nervous, unpredictable, and sometimes breathless-paced existence of the apartment tree.)

There were any number of reasons why she couldn't follow her own advice and speak to others in the apartment tree, strike up conversations, even look at them much, do more than steal infrequent glances at their faces, but the overriding one was the deep conviction that *she had no right to be in the apartment tree* and that she'd get into serious trouble if she drew attention to herself. She might even be barred from the tree forever, sentenced to the black layer. (And if that last were the ridiculous nonsense idea it sounded like—where was the court and who would pronounce sentence?—why did it give her the cold shivers and a sick depression just to mention it to herself?)

No, she *didn't* have an apartment here, she'd tell herself, or any friend in the building. That was why she never had any keys—or any money either, or any little notebooks in which she could find out things about herself, or letters from others or even bills! No, she was a homeless waif and she had nothing. (The only thing she always or almost always carried was a complete riddle to her: a brass tube slim as a soda straw about four inches long which at one end went through a-smooth cork not much bigger around than an eraser-worm—don't think of those!)

At other times she'd tell herself she needn't have any fear of being spotted, caught, unmasked, shown to be an illegal intruder by the other passers-through of the apartment tree, because she was *invisible* to them, or almost all of them. The proof of this (which was so obvious, right before your eyes, that you missed it) was simply that none of them noticed her, or spoke to her, or did her the little courtesies which they did each other, such as holding the elevator door for her. She had to move aside for them, not they for her!

This speculation about being invisible led to another special horror for her. Suppose, in her efforts to discover how old she was, she ever did manage to take off her gloves and found, not the moist hands of a young woman, nor yet the dry vein-crawling ones of a skinny old hag, but simply emptiness? What if she managed to open her coat and found herself, chin tucked in, staring down at lining? What if she looked into a mirror and saw nothing, except the wall behind her, or else only another mirror with reflections of reflections going back to infinity?

What if she were a ghost? Although it was long ago, or seemed long ago, she could recall, she thought, the dizzying chill *that* thought had given her the first time she'd had it. It fitted. Ghosts were supposed to haunt one place and to appear and disappear by fits and starts, and even then to be visible only to the sensitive few. None of the ghost stories she knew told it from the ghosts' side—what they thought and felt, how much they understood, and whether they ever knew what they were (ghosts) and what they were doing (haunting).

(And there even had been the "sensitive few" who had seemed to see her—and she looked back at them flirtatiously—though she didn't like to remember those episodes because they frightened her and made her feel foolish—whyever had she flirted? taken that risk?—and in the end made her mind go blurry. There'd been that big fat boy—whatever had she seen in him?—and before him a gentle old man, and before *him*— no, she certainly didn't have to push her memory back that far, no one could make her!)

But now that thought—that she might be a ghost—had become only one more of her familiar fancies, coming back into her mind every once in a while as regular as clockwork and with a little but not much of the original shock the idea had once given her. "Part of my repertoire," she told herself drolly. (God knows how she'd manage to stand her existence if things didn't seem funny to her once in a while.)

But most times weren't so funny. She kept coming back and coming back to what seemed after all the chief question: How *long* had her conscious life, *this* conscious life, lasted? And the only final answer she could get to this, in moments of unpanic, was that she couldn't tell.

It might be months or years. Long enough so that although not looking at their faces, she'd gotten to know the tenants of the apartment tree by their clothes and movements, the little things they said to each other, their gaits and favorite expressions. Gotten to know them well enough so that she could recognize them when they'd changed their clothes, put on new shoes, slowed down their gait, begun to use a cane. Sometimes completely new ones would appear and then slowly become old familiars—new tenants moving in. And then these old familiars might in their turn disappear—moved away, or died. My God, had she been here for decades? She remembered a horror story in which a beautiful young woman woke from a coma to find herself dying of old age. Would it be like that for her when she at last faced the mirror?

And if she *were* a ghost, would not the greatest horror for such a being be to die as a ghost?—to feel you had one tiny corner of existence securely yours, from which you could from time to time glimpse the passing show, and then be mercilessly swept out of that?

Or it might, on the other hand, be only minutes, hours, days at most—of strangely clear-headed fever dreaming, or of eternity-seeming withdrawal from a drug. Memory's fallible. Mind's capable of endless tricks. How could you be sure?

Well, whatever the truth was about the "How long?" business, she needn't worry about it for a while. The last few days (and weeks, or hours and minutes, who cared?) she'd been having a brand-new adventure. Yes, you could call it a flirtation if you wanted, but whatever you called it and in spite of the fact that it had its bad and scary parts, it had made her feel happier, gayer, braver, even more devil-may-care than she had in ages. Why, already it had revealed to her, what she'd seen in the big fat boy and in the old man before him. My goodness, she'd simply *seen* them, felt interest in, them, felt concern for them, yes, loved them. For that was the way it was now.

But that was then and this was now.

From the first time she'd happened to see Ryker (she didn't; know his name then, of course) gazing so admiringly and wonderstruck at her from the front door, she'd known he couldn't possibly mean her harm, be one of the dangerous ones who'd send her back to the hospital or the black layer, or whatever. What had surprised her was the extent of her own inward reaction. She had a friend!— someone who thought she amounted to something, who *cared*. It made her dizzy, delirious. She managed to walk only a few steps, breasting the emotional tide, before she collapsed happily into the arms of darkness.

The second time it happened almost exactly the same way only this time she was anticipating and needed only the glimpse—a flicker of her eyes his way—to assure herself that there hadn't been any mistake the first time, that he did feel that way about her, that he loved her.

By the time of their third meeting, she'd worked herself up into a really daring mood—she'd prepared a surprise for him and was waiting for him in the elevator. She'd even mischievously switched off the light (when she had the strength to do things like that, she knew she was in fine fettle), and was managing somehow to hold the door open (that surprised even her) so that she'd gradually be revealed to him as she came down the hall—a sort of hide-and-seek game. As to what happened after that, she'd take her chances!

Then when he'd walked past her, making a feeble excuse about his mailbox—that was one of the bad parts. What was the matter with him? Was he, a tenant, actually scared of her, a trespasser, a waif? And if so, how was he scared of her?—as a woman or as a possible criminal who'd try to rob or rape him, or maybe as a ghost? Was he shy, or had his smiles and admiration meant nothing, been just politeness? She almost lost her hold on the door then, but she managed not to. "Hurry up, hurry up, you old scaredy cat!" she muttered perkily under her breath. "I can't hold this door forever!"

And then someone on an upper floor buzzed the elevator, startling her, and she did lose her hold on the doors and they closed and the cage moved upward. She felt a sudden surge of hopelessness at being thwarted by mere chance, and she blacked out.

But next time she came, awake her spirits were soon soaring again. In fact, that was the time when on sheerest impulse, she'd darted into a crowded elevator after him, which was something she never did—too much chance of being forced against someone and revealing your presence that way even if invisible.

Well, *that* didn't happen, but only because she kept herself pressed as flat against the door as possible and had some luck. At the first stop she hopped out thankfully, and changing her plans simply flew up the stairs, outdistancing the creaking cage, and when he didn't get out at Twelve, went on to Fourteen, and changing her plans again (she had the feeling it was almost time to black out), she simply followed him as he plodded to his room and noted its number before she lost consciousness. That was how she learned his name—by going to the mailboxes next time and checking his number, which said: R. RYKER. Oh, she might be a stupid little orphan of the apartment tree, but she had her tricks!

That time his arrival down on the ground floor front hall caught her unawares. Another man was holding the elevator door for two other ladies and with an encouraging glance at Ryker (he smiled back!) she darted in after them (she didn't mind a *few* fellow passengers, she could dodge them), thinking the man would go on holding the door open for Ryker. But he didn't, and she hesitated to hold it open from where she was standing (it would have looked too much like magic to the others) and so that chance of a shared ride and meeting was botched.

But that one failure didn't break her general mood of self-confidence and being on top of the situation. In fact, her mind seemed to be getting sharper and her memories to be opening. She got a hunch that something had once happened on the third floor in the front hall that was important to her, and it was while brooding there about it that she had her second unexpected encounter with Ryker. He came walking down the stairs and saw her and for a moment she thought he was going to march straight up to her, but once again his courage or whatever seemed to fail him and he kept on down and in her disappointment she blacked out.

These unanticipated meetings wouldn't do, she told herself, they didn't work, so the next time Ryker arrived by the front door she was waiting for him in the lobby. Then, just as things appeared to be working out, *her* courage failed, she got a sudden terrible fit of stage fright and fled up the stairs, though managing to turn at the top of the first flight and watch. She saw him pass the elevator after a hurried inspection of it, move toward the mailboxes and back hall. But he returned from there almost at once and entered the elevator. She realized that he'd gone to the back hall to look for her and, her courage restored, she flew down the stairs, but there only time to peer once through the little elevator window at him (and he peered back) before the cage's ascent blocked the window. She waited dejectedly by the shaft, heard faintly the elevator stop at the top—and then immediately start down again. Was he coming back on her account? she asked herself, feeling dizzy, her mind wavering on the edge of blackness. She managed to hold onto her consciousness just long enough for it to tell her that, indeed, he was!—and looking anxious and expectant as he came out of the elevator—before it blacked out entirely.

Ramsey Ryker did not reenter the apartment tree from his own apartment until the next evening. Any attentive and thoughtful observer, had there been one to accompany him down in the elevator and match his measured footsteps to the front door, would have deduced two things about him.

First, from cologne-whiff overlying a faintly soapy fragrance and from gleaming jowl, spotless white collar, faintly pink scalp between strands of combed white hair, and small even tie-knot, that he had recently bathed, shaved very closely, and arrayed himself with equal care, so that except for his age you might have been sure he was going out on a romantic date.

Second, from his almost corpselike pallor, his abstracted expression, and "slow march" ritualistic movements, that the evening's business was a not altogether pleasurable or at least a very serious one.

And if the observer had in addition been an *imaginative* or perhaps merely suggestible person, he might have added these two impressions together and got the sinister total of "If ever a man could be said to have dressed himself for his own funeral…"

And if that same hypothetical observer had been on hand twenty minutes later to witness Ryker's return to the apartment tree, he would have got an additional funereal shudder from the circumstance that Ryker's lapel now sported a white nation while his left hand carefully held a small floral spay, the chief feature of which was a white orchid.

But even this observer would have been surprised at the expression of excited delight that suffused and faintly colored Ryker's pale forward-straining countenance as he entered the hall. Of course sometimes merely getting cleaned up and dressed and venturing outdoors will cheer an elderly person amazingly, but this mood change seemed to and indeed did have a more specific outside stimulus.

For Ryker saw that the circumstances of his third encounter with the Vanishing Lady had been reproduced. There was that same impression of additional gloom, a black hole opening, swiftly seen to be due to the elevator doors standing open and the cage dark, and the dim-gleaming slender figure of the Vanishing Lady in profile just inside and just beyond the column of control buttons.

But this time her posture did not seem dejected but relaxedly alive: her head was bent, it's true, but it also seemed turned a little in his direction, as if she were scanning his approach co-quettishly, there was more if anything of an elusive shimmering dim sparkle about her shoulders and her front, she held again (left hand this time, the nearer one) that mysterious little brass object he'd mistaken for a key, the total effect being surprisingly erotic, as if it were a black-and-silver drawing, "Assignation in the Shadows"; while all the while he hurried on eagerly, faster and faster, fiercely arming himself against any last-minute cringings aside, determined to let only a premature closing of its doors bar him from that elevator tonight.

Without the slightest hesitation he strode into the dark cage, bowing slightly to her as he did so, reaching his right hand toward the top of the buttons column, where the light switch was, to turn it on, and said in a low and respectful voice, "Good evening." This last came out deeper and more resonant than he'd intended, so that it had a rather sepulchral sound. And his third movement was not completed, for just as he entered, she raised her head and simultaneously reached, her black-gloved right hand and that arm across her body and the lower half of her face, apparently anticipating his intention to switch on the light, so that his own hand drew back.

He turned facing her as he stepped past her and settled his back against that of the elevator. Her outstretched arm concealed her lips, so he couldn't tell if she smiled or not, but hen gleaming eyes followed him as he moved across the cage, and at least they didn't frown. The effect was provocative, alluring.

But her outreached hand did not turn on the light. Instead its black forefinger seemed to lay itself against the flat brass between the 12 and 14 buttons. But she must have pressed one or the other of those in so doing, for the doors growled shut and the cage moved upward.

That plunged the cage in gloom, but not quite as deeply as he would have expected, for the strange pale glimmering around her neck and her black coat's closure seemed to strengthen a little, almost sparkle (real or imagined? her body's aura, could it be? or only his old eyes dazzling?) and a twinkle of other light came in by the little window as they passed the second floor. In his state of heightened awareness he dimly yet distinctly saw her right hand drop away from the button panel and her other hand join it, creep a little way into its sleeve and then in one swift backward motion strip the glove from her right hand, which then uncurled gracefully toward him palm upward through the dark between them like a slender white sash ending in five slim white ribbons of unequal length. Advancing a step and bowing his head toward it, he gently received its cool weightless length upon his own fingers, touched his lips to the smooth slim palm, and withdrawing laid across it the white orchid he'd been carrying. Another little window winked by.

She pressed the slender spray against her throat and with

her yet-gloved hand touched his as if in thanks. *She* wondered why she had pressed *between* the buttons and why the cage had responded, why she had not blacked out while drawing off her glove. Dark memories threatened opening, not without fear. She tugged a little at Ryker's hand in drawing her own away.

Emboldened, he advanced another step, bringing him almost against her. Her cat-triangular small face tilted up toward his, half of it pale, the other half dark mouth, gray gleaming eyes, shadowed orbits under slim black brows. His left hand brushed her side and slid behind her, pressed her slim back. His right sought out the fingers at her throat holding his orchid and caressed them, playing with them gently. He felt her suede-soft gloved fingers creeping at the back of his neck.

She slid, the orchid with its insubstantial spray inside her coat and her ungloved moist hand stroked his dry cheek. His hand felt out two large round buttons at her neck, tilted them through their thread-bordered slits, and the collar of her coat fell open. The diamond sparkling that had long puzzled him intensified, gushed up and poured out fountainlike, as if he had uncovered her aura's nest—or was his old heart blowing up a diamond hurricane? or his old eyes jaggedly spinning out a diamond migraine pattern? He gazed down through this ghostly scintillation, these microscopic stars, at a landscape pearly gray and cool as the moon's, the smooth valley where the orchid lodged between her small jutting breasts with their dark silver nipples, a scene that was not lost, though it swung and narrowed a little, when her small hands drew his head down to hers and their lips met in a leisurely kiss that dizzied him unalarmingly.

It occurred to him whimsically that although the pearly landscape he continued to admire might seem to stretch on and on, it had an exceedingly low black sky, an extremely low ceiling, air people would say. Now why should that fantasy carry overtones which were more sinister than amusing? he wondered idly.

It was at that moment that he became aware that he was smelling cigar smoke. The discovery did not particularly startle or alarm him, but it did awaken his other senses a little from their present great dreamy preoccupation, though not entirely. Indeed, in one sense that preoccupation deepened, for at that moment the tip of her tongue drew a very narrow line into their kiss. But at the same time, as he noted that the elevator had come to rest, that its creaking groan had been replaced by a growling

mutter which he liked still less, while a wavering ruddy glow, a
shadowed reddish flickering, was mounting the walls of the cage
from some unknown source below, and that the thin reek of cigar
smoke was becoming more acrid.

Unwillingly, wearily (he was anything but tired, yet this cost
an effort), he lifted his gaze without breaking their kiss, without
thinking of breaking it, and continuing to fondle her back and
neck, until he was looking across her shoulder.

He saw, by the red glow, that the door of the cage had opened
without his having noticed it and that the elevator was at the
fourteenth floor.

But not *quite* at the fourteenth floor, for the outer door was
closed tight and the little window in it that had the numeral 14
painted under it stood about eighteen inches higher than it should.

So the floor of the cage must be the same distance below the
floor of Fourteen.

Still unalarmed, grudging each effort, he advanced his head
across her shoulder until he could look down over it. As he
did so, she leaned her head back and turned it a little sideways,
accommodating, so that their kiss was still unbroken, meanwhile
hugging him more tightly and making muffled and inarticulate
crooning sounds as if to say "It is all right."

The space between the two floors (which was also the space
between the ceiling of Twelve and the floor of Fourteen) was
wide open, a doorway five feet wide and scarcely one foot high
in the raw wall of the shaft, and through that doorway there was
pouring into the bottom of the cage from the very low-ceilinged
thirteenth floor a pulsing crimson glow which nevertheless seemed
more steady in hue, more regular in its variations of intensity
than that of any fire.

This furnace-light revealed, clustered around their ankles but
spreading out more scatteredly to fill the elevator's carpeted floor,
a horde of dark squat forms, a milling host of what appeared to
be (allowing for the extreme foreshortening) stocky Lilliputian
human beings, some lifting their white faces to peer up, others
bent entirely to the business at hand. For instance, two pairs of
them struggled with dull metal hooks almost as large as they
were and to which stout cords were attached, others carried
long prybars, one jauntily balanced on shoulder what looked
like a white paper packet about as big (relative to him) as an
unfolded Sunday newspaper, while more than half of them held

between two fingers tiny black cylinders from one end of which interweaving tiny tendrils of smoke arose, forming a thin cloud, and which when they applied the other ends to their tiny mugs, glowed winkingly red in the red light, as if they were a swarm of hellish lightless fireflies.

It may seem most implausible to assert that Ramsey Ryker did not feel terror and panic at this extremely grotesque sight (for he realized also that he had somehow penetrated the realm of his nightmares) and highly unlikely to record that his and the Vanishing Lady's kiss continued unbroken (save for the hurried puffings and inhalations normal in such a contact), yet both were so. True, as he wormed his head back across her shoulder to its first vantage point, his heart pounded alarmingly, there was a roaring in his ears, and waves of blackness threatened to overwhelm his vision and forced their way up into his skull, while the simple shifting movement he intended proved unexpectedly difficult to execute (his head felt heavy, not so much looking over her shoulder as slumped on it)—but these were physical reactions with many causes. His chief mental reactions to the beings he'd seen clustered around their feet were that they would have been interesting at another time and that they presumably had their own place, business, and concerns in the great scheme of things, and that just now he had his own great business and concerns he must return to, as hopefully they to theirs. Also, the Vanishing Lady's caresses and murmurings of reassurance and encouragement had their helpful and soothing effects.

But when he was once more gazing down into what we may call without any sarcasm his steep and narrow valley of delights, he could no longer tell whether the ghostly silver sparks that fountained from it were inside or outside his eyes and skull, the exquisite outlines wavered and were lost in mists, his fingers fondling her neck and her low back grew numb and powerless, all power save that of vision drained from his every part, he grew lax, and with her hands solicitously supporting and guiding him, he sank by degrees, his heavy head brushing her black coat entirely open and resting successively against her naked breasts, belly, and thighs, until he was laid out upon his back corner-to-comer in the small cage, head to the front of it, feet to the back, level with the hitherto unsuspected thirteenth floor, while the Vanishing Lady in assisting him had stooped until she now sat upon her heels, her upper body erect, her chin high, having never looked down.

With a slow effortless movement she regained her full stature, her hands trailing limply down, one of them still gripping the brass tube. The jaunty homunculus lifted his white paper packet to the other, and she clipped it securely between thumb and forefinger, still without the slightest downward glance, raised it until it was before her eyes, and eagerly but carefully unfolded it.

Ryker watched her attentively from the floor. His entire consciousness, almost, had focused in on her until he saw only her face and shoulders, her busy hands and matchless breasts. They looked very clear but very far away, like something seen through the wrong end of a telescope. He was only most dimly aware of the movements closer to him, of the way the two large dull hooks were being effortfully fitted under his shoulders and beneath his armpits. He watched with great interest but no comprehension, aware only of the beauty of the sight, as she fitted the cork-protected end of the brass tube into one nostril, delicately applied the other end to the flat unfolded square of white paper, and slowly but deeply inhaled. He did not hear the distant windlass creaking nor feel the hooks tighten against his armpits as he was dragged out of the elevator into the thirteenth floor and his consciousness irised in toward nothingness.

Nor did the Vanishing Lady honor either his disappearance or his captors' with even one last glance as she impatiently shifted the brass tube to her other nostril and applied it to an edge of the diminished pile of crystals outspread on the white packet paper, the sight of which had instantly recalled to her mind the use of that tube and much more besides, not all of which she was tickled to relearn: the sullen waitings for Artie Stensor, her own entrapment by the thirteenth floor, the finding of Artie there in his new and degenerate imprisoned form, the sessions that reduced her also to such a form, her deal with the reigning homunculi, the three services (or was it four?) she'd promised them, the luring and entrapment of the other two tenants. She put all that out of her mind as she inhaled slowly, very evenly, and deeply, the mouth of the brass tube like that of some tiny reaping machine eating its way up and down the edge of the coke or "snow" or whatever else you might call the sovereign diamond sparkling dream drug, until the paper was empty.

She felt the atoms of her body loosening their hold on each

other and those of her awareness and memory tightening theirs as with a fantastic feeling of liberation she slowly floated up through the ceiling of the cage into the stale air of the dark and cavernous shaft and then rose more and more swiftly along the black central cables until she shot through the shaft's ceiling, winked through the small lightless room in which were the elevator's black motor and relays, and burst out of the apartment tree into the huge dizzying night.

South shone the green coronet of the Hilton, west the winking red light that outlined the tripod TV tower atop Sutro Crest, northeast the topaz-sparkling upward-pointing arrow of the Transamerican Pyramid. Farther east, north, and west, all lapped in low fog, were the two great bridges, Bay and Golden Gate, and the unlimited Pacific Ocean. She felt she could see, go anywhere.

She spared one last look and sorrow pang for the souls entombed—or, more precisely, *immured*—in San Francisco and then, awareness sharpening and consciousness expanding, sped on up and out, straight toward that misty, nebula-swathed multiple star in Orion called the Trapezium.

THE AUTOMATIC
PISTOL

Inky Kozacs never let anyone but himself handle his automatic pistol, or even touch it. It was blue-black and hefty and when you just pressed the trigger once, eight .45 caliber slugs came out of it almost on top of each other.

Inky was something of a mechanic, as far as his automatic went. He would break it down and put it together again, and every once in a while carefully rub a file across the inside trigger catch.

Glasses once told him, "You will make that gun into such a hair-trigger that it will go off in your pocket and blast off all your toes. You will only have to think about it and it will start shooting."

Inky smiled at that, I remember. He was a little wiry man with a pale face, from which he couldn't ever shave off the blue-black of his beard, no matter how close he shaved. His hair was black, too. He talked foreign, but I never could figure what country. He got together with Anton Larsen just after prohibition came, in the days when sea-skiffs with converted automobile motors used to play tag with revenue cutters in New York Bay and off the Jersey coast, both omitting to use lights in order to make the game more difficult. Larsen and Inky Kozacs used to get their booze off a steamer and run it in near the Twin Lights in New Jersey.

It was there that Glasses and I started to work for them. Glasses, who looked like a cross between a college professor and an automobile salesman, came from I don't know where in

New York City, and I was a local small-town policeman until I determined to lead a less hypocritical life. We used to ride the stuff back toward Newark in a truck.

Inky always rode in with us; Larsen only occasionally. Neither of them used to talk much; Larsen, because he didn't see any sense in talking unless to give a guy orders or a girl a proposition; and Inky, well, I guess because he wasn't any too happy talking American. And there wasn't a ride Inky took with us but he didn't slip out his automatic and sort of pet it mutter at it under his breath. Once when we were restfully chugging down the highway Glasses asked him, polite inquiring:

"Just what is it makes you so fond of that gun? After all, the must be thousands identically like it."

"You think so?" says Inky, giving us a quick stare from his little, glinty black eyes and making a speech for once. "Let me tell you, Glasses" (he made the word sound like 'Masses'), "nothing is alike in this world. People, guns, bottles of Scotch—nothing. Everything in the world is different. Every man has different fingerprints; and, of all guns made in the same factory as this one, there is not one like mine. I could pick mine out from a hundred. Yes, even if I hadn't filed the trigger catch, I could do that."

We didn't contradict him. It sounded pretty reasonable. He sure loved that gun, all right. He slept with it under his pillow. I don't think it ever got more than three feet away from him as long as he lived.

Once when Larsen was riding in with us, he remarked! sarcastically, "That is a pretty little gun, Inky, but I am getting very tired of hearing you talk to it so much, especially when no one can understand what you are saying. Doesn't it ever talk back to you?"

Inky smiled at him. "My gun only knows eight words," he said, "and they are all alike."

This was such a good crack that we laughed.

"Let's have a look at it," said Larsen reaching out his hand.

But Inky put it back in his pocket and didn't take it out the rest of the trip.

After that Larsen was always kidding Inky about the gun, trying to get his goat. He was a persistent guy with a very peculiar sense of humor, and he kept it up for a long time after it had stopped being funny. Finally he took to acting as if he wanted to buy it, making Inky crazy offers of one to two hundred dollars.

"Two hundred and seventy-five dollars, Inky," he said one evening as we were rattling past Bayport with a load of cognac and Irish whiskey. "That's my last offer, and you better take it."

Inky shook his head and made a funny noise that was almost like a snarl. Then, to my great surprise (I almost ran the truck off the pavement) Larsen lost his temper.

"Hand over that damn gun!" he bellowed, grabbing Inky's shoulders and shaking him. I was almost knocked off the seat. Somebody might even have been hurt, if a motorcycle cop hadn't stopped us just at that moment to ask for his hush-money. By the time he was gone, Larsen and Inky were both cooled down to the freezing point, and there was no more fighting. We got our load safely into the warehouse, nobody saying a word.

Afterward, when Glasses and I were having a cup of coffee at a little open-all-night restaurant, I said, "Those two guys are crazy, and I don't like it a bit. Why the devil do they act that way, now that the business is going so swell? I haven't got the brains Larsen has, but you won't ever find me fighting about a gun as if I was a kid."

Glasses only smiled as he poured a precise half-spoonful of sugar into his cup.

"And Inky's as bad as he is," I went on. "I tell you, Glasses, it ain't natural or normal for a man to feel that way about a piece of metal. I can understand him being fond of it and feeling lost without it. I feel the same way about my lucky half-dollar. It's the way he pets it and makes love to it that gets on my nerves. And now Larsen's acting the same way."

Glasses shrugged. "We're all getting a little jittery, although we won't admit it," he said. "Too many hijackers. And so we start getting on each other's nerves and fighting about trifles— such as automatic pistols."

"You may have something there."

Glasses winked at me. "Why, certainly, No Nose," he said, referring to what had once been done to me with a baseball bat, "I even have another explanation of tonight's events."

"What?"

He leaned over and whispered in a mock-mysterious way, "Maybe there's something queer about the gun itself."

I told him in impolite language to go chase himself.

From that night, however, things were changed, Larsen and Inky Kozacs never spoke to each other any more except in the line of business. And there was no more talk, kidding or serious, about the gun. Inky only brought it out when Larsen wasn't along.

Well, the years kept passing and the bootlegging business stayed good except that the hijackers became more numerous and Inky got a couple of chances to show us what a nice noise his automatic made. Then, too, we got into a row with some competitors bossed by an Irishman named Luke Dugan, and had to watch our step very carefully and change our route every other trip.

Still, business was good. I continued to support almost all my relatives, and Glasses put away a few dollars every month for what he called his Persian Cat Fund. Larsen, I believe, spent about everything he got on women and all that goes with them. He was the kind of guy who would take all the pleasures of life without cracking a smile, but who lived for them just the same.

As for Inky Kozacs, we never knew what happened to the money he made. We never heard of him spending much, so we finally figured he must be saving it—probably in bills in a safety deposit box. Maybe he was planning to go back to the Old Country, wherever that was, and be somebody. At any rate he never told us. By the time Congress took our profession away from us, he must have had a whale of a lot of dough. We hadn't had a big racket, but we'd been very careful.

Finally we ran our last load. We'd have had to quit the business pretty soon anyway, because the big syndicates were demanding more protection money each week. There was no chance left for a small independent operator, even if he was as clever as Larsen. So Glasses and I took a couple of months off for vacation before thinking what to do next for his Persian cats and my shiftless relatives. For the time being we stuck together.

Then one morning I read in the paper that Inky Kozacs had been taken for a ride. He'd been found shot dead on a dump heap near Elizabeth, New Jersey.

"I guess Luke Dugan finally got him," said Glasses.

"A nasty break," I said, "especially figuring all that money he hadn't got any fun out of. I am glad that you and I, Glasses, aren't important enough for Dugan to bother about, I hope."

"Yeah. Say, No Nose, does it say if they found Inky's gun on him?"

I said it told that the dead man was unarmed and that no weapon was found on the scene.

Glasses remarked that it was queer to think of Inky's gun

being in anyone else's pocket. I agreed, and we spent some time wondering whether Inky had had a chance to defend himself.

About two hours later Larsen called and told us to meet him at the hide-out. He said Luke Dugan was gunning for him too.

The hide-out is a three-room frame bungalow with a big corrugated iron garage next to it. The garage was for the truck, and sometimes we would store a load of booze there when we heard that the police were going to make some arrests for the sake of variety. It is near Bayport, about a mile and a half from the cement highway and about a quarter of a mile from the bay and the little inlet in which we used to hide our boat. Stiff, knife-edged sea- grass taller than a man, comes up near to the house on the bay side, which is north, and on the west too. Under the sea-grass the ground is marshy, though in hot weather and when the tides aren't high, it gets dry and caked; here and there creeks of tidewater go through it. Even a little breeze will make the blades of sea-grass scrape each other with a funny dry sound.

To the east are some fields, and beyond them, Bayport. Bayport is a kind of summer resort town and some of the houses are built up on poles because of the tides and storms. It has a little lagoon for the boats of the fishermen who go out after crabs.

To the south of the hide-out is the dirt road leading to the cement highway. The nearest house is about half a mile away.

It was late in the afternoon when Glasses and I got there. We brought groceries for a couple of days, figuring Larsen might want to stay. Then, along about sunset, we heard Larsen's coupe turning in, and I went out to put it in the big empty garage and carry in his suitcase. When I got back Larsen was talking to Glasses. He was a big man and his shoulders were broad both ways, like a wrestler's. His head was almost bald and what was left of his hair was a dirty yellow. His eyes were little and his face wasn't given much to expression. And that was the way it was when he said, "Yeah, Inky got it."

"Luke Dugan's crazy gunmen sure hold a grudge," I observed.

Larsen nodded his head and scowled.

"Inky got it," he repeated, taking up his suitcase and starting for the bedroom. "And I'm planning to stay here for a few days, just in case they're after me too. I want you and Glasses to stay here with me."

Glasses gave me a funny wink and began throwing a meal together. I turned on the lights and pulled down the blinds, taking a worried glance down the road, which was empty. This waiting around in a lonely house for a bunch of gunmen to catch up with you didn't appeal to me. Nor to Glasses either, I guessed. It seemed to me that it would have been a lot more sensible for Larsen to put a couple of thousand miles between him and New York. But, knowing Larsen, I had sense enough not to make any comments.

After canned corned-beef hash and beans and beer, we sat around the table drinking coffee.

Larsen took an automatic out of his pocket and began fooling with it, and right away I saw it was Inky's. For about five minutes nobody said a word. Glasses played with his coffee, pouring in the cream one drop at a time. I wadded a piece of bread into little pellets which kept looking less and less appetizing.

Finally Larsen looked up at us and said, "Too bad Inky didn't have this with him when he was taken for a ride. He gave it to me just before he planned sailing for the Old Country. He didn't want it with him any more, now that the racket's over."

"I'm glad the guy that killed him hasn't got it now," said Glasses quickly. He talked nervously and in his worst college professor style. I could tell he didn't want the silence to settle down again. "It's a funny thing. Inky giving up his gun—but I can understand his feeling; he mentally associated the gun with our racket; when the one was over he didn't care about the other."

Larsen grunted, which meant for Glasses to shut up.

"What's going to happen to Inky's dough?" I asked.

Larsen shrugged his shoulders and went on fooling with the automatic, throwing a shell into the chamber, cocking it, and so forth. It reminded me so much of the way Inky used to handle it that I got fidgetting and began to imagine I heard Luke Dugan's gunmen creeping up through the sea-grass. Finally I got up and started to walk around.

It was then that the accident happened. Larsen, after cocking the gun, was bringing up his thumb to let the hammer down easy, when it slipped out of his hand. As it hit the floor it went off with a flash and a bang, sending a slug gouging the floor too near my foot for comfort.

As soon as I realized I wasn't hit, I yelled without thinking, "I always told Inky he was putting too much of a hair trigger on his gun! The crazy fool!"

Larsen sat with his pig eyes staring down at the gun where it lay between his feet. Then he gave a funny little snort, picked it up and put it on the table.

"That gun ought to be thrown away. It's too dangerous to handle. It's bad luck," I said to Larsen—and then wished I hadn't, for he gave me the benefit of a dirty look and some fancy Swedish swearing.

"Shut up, No Nose," he finished, "and don't tell me what I can do and what I can't, I can take care of you, and I can take care of Inky's gun. Right now I'm going to bed."

He shut the bedroom door behind him, leaving it up to me and Glasses to guess that we were supposed to take out our blankets and sleep on the floor.

But we didn't want to go to sleep right away, if only because we were still thinking about Luke Dugan. So we got out a deck of cards and started a game of stud poker, speaking very low. Stud poker is like the ordinary kind, except that four of the five cards are dealt face up and one at a time.

You bet each time a card is dealt, and so considerable money is apt to change hands, even when you're playing with a ten-cent limit, like we were. It's a pretty good game for taking money away from suckers, and Glasses and I used to play it by the hour when we had nothing better to do. But since we were both equally smart, neither one of us won consistently.

It was very quiet, except for Larsen's snoring and the rustling of the sea-grass and the occasional chink of a dime.

After about an hour, Glasses happened to look down at Inky's automatic lying on the other side of the table, and something about the way his body twisted around sudden made me look too. Right away I felt something was wrong, but I couldn't tell what; it gave me a funny feeling in the back of the neck. Then Glasses put out two thin fingers and turned the gun halfway around, and I realized what had been wrong—or what I thought had been wrong. When Larsen had put the gun down, I thought it had been pointing at the outside door; but when Glasses and I looked at it, it was pointing more in the direction of the bedroom door. When you have the fidgets your memory gets tricky.

A half-hour later we noticed the gun again pointing toward the bedroom door. This time Glasses spun it around quick, and I got the fidgets for fair. Glasses gave a low whistle and got up, and tried putting the gun on different parts of the table and jiggling the table to see if the gun would move.

"I see what happened now," he whispered finally. "When the gun is lying on its side, it sort of balances on its safety catch.

"Now this little table has got a wobble to it and when we are playing cards the wobble is persistent enough to edge the gun slowly around in a circle."

"I don't care about that," I whispered back. "I don't want to be shot in my sleep just because the table has a persistent wobble. I think the rumble of a train two miles away would be enough to set off that crazy hair-trigger. Give me it."

Glasses handed it over and, taking care always to point it at the floor, I unloaded it, put it back on the table, and put the bullets in my coat pocket. Then we tried to go on with our card game.

"My red bullet bets ten cents," I said, referring to my ace of hearts.

"My king raises you ten cents," responded Glasses.

But it was no use. Between Inky's automatic and Luke Dugan I couldn't concentrate on my cards.

"Do you remember, Glasses," I said, "the evening you said there was maybe something queer about Inky's gun?"

"I do a lot of talking, No Nose, and not much of it is worth remembering. We'd better stick to our cards. My pair of sevens bets a nickel."

I followed his advice, but didn't have much luck, and lost five or six dollars. By two o'clock we were both pretty tired and not feeling quite so jittery; so we got the blankets and wrapped up in them and tried to grab a little sleep. I listened to the sea-grass and the tooting of a locomotive about two miles away, and worried some over the possible activities of Luke Dugan, but finally dropped off.

It must have been about sunrise that the clicking noise woke me up. There was a faint, greenish light coming in through the shades. I lay still, not knowing exactly what I was listening for, but so on edge that it didn't occur to me how prickly hot I was from sleeping without sheets, or how itchy my face and hands were from mosquito bites. Then I heard it again, and it sounded like nothing but the sharp click the hammer of a gun makes when it snaps down on an empty chamber. Twice I heard it. It seemed to be coming from the inside of the room. I slid out of my blankets and rustled Glasses awake.

"It's that damned automatic of Inky's," I whispered shakily. "It's trying to shoot itself."

When a person wakes up sudden and before he should, he's apt to feel just like I did and say crazy things without thinking. Glasses looked at me for a moment, then he rubbed his eyes and smiled. I could hardly see the smile in the dim light, but I could feel it in his voice when he said, "No Nose, you are getting positively psychic."

"I tell you I'd swear to it," I insisted. "It was the click of the hammer of a gun."

Glasses yawned. "Next you will be telling me that the gun was Inky's familiar."

"Familiar what?" I asked him, scratching my head and beginning to get mad. There are times when Glasses' college professor stuff gets me down.

"No Nose," he continued, "have you ever heard of witches?"

I was walking around to the windows and glancing out from behind the blinds to make sure there was no one around. I didn't see anyone. For that matter, I didn't really expect to.

"What do you mean?" I said. "Sure I have. Why, I knew a guy, a Pennsylvania Dutchman, and he told me about witches putting what he called hexes on people. He said his uncle had a hex put on him and he died afterward. He was a traveling salesman—the Dutchman that told me, I mean."

Glasses nodded his head, and then went on, sleepy-like, from the floor, "Well, No Nose, the Devil used to give each witch a pet black cat or dog or maybe a toad to follow it around and protect it and revenge injuries. Those little creatures were called familiars—stooges sent out by the Big Boy to watch over his chosen, you might say. The witches used to talk to them in a language no one else could understand. Now this is what I'm getting at. Times change and styles change—and the style in familiars along with them. Inky's gun is black, isn't it? And he used to mutter at it in a language we couldn't understand, didn't he? And—"

"You're crazy," I told him, not wanting to be kidded.

"Why, No Nose," he said, "you were telling me yourself just now that you thought the gun had a life of its own, that it could cock itself and shoot itself without any human assistance. Weren't you?"

"You're crazy," I repeated, feeling like an awful fool and wishing I hadn't waked Glasses up. "See, the gun's here where I left it on the table, and the bullets are still in my pocket."

"Luckily," he said in a stagy voice he tried to make sound like an undertaker's. "Well, now that you've called me early, I shall wander off and avail us of our neighbor's newspaper. Meanwhile you may run my bath."

I waited until I was sure he was gone, because I didn't want him to make a fool of me again. Then I went over and examined the gun. First I looked for the trade mark or the name of the maker. I found a place which had been filed down, where it might have been once, but that was all. Before this I would have sworn I could have told the make, but now I couldn't. Not that in general it didn't look like an ordinary automatic; it was the details—the grip, the trigger guard, the safety catch—that were unfamiliar. I figured it was some foreign make I'd never happened to see before.

After I'd been handling it for about two minutes I began to notice something queer about the feel of the metal. As far as I could see it was just ordinary blued steel, but somehow it was too smooth and slick and made me want to keep stroking the barrel back and forth. I can't explain it any better; the metal just didn't seem *right* to me. Finally I realized the gun was getting on my nerves and making me imagine things; so I put it down on the mantel.

When Glasses got back, the sun was up and he wasn't smiling any more. He shoved a newspaper on my lap and pointed. It was open to page five. I read:

ANTON LARSEN SOUGHT IN KOZACS KILLING
Police Believe Ex-Bootlegger Slain by Pal

I looked up to see Larsen standing in the bedroom door. He was in his pajama trousers and looked yellow and seedy, his eyelids puffed and his pig eyes staring at us.

"Good morning, boss," said Glasses slowly. "We just noticed in the paper that they are trying to do you a dirty trick. They're claiming you, not Dugan, had Inky shot."

Larsen grunted, came over and took the paper, looked at it quickly, grunted again, and went to the sink to splash some cold water on his face.

"So," he said, turning to us. "All the better we are here at the hideout."

That day was the longest and most nervous I've ever gone through. Somehow Larsen didn't seem to be completely waked up. If he'd been a stranger I'd have diagnosed it as a laudanum jag. He sat around in his pajama trousers, so that by noon he still looked as if he'd only that minute rolled out of bed. The worst thing was that he wouldn't talk or tell us anything about his plans. Of course he never did much talking, but this time there was a difference. His funny pig eyes began to give me the jim-jams; no matter how still he sat they were always moving— like a guy having a laudanum nightmare and about to run amuck.

Finally it started to get on Glasses' nerves, which surprised me, for Glasses usually knows how to take things quietly. He began by making little suggestions—that we should get a later paper, that we should call up a certain lawyer in New York, that I should get my cousin Jake to mosey around the police station at Bayport and see if anything was up, and so on. Each time Larsen shut him up quick.

Once I thought he was going to take a crack at Glasses. And Glasses, like a fool, kept on pestering. I could see a blow-up coming, plain as the absence of my nose. I couldn't figure what was making Glasses do it. I guess when the college professor type gets the jim-jams they get them worse than a dummy like me. They've got trained brains which they can't stop from pecking away at ideas, and that's a disadvantage.

As for me, I tried to keep hold of my nerves. I kept saying to myself, "Larsen is O.K. He's just a little on edge. We all are. Why, I've known him ten years. He's O.K." I only half realized I was saying those things because I was beginning to believe that Larsen wasn't O.K.

The blow-up came at about two o'clock. Larsen's eyes opened wide, as if he'd just remembered something, and he jumped up so quick that I started to look around for Luke Dugan's firing-squad—or the police. But it wasn't either of those. Larsen had spotted the automatic on the mantel. Right away as he began fingering it, he noticed it was unloaded.

"Who monkeyed with this?" he asked in a very nasty, thick voice. "And why?"

Glasses couldn't keep quiet.

"I thought you might hurt yourself with it," he said.

Larsen walked over to him and slapped him on the side of the face, knocking him down. I took firm hold of the chair I had been sitting on, ready to use it like a club. Glasses twisted on the floor for a moment, until he got control of the pain. Then he looked up, tears beginning to drip out of his left eye where he had been hit. He had sense enough not to say anything, or to smile. Some fools would have smiled in such a situation, thinking it showed courage. It would have showed courage, I admit, but not good sense.

After about twenty seconds Larsen decided not to kick him in the face.

"Well, are you going to keep your mouth shut?" he asked.

Glasses nodded. I let go my grip on the chair.

"Where's the load?" asked Larsen.

I took the bullets out of my pocket and put them on the table, moving deliberately.

Larsen reloaded the gun. It made me sick to see his big hands sliding along the blue-black metal, because I remembered the feel of it.

"Nobody touches this but me, see?" he said.

And with that he walked into the bedroom and closed the door.

All I could think of was, "Glasses was right when he said that Larsen was crazy on the subject of Inky's automatic. And it's just the same as it was with Inky. He has to have the gun close to him. That's what was bothering him all morning, only he didn't know."

Then I kneeled down by Glasses, who was still lying on the floor, propped up on his elbows looking at the bedroom door. The mark of Larsen's hand was brick-red on the side of his face, with a little trickle of blood on the cheekbone, where the skin was broken.

I whispered, very low, just what I thought of Larsen. "Let's beat it first chance and get the police on him," I finished.

Glasses shook his head a little. He kept staring at the door, his left eye blinking spasmodically. Then he shivered, and gave a funny grunt deep down in his throat.

"I can't believe it," he said.

"He killed Inky," I whispered in his ear. "I'm almost sure of it. And he was within an inch of killing you."

"I don't mean that," said Glasses.

"What do you mean then?"

Glasses shook his head, as if he were trying to change the subject of his thoughts.

"Something I saw," he said, "or, rather, something I realized."

"The gun?" I questioned. My lips were dry and it was hard for me to say the word.

He gave me a funny look and got up.

"We'd better both be sensible from now on," he said, and then added in a whisper. "We can't do anything now. Maybe we'll get a chance tonight."

After a long while Larsen called to me to heat some water so he could shave. I brought it to him, and by the time I was frying hash he came out and sat down at the table. He was all washed and shaved, and the straggling patches of hair around his bald head were brushed smooth. He was dressed and had his hat on. But in spite of everything he still had that yellow, seedy, laudanum-jag look. We ate our hash and beans and drank our beer, no one talking. It was dark now, and a tiny wind was making the blades of sea-grass whine.

Finally Larsen got up and walked around the table once and said, "Let's have a game of stud poker."

While I was clearing off the dishes he brought out his suitcase and planked it down on the side table. He took Inky's automatic out of his pocket and looked at it a second. Then he laid the automatic in the suitcase, and shut it up and strapped it tight.

"We're leaving after the game," he said.

I wasn't quite sure whether to feel relieved or not.

We played with a ten-cent limit, and right from the start Larsen began to win. It was a queer game, what with me feeling so jittery, and Glasses sitting there with the left side of his face all swollen, squinting through the right lens of his spectacles because the left lens had been cracked when Larsen hit him, and Larsen all dressed up as if he were sitting in a station waiting for a train. The shades were all down and the hanging light bulb, which was shaded with a foolscap of newspaper, threw a bright circle of light on the table, but left the rest of the room too dark to please me.

It was after Larsen had won about five dollars from each of us that I began hearing the noise. At first I couldn't be sure, because it was very low and because of the dry whining of the sea-grass, but right from the first it bothered me.

Larsen turned up a king and raked in another pot.

"You can't lose tonight," observed Glasses, smiling—and winced because the smile hurt his cheek.

Larsen scowled. He didn't seem pleased at his luck, or at Glasses' remark. His pig eyes were moving in the same way that had given us the jim-jams earlier in the day. And I kept thinking, "Maybe he killed Inky Kozacs. Glasses and me are just small fry to him. Maybe he's trying to figure out whether to kill us too. Or maybe he's got a use for us, and he's wondering how much to tell us. If he starts anything I'll shove the table over on him; that is, if I get the chance." He was beginning to look like a stranger to me, although I'd known him for ten years and he'd been my boss and paid me good money.

Then I heard the noise again, a little plainer this time. It was very peculiar and hard to describe—something like the noise a rat would make if it were tied up in a lot of blankets and trying to work its way out. I looked up and saw that the bruise on Glasses' left cheek stood out plainer.

"My black bullet bets ten cents," said Larsen, pushing a dime into the pot.

"I'm with you," I answered, shoving in two nickels. My voice sounded so dry and choked it startled me.

Glasses put in his money and dealt another card to each of us.

Then I felt my face going pale, for it seemed to me that the noise was coming from Larsen's suitcase, and I remembered that he had put Inky's automatic into the suitcase with its muzzle pointing *away* from us.

The noise was louder now. Glasses couldn't bear to sit still without saying anything. He pushed back his chair and started to whisper, "I think I hear—"

Then he saw the crazy, murderous look that came into Larsen's eyes, and he had sense enough to finish, "I think I hear the eleven o'clock train."

"Sit still," said Larsen, "very still. It's only ten forty-five. My ace bets another ten cents."

"I'll raise you," I croaked.

I wanted to jump up. I wanted to throw Larsen's suitcase out the door. I wanted to run out myself. Yet I sat tight. We all sat tight. We didn't dare make a move, for if we had, it would have shown that we believed the impossible was happening. And if a man does that he's crazy. I kept rubbing my tongue against my lips, without wetting them.

I stared at the cards, trying to shut out everything else. The hand was all dealt now. I had a jack and some little ones, and I knew my face-down card was a jack. Glasses had a king showing. Larsen's ace of clubs was the highest card on the board.

And still the sound kept coming. Something twisting, straining, heaving. A muffled sound.

"And I raise *you* ten cents," said Glasses loudly. I got the idea he did it just to make a noise, not because he thought his cards were especially good.

I turned to Larsen, trying to pretend I was interested in whether he would raise or stop betting. His eyes had stopped moving and were staring straight ahead at the suitcase. His mouth was twisted in a funny, set way. After a while his lips began to move. His voice was so low I could barely catch the words.

"Ten cents more. *I killed Inky you know*. What does your jack say, No Nose?"

"It raises you," I said automatically.

His reply came in the same almost inaudible voice. "You haven't a chance of winning, No Nose. *He didn't bring the money with him, like he said he would. But I made him tell me where he hid it in his room. I can't pull the job myself; the cops would recognize me. But you two ought to be able to do it for me. That's why we're going to New York tonight*. I raise you ten cents more."

"I'll see you," I heard myself saying.

The noise stopped, not gradually but all of a sudden. Right away I wanted ten times worse to jump up and do something. But I was stuck to my chair.

Larsen turned up the ace of spades.

"Two aces. *Inky's little gun didn't protect him, you know. He didn't have a chance to use it*. Clubs and spades. Black bullets. I win."

Then it happened.

I don't need to tell you much about what we did afterward. We buried the body in the sea-grass. We cleaned everything up and drove the coupe a couple of miles inland before abandoning it. We carried the gun away with us and took it apart and hammered it out of shape and threw it into the bay part by part. We never found out anything more about Inky's money or tried to. The police never bothered us. We counted ourselves lucky that we had enough sense left to get away safely, after what happened.

For, with smoke and flame squirting through the little round holes, and the whole suitcase jerking and shaking with the recoils, eight slugs drummed out and almost cut Anton Larsen in two.

CRAZY ANNAOJ

Two things will last to the end of time, at least for the tribes of Western Man, no matter how far his spaceships rove. They are sorcery and romantic love, which come to much the same thing in the end.

For the more that becomes possible to man, the more wildly he yearns for the impossible, and runs after witches and sorcerers to find it.

While the farther he travels, to the star-ribboned rim of the Milky Way and beyond, the more he falls in love with far-off things and yearns for the most distant and unattainable beloved.

Also, witchcraft and sorcery are games it takes two to play; the witch or sorcerer and his or her client.

The oldest and wealthiest man in the Milky Way and its loveliest girl laughed as they left the gypsy's tent pitched just outside the jewel-pillared space-field of the most exclusive pleasure planet between the galaxy's two dizzily-whirling, starry arms. The gypsy's black cat, gliding past them back into the tent, only smiled cryptically.

A private, eiderdown-surfaced slidewalk, rolled out like the red carpet of ancient cliche, received the begemmed slippers of the honeymooning couple and carried them toward the most diamond-glittering pillar of them all, the private hyperspace yacht *Eros* of the galactic shipping magnate Piliph Foelitsack and his dazzling young bride Annaoj.

He looked 21 and was 20 times that old. Cosmetic surgery and organ replacements and implanted featherweight power-prosthetics and pacemakers had worked their minor miracles. At

any one time there were three physicians in the *Eros* listening in
on the functionings of his body.

She looked and was 17, but the wisdom in her eyes was that
of Eve, of Helen of Troy, of Cleopatra, of Forzane. It was also
the wisdom of Juliet, of Iseult, of Francesca da Rimini. It was
a radiant but not a rational wisdom, and it had a frightening
ingredient that had been known to make nurses and lady's maids
and the wives of planetary presidents and systemic emperors
shiver alike.

Together now on the whispering white slidewalk, planning
their next pleasures, they looked the pinnacle of cosmic romance
fulfilled—he dashing and handsome and young, except that there
was something just a shade careful about the way he carried
himself; she giddy and slim with a mind that was all sentimental
or amorous whim, except for that diamond touch of terrifying
fixed white light in her most melting or mischievous glance.
Despite or perhaps because of those two exceptions, they seemed
more akin to the sparkling stars above them than even to the
gorgeous pleasure planet around them.

He had been born in a ghetto on Andvari III and had fought
his way up the razor-runged ladder of economic power until he
owned fleets of hyperspace freighters, a dozen planets, and the
governments of ten times that many.

She had been born in a slum on Aphrodite IV, owning only
herself. It had taken her six Terran months to bring herself to the
attention of Piliph Foelitsack by way of three beauty contests and
one bit part in a stereographic all-senses sex-film, and six more
months to become his seventeenth wife instead of one more of his
countless casual mistresses.

The beepers of social gossip everywhere had hinted discreetly
about the infatuation-potential of fringe senile megabillionaires
and the coldly murderous greed of teenage starlets. And Annaoj
and Piliph Foelitsack had smiled at this gossip, since they knew
they loved each other and why: for their matching merciless
determination to get what they wanted and keep it, and for the
distance that had been between them and was no longer. Of the
two, Annaoj's love was perhaps the greater, accounting for the
icy, fanatic glint in her otherwise nymphet's eyes.

They had laughed on leaving the drab tent of the gypsy
fortuneteller, who herself owned a small, beat-up spaceship

covered with cabalistic signs, because the last thing she had said to the shipping king, fixing his bright youthful eyes with her bleared ones, had been, "Piliph Foelitsack, you have journeyed far, very far, for such a young man, yet you shall make even longer journeys hereafter. Your past travels will be trifles compared to your travels to come."

Both Piliph and Annaoj knew that he had been once to the Andromeda Galaxy and twice to both Magellanic Clouds, though they had not told the silly old gypsy so, being despite their iron wills kindly lovers, still enamored of everything in the cosmos by virtue of their mutual love. They also knew that Piliph had determined to restrict his jauntings henceforth to the Milky Way, to keep reasonably close to the greatest geriatric scientists, and they were both reconciled, at least by day, to the fact that despite all his defenses, death would come for him in ten or twenty years.

Yet, although they did not now tell each other so, the gypsy's words had given a spark of real hope to their silly night-promises under the stars like gems and the galaxies like puffs of powder that: "We will live and love forever." Their loveliest night had been spent a hundred light-years outside the Milky Way—it was to be Piliph's last extragalactic venture—where the *Eros* had emerged briefly from hyperspace and they had lolled and luxuriated for hours under the magnifying crystal skylight of the Master Stateroom, watching only the far-off galaxies, with all of their moiling, toiling home-galaxy out of sight beneath the ship.

But now, as if the cryptic universe had determined to give an instant sardonic rejoinder to the gypsy's prediction, the eiderdown slidewalk had not murmured them halfway to the *Eros* when a look of odd surprise came into Piliph's bright youthful eyes and he clutched at his heart and swayed and would have toppled except that Annaoj caught him in her strong slender arms and held him to her tightly.

Something had happened in the body of Piliph Foelitsack that could not be dealt with by all its pacemakers and its implanted and remotely controlled hormone dispensers, nor by any of the coded orders frantically tapped out by the three physicians monitoring its organs and systems.

It took thirty seconds for the ambulance of the *Eros* to hurtle out from the yacht on a track paralleling the slidewalk and brake to a bone-jolting silent halt.

During that half minute Annaoj watched the wrinkles come out on her husband's smooth face, like stars at nightfall in the sky of a planet in a star cluster. She wasted one second on the white-hot impulse to have the gypsy immediately strangled, but she knew that the great aristocrats of the cosmos do not take vengeance on its vermin and that in any event she had far more pressing business with which to occupy herself fully tonight. She clasped the pulseless body a trifle more tightly, feeling the bones and prosthetics through the layer of slack flesh.

In two minutes more, in the surgery of the *Eros*, Piliph's body was in a dissipatory neutrino field, which instantly sent all its heat packing off at the speed of light, but in particles billions of times slimmer than the photons of heat, so that the body was supercooled to the temperature of frozen helium without opportunity for a single disruptive crystal to form.

Then without consulting the spacefield dispatching station or any other authority of the pleasure planet, Annaoj ordered the *Eros* blasted into hyperspace and driven at force speed to the galaxy's foremost geriatrics clinic on Menkar V, though it lay halfway across the vast Milky Way.

During the anxious, grueling trip, she did only one thing quite out of the ordinary. She had her husband's supercooled body sprayed with a transparent insulatory film, which would adequately hold its coolth for a matter of days, and placed in the Master Stateroom. Once a week the body was briefly returned to the dissipatory neutrino field, to bring its temperature down again to within a degree of zero Kelvin.

Otherwise she behaved as she always had, changing costume seven times a day, paying great attention to her coiffure and to her cosmetic and juvenation treatments, being idly charming to the officers and stewards.

But she spent hours in her husband's office, studying his business and working to the edge of exhaustion his three secretaries. And she always took her small meals in the Master Stateroom.

On Menkar V they told her, after weeks of test and study, that her husband was beyond reawakening, at least at the present state of medical skill, and to come back in ten years. More would be known then.

At that, Annaoj nodded frigidly and took up the reins of her husband's business, conducting them entirely from the *Eros* as it skipped about through space and hyperspace. Under her guidance the Foelitsack economic empire prospered still more than it had under its founder. She successfully fought or bought off the claims of Piliph's eleven surviving divorced wives, a hundred of his relatives and a score of his prime managers.

She regularly returned to Menkar V and frequently visited other clinics and sought out famous healers. She became expert at distinguishing the charlatans from the dedicated, the conceited from the profound. Yet at times she also consulted sorcerers and wizards and witchdoctors. Incantations in exotic tongues and lights were spoken and glowed over Philiph's frigid form, extraterrestrial stenches filled the surgery of the *Eros*, and there were focused there the meditations of holy creatures which resembled man less than a spider does—while three or four fuming yet dutiful doctors of the *Eros'* dozen waited for the crucial moment in the ceremony when they would obediently work a five-second reversal of the neutrino field to bring the body briefly to normal temperature to determine whether the magic had worked.

But neither science nor sorcery could revive him.

She bullied many a police force and paid many a detective agency to hunt down the gypsy with the black cat, but the old crone and her runic spaceship had vanished as utterly as the vital spark in Piliph Foelitsack. No one could tell whether Annaoj really believed that the gypsy had had something to do with the striking down of her husband and might be able to bring him alive, or whether the witch had merely become another counter in the sorcery game of which Annaoj had suddenly grown so fond.

In the course of time Annaoj took many lovers. When she tired of one, she would lead him for the first time into the Master Stateroom of the *Eros* and show him the filmed and frosty body of her husband and send him away without as much as a parting touch of her fingertips and then lie down beside the cold, cold form under the cold, cold stars of the skylight.

And she never once let another woman set foot in that room.

Not the humblest, nor ugliest maid. Not the greatest sculptress of Pleiades. Not the most feared and revered sorceress in the Hyades.

She became known as Crazy Annaoj, though no one thought it to her face or whispered it within a parsec of her.

* * *

When she still looked 17, though her age was 70 times that—
for sciences of geriatrics and juvenation had progressed greatly
since her husband's collapse—she felt an unfamiliar weariness
creeping on her and she ordered the *Eros* to make once more for
Menkar V at force speed.

The *Eros* never emerged from hyperspace. Most say she was
lost scuttled by Annaoj as she felt death coming on her. A few
maintain she exited into altogether another universe, where Crazy
Annaoj is still keeping up her search for the healer who can revive
Piliph, or playing her game with the doctors and witchdoctors
and with her lovers.

But in any case the gypsy's prediction was fulfilled, for in the
course of Annaoj's voyages, the body of Piliph Foelitsack had
been carried twice to Andromeda and also to two galaxies in
Virgo, three in Leo and one in Coma Berenices.

THE HOUND

DAVID LASHLEY HUDDLED THE SKIMPY BLANKETS around him and dully watched the cold light of morning seep through the window and stiffen in his room. He could not recall the exact nature of the terror against which he had fought his way to wakefulness, except that it had been in some way gigantic and had brought back to him the fear-ridden helplessness of childhood. It had lurked near him all night and finally it had crouched over him and thrust down toward his face.

The radiator whined dismally with the first push of steam from the basement, and he shivered in response. He thought that his shivering was an ironically humorous recognition of the fact that his room was never warm except when he was out of it. But there was more to it than that. The penetrating whine had touched something in his mind without being quite able to dislodge it into consciousness. The mounting rumble of city traffic, together with the hoarse panting of a locomotive in the railroad yards, mingled themselves with the nearer sound, intensifying its disturbing tug at hidden fears. For a few moments he lay inert, listening. There was an unpleasant stench too in the room, he noticed, but that was nothing to be surprised at. He had experienced more than once the strange olfactory illusions that are part of the aftermath of flu. Then he heard his mother moving about laboriously in the kitchen, and that stung him into action.

"Have you another cold?" she asked, watching him anxiously as he hurriedly spooned in a boiled egg before its heat should be entirely lost in the chilly plate. "Are you sure?" she persisted. "I heard someone sniffling all night."

"Perhaps Father—" he began. She shook her head. "No, he's all right. His side was giving him a lot of pain yesterday evening, but he slept quietly enough. That's why I thought it must be you, David. I got up twice to see, but"—her voice became a little doleful—"I know you don't like me to come poking into your room at all hours."

"That's not true!" he contradicted. She looked so frail and little and worn, standing there in front of the stove with one of Father's shapeless bathrobes hugged around her, so like a sick sparrow trying to appear chipper, that a futile irritation, an indignation that he couldn't help her more, welled up within him, choking his voice a little. "It's that I don't want you getting up all the time and missing your sleep. You have enough to do taking care of Father all day long. And I've told you a dozen times that you mustn't make breakfast for me. You know the doctor says you need all the rest you can get."

"Oh, *I'm* all right," she answered quickly, "but I was sure you'd caught another cold. All night long I kept hearing it—a sniffling and a snuffling—"

Coffee spilled over into the saucer as David set down the half-raised cup. His mother's words had reawakened the elusive memory, and now that it had come back he did not want to look it in the face.

"It's late, I'll have to rush," he said.

She accompanied him to the door, so accustomed to his hastiness that she saw in it nothing unusual. Her wan voice followed him down the dark apartment stair: "I hope a rat hasn't died in the walls. Did you notice the nasty smell?"

And then he was out of the door and had lost himself and his memories in the early morning rush of the city. Tires singing on asphalt. Cold engines coughing, then starting with a roar. Heels clicking on the sidewalk, hurrying, trotting, converging on street car intersections and elevated stations. Low heels, high heels, heels of stenographers bound downtown, and of war workers headed for the outlying factories. Shouts of newsboys and glimpses of headlines: "AIR BLITZ ON... BATTLESHIP SUNK... BLACKOUT EXPECTED HERE... DRIVEN BACK."

But sitting in the stuffy solemnity of the street car, it was impossible to keep from thinking of it any longer. Besides, the stale medicinal smell of the yellow woodwork immediately brought back the memory of that other smell. David Lashley clenched his hands in his overcoat pockets and asked himself how it was possible for a grown man to be so suddenly overwhelmed by a fear from childhood. Yet in the same instant he knew with acute certainty that this was no childhood fear, this thing that had pursued him up the years, growing ever more vast and menacing, until, like the demon wolf Fenris at Ragnorak, its gaping jaws scraped heaven and earth, seeking to open wider. This thing that had dogged his footsteps, sometimes so far behind that he forget its existence, but now so close that he could feel its cold sick breath on his neck. Werewolves? He had read up on such things at the library, fingering dusty books in uneasy fascination, but what he had read made them seem innocuous and without significance—dead superstitions—in comparison with this thing that was part and parcel of the great sprawling cities and chaotic peoples of the Twentieth Century, so much a part that he, David Lashley, winced at the endlessly varying howls and growls of traffic and industry—sounds at once animal and mechanical; shrank back with a start from the sight of headlights at night—those dazzling unwinking eyes; trembled uncontrollably if he heard the scuffling of rats in an alley or caught sight in the evenings of the shadowy forms of lean mongrel dogs looking for food in vacant lots. "Sniffling and snuffling." his mother had said. What better words could you want to describe the inquisitive, persistent pryings of the beast that had crouched outside the bedroom door all night in his dreams and then finally pushed through to plant its dirty paws on his chest. For a moment he saw, superimposed on the yellow ceiling and garish advertising placards of the streetcar, its malformed muzzle... the red eyes like thickly scummed molten metal... the jaws slavered with thick black oil....

Wildly he looked around at his fellow passengers, seeking to blot out that vision, but it seemed to have slipped down into all of them, infecting them, giving their features an ugly canine cast—the slack, receding jaw of an otherwise pretty blond, the narrow head and wide-set eyes of an unshaven mechanic returning from the night shift. He sought refuge in the open newspaper of the man sitting beside him, studying it intently without regard for the impression of rudeness he was creating. But there was a wolf in the cartoon and he quickly turned away to stare through the dusty pane at the stores sliding by. Gradually the sense of oppressive menace lifted a little. But the cartoon had established another contact in his brain—the memory of a cartoon from the First

World War. What the wolf or hound in that earlier cartoon had represented—war, famine, or the ruthlessness of the enemy—he could not say, but it had haunted his dreams for weeks, crouched in corners, and waited for him at the head of the stairs. Later he had tried to explain to friends the horrors that may lie in the concrete symbolisms and personifications of a cartoon if interpreted naively by a child, but had been unable to get his idea across.

The conductor growled out the name of a downtown street, and once again he lost himself in the crowd, finding relief in the never- ceasing movement, the brushing of shoulders against his own. But as the time-clock emitted its delayed musical bong! and he turned to stick his card in the rack, the girl at the desk looked up and remarked, "Aren't you going to punch in for your dog, too?"

"My dog?"

"Well, it was there just a second ago. Came in right behind you, looking as if it owned you—I mean you owned it." She giggled briefly through her nose. "One of Mrs. Montmorency's mastiffs come to inspect conditions among the working class, I presume."

He continued to stare at her blankly. "A joke," she explained patiently, and returned to her work.

"I've got to get a grip on myself," he found himself muttering tritely as the elevator lowered him noiselessly to the basement.

He kept repeating it as he hurried to the locker room, left his coat and lunch, gave his hair a quick careful brushing, hurried again through the still-empty aisles, and slipped in behind the socks-and-handkerchiefs counter.

"It's just nerves. I'm not crazy. But I've got to get a grip on myself."

"Of course you're crazy. Don't you know that talking to yourself and not noticing anybody is the first symptom of insanity?"

Gertrude Rees had stopped on her way over to neckties. Light brown hair, painstakingly waved and ordered, framed a serious not-too-pretty face.

"Sorry," he murmured. "I'm jittery." What else could you say? Even to Gertrude.

She grimaced sympathetically. Her hand slipped across the counter to squeeze his for a moment.

But even as he watched her walk away, his hands automatically setting out the display boxes, the new question was furiously hammering in his brain. What else could you say? What words could you use to explain it? Above all, to whom could you tell it? A dozen names printed themselves in his mind and were as quickly discarded.

One remained. Tom Goodsell. He would tell Tom. Tonight, after the first-aid class.

Shoppers were already filtering into the basement. "He wears size eleven, Madam? Yes, we have some new patterns. These are silk and lisle." But their ever-increasing numbers gave him no sense of security. Crowding the aisles, they became shapes behind which something might hide. He was continually peering past them. A little child who wandered behind the counter and pushed at his knee, gave him a sudden fright.

Lunch came early for him. He arrived at the locker room in time to catch hold of Gertrude Rees as she retreated uncertainly from the dark doorway.

"Dog," she gasped. "Huge one. Gave me an awful start. Talk about jitters! Wonder where he could have come from? Watch out. He looked nasty."

But David, impelled by sudden recklessness born of fear and shock, was already inside and switching on the light.

"No dog in sight," he told her.

"You're crazy. It must be there." Her face, gingerly poked through the doorway, lengthened in surprise. "But I tell you I— Oh, I guess it must have pushed out through the other door."

He did not tell her that the other door was bolted.

"I suppose a customer brought it in," she rattled on nervously. "Some of them can't seem to shop unless they've got a pair of Russian wolfhounds. Though that kind usually keeps out of the bargain basement. I suppose we ought to find it before we eat lunch. It looked dangerous."

But he hardly heard her. He had just noticed that his locker was open and his overcoat dragged down on the floor. The brown paper bag containing his lunch had been torn open and the contents rummaged through, as if an animal had been nosing at it. As he stooped, he saw that there were greasy, black stains on the sandwiches, and a familiar stale stench rose to his nostrils.

That night he found Tom Goodsell in a nervous, expansive mood. The latter had been called up and would start for camp in a week. As they sipped coffee in the empty little restaurant, Tom poured out a flood of talk about old times. David would have been able to listen better, had not the uncertain, shadowy shapes outside the window been continually distracting his attention. Eventually he found an opportunity to turn the conversation down the channels which absorbed his mind.

"The supernatural beings of a modern city?" Tom answered, seeming to find nothing out of the way in the question. "Sure, they'd be different from the ghosts of yesterday. Each culture creates its own ghosts. Look, the Middle Ages built cathedrals, and pretty soon there were little gray shapes gliding around at night to talk with the gargoyles. Same thing ought to happen to us, with our skyscrapers and factories." He spoke eagerly, with all his old poetic flare, as if he'd just been meaning to discuss this very matter. He would talk about anything tonight. "I'll tell you how it works, Dave. We begin by denying all the old haunts and superstitions. Why shouldn't we? They belong to the era of cottage and castle. They can't take root in the new environment. Science goes materialistic, proving that there isn't anything in the universe except tiny bundles of energy. As if, for that matter, a tiny bundle of energy mightn't mean anything.

"But wait, that's just the beginning. We go on inventing and discovering and organizing. We cover the earth with huge structures. We pile them together in great heaps that make old Rome and Alexandria and Babylon seem almost toy-towns by comparison. The new environment, you see, is forming."

David stared at him with incredulous fascination, profoundly disturbed. This was not at all what he had expected or hoped for—this almost telepathic prying into his most hidden fears. He had wanted to talk about these things—yes—but in a skeptical reassuring way. Instead, Tom sounded almost serious. David started to speak, but Tom held up his finger for silence, aping the gesture of a schoolteacher.

"Meanwhile, what's happening inside each one of us? I'll tell you. All sorts of inhibited emotions are accumulating. Fear is accumulating. Horror is accumulating. A new kind of awe of the mysteries of the universe is accumulating. A psychological environment is forming, along with the physical one. Wait, let me finish. Our culture becomes ripe for infection. From somewhere. It's just like a bacteriologist's culture—I didn't intend the pun—when it gets to the right temperature and consistency for supporting a colony of germs. Similarly, our culture suddenly spawns a horde of demons. And, like germs, they have a peculiar affinity for our culture. They're unique. They fit in. You wouldn't find the same kind any other time or place.

"How would you know when the infection had taken place? Say, you're taking this pretty seriously, aren't you? Well, so am I, maybe. Why, they'd haunt us, terrorize us, try to rule us. Our fears would be their fodder. A parasite-host relationship. Supernatural symbiosis. Some of us—the sensitive ones— would notice them sooner than others. Some of us might see them without knowing what they were. Others might know about them without seeing them. Like me, eh?

"What was that? I didn't catch your remark. Oh, about werewolves. Well, that's a pretty special question, but tonight I'd take a crack at anything. Yes, I think there'd be werewolves among our demons, but they wouldn't be much like the old ones. No nice clean fur, white teeth and shining eyes. Oh, no. Instead you'd get some nasty hound that wouldn't surprise you if you saw it nosing at a garbage pail or crawling out from under a truck. Frighten and terrorize you, yes. But surprise, no. It would fit into the environment. Look as if it belonged in a city and smell the same. Because of the twisted emotions that would be its food, your emotions and mine. A matter of diet."

Tom Goodsell chuckled loudly and lit another cigarette. But David only stared at the scarred counter. He realized he couldn't tell Tom what had happened this morning—or this noon. Of course, Tom would immediately scoff and be skeptical. But that wouldn't get around the fact that Tom had already agreed— agreed in partial jest perhaps, but still agreed. And Tom himself confirmed this, when, in a more serious, friendlier voice, he said:

"Oh, I know I've talked a lot of rot tonight, but still, you know, the way things are, there's something to it. At least, I can't express my feelings any other way."

They shook hands at the corner, and David rode the surging street car home through a city whose every bolt and stone seemed subtly infected, whose every noise carried shuddering overtones. His mother was waiting up for him, and after he had wearily argued with her about getting more rest and seen her off to bed, he lay sleepless himself, all through the night, like a child in a strange house, listening to each tiny noise and watching intently each changing shape taken by the shadows.

That night nothing shouldered through the door or pressed its muzzle against the window pane.

Yet he found that it cost him an effort to go down to the department store next morning, so conscious was he of the thing's presence in the faces and forms, the structures and machines around him. It was as if he were forcing himself into the heart of a monster. Detestation of the city grew within him. As yesterday, the crowded aisles seemed only hiding places, and he avoided the locker room. Gertrude Rees remarked sympathetically on his fatigued look, and he took the opportunity to invite her out that evening. Of course, he told himself while they sat watching the movie, she wasn't very close to him. None of the girls had been close to him—a not-very-competent young man tied down to the task of supporting parents whose little reserve of money had long ago dribbled away. He had dated them for a while, talked to them, told them his beliefs and ambitions, and then one by one they had drifted off to marry other men. But that did not change the fact that he needed the wholesomeness Gertrude could give him.

And as they walked home through the chilly night, he found himself talking inconsequentially and laughing at his own jokes. Then, as they turned to one another in the shadowy vestibule and she lifted her lips, he sensed her features altering queerly, lengthening. "A funny sort of light here," he thought as he took her in his arms. But the thin strip of fur on her collar grew matted and oily under his touch, her fingers grew hard and sharp against his back, he felt her teeth pushing out against her lips, and then a sharp, prickling sensation as of icy needles.

Blindly he pushed away from her, then saw—and the sight stopped him dead—that she had not changed at all or that whatever change had been was now gone.

"What's the matter, dear?" he heard her ask startledly. "What's happened? What's that you're mumbling? Changed, you say? What's changed? Infected with it? What do you mean? For heaven's sake, don't talk that way. You've done it to me, you say? Done what?" He felt her hand on his arm, a soft hand now. "No, you're not crazy. Don't think of such things. But you're neurotic and maybe a little batty. For heaven's sake, pull yourself together."

"I don't know what happened to me," he managed to say, in his right voice again. Then, because he had to say something more: "My nerves all jumped, like someone had snapped them."

He expected her to be angry, but she seemed only puzzledly sympathetic, as if she liked him but had become afraid of him, as if she sensed something wrong in him beyond her powers of understanding or repair.

"Do take care of yourself," she said doubtfully. "We're all a little crazy now and then, I guess. My nerves get like wires too. Goodnight."

He watched her disappear up the stair. Then he turned and ran.

At home his mother was waiting up again, close to the hall radiator to catch its dying warmth, the inevitable shapeless bathrobe wrapped about her. Because of a new thought that had come to the forefront of his brain, he avoided her embrace and, after a few brief words, hurried off toward his room. But she followed him down the hall.

"You're not looking at all well, David," she told him anxiously, whispering because Father might be asleep. "Are you sure you're not getting flu again? Don't you think you should see the doctor tomorrow?" Then she went on quickly to another subject, using that nervously apologetic tone with which he was so familiar. "I shouldn't bother you with it, David, but you really must be more careful of the bedclothes. You'd laid something greasy on the coverlet and there were big, black stains."

He was pushing open the bedroom door. Her words halted his hand only for an instant. How could you avoid the thing by going one place rather than another?

"And one thing more," she added, as he switched on the lights. "Will you try to get some cardboard tomorrow to black out the windows? They're out of it at the stores around here and the radio says we should be ready."

"Yes, I will. Goodnight, mother."

"Oh, and something else," she persisted, lingering uneasily just beyond the door. "That really must be a dead rat in the walls. The smell keeps coming in waves. I spoke to the real-estate agent, but he hasn't done anything about it. I wish you'd speak to him."

"Yes. Goodnight, Mother."

He waited until he heard her door softly close. He lit a cigarette and slumped down on the bed to try and think as clearly as he could about something to which everyday ideas could not be applied.

Question One (and he realized with an ironic twinge that it sounded melodramatic enough for a dime-novel): Was Gertrude Rees what might be called, for want of a better term, a werewolf?

Answer: Almost certainly not, in any ordinary sense of the word. What had momentarily come to her had been something he had communicated to her. It had happened because of his presence. And either his own shock had interrupted the transformation or else Gertrude Rees had not proved a suitable vehicle of incarnation for the thing.

Question Two: Might he not communicate the thing to some other person? Answer: Yes. For a moment his thinking paused, as there swept before his mind's eye kaleidoscopic visions of the faces which might, without warning, begin to change in his presence: His mother, his father, Tom Goodsell, the prim-mouthed real estate agent, a customer at the store, a panhandler who would approach him on a rainy night.

Question Three: Was there any escape from the thing? Answer: No. And yet—There was one bare possibility. Escape from the city. The city had bred the thing; might it not be chained to the city? It hardly seemed to be a reasonable possibility; how could a supernatural entity be tied down to one locality? And yet—he stepped quickly to the window and, after a moment's hesitation, jerked it up. Sounds which had been temporarily blotted out by his thinking now poured past him in quadrupled volume, mixing together discordantly like instruments tuning up for some titanic symphony—the racking surge of street car and elevated, the coughing of a locomotive in the yards, the hum of tires on asphalt and the growl of engines, the mumbling of radio voices, the faint mournful note of distant horns. But now they were no longer separate sounds. They all issued from one cavernous throat—a single moan, infinitely penetrating, infinitely menacing. He slammed down the window and put his hands to his ears. He switched out the lights and threw himself on the bed, burying his head in the pillows. Still the sound came through. And it was then he realized that ultimately, whether he wanted to or not, the thing would drive him from the city. The moment would come when the sound would begin to penetrate too deeply, to reverberate too unendurably in his ears.

The sight of so many faces, trembling on the brink of an almost unimaginable change, would become too much for him. And he would leave whatever he was doing and go away.

The moment came a little after four o'clock next afternoon. He could not say what sensation it was that, adding its straw-weight to the rest, drove him to take the step. Perhaps it was a heaving movement in the rack of dresses two counters away; perhaps it was the snoutlike appearance momentarily taken by a crumpled piece of cloth. Whatever it was, he slipped from behind the counter without a word, leaving a customer to mutter indignantly, and walked up the stair and out into the street, moving almost like a sleep-walker yet constantly edging from side to side to avoid any direct contact with the crowd engulfing him. Once in the street, he took the first car that came by, never noting its number, and found himself an empty place in the corner of the front platform.

With ominous slowness at first, then with increasing rapidity the heart of the city was left behind. A great gloomy bridge spanning an oily river was passed over, and the frowning cliffs of the buildings grew lower. Warehouses gave way to factories, factories to apartment buildings, apartment buildings to dwellings which were at first small and dirty white, then large and mansion-like but very much decayed, then new and monotonous in their uniformity. Peoples of different economic status and racial affiliation filed in and emptied out as the different strata of the city were passed through. Finally the vacant lots began to come, at first one by one, then in increasing numbers, until the houses were spaced out two or three to a block.

"End of the line," sang out the conductor, and without hesitation David swung down from the platform and walked on in the same direction that the street car had been going. He did not hurry. He did not lag. He moved as an automaton that had been wound up and set going, and will not stop until it runs down.

The sun was setting smokingly red in the west. He could not see it because of a tree-fringed rise ahead, but its last rays winked at him from the window panes of little houses blocks off to the right and left, as if flaming lights had been lit inside. As he moved they flashed on and off like signals. Two blocks further on the sidewalk ended, and he walked down the center of a muddy lane. After passing a final house, the lane also came to an end, giving way to a narrow dirt path between high weeds. The path led up the rise and through the fringe of trees. Emerging on the other side, he slowed his pace and finally stopped, so bewilderingly fantastic was the scene spread out before him. The sun had set, but high cloud-banks reflected its light, giving a spectral glow to the landscape.

Immediately before him stretched the equivalent of two or

three empty blocks, but beyond that began a strange realm that seemed to have been plucked from another climate and another geological system and set down here outside the city. There were strange trees and shrubs, but, most striking of all, great uneven blocks of reddish stone which rose from the earth at unequal intervals and culminated in a massive central eminence fifty or sixty feet high.

As he gazed, the light drained from the landscape, as if a cloak had been flipped over the earth, and in the sudden twilight there rose from somewhere in the region ahead a faint howling, mournful and sinister, but in no way allied to the other howling that had haunted him day and night. Once again he moved forward, but now impulsively toward the source of the new sound.

A small gate in a high wire fence pushed open, giving him access to the realm of rocks. He found himself following a gravel path between thick shrubs and trees. At first it seemed quite dark, in contrast to the open land behind him. And with every step he took, the hollow howling grew closer. Finally the path turned abruptly around a shoulder of rock, and he found himself at the sound's source.

A ditch of rough stone about eight feet wide and of similar depth separated him from a space overgrown with short, brownish vegetation and closely surrounded on the other three sides by precipitous, rocky walls in which were the dark mouths of two or three caves. In the center of the open space were gathered a half dozen white- furred canine figures, their muzzles pointing toward the sky, giving voice to the mournful cry that had drawn him here.

It was only when he felt the low iron fence against his knees and made out the neat little sign reading, ARCTIC WOLVES, that he realized where he must be—in the famous zoological gardens which he had heard about but never visited, where the animals were kept in as nearly natural conditions as was feasible. Looking around, he noted the outlines of two or three low inconspicuous buildings, and some distance away he could see the form of a uniformed guard silhouetted against a patch of dark sky. Evidently he had come in after hours and through an auxiliary gate that should have been locked.

Swinging around again, he stared with casual curiosity at the wolves. The turn of events had the effect of making him feel stupid and bewildered, and for a long time he pondered dully as to why he should find these animals unalarming and even attractive.

Perhaps it was because they were so much a part of the wild, so little of the city. That great brute there, for instance, the biggest of the lot, who had come forward to the edge of the ditch to stare back at him. He seemed an incarnation of primitive strength. His fur so creamy white—well, perhaps not so white; it seemed darker than he had thought at first, streaked with black—or was that due to the fading light? But at least his eyes were clear and clean, shining faintly like jewels in the gathering dark. But no, they weren't clean; their reddish gleam was thickening, scumming over, until they looked more like two tiny peepholes in the walls of a choked furnace. And why hadn't he noticed before that the creature was obviously malformed? And why should the other wolves draw away from it and snarl as if afraid?

Then the brute licked its black tongue across its greasy jowls, and from its throat came a faint familiar growl that had in it nothing of the wild, and David Lashley knew that before him crouched the monster of his dreams, finally made flesh and blood.

With a choked scream he turned and fled blindly down the gravel path that led between thick shrubs to the little gate, fled in panic across empty blocks, stumbling over the uneven ground and twice falling. When he reached the fringe of trees he looked back, to see a low, lurching form emerge from the gate. Even at this distance he could tell that the eyes were those of no animal.

It was dark in the trees, and dark in the lane beyond. Ahead the street lamps glowed, and there were lights in the houses. A pang of helpless terror gripped him when he saw there was no street car waiting, until he realized—and the realization was like the onset of insanity—that nothing whatever in the city promised him refuge. This—everything that lay ahead—was the thing's hunting ground. It was driving him in toward its lair for the kill.

Then he ran, ran with the hopeless terror of a victim in the arena, of a rabbit loosed before greyhounds, ran until his sides were walls of pain and his grasping throat seemed aflame, and then still ran. Over mud, dirt and brick, and then onto the endless sidewalks; past the neat suburban dwellings which in their uniformity seemed like monoliths lining some avenue of Egypt. The streets were almost empty, and those few people he passed stared at him as at a madman.

Brighter lights came into view, a corner with two or three

stores. There he paused to look back. For a moment he saw nothing. Then it emerged from the shadows a block behind him, loping unevenly with long strides that carried it forward with a rush, its matted fur shining oilily under a street lamp. With a croaking sob he turned and ran on.

The thing's howling seemed suddenly to increase a thousandfold, becoming a pulsating wail, a screaming ululation that seemed to blanket the whole city with sound. And as that demoniac screeching continued, the lights in the houses began to go out one by one. Then the streetlights vanished in a rush, and an approaching street car was blotted out, and he knew that the sound did not come altogether or directly from the thing. This was the long-predicted blackout.

He ran on with arms outstretched, feeling rather than seeing the intersections as he approached them, misjudging his step at curbs, tripping and falling flat, picking himself up to stagger on half-stunned. His diaphragm contracted to a knot of pain that tied itself tighter and tighter. Breath rasped like a file in his throat. There seemed no light in the whole world, for the clouds had gathered thicker and thicker ever since sunset. No light, except those twin points of dirty red in the blackness behind.

A solid edge of darkness struck him down, inflicting pain on his shoulder and side. He scrambled up. Then a second solid obstacle in his path smashed him full in the face and chest. This time he did not rise. Dazed, tortured by exhaustion, motionless, he waited its approach.

First a padding of footsteps, with the faint scraping of claws on cement. Then a snuffing. Then a sickening stench. Then a glimpse of red eyes. And then the thing was upon him, its weight pinning him down, its jaws thrusting at his throat. Instinctively his head went up, and his forearm was clamped by teeth whose icy sharpness stung through the layers of cloth, while a foul oily fluid splattered his face.

At that moment light flooded them, and he was aware of a malformed muzzle retreating into the blackness, and of weight lifted from him. Then silence and cessation of movement. Nothing, nothing at all—except the light flooding down. As consciousness and sanity teetered in his brain, his eyes found the source of light, a glaring white disk only a few feet away. A flashlight, but nothing visible in the blackness behind it. For what seemed an eternity, there was no change in the situation—himself supine and exposed upon the ground in the unwavering circle of light.

Then a voice from the darkness, the voice of a man paralyzed by supernatural fear. "God, God, God," over and over again. Each word dragged out with prodigious effort.

An unfamiliar sensation stirred in David, a feeling almost of security and relief.

"You—saw it then?" he heard issue from his own dry throat. "The hound? the—wolf?"

"Hound? Wolf?" The voice from behind the flashlight was hideously shaken. "It was nothing like that. It was—" Then the voice broke, became earthly once more. "Good grief, man, we must get you inside."

ALICE AND THE ALLERGY

THERE WAS A KNOCKING. THE DOCTOR PUT DOWN his pen. Then he heard his wife hurrying down the stairs. He resumed his history of old Mrs. Easton's latest blood-clot.

The knocking was repeated. He reminded himself to get after Engstrand to fix the bell.

After a pause long enough for him to write a sentence and a half, there came a third and louder burst of knocking. He frowned and got up.

It was dark in the hall. Alice was standing on the third step from the bottom, making no move to answer the door. As he went past her he shot her an inquiring glance. He noted that her eyelids looked slightly puffy, as if she were having another attack—an impression which the hoarseness of her voice a moment later confirmed.

"*He* knocked that way," -was what she whispered. She sounded frightened. He looked back at her with an expression of greater puzzlement—which almost immediately, however, changed to comprehension. He gave her a sympathetic, semi-professional nod, as if to say, "I understand now. Glad you mentioned it. We'll talk about it later." Then he opened the door.

It was Renshaw from the Allergy Lab. "Got the new kit for you, Howard," he remarked in an amiable Southern drawl. "Finished making it up this afternoon and thought I'd bring it around myself."

"A million thanks. Come on in."

Alice had retreated a few steps farther up the stairs. Renshaw did not appear to notice her in the gloom. He was talkative as he followed Howard into his office.

"An interestin' case turned up. Very unusual. A doctor we supply lost a patient by broncho-spasm. Nurse mistakenly injected the shot into a vein. In ten seconds he was strangling. Edema of the glottis developed. Injected ammophyllme and epmephnne—no dice. Tried to get a bronchoscope down his windpipe to give him air, but couldn't manage. Finally did a tracheotomy, but by that time it was too late."

"You always have to be damned careful," Howard remarked.

"Right," Renshaw agreed cheerfully. He set the kit on the desk and stepped back. "Well, if we don't identify the substance responsible for your wife's allergy this time, it won't be for lack of imagination. I added some notions of my own to your suggestions."

"Good."

"You know, she's well on her way to becoming the toughest case I ever made kits for. We've tested all the ordinary substances, and most of the extraordinary."

Howard nodded, his gaze following the dark woodwork toward the hall door. "Look," he said, "do many doctors tell you about allergy patients showing fits of acute depression during attacks, a tendency to rake up unpleasant memories—especially old fears?"

"Depression seems to be a pretty common symptom," said Renshaw cautiously. "Let's see, how long is it she's been bothered?"

"About two years—ever since six months after our marriage." Howard smiled. "That arouses certain obvious suspicions, but you know how exhaustively we've tested myself, my clothes, my professional equipment."

"I should say so," Renshaw assured him. For a moment the men were silent. Then, "She suffers from depression and fear?"

Howard nodded.

"Fear of anything in particular?"

But Howard did not answer that question.

About ten minutes later, as the outside door closed on the man from the Allergy Lab, Alice came slowly down the stairs.

The puffiness around her eyes was more marked, emphasizing her paleness. Her eyes were still fixed on the door.

"You know Renshaw, of course," her husband said.

"Of course, dear," she answered huskily, with a little laugh. "It was just the knocking. It made me remember *him.*"

"That so?" Howard inquired cheerily. "I don't think you've ever told me that detail. I'd always assumed—"

"No," she said, "the bell to Auntie's house was out of order that afternoon. So it was his knocking that drew me through the dark hallway and made me open the door, so that I saw his white avid face and long strong hands—with the big dusty couch just behind me, where... and my hand on the curtain sash, with which he—"

"Don't think about it." Howard reached up and caught hold of her cold hand. "That chap's been dead for two years now. He'll strangle no more women."

"Are you sure?" she asked.

"Of course. Look, dear, Renshaw's brought a new kit. We'll make the scratch tests right away."

She followed him obediently into the examination room across the hall from the office. He rejected the forearm she offered him— it still showed faint evidences of the last test. As he swabbed off the other, he studied her face.

"Another little siege, eh? Well, we'll ease that with a mild ephedrine spray."

"Oh it's nothing," she said. "I wouldn't mind it at all if it weren't for those stupid moods that go with it."

"I know," he said, blocking out the test areas.

"I always have that idiotic feeling," she continued hesitantly, "that *he's* trying to get at me."

Ignoring her remark, he picked up the needle. They were both silent as he worked with practiced speed and care. Finally he sat back, remarking with considerably more confidence than he felt, "There! I bet you this time we've nailed the elusive little demon who likes to choke you!"—and looked up at the face of the slim, desirable, but sometimes maddeningly irrational person he had made his wife.

"I wonder if you've considered it from my point of view," he said, smiling. "I know it was a horrible experience, just about the worst a woman can undergo. But if it hadn't happened, I'd never have been called in to take care of you—and we'd never have got married."

"That's true," she said, putting her hand on his.

"It was completely understandable that you should have spells of fear afterwards," he continued. "Anyone would. Though I do think your background made a difference. After all, your Aunt kept you so shut away from people—men especially. Told you they were all sadistic, evil-minded brutes. You know, sometimes when I think of that woman deliberately trying to infect you with all her rotten fears, I find myself on the verge of forgetting that she was no more responsible for her actions than any other miseducated neurotic."

She smiled at him gratefully.

"At any rate," he went on, "it was perfectly natural that you should be frightened, especially when you learned that he was a murderer with a record, who had killed other women and had even, in two cases where he'd been interrupted, made daring efforts to come back and complete the job. Knowing that about him, it was plain realism on your part to be scared—at least intelligently apprehensive—as long as he was on the loose. Even after we were married."

"But then, when you got incontrovertible proof—" He fished in his pocket, "Of course, he didn't formally pay the law's penalty, but he's just as dead as if he had." He smoothed out a worn old newspaper clipping. "You can't have forgotten this," he said gently, and began to read:

MYSTERY STRANGLER
UNMASKED BY DEATH

Lansing, Dec. 22. (Universal Press)—A mysterious boarder who died two days ago at a Kinsey Street rooming house has been conclusively identified as the uncaught rapist and strangler who in recent years terrified three Midwestern cities. Police Lieutenant Jim Galeto, interviewed by reporters in the death room at 1555 Kinsey Street...

She covered the clipping with her hand. "Please."

"Sorry," he said, "but an idea had occurred to me—one that would explain your continuing fear. I don't think you've ever hinted at it, but are you really completely satisfied that this was the man? Or is there a part of your mind that still doubts, that believes the police mistaken, that pictures the killer still at large?

I know you identified the photographs, but sometimes, Alice, I think it was a mistake that you didn't go to Lansing like they wanted you to and see with your own eyes—"

"I wouldn't want to go near that city, ever." Her lips had thinned.

"But when your peace of mind was at stake...."

"No, Howard," she said. "And besides, you're absolutely wrong. From the first moment I never had the slightest doubt that he was the man who died—"

"But in that case—"

"And furthermore, it was only then, when my allergy started, that I really began to be afraid of him."

"But surely, Alice—" Calm substituted for anger in his manner. "Oh, I know you can't believe any of that occult rot your aunt was always falling for."

"No, I don't," she said. "It's something very different."

"What?"

But that question was not answered. Alice was looking down at the inside of her arm. He followed her gaze to where a white welt was rapidly filling one of the squares.

"What's it mean?" she asked nervously.

"Mean?" he almost yelled. "Why, you little dope, it means we've licked the thing at last! It means we've found the substance that causes your allergy. I'll call Renshaw right away and have him make up the shots."

He picked up one of the vials, frowned, checked it against the area. "That's odd," he said. "HOUSEHOLD DUST. We've tried that a half dozen times. But then, of course, it's always different...."

"Howard," she said, "I don't like it. I'm frightened."

He looked at her lovingly. "The little dope," he said to her softly. "She's about to be cured—and she's frightened." And he hugged her. She was cold in his arms.

But by the time they sat down to dinner, things were more like normal. The puffiness had gone out of her eyelids and he was briskly smiling.

"Got hold of Renshaw. He was very interested. HOUSEHOLD DUST was one of his ideas. He's going down to the lab tonight and will have the shots over early tomorrow. The sooner we start, the better. I also took the opportunity to phone Engstrand.

He'll try to get over to fix the bell, this evening. Heard from Mrs. Easton's nurse too. Things aren't so well there. I'm pretty sure there'll be bad news by tomorrow morning at latest. I may have to rush over any minute. I hope it doesn't happen tonight, though."

It didn't and they spent a quiet evening—not even Engstrand showed up—which could have been very pleasant had Alice been a bit less pre-occupied.

But about three o'clock he was shaken out of sleep by her trembling. She was holding him tight.

"He's coming." Her whisper was whistly, laryngitic.

"What?" He sat up, half pulling her with him. "I'd better give you another eph—"

"Sh! What's that? Listen."

He rubbed his face. "Look Alice," after a moment, he said, "I'll go downstairs and make sure there's nothing there."

No, don't!" she clung to him. For a minute or two they huddled there without speaking. Gradually his ears became attuned to the night sounds—the drone and mumble of the city, the house's faint, closer creakings. Something had happened to the street lamp and incongruous unmixed moonlight streamed through the window beyond the foot of the bed.

He was about to say something, when she let go of him and said, in a more normal voice, "There. It's gone."

She slipped out of bed, went to the window, opened it wider, and stood there, breathing deeply.

"You'll get cold, come back to bed," he told her.

"In a while."

The moonlight was in key with her flimsy nightgown. He got up, rummaged around for her quilted bathrobe and, in draping it around her, tried an embrace. She didn't respond.

He got back in bed and watched her. She had found a chair-arm and was looking out the window. The bathrobe had fallen back from her shoulders. He felt wide awake, his mind crawlingly active.

"You know, Alice," he said, "there may be a psychoanalytic angle to your fear."

"Yes?" She did not turn her head.

"Maybe, in a sense, your libido is still tied to the past. Unconsciously, you may still have that distorted conception of sex your aunt drilled into you, something sadistic and murderous.

And it's possible your unconscious mind had tied your allergy in with it—you said it was a dusty couch. See what I'm getting at?"

She still looked out the window.

"It's an ugly idea and of course your conscious mind wouldn't entertain it for a moment, but your aunt's influence set the stage and, when all's said and done, *he* was your first experience of men. Maybe in some small way, your libido is still linked to... him."

She didn't say anything.

Rather late next morning he awoke feeling sluggish and irritable. He got out of the room quietly, leaving her still asleep, breathing easily. As he was getting a second cup of coffee, a jarringly loud knocking summoned him to the door. It was a messenger with the shots from the Allergy Lab. On his way to the examination room he phoned Engstrand again, heard him promise he'd be over in a half hour sure, cut short a long-winded explanation as to what had tied up the electrician last night.

He started to phone Mrs. Easton's place, decided against it.

He heard Alice in the kitchen.

In the examination room he set some water to boil in the sterilizing pan, got out instruments. He opened the package from the Allergy Lab, frowned at the inscription HOUSEHOLD DUST, set down the container, walked over to the window, came back and frowned again, went to his office and dialed the Lab.

"Renshaw?"

"Uh huh. Get the shots?"

"Yes, many thanks. But I was just wondering... you know, it's rather odd we should hit it with household dust after so many misses."

"Not so odd, when you consider..."

"Yes, but I was wondering exactly where the stuff came from."

"Just a minute."

He shifted around in his swivel chair. In the kitchen Alice was humming a tune.

"Say, Howard, look. I'm awfully sorry, but Johnson seems to have gone off with the records. I'm afraid I won't be able to get hold of them 'til afternoon."

"Oh, that's all right. Just curiosity. You don't have to bother."

"No, I'll let you know. Well, I suppose you'll be making the first injection this morning?"

"Right away. You know we're both grateful to you for having hit on the substance responsible."

"No credit due me. Just a..." Renshaw chuckled "... shot in the dark."

Some twenty minutes later, when Alice came into the examination room, Howard was struck, to a degree that quite startled him, with how pretty and desirable she looked. She had put on a white dress and her smiling face showed no signs of last night's attack. For a moment he had the impulse to take her in his arms, but then he remembered last night and decided against it.

As he prepared to make the injection, she eyed the hypodermics, bronchoscope, and scalpels laid out on the sterile towel.

"What are those for?" she asked lightly.

"Just routine stuff, never use them."

"You know," she said laughingly, "I was an awful ninny last night. Maybe you're right about my libido. At any rate, I've put *him* out of my life forever. He can't ever get at me again. From now on, you're the only one."

He grinned, very happily. Then his eyes grew serious and observant as he made the injection, first withdrawing the needle repeatedly to make sure there were no signs of venous blood. He watched her closely.

The phone jangled.

"Damn," he said. "That'll be Mrs. Easton's nurse. Come along with me."

He hurried through the swinging door. She started after him.

But it wasn't Mrs. Easton's nurse. It was Renshaw. "Found the records. Johnson didn't have them after all. Just misplaced. And there *is* something out of the way. That dust didn't come from there at all. It came from..."

There came a knocking. He strained to hear what Renshaw was saying.

"What?" He whipped out a pencil. "Say that again. Don't mind the noise. It's just our electrician coming to fix the bell. What was that city?"

The knocking was repeated.

"Yes, I've got that. And the exact address of the place the dust came from?"

There came a third and louder burst of knocking, which grew to a violent tattoo.

Finishing his scribbling, he hung up with a bare "Thanks," to Renshaw, and hurried to the door just as the knocking died.

There was no one there.

Then he realized. He hardly dared push open the door to the examination room, yet no one could have gone more quickly.

Alice's agonizingly arched, suffocated body was lying on the rug. Her heels, which just reached the hardwood flooring, made a final, weak knock-knock. Her throat was swollen like a toad's.

Before he made another movement he could not stop himself from glaring around, window and door, as if for an escaping intruder.

As he snatched for his instruments, knowing for an absolute certainty that it would be too late, a slip of paper floated down from his hand.

On it was scribbled, "LANSING, 1555 Kinsey Street."

SKINNY'S WONDERFUL

I BET A LOT OF THESE LADS BEEF TO YOU ABOUT THEIR
wives... you must get sick of it... but not me. I think Skinny's
wonderful. It isn't every man has a wife who is loving, hardworking,
brainy as they make them, talented seventeen different ways, and
a professional dancer. You could draw me another beer. Hot as
the hinges, isn't it? Thanks.

I started calling her Skinny because she wasn't meaty like the
other girls, though she could outlast any ten of them dancing.
They has nice enough figures if you go for that sort of thing, but
they were meaty... not in the old-time beef-trust class, but the
grits and greens and side meat showed. You know how they
round them up. Lad goes south and puts an ad in the country
papers: Girls One Hundred Dollars a Week. Likely looking ones
he asks to strip. If they will and the figure's okay they're in.

Skinny's no stripper. They always try to have one real dancer
in those shows so they can call them artistic and give the boobs'
libidos a rest. Of course Skinny always sheds a few clothes...
that's a must... but she never goes all the way. Shinny provides
the touch of imagination. She's an Aztec priestess with a glass
knife or a Russian duchess with a whip. Once she was Joan of
Arc holding a cross and her robe got burned off six times a night...
quite a lighting effect... and she does a half-and-half apache dance
where she throws herself all over the stage and kicks herself. She
was going to be Queen Theodora once with blue and gold robes
and a jeweled cross, but they told her the Irish boobs would think
it was supposed to be the Virgin Mary.

No wonder she's skinny the way she's always worked on

those routines. Rehearse, rehearse, over and over. All around the living room. Whew! You could draw me another and have one yourself this time. Okay, a shortie. Once before I knew her she was working a bog club date where the boobs sat at tables having dinner. Skinny was doing a slow backbend, bare middle, when one of the yells, "That girl looks starved. Let's give her something to eat," and he throws a roll. Right away hard rolls are skidding all over all over the stage and a few thudding on her ribs. She finished the act though. Some of those club dates are pretty terrible. They even expect the pianist to play naked. Can you imagine?

But Skinny's no stripper and be damned to my mother for calling her one. Just after we got married Skinny gave a dance recital in our back garden for some of mother's friends and a few of ours. Mother said afterwards she was trying to give Skinny every chance. It was very beautiful, blue spotlights, Greek robes; Isadora Duncan sort of thing, Skinny's really an artist. But right in the middle of one number she popped a shoulder strap. I don't see anything wrong about a breast, certainly not one of Skinny's, it's sort of tiny and tender, its makes you think of little kids. Naturally Skinny finished the act, she always does, but Mother thought, she should have stopped... made like September Morn I suppose... or worn a brassiere. Mother also said Skinny wasn't careful about drawing the alcove curtains when she changed costumes and that she shouldn't have stood on the alcove table to do it. She worries and fusses and criticizes all the time.

Skinny's nothing like that. She has a wonderful disposition. That's why I'm telling you about her. I wouldn't want to bore you with my woes. Of course she screams at me sometimes and throws the soup, but it's generally lukewarm soup, Skinny believes hot foods give you cancer... I'm a lucky man, wouldn't you say? Once she did throw some paint at me, I mean trip me and shove me into a bog slopping puddle of it. She'd got me to help her paint the living room ceiling... she's always redecorating the apartment... and I climbed on the stepladder and right away spilled a two-gallon can. She had justification that time, you must admit. It wasn't anything like the night she got mad at me in the car and started stamping on my ankle and finally hit the gas pedal. We went off the road... no bones broken though the birdcage got knocked open and the white rats escaped out of it. But that night Skinny had been drinking and I must have been beefing to her. Normally she has a wonderful disposition, it's just that she has all this energy and it has to find an outlet.

Skinny has energy enough for ten women. Did I say ten? I meant two hundred. By contrast I have what you might call a lethargic disposition, I need Skinny to balance me off.

It's not only energy. Skinny has brains. You may think I'm exaggerating, you may think I'm just a lad mooning about his girl, but I actually believe Skinny has brains enough to be president of the United States, if we had women presidents. Something like a combination of Claire Booth Luce and Bridgitte Bardot. Once an intellectual lad told Skinny she had no brains at all, but she argued him down. She's talented in all sorts of directions. Take interior decoration...

No, no, that's all right. Go ahead and serve them, it's your vocation. Hello, friend. Join me in a beer? Has it ever occurred to you, friend, that women have a nest-building instinct? Take my wife Skinny. Every six months, regular as clockwork, she has to rent a new apartment and redecorate it from vestibule to garbage can. If she doesn't she starts brooding. She does a wonderful job... white woolly rugs, low tables, dramatic simplicity. My mother's all wet when she says our places always look like night clubs when Skinny's through with them. Mother's never been inside a burlesque bar in her life.

Skinny's awfully smart about figuring out stuff to use in decorating, stuff nobody else would think of, and finding places where you can pick it up for nothing or sort of snitch it. Driftwood, big branches with leaves on, travel posters, old spotlights and gelatin from the night clubs, wicker baskets a yard across, ten-gallon green glass carboys, bricks and tiles, you name it. We can't drive past a house that's being torn down but what we have to stop and rummage for old ironwork. We generally find it too and it's always the biggest heaviest piece. She's always calling me up at the last minute to tell me to stop off somewhere on the way and bring home the damnedest things. She never stops hunting. Sometimes when it's a snitch operation she gets caught, but she always has an explanation. One night when she was tearing down flowered branches in a private forest just off the highway a watchman yelled at her and started to come running, but she screamed back that she was only going to the powder room and what sort of a filthy old Peeping Tom was he, anyway?

I'm generally along to carry the branches and tear down the bigger ones she points out.

But of course moving every six months is the real monster job. Especially lugging and repotting all these tremendous plants. Skinny hammers nails in the living room and drapes the vines around. Striped and spotted leaves bigger than your two hands. You felt you're right in the jungle.

No, we haven't any children. I suppose if we did she'd take out her nest-building instinct on them. Still, I don't know. She has an awful lot of excess energy, there might still be some left over for plants and things. Besides, she likes to entertain. She lives for her parties.

Skinny's a great little hostess. She knocks herself out getting ready for her parties... all sorts of smorgasbord spread out, a huge punchbowl with colored ice, the kitchen set up for making pizza. And she's generally stayed up housecleaning the whole night before... those are the nights we get our complaints from the neighbors, not on the party nights. Our parties are pretty quiet, even Skinny doesn't have much energy left, and then our friends are an odd lot, they're all sorts... show people, some of Mother's friends. Skinny's father's social-minded characters, some of the people from the dime store, and now my securities lads... they don't mix so well and Skinny always invites them all. You know, it's only on party nights that Skinny gets even the teeniest bit rubber-kneed drunk... it's simply that getting ready has taken it out of her. She knocks herself out giving us all a good time.

Skinny's been a wonderful wife to me. Really. Of course she hasn't been able to get along with Mother, especially when Mother didn't pass on as we expected. Certainly you can't blame Mother for that. I was happier than anybody two months ago when Mother hit eighty, but I do blame Mother for calling Skinny a communist. Unquestionably I shouldn't have hit Mother, that was a contemptible and a big mistake that I'll be paying for until I die, even if it was nothing more than an accidental flick and anyway Skinny always gets everybody around her terribly worked up. There was absolutely nothing to Mother's suspicions. Skinny's father had all sorts of upside down social ideas in the old days... as who didn't, they tell me... but now the only subversive literature you'll find in his place of business is on Russian wolfhounds. Supplying dogs and cats and birds to stabilize the American home is just about the most patriotic job a man can do, in a way, wouldn't you say? Skinny's own interest in Russia is strictly limited to music, ballet, and Orthodox Church decor. A balalaika hanging on the wall against jewel-crusted brocade, that about sums up the Soviets for Skinny, though it's true she once had the ice in the punchbowl frozen in a big red star at one of the parties Mother came to, I don't know why. Certainly the detective Mother hired to investigate Skinny never turned up anything except the lunch dates she was having with a mocky screenwriter, or so he claimed to be... but that's another story. And in a way the trouble with Mother hasn't turned out so badly. She and Skinny stay away from each other, which is a relief, and although I can't expect any lump-sum money when Mother dies. I'll get something in trust... she'll probably live to one hundred anyway... and meanwhile she puts up a little cash from time to time for me to study my new job of selling securities in preparation for getting a license to sell them. Buy you another beer?

I've been slow getting my license, I have to admit. There are all sorts of tests you have to pass and I don't have Skinny's kind of ambition though tries hard enough to give it to me. Maybe I should go back to an office job. Skinny herself is almost coming around to think there are advantages, even if no future, in a biweekly paycheck. I don't know.

Skinny's still terrifically ambitious, though. As always, not barring childhood. She ran off and got a job dancing with a carnival when she was fourteen. She looked older then, just as she looks younger now. The girls had to turn cartwheels in one number. Skinny swore she could though she knew she couldn't. That night she went out to the park and practiced. When dawn came she could turn cartwheels. That's how I sometimes think of Skinny... a little girl all alone in the park turning cartwheels at 3 A.M.

The carnival had its points, Skinny said. They had a pit of rattlesnakes in the sideshow and she got a kick out of looking down into it.

Her father wasn't much help to her... that was before the pet shop and he was saving humanity and shifting around in these free-love situations. Skinny wanted to dance in ballet... she knew it was tops, her father did give her that scrap of information... but those were depression times and the big ballet troupes weren't going strong yet. Skinny got a job dancing in the Palace lone. She held it for five years.

I imagine you've been to enough burlesque shows, friend, probably more than I have, but it was little Skinny who told me how hard those line-girls worked. Fours shows a day seven days a week and five on Saturdays. A day off when and if. Rehearsal every weekday morning, early on Fridays to fit costumes for the new show. Playing one show, rehearsing another, and learning routines for the third. Monotony for the headlined strippers, boredom for the stand-around showgirls, but those little line-dancers got their tails worked off. Because Skinny was the most active and ambitions, they put her on the end of the line where she had to dance twice as far... when the line danced off sideways into the wings she was the last to leave the stage. By the time they exited high-kicking into the other wing, the line was reversed and she was still at the on-stage end... they somehow arranged it that way, Skinny told me, though at one point she'd have to sprint from one end of the line to the other to make it come out right.

I can't speak for the showgirls, friend, but I can assure you that the girls of the burlesque line were virtuous... those routines left them with no energy for anything else. Skinny told me she'd wake up nights counting five-six and she said that when the Midnight Shambles came along on Saturday it was just that.

Skinny rose to being a specialty dancer a few times at the Palace. Her high point was a poison dance as Lucretia Borgia... she carried a bottle of green dye and dripped it in the goblets of ten showgirls. But then stage burlesque faded and Skinny got started on club dates. She auditioned for ballet a few times, but it's my honest opinion Skinny simply had more than ballet knew what to do with. Same with movies, the stage and now TV. Skinny's an endless dynamo. Another beer would go fine. Thanks.

Club dates can be anything from a company dinner for the whole family to an army of drunken apes at a so-called hunting lodge in the middle of an impenetrable forest. Business men, lodge brothers, politicos, actual fishermen, or just plain boobs, Usually the show would carry a pianist or even a band but once they had to fall back on a member of the audience who could only play the first six bars of "There'll Be a Hot Time in the Old Town Tonight"... two hours of that, over, and over, while different girls stripped, can you imagine? Sometimes they'd have an auditorium; sometimes the stage would be the back end of a panel truck. Once the apes got the idea they'd grab Skinny off the back of the truck and throw her around among them...

she'd been doing her half- and-half apache number and the year before there'd been a little stripper who'd let the apes give her the pass-around treatment. Skinny had to climb to escape. She was marooned on the roof of that truck for half and hour, but every ape that grabbed at her ankle got his fingers stamped on. So Skinny says. Oh, those club dates! All those effing club dates! as one of Skinny's earthier associates refers to them.

Sorry you have to go, friend. Gentlemen, may I buy us a beer around? I couldn't help hearing the three of you discussing the perennial problem of how to make money. Now at a modest estimate my wife Skinny thinks up in a month more plans for making money than the four of us will in all our lives. That is, if you gentlemen are anything like me. Arabian restaurants where you sit on pillows, dog walking services that also change cat boxes and clean the birdcage, a chain of friendly American motels across Mexico that specialize in New England cooking, a shoppers' escort and buying-guide service, a distressed party givers' bureau that does everything from taking unruly drunks off your hands to emptying ashtrays the next morning... you name it, Skinny's thought of it and threshed it all out... along with all the more conventional business enterprises. One new way a week of making a million dollars... that's par for Skinny.

But you can't understand how intense Skinny is about her ideas for making money unless you've seen her make a pitch. She gets some of us together, me and two or three other lads, and she hands us a drink around and then she gives us a half-hour sales talk, all about initiative and push and golden opportunity. The NAM should hire Skinny, they really should... you never heard anybody build up industry, advertising, and the rewards of success the way she does. Her face just glows. She generally tops it off with something like, "Gentlemen, I have given you your choice: sit around on your fannies all your lives in Noplace Alley or put a down payment on a five-figure address on Easy Street!" Sometimes she says six-figure.

Of course it turns out then that we all have to put up money or go out and start changing cat boxes, managing unruly drunks and transforming old grocery stores into Arabian restaurants. The other lads butter up Skinny and then back down, and I explain to her there isn't much I can do all by myself, though she sometimes keeps after me for a while.

Nothing discourages her. She needs that million-dollar plan a week just like she needs to nest-build every six months.

The puzzling thing is that with all her brains and drive Skinny's never been able to get a good job outside show business. I guess it's the same way as with ballet... anybody who might hire Skinny is scared of her. Her drive shows through. They figure that if they gave her a toehold she'd own the business in a year. Just the same, She's wonderful.

Right now she's got a job as a demonstrator at the big dime store. That's right, that red-head who's always chopping up vegetables with a patent gadget, or putting a rainbow oil-slick in china, or sample-enameling a teenager's nails ten different shades, or managing a tableful of tiny clockwork men in striped pants... that's Skinny. She gets a chance to sales talk and explain and do something all day long, but it never uses up all her energy. They say they never had anybody like her. The manager sometimes brings her home.

You see, Skinny has the touch of imagination. Another demonstrator would never have thought of the ten-shades idea, which has become a high-school fad, she tells me. Or of having the little men march off a plank and drown in a sea of green cotton wool, She put live ants in a kaleidoscope, but they wouldn't let her demonstrate that one at the store. She brought it home. It was quite weird to look into. Once she tried writing stories for *Weird Tales* but they all came back with the comment "Too horrible." Or maybe it was "Needlessly horrible." I never understood that. As that so-called screenwriter told Skinny, "Even Shakespeare got called too horrible." By Lamb, I think. Something about putting someone's eyes out on the stage. Which reminds me that one of the schemes Skinny keeps coming back to is starting an American Grand Guignol theater. She's great at thinking up weird costumes... she still gets a club date once in a while, you know. She's still got a terrific figure and she really takes care of it (it's good for a woman to be proud of her figure, I think) though I guess even if she didn't take care of it, all that energy of hers would keep her slimmed down anyway. And she's great at thinking up weird costume accessories, like a gold wire handbag with white mice in it, or fireflies in cellophane pin-ons) that's for garden parties, or having a real spider web between a tiara and a shoulder yoke, or using a live snake for a belt.

Skinny loves animals. Birds, mice, lizards and turtles, pythons (small ones), baby alligators. Right now it's golden hamsters. Of course her father running a pet shop is a big help. Sometimes it builds way up and gets to be a sort of balanced economy... the mice ate the birdseed and the blacksnake ate the mice. Once Skinny had twenty-three birds. They were kind of enjoyable flying around, except when they buzzed you, but they started pulling off the wallpaper in little ribbons and they made everybody sort of uneasy about the smorgasbord. Eventually she cut down to seven parakeets.

Some animals she has no luck with. Twice she has cats but they got out fast. The spaniel slipped its leash and we never saw him again... that was my fault. Once she had two Samoyeds. They were just her style... big and white and woolly and fierce looking. She liked to walk them. But one got run over and the other bit some people. Skinny right away had me drive the dog into the next county and sell it. The people never found out who it belonged to.

We had the same trouble with the baby alligator. Skinny left it outside one night in a puddle under a washtub to give it a little nature and it worked its way out. It bit two neighbors who were weeding their gardens before we stopped hearing about it. It had bitten me too, before I found out how fast it could move. A baby alligator's bite is the funniest thing when it's fresh... a little crescent of red drops on your hand with two bigger drops for the eyeteeth.

The boa constrictor... it was only five feet long... just lost its appetite and sort of faded. Skinny thought a vacation in Mother's garden would refresh it, but Mother refused.

Of course the animals are a lot of work, sometimes more than the plants. But Skinny gets a big kick out of them. Skinny's wonderful. Why, she...

All right, gentlemen, I'll subside. I can see that Skinny is too much for you. Especially Skinny and animals. That's all right; She's sometimes too much for me. I understand. I'll just have one more beer at the end of the bar and quietly talk to myself.

Skinny loves me too. She really does. She tries to make something out of me and that's the test. She's done everything she could to give me ambition and sober me up. She's had me take antabuse and join AA and her father gives me dianstic therapy. She's really worked on me. She loves me, all right. Of course there was that screenwriter... he said... and the time she started

to Constantinople with the Turkish medical student and those
three months she just disappeared, but those were exceptions.
And of course she gets mad at me sometimes and talks about
murdering me, but I know it's just a gag when she asks people
at parties about undetectable poisons and how do you induce a
heart attack in someone who refuses to exert himself.

Yes, that's for me. I'll take it. Hello, Skinny. Yes, I'm here.
Well, I don't know how long. All right, right away. I said right
away. Yes, I'll keep an eye out for golden hamsters the last couple
of blocks. What? Look, Skinny, I can't handle that slab all by
myself... George and Fred were going to help, they said they would,
remember? Well, that's too bad. Yes, I suppose a taxi would help,
but not enough and the driver probably wouldn't allow it. You
can still use the old coffee table top for the party tonight. I know
the new one's going to look nicer but you'll have all the rest of
your life to enjoy it. Well, it may be only three inches thick but
that's still damn heavy. I don't care if the cutter has to get rid of
all his samples. He can hold onto it a day longer... it isn't the sort
of thing a person can toss in the trashcan. I absolutely refuse...
Oh I can, Can I? Well, you know where *you* can shove it!

Draw me one more beer, will you, one for the road? Yes, that
was Skinny. Better give me a shot too, this time. I'm going to need
it. On the way home I got to pick up a gravestone.

ANSWERING SERVICE

THE OVAL BEDROOM AND BOUDOIR ROCKED WITH the wind and shook with the thunder. The curving, tempered glass of the continuous-view windows strained, relaxed, strained again. The lightning flashes showed outside only the lashing tops of the big pines against inky night. Inside they regularly drowned the clusters of rosy lights and blanched to bone the quilted, pearl-gray satin upholstery. At one end of the oval, the silvery, spiral stairway leading up to the flat roof and down to the elevator floor cast momentarily flaring, fantastic shadows across the tufted floor and the great central bed with its huge silk pillows and pearl-gray comforter.

The old lady occupying an edge of the bed looked like the bent-waist mummy of a girl freshly wrapped and hurriedly fitted with a shaggy blonde wig and blonde silk nightgown. But the brown human claw did not tremble, holding the antique-inspired, pearl- gray phone greedily close to ear and lips, while the wrinkle-webbed eye gleamed with the lightning and without it, like jewels of obsidian or black onyx.

OLD LADY: Haven't you got the doctor yet, you bitch?

ANSWERING SERVICE: No, madam. He has gone out on an emergency case. I am trying to contact his copter, but the storm is interfering with short-wave telephony.

OL: I know all about the storm. Haven't you arranged yet for my medicine to be delivered, you incompetent slut?

AS: No, madam. The copters of all regional taxi and delivery services have been grounded by the storm. There have been two deaths by frightening—excuse me, lightning. I have your Cardinal pills here now. If the madam's phone were equipped with a matter-receiver—

OL: It isn't. Stop tormenting me by holding those pills just out of reach. Haven't you got the doctor yet?

AS: No, madam. He has gone out on an emergency case. I am trying to contact his copter, but the storm—

OL: That tape is beginning to bore me. You are just a bunch of tapes, aren't you? All very cleverly keyed to whatever I say, but still just a bunch of tapes.

AS: No, madam. I am a flesh-and-blood woman, age 23, name Doris. It's true, I sometimes think I'm just a tape. I'm surrounded by miles of them, which do answer routine inquiries. Alongside my matter-transmitter and keyboard I have a tape-writer for punching out more tapes. I have a long scissors and a pot of cement for editing them. But I am truly not a tape myself, though once I took a small bottle of sleeping pills because I thought—No, no, I am a flesh-and-blood woman, age 23...

OL:... name Doris. Yes, I got that on the first spin past the transmitting head. So now we have tapes with biographies, tapes that attempt suicide and ask for sympathy, tapes that play on the customer's feelings. How charming. Here I am, an old woman, all alone in a storm, and without a single servant, ever since the government with its red tape and its oversell of democracy made it possible to hire them, or even private nurses. An old—

AS: You haven't a robot nurse, madam?

OL: Shining horrors! No! I'm just an old, old woman, all alone, dying for lack of a doctor and medicine, but privileged to listen to tapes making excuses.

AS: Please, madam, I am not—

OL: Ooooh... my heart... please, nurse, my Cardinal pills... please, tape...

AS: Madam! Madam?

OL:... my heart... I'm going... ooooh...

AS: Madam, I'm breaking the rules to say this, but if you're having a heart attack, it's essential that you relax, make no effort or outcry, waste no strength on—

OL: Oooh... yes, and tapes to help you die quietly, to leave your tortured body without making a fuss that might embarrass the powers that be. Oh, don't worry, dear tape,—and let's not have any sympathetic-anxiety spools. I'm over that spasm now and merely waiting for the next. Just an old woman alone in the midst of a dreadful storm—hear that crash?—listening to tapes and waiting to die for lack of one Cardinal pill.

AS: Madam, a phone of your rating should have a matter-receiver. Are you quite certain you have not? I will inquire of our master files—

OL: And tapes to make a sales pitch while you die. Next you'll be trying to sell me a casket and a burial plot, or even urn space in a tomb satellite. I already have the first two of those, thank you. I do not have a matter-receiver.

AS: Madam, I am not trying to sell you anything, I am trying to save your life. I have your Cardinal pills here—

OL: Stop tantalizing me.

AS: —and I am doing everything I can to get them to you. If you had a matter-receiver, I would only have to drop one of the pills in the transmitter bowl in front of me or punch out its codes, and you would have it the next microsecond. Well over 99 percent of all phones of your rating have both a matter-receiver and telekinesis glove. I will inquire—

OL: Oh yes, a telekinesis glove—so I'd be able to sign checks long-distance for silver caskets cool with pearls and orchid plots and pills and masses to be said for my soul in Chartres, no doubt. But I don't have one, ha-ha, or a matter-receiver either. Who'd swallow a pill that came over a wire, all dirty with oil and electricity? Oooh...

AS: I have programmed an inquiry, madam. It is possible that you have a matter-receiver and aren't aware of it. Please don't distress or in any way exert yourself, madam; but I must point out to you that actual matter is never transmitted over the waves or wires and that, in any case, no oil is involved. The chemical and mass-shape codes for the object are punched into the transmitter or analyzed from a sample. Only those codes travel over the wires or waves. When they reach the receiver, they instantly synthesize an exact duplicate from standard raw materials there. I am oversimplifying somewhat, but—

OL: Even tapes to give lectures, to contradict and argue with a dying customer. Very clever indeed, especially when one knows that a computer, working a billion times as fast as a mere brain, can always out-think a human being, even one who isn't dying.

AS: Madam, I am not a tape! I am a flesh-and-blood.... Oh, what's the use?

OL: That would have been the third running for that one. Is it possible that even a computer, even a tape has a little shame? Very well, my dear, we will pretend you are not a tape, but a woman: age 23, name Doris. A young woman—it's only bitchy little sexpots that get to record those tapes, isn't it? Or do they concoct them entirely nowadays from the squeal of metal and the hum of power? Anyhow, we'll pretend you're a beautiful young woman who is tormenting me with pills I can't have and with grounded delivery-copters and with doctors who have skipped off on emergency visits to their mistresses and can't be reached. Yes, a beautiful vicious young woman, dear tape. At least that will give me something definite to hate while I die here all alone, someone who could conceivably suffer as I suffer. Ooooh...

AS: Madam, I am not beautiful and I'm trying hard not to be vicious. And I'm quite as alone as you are. All alone in a tiny cubical, surrounded by yards and yards of electric circuits, until my relief turns up. Yet I can faintly hear through the air-conditioning system the same storm you're having. It's moving my way.

OL: I'm glad you're all alone. I'm glad you can hear the storm. I'm glad you're in a tiny cubical and can't get away. Then you can imagine something horrible creeping silently toward you, as death is creeping toward me, while you puff your cigarettes into the air-conditioning outlet and drink your cocktails from a flask disguised as a walkie-talkie, I imagine, and preen yourself in front of a mirror and call one of your boy friends and amuse yourself by cat-and-mousing an old woman dying—

AS: Stop, mother, please!

OL: So now I've become the mother of a tape. How interesting.

Oh, excuse me, dear, I forgot we're pretending you're a beautiful young woman; but my memory's not so good these last hours, or minutes. And besides, it startled me so to discover that now tapes—excuse me again— even have mother fixations and have been psychoanalyzed, no doubt, and—

AS: Please, madam, I'm being serious. I may not be dying, but I wish I were—

OL: You're making me feel better, dear. Thank you.

AS: —so I'm every bit as miserable as you are. I took this job because of something that happened to me when I was a very little girl. My mother had a sudden heart attack and couldn't move, and she asked me to get her medicine. But I wouldn't do it because I'd asked her for candy a half hour before and she'd refused to give me any, and so I refused to move. She always called my medicine "candy," and I didn't understand what was happening at all. I thought I was just getting even. I didn't realize she was dying. And so long afterwards I took this job so I could help other people who were in her situation and make up for my crime and so I could—

OL: Oh no, my dear, you took this job so you could repeat over and over with gloating satisfaction the hot excitement you got when you watched your mother die and knew it was you who were killing her, so you could go on and on and on refusing to give old women their medicine or get them doctors, meanwhile showering them with sticky sweet sympathy, like poison for ants, and, not content with that torture, slipping in dirty little pleas for sympathy for your own vicious, murderous self—

AS: Oh, stop, stop, stop. I'm *human!* Three point one four one six. Pi. One three five seven eleven thirteen. Primes. Two four eight sixteen—

OL: How like a machine. Nothing but numbers. Confused with food. You're going crazy, machine.

AS: Oh, stop, stop, stop! I tell you I'm flesh-and-blood—

OL: Female, age 23, name Doris.

AS: —and I'm serious about all this, and I know this isn't the job for me at all, because I'm so horribly lonely; and what you say about me is the way I suspect myself of feeling, though I'm trying as hard as I can to feel the other way, the loving way, and I'm afraid—

OL: I'm glad you can feel guilt. Love—don't make me laugh. But I'm glad you're afraid. Because then you can imagine something creeping toward you as deadly as what's creeping toward me. What if your tapes should loop out and strangle you? What if your filthy matter-transmitter should suck you in and spit you out into a red-hot volcano or at the north pole or at the bottom of the Challanger Deep or on the sun side of Mercury? What's that now?—closer than the storm, rattling the grill of your ventilation inlet? What's that coming out of the answer slot of the computer? Why are the needle points of the long narrow blades of the scissors swinging toward you?

AS: Oh, stop, stop, stop, or they'll jump at my heart! Stop, stop, stop, stop, stop—

OL: Shut up! I'm tired of pretending. I'm just an old woman dying. And you're just tapes. Yes, just tapes. I know that because I've been insulting you every way I could, and you've been taking it. A live human being wouldn't. And only a tape would call me "madam." A democratized woman—and there aren't any others under 80—would call me dearie or senior citizen. And I've made you spend an hour on me. They'd never let a human being waste her working time like that, and she wouldn't care to. But tapes?—who cares? Plug the old dame in on them and let her play with them until she dies! And finally one tape got stuck on the word stop and kept jerking back and forth there, over and over. Ooooh... ooooh... this is the end, at last... ooooh...

AS: Stop, *stop,* STOP! Madam, the master files show that your phone is equipped with a miniaturized Important Trifle matter-receiver! It's hidden in the earpiece! I will place the Cardinal pill on the bowl and—

OL: Ooooh... too late, tape... I'm dying...

AS: Please, madam. For my sake.

OL: No, tape... I'm going now... I leave the horrors to you... I'm dying... like your mother... I'm... dead...

The cadaverous old lady carefully dropped the phone, not on its prongs or the floor, but with a dull, short clatter on the edge of the thick pale marble top of the night table. She leaned back into the huge pillows. Something tiny rattled on the table top. She did not look. The phone called very faintly with an insect's voice "Madam!" and "Mother!" again and again. She did not answer.

The storm was almost over, the lightning gone, the thunder faded; but now came a different thunder, a muted thunder, a thunder that grew and made the old lady frown. It drowned the phone's faint screaming, like that of a far-off cicada.

Something shook the ceiling, then jarred it. There was a rapid tattoo of footsteps overhead, the creek and slam of a door, a clatter of footsteps down the silver stairs.

Approaching her briskly was a slim, middle-aged man carrying a black bag and shaking a few water drops off his trim gray suit.

"Well, what's it this time?" he demanded with a cheery roughness. "Used your sleeping pills up too fast, I suppose, and then worked yourself into a tantrum. I'll have you know I've delayed delivering the Governor's daughter's baby, just to make sure you keep me in your will."

She grinned at him, the tip of her nose straining toward the point of her chin.

"The sleeping pills, yes, you clever devil. Oh, and I lost my temper with your stupid answering service."

"Don't blame you there. I curse them a dozen times a day myself. Only get psychoneurotics to take that job. Everyone else demands a social working-life. Now let's just—*What's that?*"

He had stopped with a jerk and was pointing at the phone.

In one frantic scramble the old lady thrust herself halfway across the bed and halfway out of the covers and crouched, looking back. She began to tremble as the doctor was trembling. But her lips were smiling, and her eyes glittered like jet.

Flowing steadily from the small black hole in the center of the pearl-gray receiver, rilling across and dropping down past the pale marble and puddling on the pearl-gray satin comforter was a thin rippling ribbon of bright blood.

SCREAM WOLF

ALTHOUGH IT WAS A MUGGY AUGUST NIGHT IN Chicago, the Lieutenant's smile was as grim and frosty as a December, sunrise over the Loop.

"Let me see if I've got it straight so far, Mr. Groener," he said. "This apartment isn't your home. You and your wife were visiting Mrs. Labelle, an old friend. You occupied the front bedroom, just back of this living room. The back bedroom was occupied by another guest of Mrs. Labelle's—a Miss Graves, also an old friend—Mrs. Labelle had the bedroom between."

The big man sitting opposite the Lieutenant nodded dully, his face turned away from the bridge lamp cascading light on his chair.

"You went to bed about midnight," the Lieutenant continued. "Mrs. Groener had been drinking heavily. At about two you woke and wanted a cup of coffee. You went back to the kitchen, past the other two bedrooms and through the dining room. While you were heating water, you heard Mrs. Groener scream. You found the bedroom empty. There was a cigarette burning out on the end of the sill of the open window beside a glass half full of straight whiskey. Four stories straight below you made out something turquoise-colored glimmering in the back courtyard.

"Mrs. Groener had been wearing a turquoise-colored long-sleeved nightgown. You knocked on Mrs. Labelle's bedroom door and told her to call us. Then you hurried down. You were kneeling beside your wife's dead body when we arrived. Correct?"

The big man slowly turned his head into the light. His face was that of a gaunt old matinee idol under its thatch of silvered dark hair. Then he looked straight at the Lieutenant and held out a steady, spread-fingered left hand.

"Except for one point," Groener said. "When my wife screamed I didn't rush back to the bedroom. I finished making my cup of coffee and I drank it first."

The Lieutenant cocked an eyebrow. The younger blond detective who had been lounging wearily against the wall of the hallway sharply turned his wide face toward the speaker.

"Now and then Mrs. Groener used to scream," the big man explained, "when she'd been drinking heavily I'd leave the bedroom. It may have been a rebuke or summons to me, or a fighting challenge to the whiskey bottle, or simply an expression of her rather dark evaluation of life. But it had never meant anything more real than that—until tonight."

"Mrs. Groener was seeing a psychiatrist?" the Lieutenant asked harshly.

"I never was able to get her to," the big man said. "As I imagine you find in your business, Lieutenant, there's no real middle course between persuading a person to seek therapy voluntarily and having them forcibly committed to an institution. Mrs. Groener always had the energy be quite sane when necessary."

The Lieutenant grunted noncommittally. "Well, you certainly seem to have been very long-suffering about it," he said and then added sharply, "Cool, at any rate."

Groener smiled bleakly. "I'm an alcoholic myself," he said. "I know how lonely it gets way out there in the dark. I didn't used to scream, but I pounded holes in the walls, and woke up to bloody plaster-powdered knuckles... and cigarette burns between my fingers." He gave his head a little shake as if he'd been dreaming. "Thing is, I managed to quit five years ago. My wife didn't."

The long couch creaked as the Lieutenant slightly, shifted his position on the edge of the center of it. He nodded curtly.

"So when Mrs. Groener screamed," he said, "you finished making your cup of coffee and you drank it. You thought she had screamed simply because she had become unnerved by heavy drinking. You were not unduly alarmed."

Groener nodded. "I'm glad you didn't say DTs," he said. "Shows you know what it's all about. Mrs. Groener never had DTs. If she had, I'd have been able to do something about her. I took my time drinking the coffee, by the way. I was hoping she'd be passed out again by the time I got to the bedroom."

"This scream she gave—how loud would you say it was?"

"Pretty loud," Groener said thoughtfully, "Almost loud enough, I'd say, to wake the people in the flat across the court—except that people in a big city never seem to bother about a scream next door."

"Some of them don't! Then it would have sounded still louder to Mrs. Labelle, or even Miss Graves, than to you. One of them might have been waked by it, or been awake, and gone to your wife's bedroom."

"No, they wouldn't," the big man disagreed. "They were familiar with Mrs. Groener's emotional tendencies. They're both *old* friends."

"They still might have gone."

Groener shook his head. "I'd have heard them."

The Lieutenant frowned. "Has it occurred to you that one of the women may have gone to your wife *before* she screamed?"

Groener's answering gaze was stony, "I'd have certainly heard them if they had," he said.

The Lieutenant stood up and jerked his head at the blond detective, who came toward him.

"Through with me?" Groener asked.

"Yes," the Lieutenant said. "When you get back to the dining room will you ask Cohan—that's the other detective—to send in Miss Graves?"

Groener nodded and started off, his feet dragging. When he came opposite the bedroom he and his wife had occupied, he paused and his shoulders tightened wincingly. The Lieutenant looked away, but when the footsteps didn't resume, he turned quickly back. The big man had disappeared.

The Lieutenant strode to the bedroom door. Groener was standing inside, just looking. The Lieutenant started to bark a question, but just then the big man's steady left hand moved toward the bed in a slow curving gesture, as if he were caressing something invisible.

It was a bedroom with a lot of little tables and stacked cardboard boxes besides the usual furnishings—evidently used by Mrs. Labelle for storage purposes as well as guests—but a broad clear path led through the orderly clutter from the far side of the double bed to the large black square of the open window.

Standing two yards behind Groener's back, the Lieutenant now became aware of the source of a high tinkling noise that had been fretting the edges of his mind for the past half hour. A small oscillating fan was going on a table beside the bed. Hanging from a yardstick stuck in a top dresser drawer a couple of feet from it was a collection of small oblongs and triangles of thin glass hanging on strings. When the stream of air swept them they jingled together monotonously.

The Lieutenant stepped up beside Groener, touched him on the shoulder, and indicated the arrangement beside the bed. Behind them the blond detective cleared his throat uneasily.

"My wife hated all little noises at night," Groener explained. "Voice and tuned-down TVs and such. She used those Chinese windchimes to blur them out."

"Was she quite a small woman?" the Lieutenant asked softly.

"How did you know that?" Groener asked as he started for the door. The Lieutenant pointed at the dresser mirror. It was turned down so that it cut off both their heads and the big man's shoulders.

The Lieutenant and the blond detective listened to his footsteps clumping noisily down the long uncarpeted hall. They heard the frosted glass door to the dining room open and close.

The blond detective grinned. "I'll bet he learned to walk loud to please his wife," he said rapidly. "My mother-in-law does the same thing when she stays overnight with us. Claims it's so as not to scare Ursie and me— we'll know she's coming. Say, this guy's wife must have been nuttier than a fruit cake."

"There are all kinds of alkies, Zocky," the Lieutenant said heavily, "with different degrees of nuttiness and sanity. You notice anything about this room, Zocky?"

"Sure, it's not messed up much for all the stuff in it," the other answered instantly.

"That mean anything to you?"

Detective Zocky shrugged. "Takes all kinds to make a world," he said. "My mother-in-law's an ashtray-washing fanatic. Never dries 'em either."

They heard the dining room door open again. As they started back for the living room, Zocky whispered unabashed, "Hey, did you notice the near-empty fifth tucked behind the head of the bed?"

"No, I merely deduced the bottle would be there like Nero Wolfe," the Lieutenant told him. "Thanks for the confirmation. Incidentally, quite a few people have a morbid fear of dirt, including cigar ashes. It's called mysophobia. And now shut off that fan!"

Miss Graves was as tall for a woman as Groener for a man and even more gaunt, but it was a coldly beautiful gauntness. She dressed it well in a severe black Chinese dress of heavy silk that hugged her knees. Her hair was like a silver fleece.

She seemed determined to be hostile, for as she sat down she glared at the Lieutenant and said to him, "I'm a labor organizer!" as if that made them lifelong enemies.

"You are, huh?" the Lieutenant responded, thumbing a notebook and playing up to her hostility in a way that made Zocky grin behind her back. "Then what do you know about Mrs. Groener? An alcoholic, wasn't she?"

"She was a thoroughly detestable woman!" Miss Graves snapped back sharply. "The only decent thing she ever did was what she did tonight, and she did that much too late! I hated her!"

"Does that mean you were in love with her husband?"

"I—Don't be stupid, officer!"

"Stupid, my eye! There has to be some reason, since you stayed close friends—at least outwardly." He held his aggressive, forward-hunching pose a moment, then leaned back, put away his notebook, smiled like a gentle tomcat, and said culturedly, "Hasn't there now, Miss Graves? Most of these complications have a psychological basis."

She did a double-take, then the tension seemed to go out of her. "You're right, of course," she said. "I knew Mr. Groener in college, before he ever met her, and after that I saw a bit of them both from time to time, through Mrs. Labelle and others."

Her voice deepened. "I watched him misuse his best years on too many high-pressure jobs, trying to be too successful too soon—because of her. I watched him become an alcoholic because of her. Finally I saw him drag himself out of that morass, but remain tied to her more closely than ever. She was his weakness, or rather, she brought out the weakness in him."

Miss Graves shook her head thoughtfully. "Actually I no longer hated her when she killed herself—because during the last years she wasn't at all sane. It wasn't just the liquor, understand. Mrs. Groener scribbled paranoid comments in the few books she read. I found some in one I loaned her. She wrote wild complaining letters to people which sometimes cost Mr. Groener jobs.

"As for her social behavior—well, they were staying here

because they'd been put out of their last apartment on account
of her screaming and loud abusive talk. And she did all sorts of
queer little things. For instance, when I came in yesterday she
was drinking in the sunroom and she had her left wrist tied to the
arm of her chair with a scarf. I asked her why, and she giggled
something about supposing I thought she was fit to be tied. I
imagine you've seen that horrible little wind-and-glass machine
she used to blank out the sounds of reality?"

The Lieutenant nodded.

"It wasn't the first time she tried to commit suicide, either,"
Miss Graves went on thoughtfully.

"No? Mr. Groener didn't tell us anything about that."

"He wouldn't! He was always trying to cover up for her, and
he still is! It's a wonder he didn't try to hide from you that she
was an alcoholic."

"About this earlier suicide attempt," the Lieutenant prompted.

"I don't know much about it except that it happened and she
used sleeping pills."

"I take it you don't live here regularly, Miss Graves."

"Oh no! Mrs. Labelle invited me yesterday with the idea of old
friends rallying around the Groeners. It wasn't a good idea. Mrs.
Groener was hostile toward me, as always, and he was simply
miserable."

"About Mrs. Groener," the Lieutenant said. "Besides her
hostility did she seem depressed?"

Miss Graves shook her head. "No—just a little crazier than
last time. And thinner than ever, a bunch of match-sticks. Her
drinking had got to that stage. We had some drinks after dinner—
not Mr. Groener, of course—and she got very drunk and loud.
We could hear her ranting at him for a half hour after we all went
to bed—about how he shouldn't have let them be put out of their
apartment and about how he always had to be surrounded by his
old girl friends and—"

"Meaning you and Mrs. Labelle?" the Lieutenant cut in.

Miss Graves made a little grimace as she nodded. "Oh yes. Mrs.
Groener firmly believed that any other halfway good-looking
women in the same room with her husband was his mistress or
had been at some time in the past. A fixed delusion though she'd
only come out with it at a certain stage of her drinking. I knew
that, but it still upset me. I had trouble getting to sleep."

"You stayed awake?"

"No, I dozed. Her scream awakened me. I started to get up, but then I remembered it was just part of the act. I lay there and after awhile I heard Mr. Groener coming back from the kitchen."

"Had you heard him go?"

"No, that must have been while I dozed."

"Did you hear the door to the dining room open or close? It's just outside your bedroom."

"I don't believe so. No, I didn't. It must have been standing open."

"Do you sleep with your bedroom door open or closed?"

"Ope—" Miss Graves frowned. "That's strange. I thought I left it open, but it was closed when the scream woke me up."

The Lieutenant looked at her sharply. "Then are you quite sure it was Mr. Groener you heard coming back from the kitchen?"

"Certainly. I couldn't be mistaken. He always made a lot of noise, even in slippers."

The Lieutenant grunted. "And when did you finally get up?"

"When Mr. Groener came rushing into the hall and knocked on Mrs. Labelle's door and told her to call the police."

The Lieutenant stood up. "There's one more thing I've got to ask you," he said quietly. "Are you Mr. Groener's mistress—or were you once?"

"No, never," she said. "Oh, Mr. Groener was an attractive man, but she spoiled him for everyone."

"But now that she's no longer here..." The Lieutenant left that question hanging in the air and so did Mrs. Graves, though it seemed to start something working in her that almost had the look of hope. "That's all then," he told her. "Thank you. Ask Cohan to send in Mrs. Labelle."

When they were alone, Detective Zocky said, "Hey, I'll bet you got the same idea as me. There was no trigger for this suicide. But what if Groener had been having his coffee in Miss Grave's bedroom, and his old lady knew it or slipped out and caught them. That'd make a wow of a trigger."

"I take it Miss Graves is a dike no longer," the Lieutenant said. "Ambidextrous at least."

"Hell, that was just descriptive. I'd say Groener and this dame are practically the same type."

"Yes, they're both tall, good-looking people with gray hair," the Lieutenant observed drily. "Bound to start making violent love to each other every chance they get."

"Well, what the hell, it was a perfect set-up for them," Zocky persisted. "The wife passed out and Mrs. Labelle the tolerant type, no doubt. I know this Groener puts on the pious reformed-alky act, but most ex-boozers his age do that. Why, my father-in-law—" He stopped talking as the dining room door opened and high heels clicked in the hall.

Mrs. Labelle was quite as sylph-bodied as Miss Graves but she dressed it in thinner silk—crimson. Under the coiled and gleaming blonde hair her face looked much younger. Its expression was teen-age, in fact, avid and pert. But there were more tiny wrinkles around the corners of her eyes and mouth than there had been around those of Miss Graves.

"Do I sit there?" she asked, pointing at the brightly lit chair under the bridge lamp before the Lieutenant could. She took it, tucking her feet under her and carefully drawing down her skirt after giving him a flash of high leg.

"This is quite an event for me," Mrs. Labelle announced. "I've always been fascinated by police work. You must find out so many strange things about how people behave in funny situations."

"Right now I'm just looking for a few everyday facts," the Lieutenant said. "How did the Groeners happen to be staying here?"

"They'd lost their apartment without warning. I always feel very sympathetic toward them, because Mr. Labelle is an alcoholic too. We're getting divorced. He lives at a hotel. Perhaps you can tell me what makes alcoholics tick, officer. They're beyond me. I always told Mrs. Groener that if she'd just control her drinking—not stop altogether and get gloomy like her husband—but just take enough to feel bright and happy and relaxed—"

"Miss Graves now," the Lieutenant interrupted. "How did she happen to be here?"

"I invited her. I thought the Groeners ought to have all their old friends around them."

"And perhaps you were interested in seeing how people behave in funny situations," the Lieutenant said. "For instance, Mrs. Groener thinking her husband's mistress was sleeping in the same apartment."

Mrs. Labelle giggled. "Oh that," she said scornfully. "Mr. Groener chased every pretty woman in a lazy secret sort of way, but if he'd ever caught one he'd have scurried right back to his wife. I think she kept throwing it up to him just to keep him in line. I'm quite a psychologist—"

"Okay," the Lieutenant said. "Now about tonight. Did you hear the Groeners quarreling after you went to bed?"

"I wouldn't call it that. Mrs. Groener just let off steam for awhile as any woman will. I listened. It didn't make much sense in her case. But it was interesting."

"And when they quieted down you went to sleep?"

"Oh my no!" Mrs. Labelle gave a little wriggle and flirted her coiled blonde hair. "I had too many exciting things to think about."

"Good! I want you to tell me exactly what you heard in the way of footsteps and other noises. It's important you get them in the right order. Mrs. Groener quieted down. Suppose you start from there."

Mrs. Labelle leaned forward, hugging her elbows, and briefly closed her eyes in happy concentration. "First a long time passed. It must have been an hour or more because I'd almost run out of things to think about and was wondering if I shouldn't take a sleeping pill. Mrs. Groener's windchimes were beginning to get on my nerves, though I'd hardly heard them at first. Then I heard Mr. Groener go clumping down the hall.

"I called to him, because I had some hints to give him about how to handle Mrs. Groener. But my door was closed and he didn't hear me. Then I heard his footsteps stop for a moment and a door close. A moment later I heard him going on to the kitchen."

"Are you sure about that?" the Lieutenant asked "Mightn't he have been going into Miss Grave's bedroom? Think hard, please, before you answer."

Mrs. Labelle laughed. "Not a chance in the world. He's scared of her. You know why? Because she's actually been in love with him her whole life and too stuck-up to do anything about it. That's why she never married. He wouldn't have gone into her bedroom even if she'd begged him to. Anyhow, I know he must have gone on to the kitchen, because right away I heard him banging around out there making coffee. Men! After awhile it got quiet and then Mrs. Groener screamed."

Mrs. Labelle shivered and momentarily closed her eyes. "It was a pretty dreadful scream, even for her, and just a little later there was a thud, as if she'd fallen out of bed. Only it wasn't quite the same. If my window hadn't been closed, I'd have probably heard the difference better and been the one to discover her. Just suppose I'd looked out and seen her perching on the sill ten feet away! That would have been a psychological challenge! As it was, I almost did get up though I knew her tricks. But when I waited, half-expecting to hear something else, there wasn't a sound. Except the windchimes, of course."

"Think carefully, Mrs. Labelle," the Lieutenant said. "Wasn't there some other sound then? Didn't Miss Graves get up? Or didn't Mr. Groener at least start back from the kitchen or make some kind of noise?"

"No, officer, it was all quiet as death—oh, I didn't mean to say that, but it was. Mr. Groener stayed in the kitchen a long time— long enough for two or three cups of coffee, I'd say. I thought about a sleeping pill again and finally I took one and about then Mr. Groener came clumping back. I might have called to him, but I'd just taken the pill. Right after that he came charging out of the bedroom and pounded on my door and told me Mrs. Groener had jumped and to call the police. That's all." Mrs. Labelle buried her head in her arms and let out a large sigh.

"Thank you," the Lieutenant said. "Just a couple more questions now. Miss Graves said Mrs. Groener had tried suicide before. Do you know anything about that?"

Mrs. Labelle laughed. "That was a false alarm. A few months ago he found her almost passed out with an empty bottle of sleeping pills beside her. He started to force warm water down her and he'd just got the waste basket for her to throw up in when he noticed the sleeping pills scattered at the bottom of it. She just wanted to make him think she'd swallowed them. People are funny, aren't they? What's the other question?"

"Miss Graves said that yesterday she saw Mrs. Groener drinking—in your sunroom, she said—with her left wrist tied to the arm of her chair with her scarf. Know anything about that?"

"No, it sounds pointless. The sunroom's that alcove behind you, officer, with the big windows. Wait a minute—I do remember seeing Mrs. Groener do that years ago. It was *Oklahoma*. It was sold out. We were sitting in the second balcony, and she had her scarf wrapped around her wrist and the arm of her seat. I thought she'd done it without thinking."

"Huh!" The Lieutenant stood up and started to pace. He noticed Mrs. Labelle. "That'll be all," he told her. "When you go back to the dining room would you ask Mr. Groener if I could see him again?"

"I certainly will," Mrs. Labelle said, popping up with another flash of leg. She smiled and rippled her eyelids. "You gentlemen have given me some fascinating sidelights on life."

"You're certainly welcome," Zocky assured her, gazing after her appreciatively as she click-clicked down the hall. Then he said to the Lieutenant, "Well, that kills my theory of a suicide trigger. I guess Groener really is the pious type who'd never get out of line."

"Yeah," the Lieutenant agreed abstractedly, still pacing. "Yeah, Zocky, I'm afraid he is, though 'pious' may not be just the right word. Scared of stepping over the line comes closer."

"But this Labelle's a real odd cookie—reminds me of that holdup girl last month. She thinks everything's funny.'"

"You got a point there, Zocky."

"A real bright-eyes too, despite her barbiturates and booze."

"Some it takes that way, Zocky."

"Of course she's real attractive for her age, but that's not here or there."

"Maybe not, Zocky."

"You know what? When you talked to her about Groener's supposed mistress I think she thought you meant her."

"Okay, okay, Zocky!"

When Groener arrived, looking more tired than ever, the Lieutenant stopped pacing and said, "Tell me, did your wife have many phobias? Especially agoraphobia, claustrophobia, acrophobia? Those are—"

"I know," Groener said, settling himself. "Fear of open spaces, dread of being shut in, fear of heights. She had quite a few irrational fears, but not those particularly. Oh, perhaps a touch of claustrophobia—"

"All right," the Lieutenant said, cutting him short. "Mr. Groener, from what I've heard tonight your wife didn't commit suicide."

Groener nodded. "I'm glad you understand alcoholics aren't responsible for the things they do in black-out."

Horrible Imaginings

"She was murdered," the Lieutenant finished.

Groener frowned at him incredulously.

"I'll give you a quick run-down on what really happened tonight, as I see it, and you can tell me what you think," the Lieutenant said.

* * *

He started to pace again as if he were too wound-up not to. "You went for your coffee. Mrs. Labelle called to you through her door as you passed. You didn't want any of her child psychology—or anything else from her either. But it told you she was wide awake and listening to everything. Then you came to Miss Graves's bedroom and the door was open and you saw her sleeping quietly, her silver fleece of hair falling across the pillow."

Groener shook his head and moved his spread-fingered left hand sideways. But the Lieutenant continued, "It struck you how you'd wasted decades of your life caring for and being faithful to a woman who was never going to get well or any more attractive. You thought of what a wonderful life you could have had if you'd taken another direction. But that direction was closed to you now—you'd been spoiled for it. You'd built up inhibitions within yourself that wouldn't let you overturn the applecart. If you'd tried to, you'd have suffered agonies of guilt and remorse. It would have killed all enjoyment. So you closed Miss Graves's door, because you couldn't bear to watch her."

"Wait a minute—" Groener protested.

"Shut up," the Lieutenant told him dispassionately. "As you closed the door you felt a terrific spasm of rage at the injustice of it. All of that rage was directed against your wife. You'd had feelings like that before, but never had a situation brought them so tormentingly home to you. For one thing you'd just been treated like a worm by the woman you were tied to in front of the woman you desired with a consuming physical passion. It was tearing you apart. You'd come to the end of your rope of hope. Five years had fully demonstrated that your wife would never stop drinking or mentally intimidating you.

"You thought of all the opportunities of happiness and pleasure you'd passed up without benefit to her, or yourself—or anybody. You suddenly saw how you could do it now without much risk to yourself, and how afterwards perhaps everything would be different for you. You could still take the other direction. What you had in mind was bad, but your wife had been asking for it. You knew you could no longer ever get free without it. It was a partly irrational but compulsive psychological barrier that nothing but your wife's death could topple. The thought of what you were going to do filled you like black fire, so there was no room in your mind for anything else."

"Really, Lieutenant, this—"

"Shut up. Your plan hung on knowing Mrs. Labelle was awake—that and knowing that she and Miss Graves were both on to your wife's screaming trick, if that should come up. You started making coffee—and even more noise than you usually do—and then you took off your slippers and you walked back to the bedroom without making a sound. Or if you did make a few slight, creaking-floorboard sounds, you figured the wind-chimes would cover them up.

"Yes, Mr. Groener, you're a man who normally makes a lot of noise walking, so your wife wouldn't accuse you of sneaking around. So much noise, in fact, that it's become a joke among your friends. But when you want to, or even just when your mind's on something else, you walk very quietly. You did it earlier this evening right in front of me when you went in the bedroom. You disappeared that time without a sound.

"You found your wife asleep, still passed out from the drinks. You carefully moved back what light furniture and stuff there was between the bed and the wide-open window. You wanted a clear pathway and it didn't occur to you that a drunk going from the bed to the window under her own power would have bumped and probably knocked over a half dozen things."

The Lieutenant's voice hardened. "You grabbed your wife—she got out one scream—and you picked her up—she weighed next to nothing—and you pitched her out the window. Then you stood there listening a minute. This was the hump, you thought. But nobody called or got up or did anything. So for a final artistic touch you put your wife's bedtime drink and one of her burnt-out lipstick-stained cigarettes on the windowsill. You've got to watch out for artistic touches, Groener, because they're generally wrong. Then you glided back to the kitchen, finished the coffee act, and came back noisy."

The Lieutenant quit pacing and paused, but Groener just stared at him—incredulously, almost stupifiedly, but still steady as a rock. Zocky shot an apprehensive look at his superior.

"The important thing you overlooked," the Lieutenant went on relentlessly, "was that I'd find out your wife was an acrophobe, and that her dread of heights was so great, sober or drunk, that she'd tie her arm to her chair when she was merely sitting near a big window or up on a theater balcony. To suggest that such a person would commit suicide by jumping is utterly implausible.

To imply that she'd preface it by sitting or leaning on the window ledge having a last drink and smoke is absolutely unbelievable."

The Lieutenant paused and narrowed his eyes before adding, "Moreover, Mr. Groener, quietly as you walked back to the bedroom, did you really suppose you accomplished that so silently that Mrs. Labelle's sharp ears wouldn't catch the sound of your footsteps?"

Groener roused himself with an obvious effort. "I... I... This is all quite absurd, Lieutenant. Mrs. Labelle..." He made the usual gesture with his left hand. "You can't really believe that."

He looked at his left hand. So did the detectives. It was shaking and as he continued to stare it began to shake more violently. The tendons stood out whitely as he stiffened it, but the shaking didn't stop.

Groener's tight-pressed lips lengthened in a grin but the corners of his mouth wouldn't turn up. "This is embarrassing," he said. "Must be embarrassing to you too. First time I've had the shakes in five years."

But the shaking only became convulsive.

"All right," he said, closing his eyes, "I did it."

The shaking stopped.

After awhile he went on gently, "Just about as you've described it. I was insane to think I could ever get away with it. I suppose your doctor noticed that her neck had been broken before she fell. He probably deduced it from the tear in her scalp where I'd jerked her head back by the hair."

"No," the Lieutenant said, "but he will now. Zocky, would you get Cohan? Tell the ladies Mr. Groener's coming with us to make a statement at the station. Tell them he doesn't want to speak to either of them now. I imagine that's the way you want it, Groener?" The other nodded.

After Zocky went off, Groener said, "Would you tell me one thing?"

"I'll try to."

"How did you know *her* hair looked like a silver fleece?"

The Lieutenant flushed. "Oh that—please excuse it. I was just blasting away at you. The words came."

Zocky returned with the third detective. They opened the front door and started down the stairs. The Lieutenant told Cohan to go first with Groener.

Zocky said to the Lieutenant in a gruff whisper, "Hey, I gave you a right steer on that walking loud on purpose business, didn't I?"

"Yes, Zocky, you did."

"I don't like this case, though," the blond detective went on. "This Groener's not a bad guy. Think of listening to those chimes night after night!"

"If they were all bad guys, our job would be easy."

"Yeah. Say, I just realized we don't know any of their first names—not Groener's or either of the dames."

"Cohan will have them," the Lieutenant said. "But that's a very important point about detective work you've just made, Zocky. Never know their first names."

MYSTERIOUS DOINGS IN THE METROPOLITAN MUSEUM

THE TOP HALF OF THE BLADE OF GRASS GROWING IN A railed plot beside the Metropolitan Museum of Art in Manhattan said "Beetles! You'd think they were the Kings of the World, the way they carry on!"

The bottom half of the blade of grass replied, "Maybe they are. The distinguished writer of supernatural horror stories H. P. Lovecraft said in *The Shadow Out of Time* there would be a 'hardy Coleopterous species immediately following mankind,' to quote his exact words. Other experts say all insects, or spiders, or rats will inherit the Earth, but old H.P.L. said hardy coleopts."

"Pedant!" the top half mocked. " 'Coleopterous species'!" Why not just say 'beetles' or just 'bugs'? Means the same thing."

"You favor long words as much as I do," the bottom half replied imperturbably, "but you also like to start arguments and employ a salty, clipped manner of speech which is really not your own—more like that of a deathwatch beetle."

"I call a spade a spade," the top half retorted. "And speaking of what spades delve into (a curt keening signifying the loamy integument of Mother Earth), I hope we're not mashed into it by gunboats the next second or so. Or by beetle-crushers, to coin a felicitous expression."

Bottom explained condescendingly, "The president and general secretary of the Coleopt Convention have a trusty corps of early-warning beetles stationed about to detect the approach of gunboats. A coleopterous Dewline."

Top snorted, "Trusty! I bet they're all goofing off and having lunch at Schrafft's."

"I have a feeling it's going to be a great con," bottom said.

"I have a feeling it's going to be a lousy, fouled-up con," top said. "Everybody will get conned. The Lousicon—how's that for a name?"

"Lousy. Lice have their own cons. They belong to the orders *Psocoptera, Anoplura,* and *Mallophaga,* not the godlike, shining order *Coleoptera.*"

"Scholiast! Paranoid!"

The top and bottom halves of the blade of grass broke off their polemics, panting.

The beetles of all Terra, but especially the United States, were indeed having their every-two-years world convention, their Biannual Bug Thing, in the large, railed-off grass plot in Central Park, close by the Metropolitan Museum of Art, improbable as that may seem and just as the grassblade with the split personality had said.

Now, you may think it quite impossible for a vast bunch of beetles, ranging in size from nearly microscopic ones to unicorn beetles two and one-half inches long, to hold a grand convention in a dense urban area without men becoming aware of it. If so, you have seriously underestimated the strength and sagacity of the coleopterous tribe and overestimated the sensitivity and eye for detail of Homo Sapiens—Sap for short.

These beetles had taken security measures to awe the CIA and NKVD, had those fumbling human organizations been aware of them. There was indeed a Beetle Dewline to warn against the approach of gunboats—which are, of course, the elephantine, leather-armored feet of those beetle-ignoring, city-befuddled giants, men. In case such veritable battleships loomed nigh, all accredited beetles had their directives to dive down to the grassroots and harbor there until the all-clear sounded on their ESP sets.

And should such a beetle-crusher chance to alight on a beetle or beetles, well, in case you didn't know it, beetles are dymaxion-built ovoids such as even Buckminster Fuller and Frank Lloyd Wright never dreamed of, crush-resistant to a fabulous degree and able to endure such saturation shoe-bombings without getting the least crack in their resplendent carapaces.

So cast aside doubts and fears. The beetles were having their world convention exactly as and where I've told you. There were bright-green ground beetles, metallic wood-boring beetles, yellow soldier beetles, gorgeous ladybird beetles, and handsome and pleasing fungus beetles just as brilliantly red, charcoal—gray blister yellow hieroglyphs imprinted on their shining green backs, immigrant and affluent Japanese beetles, snout beetles, huge darksome stag and horn beetles, dogbane beetles like fire opals, and even that hyper-hieroglyphed rune-bearing yellow-on-blue beetle wonder of the family *Chrysomelidae* and subfamily *Chrysomelinae Calligrapha serpentine*. All of them milling about in happy camaraderie, passing drinks and bons mots, as beetles will. Scuttling, hopping, footing the light fantastic, and even in sheer exuberance lifting their armored carapaces to take short flights of joy on their retractable membranous silken wings like glowing lace on the lingerie of Viennese baronesses.

And not just U.S. beetles, but coleopts from all over the world—slant-eyed Asian beetles in golden robes, North African beetles in burnished burnooses, South African beetles wild as fire ants with great Afro hairdos, smug English beetles, suave Continental bugs, and brilliantly clad billionaire Brazilian beetles and fireflies constantly dancing the carioca and sniffing ether and generously spraying it at other beetles in intoxicant mists. Oh, a grandsome lot.

Not that there weren't flies in the benign ointment of all this delightful coleopterous sociability. Already the New York City cockroaches were out in force, picketing the convention because they hadn't been invited. Round and round the sacred grass plot they tramped, chanting labor-slogans in thick accents and hurling coarse working-class epithets.

"But of course we couldn't have invited them even if we'd wanted to," explained the Convention's general secretary, a dapper click beetle, in fact an eyed elater of infinite subtlety and resource in debate and tactics. As the book says, "If the eyed elater falls on its back, if lies quietly for perhaps a minute. Then, with a loud click, it flips into the air. If it is lucky, it lands on its feet and runs away; otherwise it tries again." And the general secretary had a million other dodges as good or better. He said now, "But we couldn't have invited them even if we'd wanted to, because cockroaches aren't true beetles at all, aren't *Coleoptera;* they belong to the order *Orthoptera,* the family *Blattidae—blat* to them! Moreover, many of them are mere German (German-Jewish, maybe?) Croton bugs, dwarfish in stature compared to American cockroaches, who all once belonged to the Confederate Army."

In seconds the plausible slander was known by insect grapevine to the cockroaches. Turning the accusation to their own Wobbly purposes, they began rudely to chant in unison as they marched, "Blat, blat, go the *Blattidae!*"

Also, several important delegations of beetles had not yet arrived, including those from Bangladesh, Switzerland, Iceland and Egypt.

But despite all these hold-ups and disturbances, the first session of the Great Coleopt Congress got off to a splendid start. The president, a portly Colorado potato beetle resembling Grover Cleveland, rapped for order. Whereupon row upon row of rainbow-hued beetles rose to their feet amidst the greenery and sonorously sang—drowning out even the guttural *blats* of the crude cockroaches—the chief beetle anthem:

> "Beetles are not dirty bugs
> Spiders, scorpions or slugs.
> Heroes of the insect realms,
> They sport winged burnished helms.
> They are shining and divine.
> They are kindly and just fine.
> Beetles do not bite or sting.
> They love almost everything."

They sang it to the melody of the Ode to Joy in the last movement of Beethoven's Ninth.

The session left many beetle wives, larval children, husbands and other nonvoting members at loose ends. But provision had been made for them. Guided by a well-informed though somewhat stuffy scribe beetle, they entered the Metropolitan Museum for a conducted tour designed for both entertainment and cultural enrichment.

While the scribe beetle pointed out notable items of interest and spoke his educational but somewhat longwinded pieces, they scuttled all over the place, feeling out the forms of great statues by crawling over them and revealing inside the many silvery suits of medieval armor.

Most gunboats didn't notice them at all. Those who did were not in the least disturbed. Practically all gunboats—though they dread spiders and centipedes and loath cockroaches—like true beetles, as witness the good reputation of the ladybug, renowned in song and story for her admirable mother love and fire-fighting ability. These gunboats assumed that the beetles were merely some new educational feature of the famed museum, or else an artistry of living arabesques.

When the touring beetles came to the Egyptian Rooms, they began to quiet down, entranced by art most congenial to coleopts by reason of its antiquity and dry yet vivid precision. They delighted in the tiny, toy-like tomb ornaments and traced out the colorful murals and even tried to decipher the cartouches and other hieroglyphs by walking along their lines, corners and curves. The absence of the Egyptian delegation was much regretted. They would have been able to answer many questions, although the scribe beetle waxed eloquent and performed prodigies of impromptu scholarship.

But when they entered the room with the sign reading SCARABS, their awe and admiration knew no bounds. They scuttled softer than mice in feather slippers. They drew up silently in front of the glass cases and gazed with wonder and instinctive reverence at the rank on rank of jewel-like beetle forms within. Even the scribe beetle had nothing to say.

Meanwhile, back at the talkative grassblade, the top half, who was in fact a purple boy tiger beetle named Speedy, said "Well, they're all off to a great start, I don't think. This promises to be the most fouled-up convention in history."

"Don't belittle," reproved the bottom half, who was in reality a girl American burying beetle named Big Yank. "The convention is doing fine—orderly sessions, educational junkets, what more could you ask?"

"Blat, blat, go the *Blattidae!*" Speedy commented sneeringly. "The con's going to hell in a beetle basket. Take that sneaky click beetle who's general secretary—he's up to no good, you can be sure. An insidious insect, if I ever knew one. An eyed elater— who'd he ever elate? And that potato bug who's president—a bleedin' plutocrat. As for that educational junket inside the museum, you just watch what happens!"

"You really do have an evil imagination," Big Yank responded serenely.

Despite their constant exchange of persiflage, the boy and girl beetles were inseparable pals who'd had many an exciting adventure together. Speedy was half an inch long, a darting purple beauty most agile and difficult for studious gunboats to catch. Big Yank was an inch long, gleaming black of carapace with cloudy red markings. Though quick to undermine and bury small dead animals to be home and food for her larvae, Big Yank was not in the least morbid in outlook.

Although their sex was different and their companionship intimate, Speedy and Big Yank had never considered having larvae together. Their friendship was of a more manly and girlish character and very firm-footed, all twelve of them.

"You really think something *outr* is going to happen inside the museum?" Big Yank mused.

"It's a dead certainty," Speedy assured her.

In the Scarab room silent awe had given way to whispered speculation. Exactly what and or who were those gemlike beetle forms arranged with little white cards inside the glass-walled cases? Even the scribe-beetle guide found himself wondering.

It was a highly imaginative twelve-spotted cucumber beetle of jade-green who came up with the intriguing notion that the scarabs were living beetles rendered absolutely immobile by hypnosis or drugs and imprisoned behind walls of thick glass by the inscrutable gunboats, who were forever doing horrendous things to beetles and other insects. Gunboats were the nefarious giants, bigger than Godzilla, of beetle legend. Anything otherwise nasty and inexplicable could be attributed to them.

The mood of speculation now changed to one of lively concern. How horrid to think of living, breathing beetles doped and brainwashed into the semblance of death and jailed in glass by gunboats for some vile purpose! Something must be done about it.

The junketing party changed its plans in a flash, and they all scuttled swifter than centipedes back to the convention, which was deep into such matters as Folk Remedies for DDT, Marine Platforms to Refuel Transoceanic Beetle Flights, and Should

There Be a Cease Fire Between Beetles and *Blattidae?* (who still went "Blat, blat!").

The news brought by the junketters tabled all that and electrified the convention. The general secretary eyed elater was on his back three times running and then on his feet again—click, click, click, click, click, *click!* The president Colorado potato beetle goggled his enormous eyes. It was decided by unanimous vote that the imprisoned beetles must be rescued at once. Within seconds Operation Succor was under way.

A task force of scout, spy, and tech beetles was swiftly sent off and dispatched into the museum to evaluate and lay out the operation. They confirmed the observations and deductions of the junketters and decided that a rare sort of beetle which secretes fluoric acid would be vital to the caper.

A special subgroup of these investigators traced out by walking along them the characters of the word Scarab. Their report was as follows:

"First you got a Snake character, see?" (That was the S.)

"Then you get a Hoop Snake with a Gap." (That was the C.)

"Then Two Snakes Who Meet in the Night and have Sexual Congress." (That was the A.)

"Next a Crooked Hoop Snake Raping an Upright or Square Snake." (The R.)

"Then a repeat of Two Snakes Who Meet in the Night, et cetera." (The second A.)

"Lastly Two Crazy Hoop Snakes Raping a Square Snake." (The B.)

"Why all this emphasis on snakes and sex we are not certain."

"We suggest the Egyptian delegation be consulted as soon as it arrives."

Operation Succor was carried out that night.

It was a complete success.

Secreted fluoric acid ate small round holes in the thick glass of all cases. Through these, every last scarab in the Egyptian Rooms were toted by carrying beetles—mostly dung beetles—down into deep beetle bunkers far below Manhattan and armored against the inroads of cockroaches.

Endless atempts to bring the drugged and hypnotized beetles back to consciousness and movement were made. All failed.

Undaunted, the beetles decided simply to venerate the rescued scarabs. A whole new beetle cult sprang up around them.

The Egyptian delegation arrived, gorgeous as pharaohs, and knew at once what had happened. However, they decided to keep this knowledge secret for the greater good of all beetledom. They genuflected dutifully before the scarabs just as did the beetles not in the know.

The cockroaches had their own theories, but merely kept up their picketing and their chanting of "Blat, blat, go the *Blattidae.*"

Because of their theories, however, one fanatical Egyptian beetle went bats and decided that the scarabs were indeed alive though drugged and that the whole thing was part of a World Cockroach Plot carried out by commando Israeli beetles and their fellow travelers. His wild mouthings were not believed.

Human beings were utterly puzzled by the whole business. The curator of the Met and the chief of the New York detectives investigating the burglary stared at the empty cases in stupid wonder.

"Godammit," the detective chief said. "When you look at all those little holes, you'd swear the whole job had been done by beetles."

The curator smiled sourly.

Speedy said, "Hey, this skyrockets us beetles to the position of leading international jewel thieves."

For once Big Yank had to agree. "It's just too bad the general public, human and coleopterous, will never know," she said wistfully. Then, brightening, "Hey, how about you and me having another adventure?"

"Suits," said Speedy.

WHEN BRAHMA WAKES

GOD SHOULDERED OPEN THE SWOLLEN BACK DOOR and amidst the plosive shower of rust and dust sneaked a quick squint upward.

There wasn't a star or planet in sight. They were all masked by an opalescent gray blanket. An invisible gray thread snaking down to His nostrils informed Him of the blanket's advanced industrial origin—not honest coal smoke so much as the sulphuric stench that was a by-product of the manufacture of plastics, high-grade fuels, and steel.

While the music of the spheres drowned by a restless, incessant throbbing like the grumbling of a thousand distant dragons and the hissing of ten thousand serpents.

God squared His chin surlily. That was the trouble with meditating on His creation, Zen or no Zen. It gave the Adversary a chance to undo it. He'd dozed off dreaming of a glittering city with silver spires climbing toward a bespangled Heaven and swarms of His happy creatures, rainbow-clad, dancing on the greensward between the skyscrapers. And while He'd slept, the Adversary had devised smog and freeways.

It was a wonder that when He'd originally rested on the seventh day, He hadn't waked on the eighth to find everything redesigned. The Adversary had been sluggish then, but now he was carrying the contest to His very door.

God backed away without closing it. There was an old cloak hanging beside it, and a slouch hat that had seen better days, and a black eyepatch dangling by its worn elastic. God's shaggy white head brushed a large, empty birdcage and set it swinging.

He'd have to re-think this Adversary business very carefully. He told Himself as He turned. Maybe He'd been too quick in letting his cozening creatures woo Him away from gnosticism and convince Him that the Adversary was only a paper devil, who'd crumple and flare to nothing like flash paper on Judgment Day, or the Japanese fleet before Pearl Harbor. Ahriman might be a better name for the Adversary, an evil strong as His own good. In which case He'd damn well better do the Persian again and be Ormazd fast.

A pair of sleazy stretch pants and an old bra hanging on the back of a kitchen chair made Him remember Venus. There was a lot to be said for polytheism, He had to admit, especially when He woke lonely as this. The trouble was He couldn't trust the pantheon, which He had fathered during his Zeus phase, to stick by Him. He had a vivid vision of Venus, last to leave Him, turning in the kitchen door, glorious in her sandals, denims, sweater, long golden hair, and inimitable vase-curves.

"It's been the most, Dad," she'd said simply, "but now I gotta drift. The beach, Dad. I always had an affinity for surf."

Nor could he trust or find security in any of His mortal creatures. He'd guided them to atomic energy and spaceflight and computers, and then thought He could turn Himself off awhile, at least for this sector of the cosmos—and He'd come back to find them almost unrecognizable: talking a jumble of new scientific and artistic and social jargon (though many of them no longer thought, they dug), haring off after extrasensory perception, creating brief rainbow microcosms in the inner space of their brains with new alphabet drugs, peering up at quasars rather than stars, tweezering out the molecules of heredity, insanity, sanity—that list was almost endless—inventing languages for machines, reducing ultimate particles to flickering clouds of sub-particles—or wavicles!—devising new human relations by the hundred (they were fantastic social inventors) and new human arts by the thousand.

Of course He could keep an eye on them all the time. He could watch each sparrow fall, each overworked ant collapse from heart failure, each microbe dissolve in the grip of a posse of leucocytes, each unstable atom give up its pale radioactive ghost, each restless particle put on its quick-change act, each idea flicker and die, not missing the one idea in a billion billion billion that lived. But would that grandiose busy-work bring Him any closer to His Creatures or really keep Him in touch with them? They'd still all go on changing and developing through the cycles of seemingly sterile repetition. And He'd be dead inside.

A scrawny black kitten came, mewing at God's shapeless, soft-soled slipper. Well, at least one of His creatures still depended on him. God levered open two triangular holes in a small can, poured the condensed milk into a dirty saucer, set it on the warped floor, and went off to inspect His four rooms.

In the small studio where He roughed out creation, the paints were dry on canvas and palette, the watercolors cracked, the copper plates eaten through by acid.

In the second room, where He recorded His directives—His Word—there was dust on the tapes and from the machine came a faint stale stench of burnt insulation.

In the third room there were cobwebs on His typewriter.

Clearly the Adversary hadn't stopped at the back door. He had invaded and disordered the whole.

He had even invaded His body, God belatedly realized. He was full of aches and pains, His tongue was thick, He had to lean down close to the typewriter to make out what He had been typing on the last sheet.

There was a web just above the paper and a tiny black spider was walking across it. God jerked back. Why the Hell had He ever created spiders? What had got into Him then? For the moment He couldn't recall. It seemed like the end of everything.

But then He reminded Himself that this wasn't the first time He'd been slammed back on His heels. This wasn't the only occasion on which He'd been made to feel small. He became aware of a warm knot of identity deep in His gullet, under His breastbone. The Adversary hadn't invaded *that* and right now that was all that mattered. He still had a mustard-seed of faith in Himself.

His lifting gaze touched a tiny Buddha of once polished, now dust-coated, reddish wood. Maybe... no!—look at the trouble the contemplative mode had got Him into. The trouble about Nirvana was He always had to come back from it. No, another time, maybe, but not now.

A chain of association flashed on in His mind, like a zigzag lightning flash. Buddha—those priests drenching themselves with gasoline and setting themselves afire—universal flames—atomic holocaust—the ultimate battle of Ragnarok—the Norse gods—

Odin! Yes, that was it! It was time that He went out on another anonymous swing, to inspect His creatures and perhaps spot one of the lesser gods here and there. Somewhere along the line, He'd remember the beach.

He returned to the kitchen and put on the eyepatch—His left eye felt as if it really needed the sleazy thing. He whipped on the slouch hat, pulling it low on his forehead, and swirled the old cloak around his shoulders.

He looked up unhappily at the empty birdcage. He really ought to have His two ravens on His shoulders when He went on His Odin-tour of inspection, but they must have flown away long ago. Someone had probably released them out of mercy—maybe Venus, just before she left. Or maybe He had.

The kitten came purring to his slipper. On a sudden inspiration, God picked it up and gently stuffed it inside his vest. Then He hurried back to the typewriter, delicately caught up the cobweb with the spider on it and laid it on His shoulder. They would have to do for his Hugin and Munin. At least they were both black.

Then God squared His shoulders, tucked His chin against His chest, pushed the back door open wide, and stepped out. He was feeling remarkably cheerful. He'd really make His rounds this time. If he happened on a rocket bound for the Moon, or Mars, or even Midgard, He'd hop aboard.

The back gate was stuck like the back door and had to be forced open. That depressed Him again, but after He'd taken a few dozen steps down the dark alley, He began to feel better.

THE GLOVE

MY MOST LITERALLY TANGIBLE BRUSH WITH THE supernatural (something I can get incredibly infatuated with yet forever distrust profoundly, like a very beautiful and adroit call girl) occurred in connection with the rape by a masked intruder of the woman who lived in the next apartment to mine during my San Francisco years. I knew Evelyn Mayne only as a neighbor and I slept through the whole incident, including the arrival and departure of the police, though there came a point in the case when the police doubted both these assertions of mine.

The phrase "victim of rape" calls up certain stereotyped images: an attractive young woman going home alone late at night, enters a dark street, is grabbed... or, a beautiful young suburban matron, mother of three, wakes after midnight, feels a nameless dread, is grabbed... The truth is apt to be less romantic. Evelyn Mayne was 65, long divorced, neglected and thoroughly detested by her two daughters-in-law and only to a lesser degree by their husbands, lived on various programs of old age, medical and psychiatric assistance, was scrawny, gloomy, alcoholic, waspish, believed life was futile, and either overdosed on sleeping pills or else lightly cut her wrists three or four times a year.

Her assailant at least was somewhat more glamorous, in a sick way. The rapist was dressed all in rather close-fitting gray, hands covered by gray gloves, face obscured by a long shock of straight silver hair falling over it. And in the left hand, at first, a long knife that gleamed silver in the dimness.

And she wasn't grabbed either, at first, but only commanded

in a harsh whisper coming through the hair to lie quietly or be
cut up.

When she was alone again at last, she silently waited something
like the ten minutes she'd been warned to, thinking that at least
she hadn't been cut up, or else (who knows?) wishing she had
been. Then she went next door (in the opposite direction to mine)
and roused Marcia Everly, who was a buyer for a department
store and about half her age. After the victim had been given a
drink, they called the police and Evelyn Mayne's psychiatrist and
also her social worker, who knew her current doctor's number
(which she didn't), but they couldn't get hold of either of the last
two. Marcia suggested waking me and Evelyn Mayne countered
by suggesting they wake Mr. Helpful, who has the next room
beyond Marcia's down the hall. Mr. Helpful (otherwise nicknamed
Baldy, I never remembered his real name) was someone I loathed
because he was always prissily dancing around being neighborly
and asking if there was something he could do—and because he
was six foot four tall, while I am rather under average height.

Marcia Everly is also very tall, at least for a woman, but as it
happens I do not loathe her in the least. Quite the opposite in fact.

But Evelyn Mayne said I wasn't sympathetic, while Marcia
(thank goodness!) loathed Mr. Helpful as much as I do—she
thought him a weirdo, along with half the other tenants in the
building.

So they compromised by waking neither of us, and until the
police came Evelyn Mayne simply kept telling the story of her
rape over and over, rather mechanically, while Marcia listened
dutifully and occupied her mind as to which of our crazy fellow-
tenants was the best suspect—granting it hadn't been done by an
outsider, although that seemed likeliest. The three most colorful
were the statuesque platinum-blonde drag queen on the third
floor, the long-haired old weirdo on six who wore a cape and
was supposed to be into witchcraft, and the tall, silver-haired,
Nazi-looking lesbian on seven (assuming she wore a dildo for the
occasion and was nuttier than a five-dollar fruit cake).

Ours really is a weird building, you see, and not just because
of its occupants, who sometimes seem as if they were all referred
here by mental hospitals. No, it's eerie in its own right. You see,
several decades ago it was a hotel with all the rich, warm inner
life that once implied: bevies of maids, who actually used the
linen closets (empty now) on each floor and the round snap-

capped outlets in the baseboards for a vacuum system (that hadn't been operated for a generation) and the two dumb-waiters (their doors forever shut and painted over). In the old days there had been bellboys and an elevator operator and two night porters who'd carry up drinks and midnight snacks from a restaurant that never closed.

But they're gone now, every last one of them, leaving the halls empty-feeling and very gloomy, and the stairwell an echoing void, and the lobby funereal, so that the mostly solitary tenants of today are apt to seem like ghosts, especially when you meet one coming silently around a turn in the corridor where the ceiling light's burnt out.

Sometimes I think that, what with the smaller and smaller families and more and more people living alone, our whole modern world is getting like that.

The police finally arrived, two grave and solicitous young men making a good impression—especially a tall and stalwart (Marcia told me) Officer Hart. But when they first heard Evelyn Mayne's story, they were quite skeptical (Marcia could tell, or thought she could, she told me). But they searched Evelyn's room and poked around the fire escapes and listened to her story again, and then they radioed for a medical policewoman, who arrived with admirable speed and who decided after an examination that in all probability there'd been recent sex, which would be confirmed by analysis of some smears she'd taken from the victim and the sheets.

Officer Hart did two great things, Marcia said. He got hold of Evelyn Mayne's social worker and told him he'd better get on over quick. And he got from him the phone number of her son who lived in the city and called him up and threw a scare into his wife and him about how they were the nearest of kin, God damn it, and had better start taking care of the abused and neglected lady.

Meanwhile the other cop had been listening to Evelyn Mayne, who was still telling it, and he asked her innocent questions, and had got her to admit that earlier that night she'd gone alone to a bar down the street (a rather rough place) and had one drink, or maybe three. Which made him wonder (Marcia said she could tell) whether Evelyn hadn't brought the whole thing on herself, maybe by inviting some man home with her, and then inventing

the rape, at least in part, when things went wrong. (Though I
couldn't see her inventing the silver hair.)

Anyhow the police got her statement and got it signed and
then took off, even more solemnly sympathetic than when they'd
arrived, Officer Hart in particular.

Of course, I didn't know anything about all this when I knocked
on Marcia's door before going to work that morning, to confirm
a tentative movie date we'd made for that evening. Though I
was surprised when the door opened and Mr. Helpful came out
looking down at me very thoughtfully, his bald head gleaming,
and saying to Marcia in the voice adults use when children are
listening, "I'll keep in touch with you about the matter. If there is
anything I can do, don't hesitate..."

Marcia, looking at him very solemnly, nodded.

And then my feeling of discomfiture was completed when
Evelyn Mayne, empty glass in hand and bathrobe clutched
around her, edged past me as if I were contagious, giving me a
peculiarly hostile look and calling back to Marcia over my head,
"I'll come back, my dear, when I've repaired my appearance, so
that people can't say you're entertaining bedraggled old hags."

I was relieved when Marcia gave me a grin as soon as the door
was closed and said, "Actually she's gone to get herself another
drink, after finishing off my supply. But really, Jeff, she has a
reason to this morning—and for hating any man she runs into."
And her face grew grave and troubled (and a little frightened
too) as she quickly clued me in on the night's nasty events. Mr.
Helpful, she explained, had dropped by to remind them about a
tenants' meeting that evening and, when he got the grisly news,
to go into a song and dance about how shocked he was and how
guilty at having slept through it all, and what could he do?

Once she broke off to ask, almost worriedly, "What I can't
understand, Jeff, is why any man would want to rape someone
like Evelyn."

I shrugged. "Kinky some way, I suppose. It does happen, you
know. To old women, I mean. Maybe a mother thing."

"Maybe he *hates* women," she speculated. "Wants to punish
them."

I nodded.

She had finished by the time Evelyn Mayne came back, very
listless now, looking like a woebegone ghost, and dropped into
a chair. She hadn't got dressed or even combed her hair. In one

hand she had her glass, full and dark, and in the other a large, pale gray leather glove, which she carried oddly, dangling it by one finger.

Marcia started to ask her about it, but she just began to recite once more all that had happened to her that night, in an unemotional, mechanical voice that sounded as if it would go on forever.

Look, I didn't like the woman—she was a particularly useless, venomous sort of nuisance (those wearisome suicide attempts!)—but that recital got to me. I found myself hating the person who would deliberately put someone into the state she was in. I realized, perhaps for the first time, just what a vicious and sick crime rape is and how cheap are all the easy jokes about it.

Eventually the glove came into the narrative naturally: "... and in order to do that he had to take off his glove. He was particularly excited just then, and it must have got shoved behind the couch and forgotten, where I found it just now."

Marcia pounced on the glove at once then, saying it was important evidence they must tell the police about. So she called them and after a bit she managed to get Officer Hart himself, and he told her to tell Evelyn Mayne to hold onto the glove and he'd send someone over for it eventually.

It was more than time for me to get on to work, but I stayed until she finished her call, because I wanted to remind her about our date that evening.

She begged off, saying she'd be too tired from the sleep she'd lost and anyway she'd decided to go to the tenants' meeting tonight. She told me, "This has made me realize that I've got to begin to take some responsibility for what happens around me. We may make fun of such people—the good neighbors—but they've got something solid about them."

I was pretty miffed at that, though I don't think I let it show. Oh, I didn't so much mind her turning me down—there were reasons enough for it that she didn't have to make such a production of it and drag in "good neighbors." (Mr. Helpful, who else?) Besides, Evelyn Mayne came out of her sad apathy long enough to give me a big smile when Marcia said "No."

So I didn't go to the tenants' meeting that night, as I might otherwise have done. Instead I had dinner out and went to the movie—it was lousy—and then had a few drinks, so that it was late when I got back (no signs of life in the lobby or lift or corridor) and gratefully piled into bed.

I was dragged out of the depths of sleep—that first blissful plunge—by a persistent knocking. I shouted something angry but unintelligible and when there was no reply made myself get up, feeling furious.

It was Marcia. With a really remarkable effort I kept my mouth shut and even smoothed out whatever expression was contorting my face. The words one utters on being suddenly awakened, especially from that matchless first sleep that is never recaptured, can be as disastrous as speaking in drink. Our relationship had progressed to the critical stage and I sure didn't want to blow it, especially when treasures I'd hoped to win were spread out in front of my face, as it were, under a semi-transparent nightgown and hastily-thrown-on negligee.

I looked up, a little, at her face. Her eyes were wide.

She said in a sort of frightened little-girl voice that didn't seem at all put on, "I'm awfully sorry to wake you up at three o'clock in the morning, Jeff, but would you keep this 'spooky' for me? I can't get to sleep with it in my room,"

It is a testimony to the very high quality of Marcia's treasures that I didn't until then notice what she was carrying in front of her—in a fold of toilet paper—the pale gray leather glove Evelyn Mayne had found behind her couch.

"Huh?" I said, not at all brilliantly. "Didn't Officer Hart come back, or send someone over to pick it up?"

She shook her head. "Evelyn had it, of course, while I was at my job—her social worker did come over right after you left. But then at supper time her son and daughter-in-law came (Officer Hart did scare them!) and bundled her off to the hospital, and she left the glove with me. I called the police, but Officer Hart was off duty and Officer Halstead, whom I talked to, told me they'd be over to pick it up early in the morning. Please take it, Jeff. Whenever I look at it, I think of that crazy sneaking around with the silver hair down his face and waving the knife. It keeps giving me the shivers."

I looked again at her "spooky" in its fold of tissue (so that she wouldn't have to touch it, what other reason?) and, you know, it began to give *me* the shivers. Just an old glove, but now it had an invisible gray aura radiating from it.

"Okay," I said, closing my hand on it with an effort, and went on ungraciously, really without thinking, "Though I wonder you didn't ask Mr. Helpful first, what with all his offers and seeing him at the meeting."

"Well, I asked *you*," she said a little angrily. Then her features relaxed into a warm smile, "Thanks, Jeff."

Only then did it occur to me that here I was passing up in my sleep-soddenness what might be a priceless opportunity. Well, that could be corrected. But before I could invite her in, there came this sharp little cough, or clearing of the throat. We both turned and there was Mr. Helpful in front of his open door, dressed in pajamas and a belted maroon dressing gown. He came smiling and dancing toward us (he didn't really dance, but he gave that impression in spite of being six foot four) and saying, "Could I be of any assistance, Miss Everly? Did something alarm you? Is there... er?..." He hesitated, as if there might be something he should be embarrassed at.

Marcia shook her head curtly and said to me quite coolly, "No thank you, I needn't come in, Mr. Winter. That will be fine. Good night."

I realized Baldy *had* managed to embarrass her and that she was making it clear that we weren't parting after a rendezvous, or about to have one. (But to use my last name!)

As she passed him, she gave him a formal nod. He hurried back to his own door, a highlight dancing on the back of his head. (Marcia says he shaves it; I, that he doesn't have to.)

I waited until I heard her double-lock her door and slide the bolt across. Then I looked grimly at Baldy until he'd gone inside and closed his—I had that pleasure. Then I retired myself, tossed the glove down on some sheets of paper on the table in front of the open window, threw myself into bed and switched out the light.

I fully expected to spend considerable time being furious at my hulking, mincing, officious neighbor, and maybe at Marcia too, before I could get to sleep, but somehow my mind took off on a fantasy about the building around me as it might have been a half century ago. Ghostly bellboys sped silently with little notes inviting or accepting rendezvous. Ghostly waiters wheeled noiseless carts of silver-covered suppers for two. Pert, ghostly maids whirled ghostly sheets through the dark air as they made the bed, their smiles suggesting they might substitute for non-arriving sweethearts. The soft darkness whirlpooled. Somewhere was wind.

I woke with a start as if someone or something had touched me, and I sat up in bed. And then I realized that something was touching me high on my neck, just below my ear. Something long, like a finger laid flat or—oh God!—a centipede. I remembered how centipedes were supposed to cling with their scores of tiny feet—and *this* was clinging. As a child I'd been terrified by a tropical centipede that had come weaving out of a stalk of new-bought bananas in the kitchen, and the memory still returned full force once in a great while. Now it galvanized me into whirling my hand behind my head and striking my neck a great brushing swipe, making my jaw and ear sting. I instantly turned on the light and rapidly looked all around me without seeing anything close to me that might have brushed off my neck. I thought I'd felt something with my hand when I'd done that, but I couldn't be sure.

And then I looked at the table by the window and saw that the glove was gone.

Almost at once I got the vision of it lifting up and floating through the air at me, fingers first, or else dropping off the table and inching across the floor and up the bed. I don't know which was worse. The thing on my neck *had* felt leathery.

My immediate impulse was to check if my door was still shut. I couldn't tell from where I sat. A very tall clothes cabinet abuts the door, shutting the view of it off from the head of the bed. So I pushed my way down the bed, putting my feet on the floor after looking down to make sure there was nothing in the immediate vicinity.

And then a sharp gust of wind came in the window and blew the last sheet of paper off the table and deposited it on the floor near the other sheets of paper *and the glove* and the tissue now disentangled from it.

I was so relieved I almost laughed. I went over and picked up the glove, feeling a certain revulsion, but only at the thought of who had worn it and what it had been involved in. I examined it closely, which I hadn't done earlier. It was rather thin gray kid, a fairly big glove and stretched still further as if a pretty big hand had worn it, but quite light enough to have blown off the table with the papers.

There were grimy streaks on it and a slightly stiff part where some fluid had dried and a faintly reddish streak that might have been lipstick. And it looked old—decades old.

I put it back on the table and set a heavy ashtray on top of it and got back in bed, feeling suddenly secure again.

It occurred to me how the empty finger of a gray leather glove is really very much like a centipede, some of the larger of which are the same size, flat and yellowish gray (though the one that had come out of the banana stalk had been bright red), but these thoughts were no longer frightening.

I looked a last time across the room at the glove, pinioned under the heavy ashtray, and I confidently turned off the light.

Sleep was longer in coming this time, however. I got my fantasy of hotel ghosts going again, but gloves kept coming into it. The lissom maids wore work ones as they rhythmically polished piles of ghostly silver. The bellboys' hands holding the ghostly notes were gloved in pale gray cotton. And there were opera gloves, almost armpit length, that looked like spectral white cobras, especially when they were drawn inside-out off the sinuous, snake-slender arms of wealthy guesting ladies. And other ghostly gloves, not all hotel ones, came floating and weaving into my fantasy: the black gloves of morticians, the white gloves of policemen, the bulky fur-lined ones of polar explorers, the trim dark gauntlets of chauffeurs, the gloves of hunters with separate stalls only for thumb and trigger finger, the mittens of ice-skaters and sleigh riders, old ladies' mitts without any fingers at all, the thin, translucent elastic gloves of surgeons, wielding flashing scalpels of silver-bright steel—a veritable whirlpool of gloves that finally led me down, down, down to darkness.

Once again I woke with a start, as if I'd been touched, and shot up. Once again I felt something about four inches long clinging high on my neck, only this time under the other ear. Once again I frantically slashed at my neck and jaw, stinging them painfully, only this time I struck upward and away. I *thought* I felt something go.

I got the light on and checked the door at once. It was securely shut. Then I looked at the table by the open window.

The heavy ashtray still sat in the center of it, rock firm.

But the rapist's glove that had been under it was gone.

I must have stood there a couple of minutes, telling myself this could not be. Then I went over and lifted the ashtray and carefully inspected its underside, as if the glove had somehow managed to shrink and was clinging there.

And all the while I was having this vision of the glove painfully humping itself from under the ashtray and inching to the table's edge and dropping to the floor and then crawling off... almost anywhere.

Believe me, I searched my place then, especially the floor. I even opened the doors to the closet and the clothes cabinet, though they had been tightly shut, and searched the floor there. And of course I searched under and behind the bed. And more than once while I searched, I'd suddenly jerk around thinking I'd seen something gray approaching my shoulder from behind.

There wasn't a sign of the glove.

It was dawn by now—had been for some time. I made coffee and tried to think rationally about it.

It seemed to boil down to three explanations that weren't wildly farfetched.

First, that I'd gone out of my mind. Could be, I suppose. But from what I'd read and seen, most people who go crazy know damn well ahead of time that something frightening is happening to their minds, except maybe paranoiacs. Still, it remained a possibility.

Second, that someone with a duplicate or master key had quietly taken the glove away while I was asleep. The apartment manager and janitor had such keys. I'd briefly given my duplicate to various people. Why, once before she got down on me, I'd given it to Evelyn Mayne—matter of letting someone in while I was at work. I *thought* I'd got it back from her, though I remember once having a second duplicate made—I'd forgotten why. The main difficulty about this explanation was motive. Who'd want to get the glove?—except the rapist, maybe.

Third, of course, there was the supernatural. Gloves are ghostly to start with, envelopes for hands—and if there isn't a medieval superstition about wearing the flayed skin of another's hand to work magic, there ought to be. (Of course, there was the Hand of Glory, its fingers flaming like candles, guaranteed to make people sleep while being burgled, but there the skin is still on the dried chopped- off hand.) And there are tales of spectral hands a-plenty—pointing out buried treasure or hidden graves, or at guilty murderers, or carrying candles or daggers—so why not gloves? And could there be a kind of telekinesis in which a hand controls at a distance the movements and actions of a glove it has worn? Of course that would be psionics or whatnot, but to me the parapsychological is supernatural. (And in that case what had the glove been trying to do probing at my neck?—strangle me, I'd think.) And somewhere I'd read of an aristocratic Brazilian murderess of the last century who wore gloves woven of spider silk, and of a knight blinded at a crucial moment in a tourney by a lady's silken glove worn as a favor. Yes, they were eerie envelopes, I thought, gloves were, but I was just concerned with one of them, a vanishing glove.

I started with a jerk as there came a measured *knock-knock*. I opened the door and looked up at the poker faces of two young policemen. Over their shoulders Mr. Helpful was peering down eagerly at me, his lips rapidly quirking in little smiles with what I'd call questioning pouts in between. Back and a little to one side was Marcia, looking shocked and staring intently at me through the narrow space between the second policeman and the door jamb.

"Jeff Winters," the first policeman said to me, as if it were a fact that he was putting into place. It occurred to me that young policemen look very *blocky* around their narrow hips with all that equipment they carry snugly nested and cased in black leather.

"Officer Hart—" Marcia began anxiously.

The second policeman's eyes flickered towards her, but just then the first policeman continued, "Your neighbor Miss Everly says she handed you a glove earlier this morning," and he stepped forward into the private space (I think it's sometimes called) around my body, and I automatically stepped back.

"We want it," he went on, continuing to step forward, and I back.

I hesitated. What was I to say? That the glove had started to spook me and then disappeared? Officer Hart followed the first policeman in. Mr. Helpful followed *him* in and stopped just inside my door, Marcia still beyond him and looking frantic. Officer Hart turned, as if about to tell Mr. Helpful to get out, but just then Officer Halstead (that was the other name Marcia had mentioned) said, "Well, you've still got it, haven't you? She gave it to you, didn't she?"

I shook and then nodded my head, which must have made me look rattled. He came closer still and said harshly and with a note of eagerness, "Well, where is it, then?"

I had to look up quite sharply at him to see his face. Beyond it, just to one side of it, diagonally upward across the room, was the top of the tall clothes cabinet, and on the edge of that there balanced that damned gray glove, flat fingers dripping over.

I froze. I could have sworn I'd glanced up there more than once when I was hunting the thing, and seen nothing. Yet there it was, as if it had flown up there or else been flicked there by me the second time I'd violently brushed something from my face.

Officer Halstead must have misread my look of terror, for he ducked his head toward mine and rasped, "Your neighbor Mr. Angus says that it's *your* glove, that he saw you wearing gray gloves night before last! What do you say?"

But I didn't say anything, for at that moment the glove slid off its precarious perch and dropped straight down and landed on Mr. Helpful's (Angus's) shoulder close to his neck, just like the hand of an arresting cop.

Now it may have been that in ducking his head to look at it, he trapped it between his chin and collarbone, or it may have been (as it looked to me) that the glove actively clung to his neck and shoulder, resisting all his frantic efforts to peel it off, while he reiterated, his voice mounting in screams, "It's not my glove!"

He took his hands away for a moment and the glove dropped to the floor.

He looked back and forth and saw the dawning expressions on the faces of the two policemen, and then with a sort of despairing sob he whipped a long knife from under his coat.

Considerably to my surprise I started toward him, but just then Officer Hart endeared himself to us all forever by wrapping his arms around Mr. Angus like a bear, one hand closing on the wrist of the hand holding the knife.

I veered past him (I vividly recall changing the length of one of my strides so as not to step on the glove) and reached Marcia just in time to steady her as, turned quite white, she swayed, her eyelids fluttering.

I heard the knife clatter to the floor. I turned, my arms around Marcia, and we both saw Mr. Angus seem to shrink and collapse in Officer Hart's ursine embrace, his face going gray as if he were an empty glove himself.

That was it. They found the other glove and the long silver wig in a locked suitcase in his room. Marcia stayed frightened long enough, off and on, for us to become better acquainted and cement our friendship.

Officer (now Detective) Hart tells us that Mr. Angus is a

model prisoner at the hospital for the criminally insane and has gone very religious, but never smiles. And he—Hart—now has the glove in a sort of Black Museum down at the station, where it has never again been seen to move under its own power. If it ever did.

One interesting thing. The gloves had belonged to Mr. Angus's father, now deceased, who had been a judge.

THE GIRL WITH THE HUNGRY EYES

ALL RIGHT, I'LL TELL YOU WHY THE GIRL GIVES ME the creeps. Why I can't stand to go downtown and see the mob slavering up at her on the tower, with that pop bottle or pack of cigarettes or whatever it is beside her. Why I hate to look at magazines any more because I know she'll turn up somewhere in a brassiere or a bubble bath. Why I don't like to think of millions of Americans drinking in that poisonous half smile. It's quite a story—more story than you're expecting.

No, I haven't suddenly developed any long-haired indignation at the evils of advertising and the national glamour-girl complex. That'd be a laugh for a man in my racket, wouldn't it?

Though I think you'll agree there's something a little perverted about trying to capitalize on sex that way. But it's okay with me. And I know we've had the Face and the Body and the Look and what not else, so why shouldn't someone come along who sums it all up so completely, that we have to call her the Girl and blazon her on all the billboards from Times Square to Telegraph Hill?

But the Girl isn't like any of the others. She's unnatural. She's morbid. She's unholy.

Oh it's 1948, is it, and the sort of thing I'm hinting at went out with witchcraft? But you see I'm not altogether sure myself what I'm hinting at, beyond a certain point. There are vampires and vampires, and not all of them suck blood.

And there were the murders, if they were murders.

Besides, let me ask you this. Why, when America is obsessed

with the Girl, don't we find out more about her? Why doesn't she
rate a *Time* cover with a droll biography inside? Why hasn't there
been a feature in *Life* or the *Post?* A Profile in the *New Yorker?*
Why hasn't *Charm* or *Mademoiselle* done her career saga? Not
ready for it? Nuts!

Why haven't the movies snapped her up? Why hasn't she been
on Information, Please? Why don't we see her kissing candidates
at political rallies? Why isn't she chosen queen of some sort of
junk or other at a convention?

Why don't we read about her tastes and hobbies, her views of
the Russian situation? Why haven't the columnists interviewed
her in a kimono on the top floor of the tallest hotel in Manhattan
and told us who her boy-friends are?

Finally—and this is the real killer—why hasn't she ever been
drawn or painted?

Oh, no she hasn't. If you knew anything about commercial art
you'd know that. Every blessed one of those pictures was worked
up from a photograph. Expertly? Of course. They've got the top
artists on it. But that's how it's done.

And now I'll tell you the *why* of all that. It's because from the
top to the bottom of the whole world of advertising, news, and
business, there isn't a solitary soul who knows where the Girl
came from, where she lives, what she does, who she is, even what
her name is.

You heard me. What's more, not a single solitary soul ever *sees*
her—except one poor damned photographer, who's making more
money off her than he ever hoped to in his life and who's scared
and miserable as hell every minute of the day.

No, I haven't the faintest idea who he is or where he has his
studio. But I know there has to be such a man and I'm morally
certain he feels just like I *said.*

Yes, I might be able to find her, if I tried. I'm not sure though—
by now she probably has other safeguards. Besides, I don't want to.

Oh, I'm off my rocker, am I? That sort of thing can't happen
in this Year of our Atom 1948? People can't keep out of sight that
way, not even Garbo?

Well I happen to know they can, because last year I was that
poor damned photographer I was telling you about. Yes, last year,
in 1947, when the Girl made her first poisonous splash right here
in this big little city of ours.

Yes, I knew you weren't here last year and you don't know

about it. Even the Girl had to start small. But if you hunted through the files of the local newspapers, you'd find some ads, and I might be able to locate you some of the old displays—I think Lovelybelt is still using one of them. I used to have a mountain of photos myself, until I burned them.

Yes, I made my cut off her. Nothing like what that other photographer must be making, but enough so it still bought this whisky. She was funny about money. I'll tell you about that.

But first picture me in 1947. I had a fourth floor studio in that rathole the Hauser Building, catty-corner from Ardleigh Park.

I'd been working at the Marsh-Mason studios until I'd gotten my bellyful of it and decided to start in for myself. The Hauser Building was crummy—I'll never forget how the stairs creaked—but it was cheap and there was a skylight.

Business was lousy. I kept making the rounds of all the advertisers and agencies, and some of them didn't object to me too much personally, but my stuff never clicked. I was pretty near broke. I was behind on my rent. Hell, I didn't even have enough money to have a girl.

It was one of those dark grey afternoons. The building was awfully quiet—even with the shortage they can't half rent the Hauser. I'd just finished developing some pix I was doing on speculation for Lovelybelt Girdles and Buford's Pool and Playground—the last a faked-up beach scene. My model had left. A Miss Leon. She was a civics teacher at one of the high schools and modelled for me on the side, just lately on speculation too. After one look at the prints, I decided that Miss Leon probably wasn't just what Lovelybelt was looking for—or my photography either. I was about to call it a day.

And then the street door slammed four storeys down and there were steps on the stairs and she came in.

She was wearing a cheap, shiny black dress. Black pumps. No stockings. And except that she had a grey cloth coat over one of them, those skinny arms of hers were bare. Her arms are pretty skinny, you know, or can you see things like that any more?

And then the thin neck, the slightly gaunt, almost prim face, the tumbling mass of dark hair, and looking out from under it the hungriest eyes in the world.

That's the real reason she's plastered all over the country today, you know—those eyes. Nothing vulgar, but just the same they're looking at you with a hunger that's all sex and something more than sex. That's what everybody's been looking for since the Year One—something a little more than sex.

Well, boys, there I was, alone with the Girl, in an office that was getting shadowy, in a nearly empty building. A situation that a million male Americans have undoubtedly pictured to themselves with various lush details. How was I feeling? Scared.

I know sex can be frightening. That cold, heart-thumping when you're alone with a girl and feel you're going to touch her. But if it was sex this time, it was overlaid with something else.

At least I wasn't thinking about sex.

I remember that I took a backward step and that my hand jerked so that the photos I was looking at sailed to the floor.

There was the faintest dizzy feeling like something was being drawn out of me. Just a little bit.

That was all. Then she opened her mouth and everything was back to normal for a while.

"I see you're a photographer, mister,' she said. 'Could you use a model?'

Her voice wasn't very cultivated.

'I doubt it,' I told her, picking up the pix. You see, I wasn't impressed. The commercial possibilities of her eyes hadn't registered on me yet, by a long shot. 'What have you done?'

Well she gave me a vague sort of story and I began to check her knowledge of model agencies and studios and rates and what not and pretty soon I said to her,

'Look here, you never modelled for a photographer in your life. You just walked in here cold.'

Well, she admitted that was more or less so.

All along through our talk I got the idea she was feeling her way, like someone in a strange place. Not that she was uncertain of herself, or of me, but just of the general situation.

'And you think anyone can model?' I asked her pityingly.

'Sure,' she said.

'Look,' I said, 'a photographer can waste a dozen negatives trying to get one half-way human photo of an average woman. How many do you think he'd have to waste before he got a real catchy, glamourous pix of her?'

'I think I could do it,' she said.

Well, I should have kicked her out right then. Maybe I admired the cool way she stuck to her dumb little guns. Maybe I was touched by her underfed look. More likely I was feeling mean on account of the way my pix had been snubbed by everybody and I wanted to take it out on her by showing her up.

'Okay, I'm going to put you on the spot,' I told her. 'I'm going to try a couple of shots of you. Understand, it's strictly on spec. If somebody should ever want to use a photo of you, which is about one chance in two million, I'll pay you regular rates for your time. Not otherwise.'

She gave me a smile. The first. 'That's swell by me,' she said.

Well, I took three of four shots, closeups of her face since I didn't fancy her cheap dress, and at least she stood up to my sarcasm. Then I remembered I still had the Lovelybelt stuff and I guess the meanness was still working in me because I handed her a girdle and told her to go back of the screen and get into it and she did, without getting flustered as I'd expected, and since we'd gone that far I figured we might as well shoot the beach scene to round it out, and that was that.

All this time I wasn't feeling anything particular in one way or the other except every once in a while I'd get one of those faint dizzy flashes and wonder if there was something wrong with my stomach or if I could have been a bit careless with my chemicals. Still, you know, I think the uneasiness was in me all the while.

I tossed her a card and pencil. 'Write your name and address and phone,' I told her and made for the darkroom.

A little later she walked out. I didn't call any good-byes. I was irked because she hadn't fussed around or seemed anxious about her poses, or even thanked me, except for that one smile.

I finished developing the negatives, made some prints, glanced at them, decided they weren't a great deal worse than Miss Leon. On an impulse I slipped them in with the pix I was going to take on the rounds next morning.

By now I'd worked long enough so I was a bit fagged and nervous, but I didn't dare waste enough money on liquor to help that. I wasn't very hungry. I think I went to a cheap movie.

I didn't think of the Girl at all, except maybe to wonder faintly why in my present womanless state I hadn't made a pass at her. She had seemed to belong to a, well, distinctly more approachable social strata than Miss Leon. But then of course there were all sorts of arguable reasons for my not doing that.

Next morning I made the rounds. My first step was Munsch's Brewery. They were looking for a 'Munsch Girl.' Papa Munsch had a sort of affection for me, though he razzed my photography.

He had a good natural judgement about that, too. Fifty years ago he might have been one of the shoestring boys who made Hollywood.

Right now he was out in the plant pursuing his favourite occupation. He put down the beaded can, smacked his lips, gabbled something technical to someone about hops, wiped his fat hands on the big apron he was wearing, and grabbed my thin stack of pix.

He was about half-way through, making noises with his tongue and teeth, when he came to her. I kicked myself for even having stuck her in.

'That's her,' he said. 'The photography's not so hot, but that's the girl.'

It was all decided. I wondered now why Papa Munsch sensed what the girl had right away, while I didn't. I think it was because I saw her first in the flesh, if that's the right word.

At the time I just felt faint.

'Who is she?' he asked.

'One of my new models,' I tried to make it casual.

'Bring her out tomorrow morning,' he told me. 'And your stuff. We'll photograph her here. I want to show you.'

'Here, don't look so sick,' he added. 'Have some beer.'

Well I went away telling myself it was just a fluke, so that she'd probably blow it tomorrow with her inexperience and so on.

Just the same, when I reverently laid my next stack of pix on Mr. Fitch, of Lovelybelt's, rose-coloured blotter, I had hers on top.

Mr. Fitch went through the motions of being an art critic. He leaned over backward, squinted his eyes, waved his long fingers, and said, 'Hmm. What do you think, Miss Willow? Here, in this light. Of course the photograph doesn't show the bias cut. And perhaps we should use the Lovelybelt Imp instead of the Angel. Still, the girl... Come over here, Binns.' More finger-waving. 'I want a married man's reaction.'

He couldn't hide the fact that he was hooked.

Exactly the same thing happened at Buford's Pool and Playground, except that Da Costa didn't need a married man's say- so.

'Hot stuff,' he said, sucking his lips. 'Oh boy, you photographers!'

I hot-footed it back to the office and grabbed up the card I'd given her to put down her name and address.

It was blank.

I don't mind telling you that the next five days were about the worst I ever went through, in an ordinary way. When next morning rolled around and I still hadn't got hold of her, I had to start stalling.

'She's sick,' I told Papa Munsch over the phone.

'She at a hospital?' he asked me.

'Nothing that serious,' I told him.

'Get her out here then. What's a little headache?'

'Sorry, I can't.'

Papa Munsch got suspicious. 'You really got this girl?'

'Of course I have.'

'Well, I don't know, I'd think it was some New York model, except I recognized your lousy photography.'

I laughed.

'Well look, you get her here tomorrow morning, you hear?'

'I'll try.'

'Try nothing. You get her out here.'

He didn't know half of what I tried. I went around to all the model and employment agencies. I did some slick detective work at the photographic and art studios. I used up some of my last dimes putting advertisements in all three papers. I looked at high school yearbooks and at employee photos in local house organs. I went to restaurants and drugstores, looking at waitresses, and to dime stores and department stores, looking at clerks. I watched the crowds coming out of movie theatres. I roamed the streets.

Evenings I spent quite a bit of time along Pick-up Row. Somehow that seemed the right place.

The fifth afternoon I knew I was licked. Papa Munsch's deadline—he'd given me several, but this was it—was due to run out at six o'clock. Mr. Fitch had already cancelled.

I was at the studio window, looking out at Ardleigh Park.

She walked in.

I'd gone over this moment so often in my mind that I had no trouble putting on my act. Even the faint dizzy feeling didn't throw me off.

'Hello,' I said, hardly looking at her.

'Hello,' she said.

'Not discouraged yet?'

'No.' It didn't sound uneasy or defiant. It was just a statement.

I snapped a look at my watch, got up and said curtly, 'Look here, I'm going to give you a chance. There's a client of mine looking for a girl your general type. If you do a real good job you may break into the modelling business.

'We can see him this afternoon if we hurry,' I said. I picked up my stuff. 'Come on. And next time if you expect favours, don't forget to leave your phone number.'

'Uh, uh,' she said, not moving.

'What do you mean?' I said.

'I'm not going out to see any client of yours.'

'The hell you aren't,' I said. 'You little nut, I'm giving you a break.'

She shook her head slowly. 'You're not fooling me, baby, you're not fooling me at all. They *want* me.' And she gave me the second smile.

At the time I thought she must have seen my newspaper ad. Now I'm not so sure.

'And now I'll tell you how we're going to work,' she went on. 'You aren't going to have my name or address or phone number. Nobody is. And we're going to do all the pictures right here. Just you and me.'

You can imagine the roar I raised at that. I was everything— angry, sarcastic, patiently explanatory, off my nut, threatening, pleading.

I would have slapped her face off, except it was photographic capital.

In the end all I could do was phone Papa Munsch and tell him her conditions. I know I didn't have a chance, but I had to take it.

He gave me a really angry bawling out, said 'no' several times and hung up.

It didn't faze her. 'We'll start shooting at ten o'clock tomorrow,' she said.

It was just like her, using that corny line from the movie magazines.

About midnight Papa Munsch called me up.

'I don't know what insane asylum you're renting this girl from,' he said, 'but I'll take her. Come around tomorrow morning and I'll try to get it through your head just how I want the pictures. And I'm glad I got you out of bed!'

After that it was a breeze. Even Mr. Fitch reconsidered and after taking two days to tell me it was quite impossible he accepted the conditions too.

Of course you're all under the spell of the Girl, so you can't understand how much self-sacrifice it represented on Mr. Fitch's part when he agreed to forgo supervising the photography of my model in the Lovelybelt Imp or Vixen or whatever it was we finally used.

Next morning she turned up on time according to her schedule, and we went to work. I'll say one thing for her, she never got tired and she never kicked at the way I fussed over shots. I got along okay except I still had that feeling of something being shoved away gently. Maybe you've felt it just a little, looking at her picture.

When we finished I found out there were still more rules. It was about the middle of the afternoon. I started down with her to get a sandwich and coffee.

'Uh uh,' she said, 'I'm going down alone. And look, baby, if you ever try to follow me, if you ever so much as stick your head out that window when I go, you can hire yourself another model.'

You can imagine how all this crazy stuff strained my temper—and my imagination. I remember opening the window after she was gone—I waited a few minutes first—and standing there getting some fresh air and trying to figure out what could be back of it, whether she was hiding from the police, or was somebody's ruined daughter, or maybe had got the idea it was smart to be temperamental, or more likely Papa Munsch was right and she was partly nuts.

But I had my pix to finish up.

Looking back it's amazing to think how fast her magic began to take hold of the city after that. Remembering what came after, I'm frightened of what's happening to the whole country—and maybe the world. Yesterday I read something in *Time* about the Girl's picture turning up on billboards in Egypt.

The rest of my story will help show you why I'm frightened in that big general way. But I have a theory, too, that helps explain, though it's one of those things that's beyond that 'certain point.' It's about the Girl. I'll give it to you in a few words.

You know how modern advertising gets everybody's mind set in the same direction, wanting the same things, imagining the same things. And you know the psychologists aren't so sceptical of telepathy as they used to be.

Add up the two ideas. Suppose the identical desires of millions of people focused on one telepathic person. Say a girl. Shaped her in their image.

Imagine her knowing the hiddenmost hungers of millions of men. Imagine her seeing deeper into those hungers than the people that had them, seeing the hatred and the wish for death behind the lust. Imagine her shaping herself in that complete image, keeping herself as aloof as marble. Yet imagine the hunger she might feel in answer to their hunger.

But that's getting a long way from the facts of my story. And some of those facts are darn solid. Like money. We made money.

That was the funny thing I was going to tell you. I was afraid the Girl was going to hold me up. She really had me over a barrel, you know.

But she didn't ask for anything but the regular rates. Later on I insisted on pushing more money at her, a whole lot. But she always took it with that same contemptuous look, as if she were going to toss it down the first drain when she got outside. Maybe she did.

At any rate, I had money. For the first time in months I had money enough to get drunk, buy new clothes, take taxicabs. I could make a play for any girl I wanted to. I only had to pick.

And so of course I had to go and pick—

But first let me tell you about Papa Munsch.

Papa Munsch wasn't the first of the boys to try to meet my model but I think he was the first to really go soft on her. I could watch the change in his eyes as he looked at her pictures. They began to get sentimental, reverent. Mama Munsch had been dead for two years.

He was smart about the way he planned it. He got me to drop some information which told him when she came to work, and then one morning he came pounding up the stairs a few minutes before.

'I've got to see her, Dave,' he told me.

I argued with him, I kidded him, I explained he didn't know just how serious she was about her crazy ideas. I pointed out he was cutting both our throats. I even amazed myself by bawling him out.

He didn't take any of it in his usual way. He just kept repeating, 'But, Dave, I've got to see her.'

The street door slammed.

'That's her,' I said, lowering my voice. 'You've got to get out.'

He wouldn't, so I shoved him in the darkroom. 'And keep quiet,' I whispered. 'I'll tell her I can't work today.'

I knew he'd try to look at her and probably come busting in, but there wasn't anything else I could do.

The footsteps came to the fourth floor. But she never showed at the door. I got uneasy.

'Get that bum out of there!' she yelled suddenly from beyond the door. Not very loud, but in her commonest voice.

'I'm going up to the next landing,' she said, 'And if that fat-bellied bum doesn't march straight down to the street, he'll never get another pix of me except spitting in his lousy beer.'

Papa Munsch came out of the darkroom. He was white. He didn't look at me as he went out. He never looked at her pictures in front of me again.

That was Papa Munsch. Now it's me I'm telling about. I talked around the subject with her, I hinted, eventually I made my pass.

She lifted my hand off her as if it were a damp rag.

'Nix, baby,' she said. 'This is working time.'

'But afterwards...' I pressed.

'The rules still hold.' And I got what I think was the fifth smile.

It's hard to believe, but she never budged an inch from that crazy line. I mustn't make a pass at her in the office, because our work was very important and she loved it and there mustn't be any distractions. And I couldn't see her anywhere else, because if I tried to, I'd never snap another picture of her—and all this with more money coming in all the time and me never so stupid as to think my photography had anything to do with it.

Of course I wouldn't have been human if I hadn't made more passes. But they always got the wet-rag treatment and there weren't any more smiles.

I changed. I went sort of crazy and light-headed—only sometimes I felt my head was going to burst. And I started to talk to her all the time. About myself.

It was like being in a constant delirium that never interfered with business. I didn't pay any attention to the dizzy feeling. It seemed natural.

I'd walk around and for a moment the reflector would look like a sheet of white-hot steel, or the shadows would seem like armies of moths, or the camera would be a big black coal car. But the next instant they'd come all right again.

I think sometimes I was scared to death of her. She'd seem the strangest, horriblest person in the world. But other times...

And I talked. It didn't matter what I was doing—lighting

her, posing her, fussing with props, snapping my pix—or where she was—on the platform, behind the screen, relaxing with a magazine—I kept up a steady gab.

I told her everything I knew about myself. I told her about my first girl. I told her about my brother Bob's bicycle. I told her about running away on a freight, and the licking Pa gave me when I came home. I told her about shipping to South America and the blue sky at night. I told her about Betty. I told her about my mother dying of cancer. I told her about being beaten up in a fight in an alley back of a bar. I told her about Mildred. I told her about the first picture I ever sold. I told her how Chicago looked from a sailboat. I told her about the longest drunk I was ever on. I told her about Marsh-Mason. I told her about Gwen. I told her about how I met Papa Munsch. I told her about hunting her. I told her about how I felt now.

She never paid the slightest attention to what I said. I couldn't even tell if she heard me.

It was when we were getting our first nibble from national advertisers that I decided to follow her when she went home.

Wait, I can place it better than that. Something you'll remember from the out-of-town papers—those maybe murders I mentioned. I think there were six.

I say 'maybe,' because the police could never be sure they weren't heart attacks. But there's bound to be suspicion when heart attacks happen to people whose hearts have been okay, and always at night when they're alone and away from home and there's a question of what they were doing.

The six deaths created one of those 'mystery poisoner' scares. And afterwards there was a feeling that they hadn't really stopped, but were being continued in a less suspicious way.

That's one of the things that scares me now.

But at that time my only feeling was relief that I'd decided to follow her.

I made her work until dark one afternoon. I didn't need any excuses, we were snowed under with orders. I waited until the street door slammed, then I ran down. I was wearing rubber-soled shoes. I'd slipped on a dark coat she'd never seen me in, and a dark hat.

I stood in the doorway until I spotted her. She was walking by Ardleigh Park toward the heart of town. It was one of those warm fall nights. I followed her on the other side of the street.

My idea for tonight was just to find out where she lived. That would give me a hold on her.

She stopped in front of a display window of Everly's department store, standing back from the glow. She stood there looking in.

I remembered we'd done a big photograph of her for Everly's, to make a flat model for a lingerie display. That was what she was looking at.

At the time it seemed all right to me that she should adore herself, if that was what she was doing.

When people passed she'd turn away a little or drift back farther into the shadows.

Then a man came by alone. I couldn't see his face very well, but he looked middle-aged. He stopped and stood looking in the window.

She came out of the shadows and stepped up beside him.

How would you boys feel if you were looking at a poster of the Girl and suddenly she was there beside you, her arm linked with yours?

This fellow's reaction showed plain as day. A crazy dream had come to life for him.

They talked for a moment. Then he waved a taxi to the kerb. They got in and drove off.

I got drunk that night. It was almost as if she'd known I was following her and had picked that way to hurt me. Maybe she had. Maybe this was the finish.

But the next morning she turned up at the usual time and I was back in the delirium, only now with some new angles added.

That night when I followed her she picked a spot under a street lamp, opposite one of the Munsch Girl billboards.

Now it frightens me to think of her lurking that way.

After about twenty minutes a convertible slowed down going past her, backed up, swung in to the kerb.

I was closer this time. I got a good look at the fellow's face. He was a little younger, about my age.

Next morning the same face looked up at me from the front page of the paper. The convertible had been found parked on a side street He had been in it. As in the other maybe-murders, the cause of death was uncertain.

All kinds of thoughts were spinning in my head that day, but there were only two things I knew for sure. That I'd got the first real offer from a national advertiser, and that I was going

to take the Girl's arm and walk down the stairs with her when
we quit work.

She didn't seem surprised. 'You know what you're doing?' she
said.

'I know.'

She smiled. 'I was wondering when you'd get around to it.'

I began to feel good. I was kissing everything good-bye, but I
had my arm around hers.

It was another of those warm fall evenings. We cut across into
Ardleigh Park. It was dark there, but all around the sky was a
sallow pink from the advertising signs.

We walked for a long time in the park. She didn't say anything
and she didn't look at me, but I could see her lips twitching and
after a while her hand tightened on my arm.

We stopped. We'd been walking across the grass. She dropped
down and pulled me after her. She put her hands on my shoulders.
I was looking down at her face. It was the faintest sallow pink
from the glow in the sky. The hungry eyes were dark smudges.

I was fumbling with her blouse. She took my hand away, not
like she had in the studio. 'I don't want that,' she said.

First I'll tell you what I did afterwards. Then I'll tell you why
I did it. Then I'll tell you what she said.

What I did was run away. I don't remember all of that because
I was dizzy, and the pink sky was swinging against the dark trees.
But after a while I staggered into the lights of the street. The next
day I closed up the studio. The telephone was ringing when I
locked the door and there were unopened letters on the floor. I
never saw the Girl again in the flesh, if that's the right word.

I did it because I didn't want to die. I didn't want the life
drawn out of me. There are vampires and vampires, and the
ones that suck blood aren't the worst. If it hadn't been for the
warning of those dizzy flashes, and Papa Munsch and the face
in the morning paper, I'd have gone the way the others did. But
I realized what I was up against while there was still time to tear
myself away. I realized that wherever she came from, whatever
shaped her, she's the quintessence of the horror behind the bright
billboard. She's the smile that tricks you into throwing away your
money and your life. She's the eyes that lead you on and on, and
then show you death. She's the creature you give everything for

and never really get. She's the being that takes everything you've got and gives nothing in return. When you yearn towards her face on the billboards, remember that. She's the lure. She's the bait. She's the Girl.

And this is what she said, 'I want you. I want your high spots. I want everything that's made you happy and everything that's hurt you bad. I want your first girl. I want that shiny bicycle. I want that licking. I want that pinhole camera. I want Betty's legs. I want the blue sky filled with stars. I want your mother's death. I want your blood on the cobblestones. I want Mildred's mouth. I want the first picture you sold. I want the lights of Chicago. I want the gin. I want Gwen's hands. I want your wanting me. I want your life. Feed me, baby, feed me.'

WHILE SET FLED

AFTER CENTURIES OF FEAR AND RUMOR, THE Hyborean tribes were streaming southward in a holocaust of destruction and conquest. The northern marches of Set had been breached and the broken armies of Tuthothomes XX were in full flight, nor would they be rallied until they reached the Styx and ancient Khemi—that great stand which saved the old Southern Kingdom was yet to be made. Meanwhile, the rich northern provinces of Set were doomed.

Nuthmekri was a craftsman of little fame, yet he chose to stay behind while greater artists fled. All yesterday the castle had been frantically a-bustle as the servitors of his patron Megshastes prepared for the flight southward too long delayed. Hurried footsteps, stumblings, strained puffings of slaves seeking to carry too much too swiftly, impatient, shinny and stomp in the courtyard of horses harnessed and hitched too soon, creaking of overladen wagons, now and then a hallow snap as lashings parted that had been drawn too tight over loads too high—shouts, curses, wailings, and commands. Now all was delightfully quiet.

It was only a small statuette that Nuthmekri was preparing to cast, yet its form seemed to him perfect. The sand mold was ready, the little furnace was aglow, and now Nuthmekri reached for an ingot of bronze. But there disappointment awaited him. His chest of metals was empty. Some slave must have looted it last night while he strolled in the meadows. Perhaps the fellow had heard the Hyboreans coveted bronze beyond all else and would sometimes show mercy to a man who gave it to them.

Nuthmekri's eyes roved questingly about his small tower room.

There were a few statuettes and pleasingly shaped implements
and utensils. These he passed over. High on one bare wall hung
an ancient sword of bronze, dusty, cobwebbed fast, almost black.
Putting stool on table, Nuthmekri was enabled to climb up and
detach it.

Holding the antique weapon in his hand, Nuthmekri moved
to the window. Through the narrow embrasure he could make
out a nearby hilltop in the hot sunlight and a road crossing it.
Suddenly there puffed up a cloud of dust, and horsemen burst
from it—ragged fellows on small bony mounts, with bows and
circular shields and spears on whose barbed blades Nuthmekri
fancied he could discern the lust of blood. There came to his ears
a faint eager shouting.

Nuthmekri stiffened and for a moment he gripped the old
sword like a fencer. Then he smiled bitterly and shook his head
and while the horde continued to pour across the hilltop, turned
away from the window to the furnace and sheathed the sword
in the narrow, glowing crucible. The slim, unbroken object was
a long time melting. Again noise filled the castle—wild laughter,
stampings, treadings, smashings and breakings, snarling curses of
disappointment as signs of the previous looting were uncovered
(an owner's self-looting—unforgivably mean and cheap—and in
this Nuthmekri agreed with them) yells as edibles and potables
came to light, ludicrous and unintelligible howlings the emotional
significance of which only a barbarian mind could hope to
comprehend.

By jerky stages the sword descended into the crucible. Then
the guard rested against the rosy lip, Nuthmekri took up the
tongs and prepared to pour.

There was a heavy tramping on the tower stairs and a jabbering
that increased in volume, then a jerking and pounding at the door,
which was unlocked and only failed to open because it was being
tried the wrong way—pushed instead of pulled. In the center of
the shadowy room the crucible made a little sun. From it there
jetted into the mold a slim perfect stream, blindingly white.

The door was jerked open. For a moment the barbarians
stood there, puzzled. Then one—perhaps he had seen molten lead
poured on his fellows when they stormed the march fortresses—
lunged forward and with one great swipe of his notched yet
razor-sharp longsword cut off Nuthmekri's head.

In the pulsing crimson fountain that arched up lazily fell

finally straight upon the mold. There was a hissing and a puff of steam. The barbarian drew back a step. Then something tickled his primeval sense of humor. He laughed loud and harshly and long.

The sand mold split from its bloody drenching and fell away from the tiny, black scaled figure, still faintly glowing, of a slim, and robed and hooded woman, who regarded the intruders enigmatically. Her head was complete yet no spike of waster metal stuck up from it—Nuthmekri had poured just enough and no more.

Nuthmekri's body stopped writhing. His fingers uncurled from the tongs. A tiny branch of the metal from the fallen crucible ran along his arm, hardening almost instantly.

But the slayer of the sculptor was laughing at one of those circumstances. What had struck him as very funny was that the slim shining stream of the statuette's pouring had been neatly twitched off by his victim a full three red-jetting heartbeats after the Hyborean's sword had shorn through Nuthmekri's neck.

DIARY IN THE SNOW

JAN. 6: TWO HOURS SINCE MY ARRIVAL AT LONE Top, and I'm still sitting in front of the fire, soaking in the heat. The taxi ride was hellishly cold and the breathtaking half-mile tramp through the drifts with John completed my transformation to an icicle. The driver from Terrestrial told me this was one of the loneliest spots in Montana, and it surely looked like it—miles and miles of tenantless, starlit snow with mysterious auroral splotches and ghostly beams flickering to the north—a beautiful, if frightening sight.

And I've even turned the cold to account! It suggested to me that I put my monsters on a drearily frigid planet, one that is circling a dead or dying sun. That will give them a motivation for wanting to invade and capture the Earth. Good!

Well, here I am—a jobless man with a book to write. My friends (such as they are, or were) never believed I'd take this step, and when they finally saw I was in earnest, they tried to convince me I was a fool. And toward the end I was afraid I'd lose my nerve, but then—it was as if forces beyond my knowledge or control were packing my bag, insulting my boss, and buying my ticket. A very pleasant illusion, after weeks of qualms and indecision!

How wonderful to be away from people and newspapers and advertisements and movies—all that damnable intellectual static! I confess I had a rather unpleasant shock when I first came in here and noticed the big radio standing right between the fireplace and window. How awful it would be to have that thing blatting at you in this cabin, with no place to escape except the tiny storeroom. It would be worse than the city! But so far John hasn't turned it on, and I have my fingers crossed.

John is a magnificent host—understanding as well as incomparably generous. After getting me coffee and a snack, and setting out the whiskey, he's retired to the other armchair and busied himself with some scribbling of his own.

Well, in a moment I'll talk as much as he wants to *(if* he wants to) though I'm still reverberating from my trip. I feel as if I'd been catapulted out of an intolerable clangor and discord into the heart of quietness. It gives me a crazy, lightheaded feeling, like a balloon that touches the earth only to bounce upward again.

Better stop here though. I'd hate to think of how quiet a quietness would have to be, in order to be as much quieter than this place, as this is quieter than the city!

A man ought to be able to listen to his thoughts out here—really hear things.

Just John, and me—and my monsters!

Jan. 7: Wonderful day. Crisp, but no wind, and a flood of yellow sunlight to put a warmth and dazzle into the snow banks. John showed me all around the place this morning. It's a snug little cabin he's got, and a good thing too!—because it's quite as lonely as it seemed last night. No houses in sight, and I'd judge there hasn't been anything down the road since my taxi—the marks where it turned around stand out sharply. John says a farmer drives by, though, every two days—he has an arrangement with him for getting milk and other necessities.

You can't see Terrestrial, there are hills in the way. John tells me that power and telephone wires have never gotten closer than six miles. The radio runs on storage batteries. When the drifts get bad he has to snowshoe all the way into Terrestrial.

I confess I feel a little awestruck at my own temerity—a confirmed desk-worker like myself plunging into a truly rugged environment like this. But John seems to think nothing of it. He says I'll have to learn to snowshoe. I had my first lesson this morning and cut a ludicrous figure. I'll be virtually a prisoner until I learn my way around. But any price is worth paying to get away from the thought-destroying din and soul-killing routine of the city!

And there's a good side to the enforced isolation—it will make me concentrate on my book.

Well, that does it. I've popped the word, and now I'll have

to start writing the thing itself—and am I scared! It's been so long since I've finished anything of my own— even attempted it. So damned long. I'd begun to be afraid (begun, hell!) that I'd never do anything but take notes and make outlines—outlines that became more and more complicated and lifeless with the years. And yet there were those early fragments of writing from my school days that ought to have encouraged me. Even much later, when I'd developed some literary judgement, I used to think those fragments showed flashes of real promise—until I burned them. They should have given me courage—at any rate, something should have—but whatever promising ideas I'd have in the morning would be shredded to tatters by that horrible hackwriting job by the time night came.

And now that I have taken the plunge, it seems hilariously strange that I should have been driven to it by an idea for a fantasy story. The very sort of writing I've always jeered at— childish playing around with interplanetary space and alien monsters. The farthest thing you could imagine from my wearisome outlines, which eventually got so filled up with character analysis (or even—Heaven help me—psychoanalysis) and dismal authentic backgrounds and "my own experience" and just heaps of social and political "significance" that there wasn't room for anything else. Yes, it does seem ludicrously paradoxical that, instead of all those profound and "important" things, it should have been an idea about black-furred, long-tentacled monsters on another planet, peering unwinkingly at the earth and longing for its warmth and life, that so began to sing in my mind, night and day, that I finally got the strength to sweep aside all those miserable little fences against insecurity I'd been so painfully long in building—and take a chance!

John says it's natural and wholesome for a beginning writer to turn to fantasy. And he's certainly made a go of that type of writing himself. (But he's built up his ability as courageously and doggedly through the years as he has this cabin. In comparison, I have a long, long way to go.)

In any case, my book won't be a cheap romance of the fabulous, despite its "cosmic" background. And when you get down to that, what's wrong with a cosmic background? I've lived a long time now with my monsters and devoted a lot of serious thought to them. I'll make them real.

That night: I just had an exhilaratingly eerie experience. I'd stepped outside for a breather and a look at the snow and stars, when my attention was caught by a beam of violet light some distance away. Though not exactly bright, it had a jewelly gleam and seemed to go up into the sky as far as I could see, without losing any of its needlelike thinness—a very perplexing thing. It was moving around slowly as if it were questing for something. For a shivery moment I had the feeling it came from the stars and was looking for me.

I was about to call John when it winked out. I'm sorry he didn't see it. He tells me it must have been an auroral manifestation, but it certainly didn't look anywhere near that far away—I believe auroras are supposed to be high in the stratosphere, where the air is as rarified as in a fluorescent tube—and besides I always thought they were blotchy. However, I suppose he must be right—he tells me he's seen some very queer ones in past years, and of course my own experience of them is practically nil.

I asked him if there mightn't be some secret military research going on nearby—perhaps with atomic power or some new kind of searchlight or radar beam—but he scouted the idea.

Whatever it was, it stimulated my imagination. Not that I need it! I'm almost worried by the degree to which my mind has come alive during my few hours at Lone Top. I'm afraid my mind is becoming too keen, like a knife with such a paper-thin edge that it keeps curling over whenever you try to cut something....

Jan. 9: At last, after several false starts, I've made a real beginning. I've pictured my monsters holding conclave at the bottom of a fantastically deep crack or canyon in their midnight planet. Except for a thin, jagged-edged ribbon of stars overhead, there is no light—their hoard of radiation is so depleted that ages ago they were forced to stop wasting any of it on the mere luxury of vision. But their strange eyes have become accommodated to starlight (though even they, wise as they are, do not know how to get any real warmth out of it) and they can perceive each other vaguely—great woolly, spidery shapes crouched on the rocks or draped along the ragged walls. It is unimaginably cold there— their insulating fur is bathed in a frigidity akin to that of interstellar space. They communicate by means of though—infrequent, well- shaped thoughts, for even thinking uses up energy. They recall their glorious past—their spendthrift youth, their vigorous prime. They commemorate the agony of their eon-long battle against the cold. They reiterate their savage and unshakable determination to survive.

It's a good piece of writing. Even honest John says so, although twitting me sardonically for writing such a wild sort of tale after many years of politely scorning his fantastic stories.

But it was pretty bad for a while there, when I was making those false starts—I began to see myself crawling back in defeat to the grinning city. I can confess now that for years I've been afraid that I never had any real creative ability, that my promising early fragments were just a freak of childhood. Children show flashes of all sorts of odd abilities which they lose when they grow up— eidetic imagery, maybe even clairvoyance, things of that sort. What people praised in those first little stories of mine was a rich human sympathy, an unusually acute insight into adult human motives. And what I was afraid of was that all this had been *telepathy*, an unconscious picking up of snatches of thought and emotion from the adult minds around me— things that sounded very genuine and impressive when written down, especially by a child, but that actually required no more creative ability than taking dictation. I even developed an acute worry that some day I'd find myself doing automatic writing! Odd, what nonsensical fears an artist's mind will cook up when it's going through a dry period—John says it's true of the whole fraternity.

At any rate, the book I'm now writing disposes in a laughably complete fashion of that crazy theory. A story about fabulous monsters on a planet dozens of light-years away can't very well be telepathy!

I suppose it was the broadcast last night that started me thinking again about that silly old notion. The broadcast wasn't silly though—a singularly intelligent discussion of future scientific possibilities—atomic energy, brain waves, new methods of radio transmission, that sort of thing—and not popularized for an oafish audience, thank God. Must be a program of some local university—John says *now* will I stop disparaging all educational institutions not located in the east!

My first apprehensions about the radio turned out to be completely groundless—I ought to have known that John isn't the sort of person to go in for soap operas and jazz. He uses the instrument intelligently—just a brief daily news summary (*not* a long-winded "commentary"), classical music when available, and an occasionally high-grade lecture or round-table discussion.

Last night's scientific broadcast was new to him though— he was out at the time and didn't recognize the station from my description.

I'm rather indebted to that program. I think it was while listening to it that the prologue of my story "jelled." Some chance word or thought provided a crystallization point for my ideas. My mind had become sufficiently fatigued—probably a reaction to my earlier over-keenness—for my churning ideas to settle into place. At any rate, I was suddenly so tired and groggy that I hardly remembered the finish of the program or John coming in or my piling off to bed. John said I looked out on my feet. He thought I'd taken a bit too much, but I referred him to the impartial judgement of the whiskey bottle, and its almost unchanged level refuted the base calumny!

In the morning I woke up fresh as a youngster and ripped off the prologue as if I'd been in the habit of turning out that much writing daily for the past ten years!

Had another snowshoe lesson today and didn't do much better— I grudge all time spent away from my book. John says I really ought to hurry up and learn, in case anything should happen to him while we were cut off from Terrestrial—small chance with reliable John! The radio reports a big blizzard farther east, but so far it hasn't touched us—the sun is bright, the sky dark blue. A local cold snap is predicted.

But what do I care how long I'm confined to the cabin. I have begun to create my monsters!

That night: I'm vindicated! John has just seen my violet beam, confirmed its non-auroral nature, and gone completely overboard as to its nearness—he claimed at first that it was actually hitting the cabin!

He was approaching from the south when he saw it— apparently striking the roof in a corruscation of ghostly violet sparks. He hurried up, calling to me excitedly. It was a moment before I heard him—I'd just caught the mumbly beginning of what seemed to be another of those interesting scientific broadcasts (must be a series) and was trying to tune in more clearly and having a hard time, the radio being mulish or my own manipulations inadequate.

By the time I got outside the beam had faded. We spent several chilly minutes straining our eyes in all directions, but saw nothing except the stars.

John admits now that the beam seeming to strike the roof must have been an optical illusion, but still stoutly insists that it was fairly near. I have become the champion of the auroral theory! For, thinking it over, I can see that the chances are it is some bizarre auroral phenomenon—Arctic and Antarctic explorers, for instance, have reported all sorts of peculiar polar lights. It is very easy to be deceived as to distance in this clear atmosphere, as John himself has said.

Or else—who knows?—it might be some unusual form of static electricity, something akin to St. Elmo's fire.

John has been trying to tune in on the program I started to catch, but no soap. There seems to be a lot of waily static in that sector of the dial. He informs me in his sardonic way that all sorts of unusual things have begun to happen since my arrival!

John has given up in disgust and is going to bed. I think I'll follow his example, though I may have another try at the radio first—my old dislike of the brute is beginning to fade, now that it's my only link with the rest of the world.

Next morning—the 10th: We've got the cold snap the radio predicted. I don't notice much difference, except it took longer to get the place warm and everything was a little tightened up. Later on I'm going to help John split firewood—I insisted on it. He enquired with mild maliciousness whether I'd succeeded where he failed at catching the tail-end of that scientific broadcast—said the last thing he heard going to sleep was moany static. I admitted that, as far as I knew, I hadn't—sleep must have struck the sledge-hammer blow it favors in this rugged locality while I was still twisting the dial; my memories of getting to bed are rather blurry, though I vaguely recall John sleepily snarling at me, "For God's sake turn down the radio."

We did run across one more odd phenomenon, though—or something that could pass for an odd phenomenon with a little grooming. In the middle of breakfast I noticed John looking intently over my shoulder. I turned and after a moment saw that it was something in the frost on the window by the radio. On closer examination we were considerably puzzled.

There was a queer sinuous pattern in the frost. It was composed of several parallel rows of tiny, roughly triangular humps with faint, hairlike veins going out to either side, all perceptibly thicker than the rest of the frost. I've never seen frost deposited in a pattern like it. The nearest analogy that occurs to me—not a very accurate one—is a squid's tentacle. For some reason there comes to my mind that description in *King Lear* of a demon glimpsed peering down from a cliff: "Horns whelk'd and wav'd like the enridged sea." I got the impression the pattern had been formed by an object *even colder than the frost* resting lightly against the glass, though that of course is impossible.

I was surprised to hear John say he thought the pattern was in the glass itself, but by scraping off a portion of the frost he did reveal a very faint bluish or lavender pattern which was rather similar.

After discussing various possibilities, we've decided that the cold snap—one of the most sudden in years, John says—brought out a latent imperfection in the glass, touching off some change in molecular organization that absorbed enough heat to account for the difference in thickness of the frost. The same change producing the faint lavender tint—if it wasn't there before.

I feel extraordinarily happy and mentally alive today. All these "odd phenomena" I've been noting down don't really amount to a hoot, except to show that a sense of strangeness, a delightful feeling of adventurous expectancy, has come back into my life— something I thought the city had ground out of me forever, with its blinkered concentration on "practical" matters, its noisy and faddish narrow-mindedness.

Best of all, there is my book. I have another scene all shaped in my mind.

Before supper: I've struck a snag. I don't know how I'm going to get my monsters to Earth. I got through the new scene all right— it tells how the monsters have for ages been greedily watching the Earth and several other habitable planets that are nearby (in light-years). They have telescopes which do not depend on lenses, but amplify the starlight just as a radio amplifies radio waves or a public address system the human voice. Those telescopes are extraordinarily sensitive—there are no limits to what can be accomplished by selection and amplification—they can see houses and people—they tune in on wave-lengths that are not distorted by our atmosphere—they catch radio-type as well as visual-type waves, and hear our voices—they make use of modes of radiation which our scientists have not yet discovered and which travel at many times the speed of the slower modes, almost instantaneously.

But all this intimate knowledge of our daily life, this

interplanetary voyeurism, profits them not in the least, except to whet their appetites to a bitter frenzy. It does not bring them an iota of warmth; on the contrary, it is a steady drain on their radiation bank. And yet they continue to spy minutely on us... watching... waiting... for the right moment.

And that's where the rub comes. Just what is this right moment they are waiting for? How the devil are they ever going to accomplish the trip? I suppose if I were a seasoned science-fiction writer this difficulty wouldn't even faze me—I'd solve it in a wink by means of space-ships or the fourth dimension, or what not. But none of those ideas seem right to me. For instance, a few healthy rocket blasts would use up what little energy they have left. I want something that's really plausible.

Oh well, mustn't worry about that—I'll get an idea sooner or later. The important thing is that the writing continues to hold up strongly. John picked up the last few pages for a glance, sat down to read them closely, gave me a sharp look when he'd finished, remarked, "I don't know what *I've* been writing science-fiction for, the past fifteen years," and ducked out to get an armful of wood. Quite a compliment.

Have I started on my real career at last? I hardly dare ask myself, after the many disappointments and blind alleys of those piddling, purposeless city years. And yet even during the blackest periods I used to feel that I was being groomed for some important or at least significant purpose, that I was being tested by moods and miseries, being held back until the right moment came.

An illusion?

Jan. 11: This is becoming very interesting. More odd patterns in the frost and glass this morning—a new set. But at twenty below it's not to be wondered that inorganic materials get freakish. What an initial drop in temperature accomplished, a further sudden drop might very well repeat. John is quite impressed by it though, and inclined to theorize about obscure points in physics. Wish I could recall the details of last night's scientific broadcast—I think something was said about low temperature phenomena that might have a bearing on cases like this. But I was dopey as usual and must have dozed through most of it—rather a shame, because the beginning was very intriguing: something about wireless transmission of power and the production of physical effects at far distant points, the future possibilities of some sort of scientific "teleporta- tion." John refers sarcastically to my "private university"—he went to bed early again and missed the program. But he says he half woke at one time and heard me listening to "a lot of nightmarish static" and sleepily implored me either to tune it better or shut it off. Odd—it seemed clear as a bell to me, at least the beginning did, and I don't remember him shouting at all. Probably he was having a nightmare. But I must be careful not to risk disturbing him again. It's funny to think of a confirmed radio-hater like myself in the role of an offensively noise-hungry "fan."

I wonder, though, if my presence is beginning to annoy John. He seemed jumpy and irritable all morning, and suddenly decided to get worried about my pre-bedtime dopeyness. I told him it was the natural result of the change in climate and my unaccustomed creative activity. I'm not used to physical exertion either, and my brief snowshoeing lessons and woodchopping chores, though they would seem trivial to a tougher man, are enough to really fag my muscles. Small wonder if an overpowering tiredness hits me at the end of the day.

But John said he had been feeling unusually sleepy and sluggish himself toward bedtime, and advanced the unpleasant hypothesis of carbon monoxide poisoning—something not to be taken lightly in a cabin sealed as tightly as this. He immediately subjected stove and fireplace to a minute inspection and carefully searched both chimneys for cracks or obstructions, inside and out. Despite the truly fiendish cold—I went outside to try and help him, arid got a dose of it—brr! The surrounding trackless snowfields looked bright and inviting, but to a man afoot—unless he were a seasoned winter veteran— lethal!

Everything proved to be in perfect order, so our fears were allayed. But John continued to rehearse scare stories of carbon monoxide poisoning, such as the tragic end of Andre's balloon expedition to the Arctic, and remained fidgety and restless—and all of a sudden he decided to snowshoe into Terrestrial for some spare radio parts and other unnecessary oddments. I asked him wasn't the bi-weekly trudge down to meet the farmer's car enough for him, and why in any case pick the coldest day of the year? But he merely snorted, "That all you know about our weather?" and set out. I'm a bit bothered, though he certainly must know how to take care of himself.

Maybe my presence does upset him. After all, he's lived alone here for years, except for infrequent trips—practically a hermit.

Having someone living with him may very well disorder his routine of existence—and of creative work—completely. Added to that, I'm another writer—a dangerous combination. It's quite possible that, despite our friendship (friendship would have nothing to do with it), I get on his nerves. I must have a long talk with him when he returns and sound him out on this—indirectly, of course.

But now to my monsters. They have a scene that is crying out in my brain to be expressed.

Later: The snag in my writing is developing into a brick wall. I can't seem to figure out *any* plausible way of getting my monsters to Earth. There's a block in my mind whenever I try to think in that direction. I certainly hope it's not going to be the way it was with so many of my early stories—magnificently atmospheric prologues that bogged down completely as soon as I was forced to work out the mechanics of the plot; and the more impressive and evocative the beginning, the more crushing the fall—and the more likely it would be to hinge on some trifling detail that persisted in thwarting my inventiveness, such as how to get two characters introduced to each other or how does the hero make a living.

Well, I won't let it defeat me this time! I'll go right ahead with the later portion of the story, and then sooner or later I'll just *have* to think through the snag.

I thought I had the thing licked when I started this noon. I pictured the monsters with a secret outpost established on Earth. Using Earth's energy resources, they are eventually able to work out a means of transporting their entire race here—or else dragging off the Earth and Sun to their own dead solar system and sacred home planet across the trackless light-years of interstellar space, like Prometheus stealing fire from heaven, humanity being wiped out in the process.

But, as should have been obvious to me, that still leaves the problem of getting the outpost here.

The section about the outpost looks very good though. Of course the pioneer monsters will have to keep their presence hidden from humanity while they "try out" our planet, become acclimated to Earth, develop resistance to inimical bacteria strains, et cetera, and measure up man from close range, deciding on the best weapons to use against him when the time for extermination arrives.

For it won't be entirely a one-sided struggle. Man won't be

completely powerless against these creatures. For instance, he could probably wipe out the outpost if he ever discovered its existence. But of course that won't happen.

I envisage a number of shivery scenes—people getting glimpses of the monsters in far, lonely places—seeing spidery, shadowy shapes in deep forests—coming on hurriedly deserted mountain lairs or encampments that disturbingly suggest neither human beings nor animals—strange black swimmers noted by boats off the usual steamship lanes—engineers and scientists bothered by inexplicable drains on power lines and peculiar thefts of equipment—a vague but mounting general dread—the "irrational" conviction that we are being listened to and spied on, "measured for our coffins"—eventually, as the creatures grow bolder, dark polypous forms momentarily seen scuttling across city roofs or clinging to high walls in the more poorly lighted sections, at night—black furry masks pressed for an instant against windowpanes—

Yes, it should work out very nicely.

I wish John would get back though. It's almost dark, and still no sign of him. I've popped out several times for a look-see, but there's nothing except his snowshoe tracks going over the hill. I confess I'm getting a bit edgy. I suppose I've frightened myself with my own story—it wouldn't be the first time that's happened to a writer. I find myself looking quickly at the window, or listening for strange sounds, and my imagination insists on playing around unpleasantly with the "odd phenomena" of the past few days—the violet auroral beam, the queer patterns in the frost, my silly notions about telepathic powers. My mental state is extraordinarily heightened and I have the illusion, both pleasurable and frightening, of standing at the doorway of an unknown alien realm and being able to rend the filmy curtain with a twitch of my finger if I choose.

But such nervousness is only natural, considering the isolation of the place and John's delay. I certainly hope he isn't going to snowshoe back in the dark—at a temperature like this any accident or misjudgement might have fatal consequences. And if he did get into trouble I wouldn't be any help to him.

As I get things ready for supper, I keep the radio going. It provides a not unpleasant companionship.

Jan. 12: We had quite a high old time last night. John popped in well past the supper hour—he'd gotten a ride with his farmer.

He had a bottle of fantastically high-proof rum with him (he says when you have to pack your liquor, you want as much alcohol and as little water as possible) and after supper we settled down for a long palaver. Oddly I had trouble getting into the spirit of the evening. I was restless and wanted to be fiddling with my writing, or the radio, or something. But the liquor helped to lull such nervous impulses, and after a while we opened our minds to each other and talked about everything under the sun.

One thing I'm glad we settled: any ideas I had about my presence annoying John are pure moonshine. He's pleased to have a comrade out here, and the fact that he's doing me a big favor really makes him feel swell. (It's up to me not to disappoint his generosity.) And if any further proof were needed, he's started a new story this morning (said he's been mulling it in his mind the past couple of days—hence his restlessness) and is typing away at it like sixty!

I feel very normal and down-to-earth this morning. I realize now that during the past few days I have been extraordinarily keyed up, both mentally and imaginatively. It's rather a relief to get over a mental binge like that (with the aid of physical binge!) but also faintly depressing—a strange bloom rubbed off things. I find my mind turning to practical matters, such as where am I going to sell my stories and how am I going to earn a living writing when my small savings give out? John and I talked about it for quite a while.

Well, I suppose I should be getting to my writing, though for once I'd rather knock around in the snow with John. The weather's moderated.

Jan. 13—evening: Got to face it—my writing has bogged down completely. It's not just the snag—I can't write *anything* on the story. I've torn up so damn many half pages! Not a single word rings true, or even feels true while I'm writing it—it's all fakey. My monsters are miserable puppets or papier-mâch and moth- eaten black fur.

John says not to worry, but *he* can talk that way—*his* story is going great guns; he put in a herculean stint of typing today and just now rolled into bed after a couple of quick drinks.

I took his advice yesterday, spent most of the day outdoors, practicing snowshoeing, chopping wood, et cetera. But it didn't make me feel a bit keener this morning.

I don't think I should have congratulated myself on getting

over my "mental binge." It was really my creative energy. Without it, I'm no good at all. It's as if I had been "listening" for my story and contact had been suddenly broken off. I remember having the same experience with some of my earlier writing. You ring and ring, but the other end of the line has gone dead.

I don't think the drinking helps either. We had another bottle session last night—good fun, but it dulls the mind, at least mine. And I don't believe John would have stopped at a couple even this evening, if I hadn't begged off.

I think John is worried about me in a friendly way-considers me a mild neurotic case and dutifully plies me with the more vigorous animal activities, such as snowshoeing and boozing. I catch a clinical look in his eyes, and then there's the way he boosts the "healthy, practical outlook" in our conversations, steers them away from morbid topics.

Of course I'm somewhat neurotic. Every creative artist is. And I did get a bit up in the air when we had our carbon monoxide scare—but so did he! Why the devil should he try to inhibit my imagination? He must know how important it is to me, how crucial, that I finish this story.

Mustn't force myself, though. That's the worst thing. I ought to turn in, but I don't feel a bit sleepy. John's snoring—damn him!

I think I'll fish around on the radio—keep it turned low. I'd like to catch another of those scientific programs—they stimulate my imagination. Wonder where they come from? John brought a couple of papers and I looked through the radio sections, but couldn't find the station.

Jan. 14: I'd give a good deal to know just what's happening here. More odd humpy patterns this morning—there's been another cold snap—and they weren't altogether in the frost. But first there was that crazy dual sleepwalking session. There may be something in John's monoxide theory—at any rate *some* theory is needed.

Late last night I awoke sitting up, still fully clothed, with John shaking me. There was a frozen, purposeful look on his face, but his eyes were closed. It was a few moments before I could make him stop pushing at me. At first he was confused, almost antagonistic, but after a while he woke up completely and told me that he had been having a fearful nightmare.

It began, he said, with an unpleasant moaning, wailing sound that had been torturing his ears for hours. Then he seemed to wake up and see the room, but it was changed—it was filled with violet sparks that showered and fell and rose again, ceaselessly. He felt an extreme chill, as of interstellar space. He was seized by the fear that something horrible was trying to get into the cabin. He felt that somehow I was letting it in, unknowingly, and that he must get to me and make me stop, but his limbs were held down as if by huge weights. He remembers making an agonizing, protracted effort.

For my part, I must have fallen asleep at the radio. It was turned on low, but not tuned to any station.

The sources of his nightmare are pretty obvious: the violet auroral beam, the "nightmarish" (prescient!) static of a few evenings ago, the monoxide fear, his partially concealed worry about me, and finally the rather heavy drinking we've both been doing. In fact, the whole business is nothing so terribly out of the way, except for the tracks—and how, or why, they should tie in with the sleepwalking session I haven't the ghost of an idea.

They were the same pattern as before, but much thicker— great ridgy welts of ice. And I had the odd illusion that they exuded a cold more intense than that of the rest of the frost. When we had scraped them away—a difficult job—we saw that the glass reproduced the pattern more distinctly and in a more pronounced hue. But strangest of all, we have traced what certainly seems to be a faint continuation on the inner windowsill, where the tracks take the form of a cracking and *disintegration* of the paint—it flakes off at a touch and the flakes, faintly lavender, crumble to powder. We also think we've found another continuation on the back of the chair by the window, though that is problematic.

What can have produced them is completely beyond us. Conceivably one of us might have "faked" them in some bizarre sleepwalking state, but how?—there's no object in the cabin that could produce that sinuous, chainy pattern with hairlike border. And even if there were, how could we possibly use it to produce a ridged pattern? Or is it possible that John is engineering an elaborate practical joke—no, it couldn't be anything like that!

We carefully inspected the other windows, including the one in the storeroom, but found no similar patterns.

John is planning to remove the pane eventually and submit it to a physicist for examination. He is very worked up about the thing. I can't quite make him out. He almost seems frightened. A few minutes ago he vaguely suggested something about our going into Terrestrial and rooming there for a few days.

But that would be ridiculous. I'm sure there's nothing inexplicable about this business. Even the matter of the tracks must have some very simple explanation that we would see at once if we were trained physicists.

I, for one, am going to forget all about it. My mind's come alive on the story again and I'm itching to write. Nothing must get in the way.

After supper: I feel strangely nervous, although my writing is going well again, thank God! I think I've licked the snag! I still don't see how I'm going to get my monsters to the Earth, but I have the inward conviction that the right method will suddenly pop into my mind when the time comes. Irrational, but the feeling is strong enough to satisfy me completely.

Meanwhile I'm writing the sections immediately before and after the first monster's arrival on Earth—creeping up on the event from both sides! The latter section is particularly effective. I show the monster floundering around in the snow (he naturally chooses to arrive in a cold region, since that would be the least unlike the climate of his own planet). I picture his temporary bewilderment at Earth's radiation storms, his awkward but swift movements, his hurried search for a suitable hiding place. An ignorant oaf glimpses him or his tracks, tells what he has seen, is laughed at for a superstitious fool. Perhaps, though, the monster is forced to kill someone....

Odd that I should see all that so clearly and still be completely blind as to the section immediately preceding. But I'm convinced I'll know tomorrow!

John picked up the last pages, put them down after a moment. "Too damned realistic!" he observed.

I should be pleased, and yet now that I'm written out for the day I suddenly find myself apprehensive and—yes—frightened. My tired, overactive mind persists in playing around in a morbid way with the events of last night. I tell myself I'm just frightening myself with my story, "pretending" that it's true—as an author will—and carrying the pretense a little too far.

But I'm very much afraid that there's more to it than that— some actual thing or influence that we don't understand.

For instance, on rereading my previous entries in this diary,

I find that I have omitted several important points—as if my unconscious mind were deliberately trying to suppress them.

For one thing, I failed to mention that the color in the glass and on the windowsill was identical with that of the violet beam.

Perhaps there is a natural connection—the beam a bizarre form of static electricity and the track its imprint, like lightning and the marks it produces.

This hint of a scientific explanation ought to relieve me, I suppose, but it doesn't.

Secondly, there's the feeling that John's nightmare was somehow partly real.

Thirdly, I said nothing about our instant fear, as soon as we first saw the patterns in the frost, that they had been produced by some, well, creature, though how a creature could be colder than its environment, I don't know. John said nothing, but I knew he had exactly the same idea as I: that a groping something had rested its chilled feeler against the windowpane.

The fear reached its highest pitch this morning. We still hadn't opened our minds to each other, but as soon as we had examined the tracks, we both started, as if by unspoken agreement, to wander around. It was like that scene reproduced so often in movies—two rivals are looking for the girl who is the object of their affections and who has coyly gone off somewhere. They begin to amble around silently, upstairs and down, indoors and out. Every once in a while they meet, start back a bit, nod, and pass each other by without a word.

That's how it was with John and me and our "creature." It wasn't at all amusing.

But we found nothing.

I can tell that John is as bothered by all this as I am. However, we don't talk about it—our ideas aren't of the sort that lend themselves to reasonable conversation.

He says one thing—that he wants to see me in bed first tonight. He's taking no chances of a repetition of the events that led up to the sleepwalking session. I'm certainly agreeable—I don't relish an experience like that any more than he does.

If only we weren't so damnably isolated! Of course, we could always get into Terrestrial at a pinch—unless a blizzard cut us off. The weatherman hints at such a possibility in the next few days.

John has kept the radio going all day, and I must confess I'm wholeheartedly grateful. Even the inanest program creates an illusion of social companionship and keeps the imagination from wandering too far.

I wish we were both in the city.

Jan. 15: This business has taken a disagreeable turn. We are planning to get out today.

There is a hostile, murderous being in the cabin, or somehow able to enter it at will without disturbing a locked door and tight-frozen windows. It is something unknown to science and alien to life as we know it. It comes from some realm of eternal cold.

I fully understand the extraordinary implications of those words. I would not put them down if I did not think they were true.

Or else we are up against an unknown natural force that behaves so like a hostile, murderous being that we dare not treat it otherwise.

We are waiting for the farmer's car, will ride back with him. We considered making the trip afoot, setting out at once, but John's injury and my inexperience decided us against it.

We have had another sleepwalking session, only this one did not end so innocuously.

It began, so far as we are able to reconstruct, with John's nightmare, which was an exact repetition of the one he had the night before, except that all the feelings, John says, were intensified.

Similarly, my first conscious sensations were of John shaking me and pushing at me. Only this time the room was in darkness, except for red glints from the fireplace.

Our struggle was much more violent. A chair was overturned. We slewed around, slammed against the wall, the radio slid to the floor with a crash.

Then John quieted. I hurried to light the lamp.

As I turned back, I heard him grunt with pain.

He was staring stupidly at his right wrist.

Encircling it like a double bracelet, deeply indenting it, were marks, like those in the frost.

The indented flesh was purplish and caked with frozen blood.

The flesh to either side of the indentation was white, cold to my touch, and covered with fine hairlike marks of the same violet hue as in the beam and the glass.

It was a minute before the crystals of blood melted.

We disinfected and bandaged the wound. Swabbing with the disinfectant had no effect on the violet hairlines.

Then we searched the cabin without result, and while waiting for morning, decided on our present plans.

We have tried and tried to reconstruct what else happened. Presumably I got up in my sleep—or else John pulled me out of bed—but then... ?

I wish I could get rid of the feeling that I am unconsciously in league with the being or force that injured John—trying to let it in.

Strangely, I am just as eager as yesterday to get at my writing. I have the feeling that once I got started, I would be past the snag in no time. Under the circumstances, the feeling disgusts me. Truly, creative ability fattens on horror in a most inhuman fashion.

The farmer's car should be here any minute. It looks dark outside. I wish we could get a weather broadcast but the radio is out of commission.

Later: Can't possibly get away today. A tremendous blizzard literally burst on us a few minutes after I finished writing the last entry. John tells me he was almost certain it was coming, but hoped it would miss us at the last moment. No chance of the farmer now.

The fury of the storm would frighten me, were it not for the other thing. The beams creak. The wind screams and roars, sucking heat out of the place. A freakishly heavy gust just no\v came down the fireplace chimney, scattering embers. We are keeping a bigger fire in the stove, which draws better. Though barely sunset, we can see nothing outside, except the meager reflections of our lights on the blasts and eddies of snow.

John has been busy repairing the radio, despite his bad hand—we must find out how long the storm is expected to last. Although I know next to nothing of the mechanism, I have been helping him by holding things.

Now that we have no alternative but to stay here, we feel less panicky. Already the happenings of last night are beginning to seem incredible, remote. Of course, there must be some unknown force loose in this vicinity, but now that we are on guard, it is unlikely that it can harm us again. After all, it has only showed itself while we were both asleep, and we are planning to stay awake tonight—at least one of us. John wants to watch straight through. I protested because of his wounded hand, but he says it doesn't hurt much—just a dull throb. It isn't badly swollen. He says it still feels as though it were faintly anaesthetized by ice.

On the whole the storm and the sense of physical danger it brings have had a stimulating effect on me. I feel eager to be doing something. That inappropriate urge to be working at my story keeps plaguing me.

Evening: About to turn in for a while. All of a sudden feel completely washed up. But, thank Heaven, the radio is going at last. Some ultra-inane program, but it steadies me. Weather report that the blizzard may be over tomorrow. John is in good spirits and on the alert. The axe—best weapon we can muster—leans against his chair.

Next day—Must put down coherent record events just as happened. *May need it*—though even if accused, don't see how they can explain how I made the marks.

Must stay in cabin! Blizzard means *certain* death. *It* can be escaped from—possibly.

Mustn't panic again. Think I escaped serious frostbite. No question about sprained or badly strained ankle. No one could get to Terrestrial. Crazy for me to try. Merest luck I found the cabin. Must keep myself in hand. Must! Even if it is here watching me.

To begin, last night. First—confused dreams snow and black spidery monsters—reflection of my book. Second—sleepwalking—blackness and violet sparks—John—violent surging movements—falling through space—breath of searing cold—crash—sudden pain—flood of white sparks—blackout.

Third—this morning. Weak—terribly feverish—staring at wall—pattern in grain of wood—*familiar*—pattern jumped to nearer surface—John's head and back—no surprise or horror, at first—muttered, "John's sick too. Gone to sleep on the floor, like me."—*recognized pattern.*

•Worked over him an hour—longer—hopeless—skull eaten in—hair dissolved—falls to powder at touch—violet lines—track twisted downward—shirt eaten through—spine laid bare—flesh near track snow white and icy to touch, much colder than cabin— trembling all the while, partly from cold—blizzard still raging—both fires out—got them going—searched cabin—John's body into storeroom—covered—coffee—crazy itch to write—tried to work on smashed radio—had to keep doing something—hands moving faster and faster—began to tremble—more and more—threw on clothes—strapped on snowshoes—out into the blizzard—full force of wind—knocked down twice—tried to go on by crouching—snowshoes tangled— down a third time—pain—struggled like something'd caught me—more pain—lay still—face lashed by ice—had to get back—crawled—crawled forever—no feeling—glimpsed open door of cabin, *behind* me—made it—

I must keep control of myself. I must keep my thoughts logical. Reconstruct!

John asleep. What made him sleep? Meanwhile, am I letting the thing in? How? He starts up suddenly. Struggles with the thing and me. Knocks me down. Is caught like Laocoon. Strikes with the axe. Misses. Hits the radio. No chance for a second blow. Squeezed, frozen, corroded to death.

Then? I was helpless. Why did it stop?

Is it sure of me and saving me for tonight? Or does it need me? At times I have the crazy feeling that the story I have been writing is true—that one of my monsters killed John—that I am trying to help them reach the Earth.

But that's mental weakness—an attempt to rationalize the incredible. This is not fantasy— it's *real* I must fight any such trends toward insanity.

I must make plans. As long as the blizzard lasts, I'm trapped here. It will try to get me tonight. I must keep awake. When the blizzard lifts, I can try smoke signals. Or, if my ankle improves, attempt it to Terrestrial along the road. The farmer ought to be coming by, though John did say that when the roads are blocked—John—

If only I weren't so completely alone. If only I had the radio.

Later: Got the radio going! A miracle of luck—I must have absorbed more knowledge than I realized, helping fix it yesterday. My fingers moved nimbly, as if they remembered more than my conscious mind, and pretty soon I had all the smashed parts replaced with spares.

It was good to hear those first voices.

The blizzard will end tonight, it is predicted.

I feel considerably reassured. I fully realize the dangers of the coming night, but I believe that with luck I'll be able to escape them.

My emotions are exhausted. I think I can face whatever comes, coolly and calmly.

I would be completely confident except for that persistent, unnerving feeling that a segment of my unconscious mind is under the control of something outside myself.

My chief fear is that I will yield to some sudden irrational impulse, such as the urge to write, which at times becomes incomprehensibly intense-I feel I *must* complete the "snag section" of my story.

Such impulses may be traps, to get me off guard.

I'll listen to the radio. Hope I find a good, steadying program. That fantastic urge to finish my story!

> *(The first lines of the next entry in Alderman's diary are wholly unintelligible—a frantic, automatic scribbling done in great haste. At several places the penpoint has penetrated the paper. Abruptly the message becomes coherent, although the writing speed seems, if anything, to increase. The transition is startling, as though a gibbering lunatic had suddenly put on the glib semblance of sanity. The change in person is also noteworthy, and obviously related to the last line of the preceding entry.)*

The spider-creature noted that contact had been reestablished and coolly asked for more power, although it meant draining the last reserves. It would not do to undershoot the mark this time— there was not enough left for another attempt.

They should succeed, however. The interfering biped had been eliminated, and the other biped was responding beautifully.

How long this moment had been anticipated! How many eons had been spent waiting for the emergence of sufficiently intelligent animals on that faraway planet and their development of adequate radiation exciters—maddeningly slow processes even with telepathic urging! How long, too, at the end, it had taken to select and mold one of the bipeds into a suitably sensitive subject! For a while it had seemed that he was going to escape them by hiding among the crude thought-storms of his duller fellows, but at last he had been tempted into the open. Conditions were right for the establishment of that delicate admixture of physical and mental radiations which opened the door between the stars and built the web across the cosmic chasms.

And now the spider-creature was halfway across that web. Five times already he had crossed it, only to be repulsed at the very end. He must not fail this time. The fate of the world hung on it.

The tractable biped's mind was becoming restive, though not as yet to an alarming degree. Because his conscious mind could not bear the reality of what he was doing, the biped was inscribing it as a fictional account—his customary rationalization.

And now the spider-creature was across the bridge. His transmuted flesh tingled as it began to reassemble, shuddered at the first radiation blasts of this raw, hot planet. It was like being reborn.

The biped's mind was in turmoil. Obviously the crasser, planet- tethered portion of it was straining to gain control and would soon over-power the more sensitive segment—but not soon enough. Dispassionately the spider-creature scanned it and noted: an almost unendurable horror, the intent to set fire to its habitation with an inflammable oil in an effort to injure the invader (that was good—it would destroy evidence), and the further intent to flee as soon as it regained control of its body (that must be prevented—the biped must be overtaken and eliminated; its story would not be believed, but alive it constituted a danger, nevertheless).

The spider-creature broke free, its crossing accomplished. As the mental portion of it underwent the final transformation, it felt its control of the biped's mind snap and it prepared for pursuit.

At that first moment of exultation, however, it felt a twinge of pity for the small, frantic, doomed animal that had helped alter so signally the destiny of its planet.

It could so easily have saved itself. It had only to have resisted one of the telepathic promptings. It had only to have maintained its previous detestation of the voice of the herd. It had only not to have undone the work of defensive sabotage its comrade, in dying, had achieved. It had only not to have repaired the radio.

Final Comment by Willard P. Cronin, M.D., Terrestrial, Montana: The fire at John Wendle's residence was noted at 3:00 A.M. on the morning of January 17th, shortly after the blizzard ended. I was a member of the party that immediately set out to render aid, and was among the first to sight the gutted cabin. In its ruin was discovered a single, badly- charred body, later identified as that of Wendle. There were indications that the fire had been started by the deliberate smashing of a kerosene lamp. It should be obvious to any rational person that Thomas Alderman's "diary" is the work of an insane mind, and almost certainly fabricated in an effort to shift to other and fabulous shoulders the guilt for a murderous crime, which he also sought to conceal entirely—by arson.

Interrogation of Alderman's former city associates confirms the picture of a weak-minded and antisocial dreamer, a miserable failure in his vocation. Very possibly the motive for his crime was jealousy of a fellow hackwriter who, although his stories were largely a puerile bilge of pseudoscience designed for immature minds, had at least some small financial success. As for the similarly childish "story" that Alderman claimed to be writing, there is no evidence that it even existed, though it is impossible, of course, to disprove that it did indeed exist and was destroyed in the fire.

Most unfortunately, some of the more lurid details of the "diary" have been noised around in Terrestrial, giving rise to scare stories among the more ignorant and credulous inhabitants.

It is equally unfortunate that an uneducated and superstitious miner named Evans, a member of the rescue party and of the group that followed Alderman's footprints away from the charred cabin, should have strayed from that group and shortly returned in panic with a wild account of having found a set of "big, sprawly, ropey tracks" paralleling Alderman's trail. Doubly unfortunate that a sudden resumption of the snowfall prevented his yarn from being disproved by such visual evidence as even the most brutish minds must accept.

It is no use pointing out to such low-grade mentalities that no reputable citizen of

Terrestrial has seen anything in the least out of the ordinary in the snowfields, that no unusual auroras whatever have been reported by meteorologists, and that there were no radio broadcasts which could possibly have agreed, either in hour or content, with those "scientific programs" of which Alderman made so much. With the exasperating and ludicrous consistency characteristic of epidemics of mass hallucination, stories of "strange tracks" in the snow and distant fleeting glimpses of "a big black spidery thing" continue to trickle in.

One wishes, with an understandably angry fervor, that the whole episode could have had the satisfying and all-decisive conclusion that the public trial of Thomas Alderman would have provided.

That, however, was not to be. About two miles from the cabin, the group following Alderman's footprints came upon his body in the snow. The expression on his frozen face was sufficient in itself to prove his insanity. One stiff hand, half buried in the snow, clutched the notebook containing the "diary." On the back of the other, which was clapped to his frosted eyes, was something that, although furnishing more fuel for the delusions of morons like Evans, provides the educated and scientific intellect with a clue as to the source of one of the more bizarre details in Alderman's fabrication.

This thing on the back of his hand obviously must have been a crude bit of tattooing, though so old and inexpertly done that the characteristic punctures and discrete dye granules were not apparent
A few wavy violet lines.

THE GHOST LIGHT

AFTERWARDS WOLF AND TERRI COULDN'T DECIDE whether little Tommy's slightly off-beat request about the green and blue night light (that later came to be called the ghost light) had come before or after the first dinner table talk about ghosts with the white- haired old man (Wolf's widowed professor emeritus father, Cassius Kruger, a four-years reformed alcoholic) in the living room of the latter's dark, too big, rather spooky house on the steep wooded hillside of canyon-narrow Goodland Valley up in Marin County just north of San Francisco that was subject to mud slides during seasons of heavy rain.

For one thing, there'd been more than one such conversation, scattered over several evenings. And they'd been quite low key and unscary, at least at first, more about memorable literary ghost stories than real or purported ghosts, so that neither Terri nor Wolf had been particularly worried about Tommy being disturbed by them.

Little Tommy Kruger was a solemn, precocious four-year-old whose rather adult speech patterns hadn't yet been corrupted by school and the chatter of other kids. Although not particularly subject to night terrors, he'd always slept with a tiny light of some sort in the room, more his mother's idea than his. In his bedroom at his grandfather's this was a small, weak bulb plugged in at floor level and cased in tiny panes of dark green and deep blue glass set in tin edges crafted in Mexico.

When in the course of the putting-to-bed ritual on the second or third (or maybe fourth) night of their visit Wolf knelt to switch on the thing, Tommy said, "Don't do that, Pa. I don't want it tonight."

Wolf looked up at his tucked-in son questioningly.

Terri had a thought based on her own unspoken feeling about the light. "Don't you like the colors, Tommy?" she asked. "Wolf, there's a plug-in fixture like this one, only with milky white glass, under that strange old painting of your mother in the living room. I'm sure your father wouldn't mind if we changed—"

"No, don't do that," Tommy interrupted. "I don't mind these colors at all, Ma, really. I just don't want a light tonight."

"Should I take this one away?" Wolf asked.

"No, don't do that, Pa, please. Leave it there, but don't turn it on. But leave the door to the hall open a little."

"Right," his father affirmed vigorously.

When good-night kisses were done and they were safely beyond Tommy's hearing, Wolf said, "I guess Tom's decided he's too grown up to need a light to sleep by."

"Maybe. Yes, I guess so," Terri agreed somewhat reluctantly. "But I'm glad it's off, anyhow. Loni said it gave the room a corpse look, and I thought so too." Loni Mills was Terri Kruger's attractive younger sister. She'd come with them on their visit to meet Wolf's father, but had decided the day before that she needed to get back to campus a couple of days before winter vacation ended at the Oregon college where she was a sophomore.

Terri added, frowning, "But why did he make a thing of your not taking the fixture away?"

"Obvious." Wolf grinned. "Little guy's keeping his options open. So if he should get scared, it's there to turn on. Good thinking. Also shows the colors don't bother him. Why'd Loni think of blue and green as corpse colors, I wonder?"

"You've seen a fresh drowned person, haven't you?" Terri responded lightly. "But why don't you ask Cassius that one? It's the sort of question gets him talking."

"Right," Wolf agreed without rancor. "Maybe I will."

And true enough, there'd been a couple of times during the visit (though not as many as Wolf had feared) when conversation had languished and they'd been grateful for any topic that would get it going again, such as oddities of psychology, Cassius' academic field, or ghost stories, in which they all seemed to share an interest. Matter of fact, the visit was for Wolf one of ultimate reconciliation with his father after a near-separation from both parents for a period of twenty years or so, while Terri was meeting her father- in-law, and Tommy his grandfather, for the first time.

The background for this was simply that the marriage of Wolf's father and mother, Cassius Kruger and Helen Hostelford, had progressively become, after Wolf's early childhood, a more and more unhappy, desperately quarrelsome, and alcoholic one, full of long, cold estrangements and fleeting reconciliations, yet neither partner had had the gumption to break it off and try something else. At the earliest teen age possible, Wolf (it was short for Wolfram, a fancy of his father) had wisely separated himself from them and largely gone it on his own, getting a degree in biology and working up a career in veterinary medicine and animal management, feeling his way through an unsuccessful early marriage and several living arrangements, until he'd met Terri. His mother's death several years back from a mixture of alcohol and barbiturate sleeping pills hadn't improved his relationship with his father—the opposite, rather, since he'd been somewhat closer to Helen and inclined to side with her in the unutterably wearisome marriage war—but then the old man, whom he'd expected to go downhill fast once he was alone, had surprised him by pulling out of his alcoholism (which had again and again threatened to end his academic career, another wearisomely repetitive series of crises) by the expedient of quitting drinking entirely and slowly rebuilding the wreckage of his body into at least a fairly good semblance of health.

Wolf had been able to keep tabs on his father's progress through letters he got from an old crony of his mother, a gossipy and humorous theatrical widow named Matilda "Tilly" Hoyt, who was also a Marin resident not far from Goodland Valley and kept in touch with the old man after Helen's death; and from infrequent, cold-bloodedly short hello-good-bye solo visits he paid Cassius to check up on him that came from a dim unwilling feeling of responsibility and from an incredulous and almost equally unwilling feeling of hope.

After several years, his father's repeated good showings, his own reawakening good memories from early childhood before the marriage war had started, the old man's seemingly sincere, even enthusiastic, interest in Wolf's profession and all his son's life, for that matter, plus some encouragement from Terri, worked a perhaps inevitable change in Wolf. He talked more with Cassius on his solo visits and found it good, and he began to

think seriously of accepting the old man's repeated invitation to
bring the new family to visit.

He talked it over first with Tilly Hoyt, though, calling on her
at her sunny cottage nearer the beach and the thundering, chill,
swift-currented Pacific than the treacherous brown hills which
rains could rumble.

"Oh, yes, he's changed, all right," she assured Wolf, "and as
far as the liquor goes, I don't think he's had a drop since two or
three months after Helen died. He's got some guilt there, I think,
which showed in odd ways after she died, like his bringing down
from the attic that weird painting of her by that crazy French-
Canadian—or was it Spanish-Mexican?—painter they used
to have around." She searched Wolf's eyes unhappily, saying,
"Cassius was pretty rough with Helen when he got very drunk,
but I guess you know about that."

Wolf nodded darkly.

She went on, "God knows I got my share of black eyes from
Pat when he was still around, the bum." She grimaced. "But I
gave as good as I got, I sincerely hope, and somehow though
we were fighting all the time, we were always making up a little
more of the time. But with Helen and Cassius anything like that
seemed to cut deeper, down to the bone, take longer to heal, they
were both such nice, idealistic, goofy, perfectionist people in their
ways, couldn't accept the violence that was in them. And the fault
wasn't always on Cassius' side. Your mother wasn't the easiest
person to get on with; she had a bitter streak, a cold-as-death
witch thing, but I guess you know that too. Anyway, now Cassius
is, well, what you might call... chastened." She curled her lip in
humorous distaste at the word and went on briskly, "I know he
wants to meet your new family, Wolf. Whenever I see him he talks
a lot about Tommy—he's proud as anything to be a grandfather,
and about Terri too, even Loni—he's always showing me their
pictures—and he positively makes a hero of you."

So Wolf had accepted his father's invitation for himself and
Terri and Tom and Loni, and everything had seemed to work
out fine from the start. The days were spent in outings around
the Bay, both north and south of the Golden Gate and east into
the Napa wine country and Berkeley-Oakland, outings in which
Cassius rarely joined and Wolf enjoyed playing tour guide, the
evenings in talking about them and catching up on the lost years
and comfortably growing a little closer. The old man had spread

himself and not only had his cavernous place cleaned up but also had the Latino couple, the Martinezes, who looked after it part time, stay extra hours and cook dinners. In addition he had a couple of neighbors over from time to time, while Tilly was an almost constant dinner guest, and he insisted on serving liquor while not partaking of it himself, though he did nothing to call attention to the latter. This so touched Wolf that he hadn't the heart to say anything about his father's almost constant cigarette smoking, though the old man's occasional emphysemic coughing fits worried him. But the other old people smoked too, Tilly especially, and on the whole everything went so well that neither Loni's premature departure nor the occasional silences that fell on their host cast much of a damper.

The talk about ghost stories had started just after dinner at the big table in the living room with the masklike painting of Wolf's mother Helen with the little white light below it, looking down on them from the mantelpiece on which there also stood the half dozen bottles of sherry, Scotch, and other liquors Cassius kept for his guests. The conversation had begun with the mention of haunted paintings when Wolf brought up Montague Rhodes James' story, "The Mezzotint."

"That's the one, isn't it," Terri had said helpfully, "where an old engraving changes over a couple of days when several different people look at it at different times, and then they compare notes and realize they've been witnessing the re-enactment of some horror that happened long ago, just before or just after the print was engraved?"

"You know, that's so goddam complicated," Tilly objected, but "Yes, indeed!" Cassius took up enthusiastically. "At first the ghost is seen from the rear and you don't know it's one; it's just a figure in a black hood and robe crawling across the moonlit lawn toward a big house."

"And the next time someone sees the picture," Wolf said, picking up the account, "the figure is gone, but one of the first-floor windows of the house is shown as being open, so that someone looking at the picture then observes, 'He must have got in.'"

"And then the next to last time they look at the picture and it's changed," Terri continued, "the figure's back and striding away from the house, only you can't see much of its face because of the hood, except that it's fearfully thin, and cradled in its arms it's got this baby it's kidnapped..." She broke off abruptly and a little uncertainly, noticing that Tommy was listening intently.

"And then what, Ma?" he asked.

"The last time the picture changes," his father answered for her, his voice tranquil, "the figure's gone and whatever it might have been carrying. There's just the house in the moonlight, and the moon."

Tommy nodded and said, "The ghost stayed inside the picture really, just like a movie. Suppose he could come out, sort of off the picture, I mean?"

Cassius frowned, lighting a cigarette. "Ambrose Bierce got hold of that same idea, Tommy, and he wrote a story, a shorter one, about a picture that changed, only as in the James story no one ever saw it at the moment it changed. The picture was mostly calm ocean with the edge of a beach in the foreground. Out in the distance was a little boat with someone in it rowing toward shore. As it got closer you could see that the rower was a Chinaman with long snaky moustaches—"

"Chinaperson," Loni corrected and bit her lip.

"Chinaperson," Cassius repeated with a nod and a lingering smile at her. "Anyhow as he beached the boat and came toward the front of the picture you could see he had a long knife. Next time someone looked at it, the picture was empty except for the boat in the edge of the wavelets. But the time after that the Chinaperson was back in the boat and rowing away. Only now lying in the stern of the boat was the corpse of the... person he'd killed. Now I suppose you could say he got out of the picture for a while."

Shaking his head a little, Tommy said, "That's good, but I don't mean that way 'zactly, Grandpa. I mean if you saw him step or float out of the picture, come *off* the picture like, same size and everything as in the picture."

"That would be something," Wolf said, catching his son's idea. "Mickey Mouse, say, mouse life-size—no, comic book size— waltzing around on the coffee table. That tiny, his squeak might be too high to hear."

"But Mickey Mouse isn't a ghost, Pa," Tommy objected.

"No," his grandfather agreed, "though I remember an early animation where he challenged a castle run by ghosts and fought a duel with a six-legged spider. But that surely is an interesting idea of yours, Tommy," he went on, his gaze roving around the room and coming to rest on the large reproduction of Picasso's "Guernica" that dominated one wall, "except that for some pictures," he said, "it wouldn't be so good if their figures came out of the frames and walked, or floated."

"I guess so," Tommy agreed, wrinkling his nose at the looming bull man and the other mad faces and somber patterns in Picasso's masterpiece.

Terri started to say something to him; then her eyes shifted to Cassius. Wolf was watching her.

Loni yielded to the natural impulse to look around at the other pictures, gauging their suitability for animation. She hesitated at the dark backgrounded one which showed the head only, all by itself like a Benda mask, of a rather young Helen Kruger with strange though striking flesh tones. She started to make a remark, but caught herself.

But Tommy had been watching her and, remembering something he'd overheard before dinner, guessed what she might have been going to say and popped out with, "I bet Grandma Helen would make a pretty green ghost if she came out of her frame."

"Tommy..." Terry began, while, "I didn't—" Loni started involuntarily to protest, when Cassius, whose eyes had flashed rekindling interest rather than hurt at Tommy's observation, cut in lightly and rapidly, yet with a strange joking or mocking intensity (hard to tell which) that soon had them all staring at him, "Yes, she would, wouldn't she? Tiny flakes of pink and green paint come crackling off the canvas without losing their configuration as a face.... Esteban always put a lot of, some said too much, green in his flesh—he said it gave it life.... Yes, a whole flight, or flock, or fester, or flutter, or flurry, yes *flurry* of greenish flakes floating off and round about in formation, swooping this way and that through the air, as though affixed to an invisible balloon responding to faintest air currents, a witches-sabbath swirling and swarming.... And then, who knows? Perhaps, their ghost venture done, settling rustlingly back onto the canvas so perfectly into their original position that not the slightest crack or faintest irregularity would be evidence of—"

He broke off suddenly as an inhalation changed into a coughing fit that bent him over, but before anyone had time to voice a remark or move to assist him, he had mastered it, and his strangely intent eyes searched them and he began to speak again, but in an altogether different voice and much more slowly.

"Excuse me, my dears. I let my imagination run away with me. You might call it the intoxication of the grotesque? I encouraged Tommy to indulge in it too, and I ask your pardons." He lit another cigarette as he went on speaking measuredly. "But let me say in extenuation of our behavior that Esteban Bernadorre was a very strange man and had some very strange ideas about color and light and pigments, strange even for a painter. Surely you must remember him, Wolf, though you weren't much older than Tommy here when that painting of Helen was executed."

"I remember Esteban," Wolf said, still studying his father uneasily and revolving in his mind the words the old man had poured out with such compulsive rapidity and then so calculatedly, as if reciting a speech, "though not so much about his being a painter as that he was able to fix a toy robot I'd broke, and that he rode a motorcycle, oh yes, and that I thought he must be terribly old because he had a few grey hairs."

Cassius chuckled. "That's right, Esteban had that mechanical knack so strange in an artist and always had some invention or other he was working on. In his spare time he panned for gold—oh, he was up to every sort of thing that might make him money—the gold-panning was partly what the motorcycle was for, to take him up into the little canyons where the little goldiferous streams are. I remember he talked about vibrations— vibes—before anyone else did. He used to say that all vibrations were one and that all colors were alive, only that red and yellow were the full life colors—blood and sunlight—while blue was the death, no, life-in-death color, the blue of empty sky, the indigo of outer space...." He chuckled again, reflectively. "You know," he said, "Esteban wasn't really much of a draftsman; he couldn't draw hardly anything worth a damn except faces; that's why he worked out that portrait technique of making faces like hanging Benda masks; that way he never got involved in hands or ears or other body parts he was apt to botch."

"That's strange," said Wolf, "because the only other one of his pictures I seem to remember now from those days—I think now that it had some influence on my life, my choice of profession— was one of a leopard."

Cassius' sudden laugh was excited. "You know, Wolf," he said, "I believe I've got that very picture up in the attic! Along with some other stuff Esteban asked me if he could store there. He was going to send for them or come back for them but he never did. In fact it was the last time I ever saw him, or heard from him for that matter. It's not a good picture, he never could sell it, the anatomy's all wrong and somehow a lot of green got into it that shouldn't have. I'll take you up and show it to you, Wolf, if you'd like. But tomorrow. It's too late tonight."

"That's right," Terri echoed somewhat eagerly. "Time for bed, Tommy. Time for bed long ago."

And later, when she and Wolf were alone in their bedroom, she confided in him, "You know, your father gave me a turn tonight. It was when he was talking about those dry flakes of green paint vibrating in the air in the shape of a face. He dwelt on them so! I think imagining them brought on his coughing fit."

"It could have," Wolf agreed thoughtfully.

The third-floor attic was as long as the house. Its front window seemed too high above the descending hillside, its rear one too close to it, shutting off the morning sunlight. Cassius piloted Wolf through the debris of an academic lifetime to where a half dozen canvases, some of them wrapped in brown paper, were stacked against the wall behind a kitchen chair on which rested a dust-filmed chunky black cylindrical object about the size and shape of a sealed-in electric generator.

"What's that?" Wolf asked.

"One of Esteban's crazy inventions," his father answered offhandedly, as he tipped the canvases forward one by one and peered down between them, hunting for the leopard painting, "some sort of ultrasonic generator that was supposed to pulverize crushed ore or, no, maybe agitate it when it was suspended in water and get the heavier gold flakes out that way, a mechanical catalyst for panning or placering, yes, that was it!" He paused in his peering search to look up at Wolf. "Esteban was much impressed by a wild claim of the aged Tesla (you know, Edison's rival, the inventor of alternating current) that he could build a small, portable device that could shake buildings to pieces, maybe set off local earthquakes, by sympathetic vibrations. That ultrasonic generator there, or whatever he called it, was Esteban's attempt in the same general direction, though with more modest aims—which is a sort of wonder in itself considering Esteban's temperament. Of course it never worked; none of Esteban's great inventions did." He shrugged.

"He fixed my robot," Wolf mused. Then, somewhat incredulously, his voice rising, "You mean he left it here with you, and the other stuff, and actually never came back for it, even wrote? And you didn't do anything about it either, write him at least?"

Cassius shrugged more broadly. "He was that sort of person. As for me, I think I tried to write him once or twice, but the letters came back. Or weren't answered." He smiled unhappily and said softly, "Alcohol's a great forgettery, you know, a great eraser, or at least blurrer, softener...." With a small gesture he indicated the shelves of books, the piled boxes of old files and papers between them and the ladder to the second floor. "Alcohol's washed through everything up here—the university, Helen, Esteban, all my past—and greyed it all. That's alcohol dust on the books." He chuckled and his voice briskened. "And now to things of today. Here's the picture I promised you."

He straightened himself, drew a canvas on which he'd been keeping his hand out of the stack with a flourish, wiped it off on his sleeve, and faced it to Wolf.

It was a medium-size oil painting, wider than high, of a golden leopard with black spots like tiny footprints, stretched out on a branch in a sea, a flood, of green leaves. You knew it was high in the tree because the branch was thin and the green sunlight the leaves transmitted was bright, so all-suffusingly bright that it gave a greenish cast to the leopard's sleek fur, Cassius had been right about that. And also about the bad anatomy too, for Wolf at once noted errors of muscle placement and underlying bony structure.

But the face! Or muzzle or mask, rather, that was as magnificent as memory had kept it for him, a wonderfully savage sensitive visage, watchful and wild, the quintessence of the feline....

Cassius was saying, "You can see he's even got the eyes wrong, giving them circular pupils instead of slits."

"In that one point he happens to be right," Wolf said, happy to get in a word for the man who, he was beginning to remember, had been something of a childhood hero to him. "The leopard does not have slit eyes like a house cat, but pupils exactly like ours. It's that detail which gives him a human look."

"Ah so," Cassius conceded. "I didn't know that. Live and learn. He should have painted just that, used the mask trick he did with his pictures of people."

Wolf's gaze and mind returned to the black object. He looked it over more closely without handling it, except to brush off dust here and there. "How the devil was it supposed to be powered? I can't see any place for plugging in wires, just the one switch on top, which indicates it was run by electricity."

"Batteries, I think he told me," the old man said, and, bolder or less cautious than his son, reached over and pushed the switch.

It was, at first, to Wolf holding it, as if a very distant unsuspected ponderous beast had roused and begun to tramp toward them across unimagined miles or light years. Under his hands the black cylinder shook a little, then began to vibrate faster and faster, while in his ears a faint buzzing became a humming and then a higher and higher pitched whine.

The unexpectedness of it paralyzed Wolf for a moment, yet it was he rather than his father who thrust back the switch and turned off the thing.

Cassius was looking at it in mild surprise and with what seemed to be a shade of reproach. "Well, fancy that!" he said lightly. "Esteban returning to us through his works. I never dreamed—This seems to be my morning for misjudging things."

"Batteries that last *twenty* or more years—?" Wolf uttered incredulously and then didn't know how to go on.

His father shrugged, which was not the answer Wolf was looking for, and said, "Look, I'm going to take this picture downstairs. I agree it has possibilities. Could you carry that... er... thing? I know it's too heavy for me, but perhaps we should have a look at it later. Or something..." he trailed off vaguely.

Wolf nodded curtly, thinking, *Yes, and shut it away safely where neither Tommy nor anyone else can get their eager little unthinking hands on it.* He found himself strangely annoyed by his father's irresponsibility, or over-casualness, or whatever it was. Up to now the old man had seemed to him such a *normal* sort of reformed or arrested alcoholic. But now—? He hefted the black cylinder. It *was* heavy.

He found himself wondering, as he followed the slow-moving Cassius to the front of the attic, what other time bombs there might be, in the old man's mind as well as the house, waiting to be detonated.

But his thoughts were somewhat diverted when he glanced out the front attic window. A short way down the hillside and to the side of the house amongst the nearest trees and further fenced by tall shrubs was a grassy bower that was bathed in sunlight and into which he could look down from his vantage point. Sprawled supine at its center on a long black beach towel was Loni clad in black wraparound sunglasses, a quite splendid sight which somehow reminded Wolf of a certain wariness Terri had had of her then thirteen-year-old sister during their courtship and also reminded him perhaps to tell the girl a cautionary tale or two about the Trailside Murderer who had terrified Marin County some years back.

When he got the black cylinder downstairs he set it, at Cassius' direction, on the high mantelpiece, which would at least put it out of Tommy's reach, and as an extra precaution taped the switch in the off position with two short lengths of friction adhesive. The old man had propped the painting on a straight-backed chair standing against the wall nearby.

Wolf's speculations about Cassius and the house were further driven from his mind, or to its shadowy outer reaches at any rate, by the day's activities when he drove Terri and Tommy up into Sonoma County through the Valley of the Moon to the Jack London Museum and led them through the big trees to the fire-darkened gaunt stone ruins of London's Wolf House. (Tommy made a solemn joke of calling it "Pa House," while Wolf promised to show him some real wolves at Golden Gate Park tomorrow.)

That must have been the day, Wolf figured out later, of Loni's impulsive departure for her Oregon college, for she wasn't there the next morning to hear Cassius' dream of the giant spider and Esteban (though Tilly was, who'd come over early to share their late breakfast). It was also the day when Weather confirmed that the big storm front building up in the North Pacific had veered south and was headed for San Francisco.

Cassius prefaced his account of the night's somnial pageantry with some nervous and veering verbal flamboyancies. He seemed a bit hollow-eyed and overwrought, as if sleep hadn't rested him and he were clowning around and gallumphing to hide the fact, and for the first time Wolf found himself wondering whether their visit hadn't begun to tire the old man.

"Never dream these days," Cassius grumbled, "just feelings and flashes, as I think I've told you, Terri, but last night I sure had a doozie. You brought it on me, Wolf, by making me go up to the attic and look at that old stuff of Esteban's I'd forgotten was there." He nodded toward the black cylinder and green-flooded leopard painting. "Yes, sir, Tommy, your Pa gave me one doozie of a dream." He paused, wrinkled his nose, and looked comically sideways at Wolf. "No, that isn't true at all, is it? I was the one who told you about it and led you up there. I brought it all on myself! See, Tommy, never trust what your Grandpa says, his mind's slipping.

"Anyhow," he launched out, "I was standing in the front attic window, which had become French windows nine feet tall with yellow silk drapes, and I was working away on a big kirschwasser highball. I sometimes drink in my dreams," he explained to Terri. "It's one of my few surviving pleasures. Sometimes wake up dream-drunk for a blessed moment or two.

"Around me in my dream the whole house was jumping, first floor, second floor, attic turned ballroom. People, lights, music, the tintinnabulation of alcoholic crystal. Benighted Goodland Valley resounded with the racket from stem to stern. Even the darkness jumped. I realized that your Grandma, Tommy, was giving one of her huge parties, to which she invited everyone and which generally bored me stiff." He looked surprised and tapped himself on his mouth. "That's another lie," he said. "I enjoyed those parties more than she did. She gave them just to please me. Keep remembering what I told you about trusting your Grandpa, Tommy.

"Anyway," he went on, "there I was carousing on the edge of nothing, leaning against the friendly dark outside, for the French windows were pure ha-ha." He explained to Tommy, "That's a place in a British fancy garden where there should be a flight of steps, but isn't. You start down it and—boomp. Hence ha-ha. Very funny. The British have a wonderfully subtle sense of humor.

"But in my dream I was gifted with an exquisite sense of balance. I could easily have walked a tightwire from where I was to the opposite crest of the valley, balancing myself with sips of kirsch and soda, if my dream had only provided one. But just then I felt something tug at my trousers, trying to topple me forward.

"I looked down at my leg, and there was a naked baby no higher than my knee, a beautiful cherub straight out of Tiepolo or Titian, but with a nasty look on her cute little face, yanking ineffectually at my pant leg with both hands. I looked straight down the outside of the house and saw, just below me way down there, a new cellar door of the slanting flat kind thrown wide open, revealing a short flight of steps leading down into the basement, from which light was pouring, as if the party were going on there too.

"But a green tinge in that light telegraphed 'Danger!' to my brain, and that was no lie for suddenly there was rearing out of the cellar up toward me a huge green and yellow spider with eight glaring jet black eyes and terribly long legs, the first pair so super long, like the two tentacular arms of a squid, that they could reach the attic.

"At that moment I felt something that made me look back at my leg, and I saw that the cherub had let go of my pants and was starting to overbalance and fall (she had no wings as a proper cherub should).

"With one hand I steadied the baby-skinned creature and with the back of the other (oh, my balance was positively miraculous) I knocked aside the spider leg that was about to touch the cherub.

"At the same instant I saw that the monster was only a large pillow toy made of lustrous stuffed velvet, the eyes circles of black sequins, and that the whole business was a put-on, a party joke on me."

Cassius took a swallow of cold coffee and lit another cigarette. "Well, that ended that part of the dream," he said, "and the next I knew I was standing on the dark hillside beside the house, the party still going on, and calculating how many inches the hill had shifted down and forward during the last rain (it never has, you know, not an iota) and wondering what the next rain was going to do to it—guess I was anticipating today's weather forecast—when I heard someone call my name softly.

"I looked down the hillside to the road and saw a small closed car, one of those early Austins or maybe a Hillman Minx, drawing up to park there. And, this is a funny part, although it was black night, I could see the driver silhouetted inside, as if by an impossibly belated sunset afterglow, and although he was wearing a big white motorcycle crash helmet I identified him at once—something about his posture, the way he held himself—as Esteban Bernadorre, whom I haven't seen for almost a quarter of a century.

"'Esteban?' I called hoarsely, and from the tiny car came the quiet, clipped, clearly enunciated response, 'Certainly, I will be happy to coffee with you, Cassius.'

"Next thing I knew I was walking uphill toward the house with Esteban close beside me. As we approached the open door, which was filled with a knot of animatedly conversing drinkers—a sort of overflow from the hubbub inside—I realized Esteban was still wearing his crash helmet, oversize gauntlets too, and that I still hadn't greeted him properly.

"Preparatory to introducing him to the others, I swung in front of him, offering my hand and trying to discern his face in the cavernous seeming helmet's depths. He drew off his gauntlet and shook hands. His hand was oversize, as its glove had been, and wet, gritty, and soft all at once. After shaking mine, he lifted his hand and made the motion of wiping the back of it across his eyes, and I saw it was composed of wet grey ashes except where the wiping motion had bared a narrow edge of pink flayed flesh. And at the same time I saw that his eyes were nothing but charred black holes, infinitely deep, and his whole face granular black char wet as the ashes.

"I swiftly turned to check how much, if anything, those in the door had seen, for we were now quite close to them. I saw that the centralmost carouser was Helen, my dear wife, looking very dashing in a silver lame evening dress.

"She said to me, gesturing impatiently with her empty glass, 'Oh, we're *quite* familiar with Esteban's boundless self-pity and self-dramatizing tricks. You should know him by now. He's forever parading his little wounds and making a big production of them.'

"At that moment I remembered that Helen was really dead, and that woke me up, as it generally does."

And with that Cassius blew out his breath in a humorously intended sigh of achievement and looked around for applause. Instead he encountered something close to stony gazes from Terri and Tilly too, Wolf looked both doubtful and slightly embarrassed, while Tommy's face had lost the excited smile it had had during the cherub-spider part of the dream, and the child avoided his grandfather's gaze. The four faces, for that matter, were a study in varieties of avoidance.

"Well," the old man grumbled apologetically after a moment, "I guess I should have realized beforehand that that was an X-rated dream. Not on account of sex or violence, but the horrifies, you might say. I'm sorry, ladies, I got carried away. Tommy, Gramps is not only a liar, he never knows when to stop. I thought my dream was a pretty good show, but I guess it overdid on the unexplained horrifies. They can be tricky, not to everyone's taste."

"That's true enough," Wolf said with a placating little laugh as Cassius went off into the kitchen to raise mild hell with the Martinezes about something. Wolf was glad to turn his attention to getting the day's drive to Golden Gate Park under way. That boiled down to plans for Tom and himself, since Terri decided she was tired from yesterday and wanted to gossip with Tilly, maybe drive over to the older woman's place. This didn't exactly displease Wolf, as the thought had struck him that Terri might be as tired as his father of their visit, maybe more so, and a day with Tilly Hoyt might set that right, and in any case give him time to rethink his own thoughts.

Tommy was uncommonly silent during the drive down, but a rowboat ride on Stow Lake and a visit to the buffaloes got him cheerful and moderately talkative again. Wolf couldn't produce any live wolves but at least found the kid a group of stuffed ones at the Academy of Sciences, while both of them enjoyed the speeding, circling dolphins at the Steinhart Aquarium, the only seemingly simplistic Bufano animal sculptures in the court outside, and the even more simplified, positively sketchy food in the cafeteria below.

Emerging in the court again, their attention was captured by the hurrying hungry clouds, which devoured the red skeletal Sutro TV tower as they watched.

"Pa, are clouds alive?" Tommy asked.

"They act that way, don't they?" Wolf agreed. "But, no, they're no more alive than, say, the ocean is, or mountains."

"They're made of snowflakes, aren't they?"

"Some of them are, Tom. Mostly high, feathery ones called cirrus. Those're made of ice flakes, you could say, tiny needles of ice. But these we're looking at are just water, billions of billions of tiny drops of water that sail through the air together."

"But drops of water aren't white, Pa. Milk clouds would be white."

"That's true, Tom, but the drops of water are tremendously tiny, droplets you call them, and at a distance they do look white when sunlight or just a lot of sky light hits them."

"What about small clouds, Pa, are they alive? I mean clouds small enough to be indoors, like smoke clouds or paint clouds, clouds of flakes or paint flakes. Grandpa can blow smoke clouds like he showed me."

"No, those clouds aren't alive either, Tom. And you don't say smoke flakes or paint flakes, though there might be flakes of soot in heavy smoke and you could blow a sort of cloud of droplets— droplets, not flakes—from a spraypaint can, but I wouldn't advise it."

"But Grandpa told about a little cloud of paint flakes flying off a picture."

"That was just in a story, Tom, and an imaginary story at that. Pretend stuff. Come on, Tom, we've looked at the sky enough for now."

But the day, which had started in sunlight, continued to grow more and more lowering until, after their visit to the Japanese Tea Garden, whose miniaturized world appealed to Tom and where he found a little bridge almost steep enough to be a ha-ha, Wolf decided they'd best head for home.

The rain held off until they were halfway across the Golden Gate If Bridge, where it struck in a great squally flurry that drenched and I locked the car, as if it were a wet black beast pouncing. And although they were happily ahead of thick traffic, the rain kept up all the way to Goodland Valley, so that Wolf was relieved to get his Volks into the sturdy garage next to Cassius' old Buick, and hurry up the pelting slippery hill with Tommy in his arms. During their absence, things had smoothed out at the old man's place, at least superficially; and mostly by simplification—the Martinezes had both departed early to their home in the Mission after getting dinner into the oven, while Tilly, who'd been going to stay for it, had decided she had to get to her place to see to its storm defenses so there were only the four of them that ate it.

By this time the rain had settled down to a steady beat considerably less violent than its first onset. Wolf could tell from Terri's manner that she had a lot she wanted to talk to him about, but only when they were alone, so he was glad the Golden Gate Park talk both lasted out the meal and trailed off quickly afterwards (while the black cylinder on the mantelpiece and the green leopard painting under it stood as mute signs of all the things they weren't talking about), so they could hurry Tommy, who was showing signs of great tiredness, off to bed, still without night light, say good-night to Cassius, who professed himself equally weary, and shut their bedroom door behind them.

Terri whipped off her dress and shoes and paced up and down in her slip.

"Boy, have I got a lot to tell you!" she said, eyeing Wolf excitedly, almost exultantly, somewhat frightenedly, and overall a bit dubiously.

"I take it this is mostly going to be stuff got from Tilly today?" he asked from where he sat half-reclining on the bed. "That's not to put it down. I've always trusted what she says, though she sure loves scandal."

Terri nodded. "Mostly," she said, "along with an important bit from Loni I've been keeping back from you, and some things I just worked out in my head."

"So tell," he said with more tranquility than he felt.

"I'll start with the least important thing," she said, approaching him and lowering her voice, "because in a way it's the most pressing, especially now that it's raining. Wolf, the hill under and back of this house—and all of Goodland Valley for that matter (they really should call it Goodland Canyon, it's so constricted and overhung!)—isn't anywhere near as stable as your father thinks it is, or keeps telling us it is. Why, every time a heavy rain keeps on, the residents are phoned warnings to get ready to evacuate, and sometimes the highway police come and make them, or try to. Wolf, there have been mudslides around the Bay that smashed through and buried whole houses, and people caught in them and their bodies never recovered. Right in places like this. There was a slide in Love Canyon, and in other places."

Wolf nodded earnestly, lips pressed together, eyeing his aroused wife. "That doesn't altogether surprise me. I've known about some of that and I certainly haven't believed everything Cassius has to say about the stability of this hillside, but there seemed no point in talking about it earlier."

She went on, "And Tilly says the last times there've been warnings, Cassius has gone down and stayed at her place. We've never heard a word about that. She says it looks like it might happen again, and we'll have to be ready to get out too."

"Of course. But the warnings haven't come yet and the rain seems to be tapering off. Oh, I guess Cassius is pretty much like the other residents in spots like this. Won't hear a word against their homes, they're safe as Gibraltar, anyone who says different is an alarmist from the city or the East or LA, an earthquake nut, but when the rains and warnings come, everything's different, no matter how quick they forget about it afterwards. Believe me, Terri, I could feel that myself when I drove back this afternoon and rushed up this soggy hill with Tom." He paused. "So what's the other stuff?"

She started to pace again, biting her lip, then stopped and eyed him defiantly. "Wolf," she said, "this is one of those things I can't talk about without cigarettes. And if you don't like it, too bad!"

"Go ahead and smoke," he directed her.

As she dug out a pack, ripped off its top, and lit up, she confessed, "I started smoking Tilly's when she was telling me things at her place, and when she drove me back here, I picked up a couple of packs on the way; I knew I'd be needing them.

"Well, look, Wolf, before Loni left she told me, after I'd agreed not to tell you, that one of the reasons she was leaving early was that your father had been... well... bothering her."

"You know, that doesn't altogether surprise me either," Wolf responded. "Depending, of course, on how far his bothering went and how she behaved." And he told Terri about seeing Loni sunbathing yesterday morning and how Cassius could have as easily seen her too, and probably did, finishing with "And, Terri, it was really a most stimulating sight: sweet black-masked nubility sprawled wide open to the wild winds and all that."

"The little fool!" Terri hissed, quickly supplementing that with, "Though why a woman in this day and age shouldn't be able to sunbathe where and whenever she wants to, I don't know. But Loni didn't, wouldn't, tell me exactly how far your father tried to go, though I got the impression there was something that really shook her. But she and I have never been terribly close, as I think you know. That's one reason why it became important what Tilly had to tell me on the subject."

"Which was?" Wolf prompted.

Lighting another cigarette and puffing furiously, Terri said, "When we got to talking over lunch at her place, the conversation somehow got around to your father and sex—I guess maybe I hinted at what Loni told me—and she came right out with (remember how rough she often talks), 'Cassius? He's an indefatigable old lecher!' and when I tactfully asked her if he'd made advances toward her, she whooped and said, 'Me? My dear, I'm much too ancient for him. Cassius, I'll have you know, is only turned on by the college freshman and *especially* high-school junior types.'"

Wolf scowled despondently. Somehow he'd not expected his own lather to be so ordinary, so humdrum, in his psychology.

You'd think a recovered alcoholic would have gained some mellowness, some dignity. He shrugged.

Terri went on, "Of course I asked for more. It turned out that Tilly knew a local girl in the latter (I mean, high-school) category. A tough, outspoken girl rather like she'd once been herself, I gather. Well, it seems Cassius' advances were an old story to this girl and to another of her female classmates too — they'd compared notes. She made a sort of joke out of the old man's attempts at 'romance,' as she called them, though they sounded like more. She told Tilly, 'Mr. Kruger? First he reads poetry to you and talks about nature and tells you how beautiful and young and fresh you are, maybe offers you a drink. Then he carries on about his dead wife and how terribly lonely he is, life over for him and all that. Then if you're still listening he begins to hint about how he's been completely impotent for years and years, and how dreadful that is, but you're so wonderful and if you'd only deign to touch him, if you'd just be a little bit kind, it would only take the tiniest touch, that's all an old man needs — a tiny touch below the belt — Well, if you fall for that and begin thinking, "A good deed. Why not?" why, then you'll find him telling you he has to touch *you* just the tiniest bit to balance things out, to make them right, at the same time he's clamping down on you with kisses, cutting off your breath, and before you know it he's got one hand down your blouse... Now I won't say that all happened to me, Ms. Hoyt, but it's sure what Mr. Kruger has in mind when he gets romantic and recites poetry and begs for the slightest touch of your beeyootiful fingers.'"

"Oh God," Wolf sighed, drawing it out. "To see ourselves as others see us." He shook his head from side to side. "What else? What next? There is something more?"

"There is," she confirmed, "and it's the most important part. But I want to get my mind straightened about it first, and that performance wore me out." And she did look a bit frazzled. "Oh hell," she said, stubbing out her cigarette and wetting her lips dry with talking, "Let's screw."

They did.

Considerably later she sat up in bed, seemed to think for a while, then with a dissatisfied sigh got up, slipped on her robe, lit another cigarette, and came back and sat on the side of the bed smiling at Wolf. The sound of the rain had sunk to a barely audible patter and the wind seemed to have died.

"You know," she said, "that should have made it easier for me to tell you the rest, but somehow it hasn't exactly.

"The thing was," she went on, her voice picking up as she began to reconstruct, "that I'd suddenly realized that repeating to you those things that girl told Tilly that Cassius did to her, or tried to do, was getting *me* excited, which made me ask myself how much of my indignation at your father was honest. That's what I wanted to straighten out in my mind, especially when Tilly (and the girl too apparently) seemed to treat it half as a joke, or one quarter at any rate, one of the grotesque indecencies you expect from practically all men, or at least all old men.

"Well, it's not too clear in my mind yet, the real reasons for my indignation, or at least my being upset. I'll try to keep it simple. It seems to boil down to two things, and one of them has nothing to do with sex at all. It's this, I just can't get out of my mind two or three of the horrible stories your father told in Tommy's presence. He made them so vivid, he seemed to gloat on them so, as if he were trying to infect that child—and all of us!—with dreads and superstitions. And the way he watched Tommy while he told them. That horrible dream of the burnt-to-ashes Esteban. And especially the way he described your mother's face coming off the painting and ghosting around the room as a cloud of green paint flakes. I'm sure Tommy's been thinking about that ever since."

"You know, that's true," Wolf said, sitting up, his face serious. And he told Terri the questions Tommy had asked him at the park about clouds being alive.

"You see," she said, nodding, as he finished, 'Tommy's got flakes on his mind, that horrible vibrating cloud-face of pinky-green flakes. Ugh!" She shivered her revulsion.

"The other thing," she went on, "*is* about sex, or at least starts with sex. Now after Tilly told me about that girl, I naturally asked her how soon after your mother's death Cassius had started to hunt high-school girls, or younger women at any rate. She whooped a little again and told me he'd always been that way, that it sometimes got obvious at those big parties your mother gave, and that she thought Cassius had been attracted to your mother in the first place because she was such a small, slight woman and always stayed somewhat girlish looking. 'Helen knew about Cassius' chasing, of course,' Tilly said. 'It was one of the things we used to drink about. At first we had both our husbands to rake over the coals. I was the most outspoken, but

Helen was more bitter. Then Pat died and there was only Cassius
for us to gripe at, mostly for his drunken pawings at parties, his
dumb little infatuations with whatever young Muff happened to
be handy.' Wolf, I don't like to ask you about this, but does that
fit at all with your memories of your father's behavior then?"

He winced but nodded. "Yes, during the last couple of years
before I lit out on my own. God, it all seemed to me then so
adult-dumb, so infantile and boring, adult garbage you wanted
to get shut of."

Terri continued, "Tilly said that after you left, Cassius and
Helen made up for a while, but then their battling got still more
bitter and more depressing. Twice Helen took too many sleeping
pills, or Cassius thought she did, and rushed her the morning
after to the hospital to have her stomach pumped out, though
Helen didn't recall overdosing those two times, just that she
blacked out. But then there came this Sunday morning when
Cassius called up Tilly about ten or so, sounding very small and
frightened, but rational-seeming, and begging her to come over,
because he thought that Helen was dead, but he wasn't absolutely
sure, and—get this!—he didn't know either whether he had killed
her, or not! Helen's doctor was coming, he'd already called him,
but would Tilly come over?

"She did, of course, and of course got there before the
doctor—Sunday mornings!—and found Helen lying peacefully
in bed, cold to the touch, and the bedroom a minor mess with
unfinished drinks and snacks set around and a couple of empty
sleeping pill bottles with their contents, or some of their contents,
scattered over the bed and floor, a snowfall of red-and-blue
Tuinal capsules. And there was Cassius in bathrobe and slippers
softly jittering around like an anxious ghost, keeping himself
tranquilized with swallows of beer, and he was telling her over
and over this story about how everything had been fine the night
before and he'd taken two or three pills, enough with the drinks
to knock him out, and then just as he was going under Helen had
started this harangue while flourishing a bottle of sleeping pills,
and he couldn't for the life of him remember whether she'd been
threatening to commit suicide or just bawling him out, maybe for
having taken the pills himself so as not to have to listen to her,
and he'd tried to get up and argue with her, stop her from taking
the pills if that was what she intended, but the pills he'd taken
were too much for him and he simply blacked out.

"Next he remembered, or thought he remembered, waking in the dark in bed and talking and then sleeping with, and then arguing with Helen and shaking her by the shoulders (or maybe strangling her! he wasn't sure which) and then passing out again. But he wasn't too sure about any of that, and if there had been talk between them, he couldn't recall a word of it.

"When he next woke up it was fully light and he felt very tranquil and secure, altogether different. Helen seemed to be sleeping peacefully, and so he slipped out of bed and made himself some coffee and began to tidy up the rest of the house, returning at intervals to check if Helen had woke up yet and wanted coffee. The second time it struck him that she was sleeping too peacefully, he couldn't see her breathing, she didn't wake up to being called or shaken, and he tried the mirror and feather tests and they didn't work, so he'd called her doctor and then Tilly.

"Tilly was sick about Helen and coldly enraged with Cassius, his pussyfooting around so coolly especially infuriated her, but on the other hand she couldn't see any bruises or signs of strangulation on Helen, or other form of violent death, and there were no signs of a struggle or any particular kind of commotion except for the scattered pills (she picked up some of those and stashed them in her bag with the thought that she might be needing them herself), and after a bit she found herself sympathizing with Cassius while still furious with him—he was being such a dumb ox!—and behaving toward him as she would have to her own husband Pat in a similar fix.

"For instance, she said to him, 'For God's sake don't talk about strangling Helen when the doctor comes unless you're really sure you did it! Don't tell him anything you're not sure of!' But she couldn't tell how much of this was really registering on him; he still seemed to be nursing a faint crazy hope that the doctor might be able to revive Helen, and muttering something about stories by Poe and Conan Doyle."

"'Premature Burial' and 'The Resident Patient,'" Wolf said absently. "About catalepsy."

"About then Helen's doctor came, a very cautious-acting young man ('My God, another pussyfooter,' Tilly said to herself) but he pronounced Helen dead quickly enough, and soon after the doctor a couple of policemen arrived, from San Rafael, she thought, whom the doctor had called before starting out.

"Maybe the appearance of the cops threw a scare into Cassius,

Tilly said, or at least convinced him of the seriousness of the situation, for there wasn't any mention of strangling in what he told the three of them, nothing at all about maybe waking in the dark, it all sounded to Tilly more cut and dried, more under control. And when he mentioned the two previous times that Helen had overdosed, the doctor casually confirmed that.

"The doctor had another look at Helen and they all poked around a bit. What seemed to bother the doctor most were the scattered sleeping pills, they seemed to offend his sense of propriety, though he didn't pick them up. And the two cops were quite respectful— your father does have quite a presence, as Tilly says—although the younger one kept being startled by things, as though the like had never happened before, first by Cassius not realizing at once when he got up that Helen was dead, then by Tilly just being there (he gave her a very funny look that made her wonder if that was what being a murder suspect was like), things like that.

"About then the ambulance the doctor had called arrived to take off Helen's body and he and the cops drove off right afterwards."

She paused at last. Wolf said earnestly, "Cassius never told me any of that—nothing about his suspicions of himself, I mean, nor about the doctor calling in the police at first. Nor did Tilly tell me—but of course you know that."

Terri nodded. "She said she didn't want to rake up things long past just when you were getting reconciled to your father and after he'd managed to quit drinking."

"But what happened?" Wolf demanded. "I mean at the time? As I think you know, Cassius didn't write me about my mother's death until after the funeral, and then only the barest facts."

"Exactly nothing happened," Terri said. "That's what made it seem so strange, at least at the time, Tilly told me—as if that weird and frantic morning of Helen's death had never happened. The autopsy revealed a fatal dose of barbiturate without even figuring in the alcohol, Cassius did call and tell her that much. And she saw him briefly at the funeral. They weren't in touch again after that for almost a year, by which time he'd been six months sober. Their new friendship was on the basis of 'Forget the past.' They never spoke of the morning of Helen's death again, and in fact not often of Helen. Tilly told me she'd almost forgotten Helen in a sort of way and seldom thought of her, until about six months ago when Cassius brought Esteban's painting of Helen down from the attic and hung and lighted it—"

"He could have been anticipating our visit," Wolf said thoughtfully.

Terri nodded and continued, "—and a couple of times since when Tilly came calling and noticed he'd hung a towel over it, as if he didn't want it watching him, at least for a while—"

At that instant there was a great flash of white light that flooded the room through the window curtains and simultaneously a ripping *craaackl* of thunder that catapulted Terri across the bed into Wolfs arms. As their hearing returned, it was assaulted by the frying sound of thick rain.

Murmuring reassurances, Wolf disengaged himself, got up, and shouldered hurriedly into his robe. Terri had the same thought: *Tommy.*

The door opened and Tommy hurtled in, to stop and look back and forth between them desperately. His facewas white, his eyes were huge.

He cried out, losing three years of vocabulary from whatever shock, "Ma take me! No, *Pa* take me! 'Fraid *Flakesma!*"

Wolf scooped him up, submitted to being grappled around the neck, speaking and cuddle-patting reassurances about as he would have to a frightened monkey. Terri started to take him from Wolf or at least add her embraces to his, but restrained herself, uneasily watching the open door.

White lightning washed the room again, followed after a second by another loud but lesser ripping *crack!*

As if the thunder had asked a question, Tommy drew his head back from Wolfs cheek a little and pronounced rapidly but coherently, regaining some vocabulary but continuing to coin new expressions under the pressure of fear: "I woke up. The ghost light was on! It made Grandma Flakesma come in after me, ceiling to floor! Pa, it brings her! Her green balloon face buzzed, Pa!"

Gathering her courage, which a new-sprouted anger reinforced, Terri moved toward the door. By the time she reached Tommy's room she was almost running.

The green and blue night light was on, just as Tommy'd said. Its deathly glow revealed a scattered trail of pillows, sheet, and blanket from the abandoned bed to her feet.

Behind her, footsteps competed with the pounding rain.

As she heard Cassius ask, "Where's Tommy? In Wolf's bedroom, Terri? Did the thunder scare him?" she stooped and switched off the offending globe with a vicious jab.

Then, as she hurried past the whitely tousle-headed old man mummy-wrapped in a faded long brown bathrobe, she snarled at him, "Your poisonous night light gave Tommy a terrible nightmare!" and rushed downstairs without listening to his stumbling responses.

In the dark living room the portrait of Helen Hostelford Kruger by Esteban Bernadorre was softly spotlighted by the pearly bulb just below its frame. As Terri advanced toward it, moving more slowly and deliberately now, breathing her full-blown anger, its witch face seemed to mock her. She noticed a subtlety that she'd previously missed: the narrowed eyes were very darkly limned, so that they sometimes seemed to be there but sometimes not, as though the portrait itself might be that of a taper-chinned witch mask greenish flesh-pink and waiting for eyes to fill it—and maybe teeth.

After glaring at it for a half dozen pounding heartbeats while thunder crackled in the middle distance, her fists clenching and unclenching, she contented herself with switching off its milky light—poison milk!—with a just audible "Flakesma!" like a curse and hurrying back upstairs.

In the hall there she passed Cassius coming out of "Wolf's bedroom," as he'd called it. She spared him a glare, but he, agitated looking and seemingly intent on wherever he was heading, hardly appeared to notice.

Wolf had Tommy tucked into the middle of their bed and was sitting close beside him. "Tom's going to spend the rest of the night with us," he told her. "Big family reunion and all."

"Oh, that's nice," she said, forcing a smile and bidding anger depart, at least from her features and tumultuous bosom.

"I've already invited him and he's accepted," Wolf went on, "so I guess you haven't any say in the matter."

"But we really want you, Ma," Tommy assured her anxiously, sitting up a little.

She plopped down on the other side, saying, "And I'm delighted to accept," as she hugged and kissed him.

Straightening up, she informed Wolf, "I turned that light off," and Tommy's face changed a little, and Wolf said lightly, "You mean that ghost light in Tom's room? A good idea. He and I have been talking about that a bit, and about ghosts and visions of all sorts, and thunderstorms, and flying cabbages and specter kings, and why if the sea were boiling hot we'd have fish stew."

"And wings for pigs," Tommy added with a pallid flicker of enthusiasm. "Space Pigs."

"Incidentally," Wolf remarked, "we discovered how the ghost light came to be on. No witchcraft at all. Cassius told us. It seems he was passing Tom's room on his way to bed and saw it was out, and not knowing that Tom had given up sleeping with a night light—"

"I might have known your father'd be the one!" Terri interjected venomously, yet midway through that statement recalled the command she'd given her anger, and managed to mute it somewhat.

"—and thinking to do a good turn he quietly stole in, so as not to wake Tom, and switched it on," Wolf finished, widening his eyes a little at Terri, warningly. "See? No mystery at all."

Then Wolf got up, saying, "Look, you guys, I want to check on what that storm's up to. I've been telling Tom how rare such storms are out here, and usually feeble when they do come. While I'm gone, Terri, why don't you tell Tom about the real humdingers they have in the Midwest that make even this one seem pretty tame? I'll be back soon."

Passing Tom's room he smelled fresh cigarette smoke.

Cassius was kneeling by the night light with his back to the door. He shoved something into his pocket and stood up. He looked haggard and distraught. He started to make an explanation to Wolf, but the latter with a warning nod toward the room where Terri and Tommy were, and not trusting himself to talk, motioned his father in the opposite direction downstairs, and followed him.

The interval gave the old man time to compose his thoughts as well as his features. When they faced each other in the living room, Cassius began, "I was replacing the night light that frightened Tommy with the white one from under Helen's picture." He gestured toward where the mask painting hung, now without its own special illumination. "Didn't want to leave the slightest opportunity for that nightmare, or whatever, to recur.

"But, Wolf," he immediately went on, his voice deepening, "what I really want to tell you is that I've been lying to you in more than one way while you've been here, at least lying in the sense of withholding information, though it didn't seem important to start with and was done, at least in part, with good intentions. Or at least I could make myself believe that, until now."

Wolf nodded without comment, dark- and suspicious-visaged.

"The littlest lie was that I haven't been dreaming much lately except for that bitch of a one about Esteban. The truth is that for the past six months or so I've been having horrible dreams in which Helen comes back from the dead and hounds and torments me, and especially dreams—green dreams, I call 'em—in which her face tonics off that picture and buzzes around me whispering and wailing like green-eyed skulls used to when I had nightmares as a boy, and threatening to *strangle* me—remember that!...

"... for the most obvious reason for these dreams leads us straight hack to my larger lie—again, a lie by withholding information: that ever since Helen's death I've had this half-memory, half-dread, that back in the horrible grey world of alcohol and blackout I contributed *more actively* to her death than just by not waking and getting her to the hospital in time to be pumped out.

"Sometimes the memory-dread has almost faded away (almost, sometimes, as if it could vanish forever), sometimes it's been real as a death-sentence—and especially since I've started this green-dreaming." Underlying all that has been the unnerving suspicion or conviction that somewhere in my mind is the memory of what really happened if only I could find a way to get back to it, through past alcoholic mists and blackout, maybe by fasting and exhaustion and sheer deprivation, maybe by drinking my way to it again or taking some stronger drug, maybe by mind-regression or psychoanalysis or some other awareness-broadening pushed to an extreme, maybe even by giving my dreams and dreads to another, to see what he'd find in them— Wolf, it's the sudden realization that I may have been trying (unknowingly!) to do that to Tommy—and to all of you, for that matter, but especially to Tommy—to use him as a sort of experimental subject, that shattered me tonight."

By this time Wolf also had had the opportunity to compose his thoughts and feelings somewhat, get over the worst of his anger at Tommy being terrorized, whether accidentally or half intentionally. Nor was he moved to sound off violently when Cassius, lighting another cigarette, had a coughing fit. But he'd also had time to make some decisions with which he knew Terri would concur.

"Don't worry any more about the night light," he began. "Tommy's sleeping with us. And tomorrow we'll be taking off, whether the rain forces us to get out (and you too maybe!) or not. It's been a good visit in a lot of ways, but I think we've pushed it too far, maybe all of us have done that. As for your dreams and guilts and worries, what can I say?" A wry note came into his voice for a moment, "After all, you're the psychologist! I do know there was something damn funny, something strange, about the scare Tommy got tonight, but I don't see where discussing it could get us anywhere, at least tonight."

Before Cassius could reply, the phone rang. It was Tilly for Cassius, and for Wolf too before she'd finished, to tell them that the TV said "the authorities" had begun to phone people in several areas including Goodland Valley to tell them to be ready to evacuate to safer places if the weather situation worsened and a second or general order came, and had they been phoned yet? Also to remind them that they were all, not just Cassius, invited down to her place, which was holding out pretty well, although there was a leak in her kitchen and a seepage in her garage.

When she finally got off the line, with messages to Terri and last admonitions to them all, Cassius tried to restart the conversation, but his mind had lost the edge it had had during his brief confession, if you could call it that, and he seemed inclined to ramble. Before he'd gotten anywhere much the phone rang again, this time with the official message Tilly had told them to expect, and there was that to respond to.

That ended their attempts at any more talk. Wolf went upstairs, while Cassius allowed he probably needed some rest too.

Outside the thunderstorm had moved into the far distance, but the rain was keeping up with a moderate pelting.

Wolf found Tom and Terri in bed, her arm around him, and with their eyes closed. She opened hers and signed to Wolf not to talk, she'd just got the boy asleep.

Wolf brought his lips close to her cheek. "We'll be leaving tomorrow," he whispered. "Stay somewhere in San Francisco. Okay?"

She nodded and smiled agreement and they softly kissed goodnight and he went around and carefully slid into bed on the other side of Tommy.

That was the ticket, Wolf told himself. Leave tomorrow and let the storm decide how fast they moved, the storm and (he grinned to himself) "the authorities." Right now the former seemed to be slackening and the latter to have signed off for the night. This lazy thought pleased him and suited his weariness. What had really happened the past few days, anyway? Why, he'd simply pushed his reconciliation with his father too far, involved himself too much in the old man's ruined life-end, and as a result got Tommy and Terri (and Loni too!) entangled in the dismal wreckage of a marriage (and all its ghosts) which was all Cassius could ever be to anyone. And the solution to this was the same as it had been when Wolf was a youngster: get away from it! Yes, that was the ticket.

His thoughts in the dark grew desultory, he dozed, and after a while slumbered.

Morning revealed the storm still firmly in charge of things. No thunder-and-lightning histrionics, but its rain persistently pelted. TV and radio glumly reported a slowly worsening weather situation.

The Martinezes called in early to say they wouldn't be making it. They had storm troubles of their own down in the city.

Wolf took that call. Overflowing ashtrays told him Cassius had been up most of the night and he let the old man sleep. He made breakfast for the rest of them and served it in the kitchen. Simpler that way, he told himself, and avoided confrontation of Tommy with a certain painting.

Tilly called with updatings of last night's news and admonitions. Terri took that call and she and the older woman spun it out.

Packing occupied some more time. Wolf didn't want to rush things, but it seemed a chore best gotten out of the way.

He gave Terri the job of making them reservations at a San Francisco hotel or motel. She settled down with the phone and big directory.

Taking a rain-armored Tommy with him, he went down to the garage and found, as he'd feared, that the gas tank was a little too near empty for comfort. They drove to the nearest gas station that was open (the first and second weren't) and filled her up, made all other checks. Wolf noted that the big flashlight he kept in the glove compartment was dim and he bought new batteries for it.

Driving back, he took more note of the rain damage: fallen

branches, scatters of rock and gravel, small runs of water crosswise of the road. In the garage he reminded himself to check out Cassius' Buick somehow before they left.

Terri had managed to make them a reservation at a motel on Lombard after getting "No vacancies" from a half dozen other places.

Cassius was up and on his best best behavior, though rather reserved (chastened? to borrow Tilly's word) and not inclined to talk much except to grumble half comically that people as usual were making too much of the storm and its dangers, decry the TV and radio reports, and in general put on a crusty-old-man act. However, he seemed quite reconciled to Wolfs departure and the visit's end, and also, despite his grumbles, to his own going down to Tilly's to stay out the end of the storm.

Wolf took advantage of this mood of acquiescence to get Cassius to go down to the garage with him and check out the Buick and its gas supply. Once there, and the Buick's motor starting readily enough, Wolf badgered the old man into backing it out of the garage and then into it again, so the car'd be facing forward for easiest eventual departure. Cassius groused about "having to prove to my own son I can still drive," but complied in the end, though in no more mood than before for any close conversation.

Back once more in the house, there came at long last the expected phone call with the order, or rather advisement, that all dwellers in it get out of Goodland Valley. Wolf carried their bags and things down to the car, while Cassius, still grumbling a little, prepared an overnight bag and made a call to Tilly, telling her he would be arriving shortly.

"But I'm not going to get out until you're all on your way," he gruffly warned his son's family. "Enough's enough. If I left at the same time you did, I'd lose completely the feeling—a very good one, let me assure you!—of having been your host in my own house for a most pleasant week."

Except for that show of warmth, Cassius continued his reserve in his good-bye, contenting himself with silently shaking hands first with Wolf, then Tommy, and giving each a curt nod of approval. Terri saw a tear in his eye and was touched, she felt a sudden swing in her feelings toward him, and impulsively threw her arms around his neck and kissed him. He started to wince away from her, then submitted with some grace and a murmured "M'dear. Thank you, Terri."

Wolf noted on her face a look of utter surprise and shock, but it was quickly replaced with a smile. It stuck in his mind, though he forgot to ask her about it, mostly because as they were pulling out of the garage, a highway patrol car stopped across the road and hailed them.

"Are you leaving the Kruger residence?" one of the officers asked, consulting a list, and when Wolf affirmed that, continued with, "Anyone else up there?"

"Yes, my father, the owner," Wolf called back. "He's leaving shortly, in another car."

They thanked him, but as he drove off, he saw them get out and start trudging up the hill.

"I'm glad they're doing that," he told Terri. "Make sure Cassius is rooted out."

But the incident left a bad taste in his mouth, because it reminded him of what he'd heard about the two policemen calling there the morning after his mother died.

At the first sizable intersection a roadblock was being set up to stop cars entering Goodland Valley. That didn't hold them back, but the drive into San Francisco took half again as long as he'd anticipated, what with the rain and slow traffic and a mudslide blocking two lanes of the freeway near Waldo Tunnel just north of the bridge.

Lombard Street, when they reached it just south of the bridge, reminded Wolf and Terri of western towns built along main highways in the days before freeways. Wide, but with stoplights every block and the sides garish with the neon of gas stations, chain restaurants, and motels. They located theirs and checked in with relief. Tommy had been starting to get cranky and the storm was making late afternoon seem like night.

Only Terri didn't seem to Wolf as relieved as she should be. Tommy was running a bath for himself and his boats. Wolf asked her, "Something bothering you, Hon?"

She was scowling nervously at the floor. "No, I guess I've just got to tell you," she decided reluctantly. "Wolf, when I kissed your father—"

"I know!" he interjected. "I was going to ask you about it, if he'd goosed you, tried to cop some other sort of feel, or what? You looked so strange."

"Wolf," she said tragically, "it was simply that his breath was reeking with alcohol. That was why he was making such a point of keeping a distance from us all day."

"Oh God," he said despondently, closing his eyes and slumping.

"Wolf," she went on in a small voice after a moment, "I think we've got to call up Tilly to check if he ever got there."

"Of course," he said, springing to the phone. "I guess we were going to do that in any case."

He got through to the Marin lady after some odd delays and found their worry realized: Cassius had not arrived. Wolf cut short Tilly's counter-questions with "Look, Til, I'll try to call him at the house, then get back to you right away."

This time the response was quicker. The number he was trying to reach was out of service due to storm damage.

He tried to call Tilly back and this time, after still more delays, got the same response as when he'd tried to call his father.

"All over Marin County the phones are going out," he told Terri, trying to put a light face on bad news. "Well, Hon," he went on, "I don't think I'm left much choice. I've just got to go back up there."

"Oh no, Wolf," she said apprehensively, "don't you think you should try calling the police first, at least? Cassius may still be at the house, I suppose, but then again he may simply have driven off somewhere else, anywhere, maybe to some bar. How can you know?"

He thought a bit, then said, "Tell you what, Hon. I'll go down to the coffee shop and have a couple of cups and a Danish or something; meanwhile you try calling the police. You may be able to find out something, they seem to have pretty good organization on this storm thing."

When he got back some twenty minutes later, she was on the phone. "Shh, I think I'm finally getting something," she told him. She listened concentratedly, nodded sharply twice, asked, "About the mudslides?" nodded at the answer she got to that, and finally said, "Yes, I've got that. Thank you very much, officer," and put down the phone.

"Nothing specifically on any Kruger," she told Wolf, "but there arc still holdouts in Goodland Valley, houses that won't vacate. And, at latest available report, there's been no major earth movement there, though they're expecting one at any time,

it's 'a real and present danger.' Wolf, I still don't think you should
go, just on the chance he'll be there."

She was watching him intently, as was a moist and robed
Tommy in the bathroom door.

Grinning sympathetically, he shook his head. "Nope, got to
go," he said. "I'll be cautious as hell, on the watch every second.
Maybe just have to check the garage."

Outside, thunder rumbled. "That's my cue," he said and
got out of the room as quickly as he could, and by the time
he'd got the Volks on the bridge again, its gas tank once more
topped off, he was feeling pretty good. Caffeine had done its
work, thunderstorms always gave him a high, and now that he
had only Cassius to worry about, everything was wonderfully
simplified. It was great to be outdoors, alone, the city behind
him, space around him, water under him, with lightning to reveal
vividly every ten seconds or so the multiple mazy zigzag angles
of the marvelous structure the Volks was traversing, and thunder
to shake his bones. And himself free on a quixotic errand that
had to be carried out but that really didn't matter all that much
when you got down to it, since worry about Cassius was hardly
to be compared with worry about Tommy or Terri, say. Oh,
this storm was good, though awfully big, much too big for any
sentimentalities or worrisome petty human concerns. It washed
those away, washed away his own concern about whether he
was being, had been, a good son (or husband or father, for that
matter) and whether he was being wise to make this trip or not,
washed away Terri's and Tilly's concern as to what indignities,
exactly, Cassius had visited on Loni, washed away Cassius' own
dreadful wondering as to whether or not he'd strangled his wife
in a blackout, washed all those away and left only the naked
phenomena, the stuff of which it, the storm itself, was composed,
and all other storms, from those in teapots and cyclotrons to
those out at the ends of the universe, that blustered through
whole galaxies and blew out stars.

This almost suspiciously exalted state of mind, this lightning
high, stuck with Wolf after the Volks had got across the bridge
and come to the first traffic hold-up, the one a little beyond the
Waldo tunnel. It was worse this time, tour lanes were blocked,
and took longer to get past; they were only letting cars through in
one direction at a time. But now that his mind had time to move
around, free for seconds and minutes from the task of driving, he

found that it was drawn to *phenomena* and awarenesses rather than worries and *concerns*. For instance, those so-alike dreams Cassius and Tommy had had (they'd both used the same word "buzz" of the swooping green face), he now found himself simply lost in wonder at the coincidence. Could one person transmit his dreams to another? Could they travel through flesh and skin? And would they look like dreams if you saw them winging through darkness?

And that black sonic generator, or whatever, Esteban was supposed to have invented, how shockingly it had come alive in his hands when Cassius had thrown the switch—that strong and deep vibration! Whatever had made it work after a quarter century of disuse? And why had the puzzle of that slipped completely from his mind? He knew one thing: if he got the chance tonight, he'd certainly glom onto the black cylinder and bring it away with him!

And the color green, the witch green and death blue of Tommy's ghost light, were colors more than the raiments of awareness, the arbitrary furniture of the mind? Were they outside the mind too: feelings, forces, the raw stuff of life? and could they kill? Wave motions, vibrations, *buzzings*—vibes, vibes, vibes, vibes.

In such ways and a thousand others his thoughts veered and whirled throughout the trip, while thunder crackled and ripped, lightning made shiny sheets of streets awash, unceasing rain pattered and pelted.

Then, not more than a mile from Goodland Valley, all streetlights, all store lights, all house lights were simultaneously extinguished. He told himself this was to be expected, that power failures were a part of storms. Moreover, the rain did at last seem to be lessening.

Just the same he found it reassuring when the stationary headlights and red lanterns of the roadblock appeared through the rain mist.

He'd been intending to explain about Cassius, but instead he found himself whipping out his veterinary identifications and launching into a story about this family in Goodland Valley that had a pet jaguar and wouldn't vacate without it and so couldn't move until he'd arrived and administered an anesthetic shot.

Almost to his chagrin they passed him through with various warnings and well wishings before he'd said much more than the words "pet jaguar." Evidently exotic pet carnivores were an old story in Marin County.

He wondered fleetingly if he'd been inspired to compose the lie in honor of Esteban Bernadorre, who'd been a mine of equally unlikely anecdotes, some of them doubtless invented only to please an admiring and credulous boy.

He followed his headlights up the slight grade leading into Goodland Valley, thankful the rain continued to slacken though lightning still flared faintly with diminished thunder from time to time, providing additional guidance. After what was beginning to seem too long a time, he caught sight of a few dim house lights in the steep hills close on each side (he'd got out of the area of the power failure, he told himself) and almost immediately afterwards his headlights picked up Cassius' garage with one door lifted open as he'd left it. Vie nosed the Volks into it until he could see the dark shape of Cassius' Buick.

On another sudden inspiration he reversed the direction of the Volks as he backed it out, so that it faced downgrade, the way he'd come. He parked it, setting the hand-brake, nearer the narrow road's center than its side. He took the flashlight from the glove compartment and got out on the side facing the house, leaving the headlights on, the motor idling, and the door open.

A fingering tendril of wind, startlingly chill, made him shiver.

But was the shiver from the wind alone? Staring uphill, straining his eyes at the dim bulk of the house, he saw a small greenish glow moving behind the windows of the second floor, while halfway between him and the house there stood a dark pale-headed figure. White-haired Cassius? Or a white crash helmet?

A flare of lightning brighter than those preceding it showed the swollen hillside empty and the windows blank.

Imagination! he told himself.

Thunder crashed loudly. The storm was getting nearer again, coming back.

He switched on the flashlight and by its reassuringly bright beam rapidly mounted the hill, stamping each step firmly into the soggy ground.

The front door was ajar. He thrust it open and was in the short hall that held the stairs to the second floor and led back to the living room.

As he moved forward between stairs and wall, he became aware of a deep and profound vibration that gave the whole house a heavy tremor; it was in the floor under his feet, the wall his hand groped, even in the thick air he breathed. While his ears were assaulted by a faint thin screaming, as of a sound too shrill to be quite heard, a sound to drive dogs mad and murder bats.

Midway in his short journey the house lurched sharply once, so he was staggered, then held steady. The deep vibration and the shrill whatever-it-was continued unchanging.

He paused in the doorway to the living room. From where he stood he had a clear view of the fireplace midway in the far wall, the mantelpiece above it, the two windows to either side of it that opened on the hill behind the house, a small coffee table in front of the fireplace, and in front of that an easy chair facing away from him. Barely showing above the back of the last was the crown of a white-haired head.

The bottles on the mantelpiece had been transferred to the coffee table, where one of them lay on its side, so that the mantelpiece itself was occupied only by the stubby black cylinder of Esteban's sonic generator and by his painting of Helen, which seemed strangely to have a pale grey rag plastered closely across it.

Wolf at first saw all these things not so much by the beam of his flashlight, which was directed at the floor from where his hand hung at his side, as by the green and blue glow of the ghost light beneath the oddly obscured painting.

Then the white glare of a lightning flash flooded in briefly from behind him through the open door and a window above the stairs, though strangely no ray of it showed through the windows to either side of the fireplace, followed almost immediately by a crash of thunder.

As though that great sound had been a word of command, Wolf strode rapidly toward the fireplace, directing the flashlight ahead of him. With every step forward the deep vibration and the super-shrill whine increased in intensity, almost unbearably.

He stopped by the coffee table and shone his flashlight at Esteban's invention. Torn-away friction tape dangled from the switch, which had been thrown on.

He shifted the beam to the painting and saw that what he had thought grey rag was the central area of bare canvas from which every last flake of paint had vanished, or rather *been shaken* by the vibrations from the cylinder beside it. For he could see now that the stripped canvas was quivering rapidly and incessantly like an invisibly beaten drumhead.

But the mantelpiece beneath the painting was bare. It showed no trace of fallen flakes.

As he swung the bright beam around to the easy chair, flashing in his mind on how the slim pinkish-green witch mask had swooped and buzzed through Cassius' and Tommy's dreams, it passed slowly across the nearest window, revealing why the lightning flash hadn't shone through it. Beyond the glass, close against it from top to bottom, was wet dirt packed solid.

The beam moved on to the easy chair. Cassius' hands gripping its arms and his head, pressed in frozen terror into the angle between back and side, were all purplish, while the whites of his bulging eyes were shot with a lacework of purple.

The reason for his suffocation was not far to seek. Stuffing his nostrils and plastered intrusively across his grimacing lips were tight-packed dry flakes of greenish-pink oil paint.

With a muted high-pitched crackle the two windows gave way to huge dark-faced thrusts of mud.

Wolf took off at speed, his flashlight held before him, raced down the lurching hall, out the open front door, down the splashing hill toward the lights of the Volks, and through its door into the driver's seat.

Simultaneously releasing the hand-brake, shifting the gear lever, and giving her throttle, he got away in a growling first that soon changed to a roaring second. A last sideways glimpse showed the house rushing down toward him in the grip of a great moving earth-wall in which uprooted trees rode like logs in a breaking-up river jam.

For critical seconds the end of the earth-wave seemed to Wolf's eye on a collision course with the hurtling Volks, but then rapidly fell behind the escaping car. He'd actually begun to slow down when he started to hear the profound, long-drawn rumbling roar of the hill burying forever Goodland Valley and all its secrets.

About the Author

Fritz Leiber is considered one of science fiction's legends. Author of a prodigious number of stories and novels, many of which were made into films, he is best known as creator of the classic Lankhmar fantasy series. Fritz Leiber has won awards too numerous to count, including the coveted Hugo and Nebula, and was honored as a lifetime Grand Master by the Science Fiction Writers of America. He died in 1992.

OPEN ROAD
INTEGRATED MEDIA

Open Road Integrated Media is a digital publisher and multimedia content company. Open Road creates connections between authors and their audiences by marketing its ebooks through a new proprietary online platform, which uses premium video content and social media.

CPSIA information can be obtained
at www.ICGtesting.com
Printed in the USA
JSHW021246100123
35997JS00002B/175